The Irish Book Club of Dublin (Ohio)

The Irish Book Club of Dublin (Ohio)

Robin Strachan

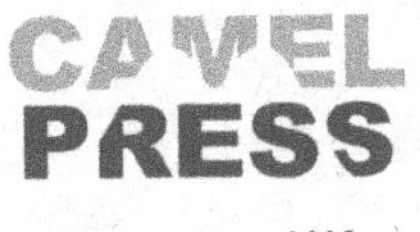

Kenmore, WA

A Camel Press book published by Epicenter Press

Epicenter Press
6524 NE 181st St.
Suite 2
Kenmore, WA 98028

For more information go to:
www.Camelpress.com
www.Coffeetownpress.com
www.Epicenterpress.com
www.robinstrachanauthor.com

This is a work of fiction. Names, characters, places, brands, media, and incidents are either the product of the author's imagination or are used fictitiously.

Cover design by Scott Book
Design by Melissa Vail Coffman

The Irish Book Club of Dublin (Ohio)
Copyright © 2023 by Robin Strachan

Library of Congress Control Number: 2022946246

ISBN: 978-1-68492-087-7 (Trade Paper)
ISBN: 978-1-68492-088-4 (eBook)

Dedicated to
All the strong, smart, capable women I know.
May we know each other in every lifetime.

Acknowledgments

The idea for this book dropped out of the sky one evening at a favorite restaurant in Dublin, Ohio. The title came to me as clearly as if someone had spoken it. With an affinity for anything Irish, I'm drawn to the historic section of Dublin like a bear cub to honey. Each year, Dublin hosts its annual Irish Festival, when visitors come to enjoy food and fun in the town named by its founder for his birthplace in Ireland. Having made the decision to set the story in Dublin, I needed a character who belonged there.

Laura Fisher, the main character in this novel, starts out as the wife of a pastor who abuses her and their sons. After losing one son in a suspicious accident, Laura wants to know the truth. But her husband seems only too willing to forgive and forget.

She dreams of a better life, but how can she? In a twist of fate, she is free, though she will need to overcome shame and a lack of self-confidence that follow her as she leaves the small town where she grew up and moves to Dublin. There, she forges a new life. But overcoming fear and traumatic memories takes time and support.

As with any book, many people contribute ideas. Thanks go to Carol Bouma, a soul sister who spent time discussing this character and providing ideas for Laura's new business as a second-hand store owner. Long-time friend Dr. Liz Kramer-Brent is always ready to discuss a story and how it can take shape in interesting ways.

A very special thank you goes to Dr. Carol Clinton who, with her Irish husband Chris, was an honorary chair of Dublin's Irish Festival.

The 2019 Irish Festival was so much fun, I'll definitely go again. I should mention that Carol also chaired the campaign to build the new Dublin library.

To my readers who inspire me with their own stories of survival through desperate times, thank you for believing that every story can have a happy ending.

Chapter One

Turning the knob on the front door to Serendipities, a second-hand store in Parmenter, Ohio, Laura Fisher barely registered the jangling of the brass bell that hung by a worn leather strap. Serendipities was the town's thrift and consignment store. It was also Laura's favorite place.

She had stopped by on Monday. Today was only Wednesday, but she felt restless and welcomed a diversion from her weekly chores. As long as dinner was on the table on time, she could let a few things slide.

"Oh, hello, Laura! I was hoping to see you today." Marjorie, the shop's owner, hurried to greet the shy, quiet woman dressed in a drab gray skirt, well below the knee, and high-necked white blouse.

Laura smiled shyly. "I couldn't resist stopping by."

"Not much new since the last time you were here." Marjorie chuckled and slid a long gray box across the counter. "These arrived this morning. How should I display them?"

Laura approached the counter and peered into the box that contained a set of tall pewter candlesticks. Her eyes lit up. "They'd be perfect with . . ." She surveyed the room before spying the items she sought. She knew the inventory almost as well as Marjorie.

Nearly skipping across the creaky hardwood floor to the back of the store, she selected a world globe in shades of beige and brown on a brass stand, along with a smaller glass snow globe containing a silver miniature of the Eiffel Tower. Carrying these items to the fireplace, she arranged the snow globe and the pewter candlesticks on the right side of the mantel. The world globe on its brass stand went on the left.

She tapped the nail of her index finger against her lips, considering the effect. "It needs one more thing for the center, something tall and colorful."

Hurrying to the back corner of the store, where paintings in a variety of sizes and frames leaned against one wall, she selected a vertical painting resplendent with turquoise, yellow, and rosy abstract flowers. "There!"

"You've got the touch," Marjorie said. She smiled fondly at the younger woman whose cheeks flushed becomingly at her praise. "You should be an interior designer. Matter of fact, I think you already are."

"Oh, no. I'm just playing." Laura shook her head vehemently and tucked a wisp of flyaway hair behind her ear.

As usual, her nearly waist-length chestnut-colored hair was arranged in a tight bun fastened, it seemed, by habitual discipline alone. Periwinkle-blue eyes, her most striking feature, were the same hue as the bluish-purple flowers that grew in profusion in summer months. Even if she had worn mascara—not allowed in their ultra-conservative church or at home, for that matter—Laura had no need of it, for her dark lashes were naturally long and thick.

As usual, she was dressed in the drab clothing and sensible, low-heeled black shoes her pastor husband favored. In their strict Apostolic Pentecostal faith, women were forbidden to cut their hair short or wear pants, for it was considered a sin to dress like men. Yet, rather than appearing dowdy, Laura wore her simple clothing with an innate dignity that exuded grace. She frequently turned heads, though she never noticed.

Reverend Jedediah Fisher was a controlling husband, intent on hiding his younger wife's physical attributes. His attempts were in vain. Despite the modest high-necked blouses and plain house dresses he insisted on, Laura had a lovely figure.

Now thirty-nine, she had married Jed when she was eighteen, just a week after graduating from the church's elementary-secondary school. Jed was the church's youth pastor and taught natural science. God created the world in seven days, and Adam and Eve were the first humans. He gave Laura a 'D' on a test when she mentioned dinosaurs in an essay question.

"Dinosaurs are a myth taught by a secular society," he wrote in red marker on her paper.

In not quite two-and-a-half years, she bore him two sons. The brown-haired, blue-eyed little boys were her proudest accomplishments. They brought joy and laughter to her days, making up for the love and affection that never materialized in her marriage. If being Jed's wife didn't bring all that she might have desired, she adored motherhood and did everything she could to make sure Michael and Andrew had happy childhoods.

She took her boys to the library every Friday for story hour. There, they learned to devour books the way their mother did, hauling as many as their little arms could carry. On nice days, she took them on nature walks. Afterward, armed with glue, glitter, crayons, and scraps of fabric, they created pine cone houses inhabited by stick people. In winter, they rode sleds down a bunny slope behind their house until wet clothing and cold fingers and toes sent them scurrying into the house for cocoa and homemade cookies.

Andrew, the youngest, was now a freshman at Ohio State majoring, it seemed, in sowing his wild oats. Laura recalled how he had balked the night Jed outlined plans for his life: seminary followed by an associate pastoral assignment at Jed's church. Although Andrew was a compliant enough church-goer, he had no intention of following in his father's footsteps.

Instead, he diligently applied for every community and state scholarship available, determined to attend Ohio State. To Laura's relief, a local foundation awarded him a generous scholarship that covered a significant portion of his tuition at Ohio State. Andrew promised his father he'd consider a role as church elder after he completed his degree. Laura knew, however, that this outcome was doubtful. Andrew would never return to Parmenter.

All along, it was Michael, their oldest son, who was a much better candidate for a life of religious service—as a music minister. He was gifted in keyboard and composition. But Michael had died six years earlier.

There wasn't a day that went by that Laura didn't think of him. She believed he was with her in spirit—was certain that she had experienced his presence one day at the very lake where he had died that hot August day. She hardly mentioned him anymore, although Marjorie understood that grief was behind her friend's perpetually haunted eyes.

Reading and home design activities kept Laura from succumbing to a depression so deep, she might never have recovered. After a period of seclusion, she resurfaced, showing up at Serendipities one afternoon, to

Marjorie's relief. She seemed to be searching for something. Marjorie could only guess that it was a purpose, a reason to go on.

Laura visited Serendipities at least three times a week, not always to buy. Mostly, she imagined how the items she saw could be arranged in someone's home. She had a knack for finding old or slightly imperfect items and giving them a second chance to shine. Something old could become new again. *Feathering nests* was how she thought of it. Her newest project was redecorating her mother's nondescript room at the county nursing home.

She felt it was the least she could do. After such a hardscrabble life and marriage to a cold, difficult man, her mother deserved a more comfortable existence. Laura had been the only child her mother was able to carry to term. It was only natural they would share a close bond.

In truth, Laura still harbored guilt that she couldn't invite her to live with her and Jed, especially now that Andrew was away at college. The quiet elderly woman was no trouble at all. But Jed wasn't in favor of the idea. Laura tried to appeal to his more pastoral sense of care and concern for a family member in need, to no avail. He wouldn't budge. But maybe this was for the best. Perhaps it was better her mother never saw what went on behind the careful façade Laura constructed.

Jed didn't say much if she shopped for small items for their home or as gifts for his parishioners. He indulged Laura this one pastime—permitted it if she didn't take too much satisfaction in her womanly art, as he called it, or exhibit any pride in accomplishment. Pride was the devil's work.

He doled out her weekly allowance for groceries and household necessities. With careful management of the family's food budget, Laura usually had a little money left over. She stored these precious coins and bills in a safe place. "Squirreling them away" was how she thought of her savings, comparing her situation with that of the chattering squirrels hard at work in their back yard. They hid food for the winter in a hollow stump near the detached garage. Laura planted flowers around it, helping the squirrels protect their hard-won gains.

She hid other things, too. Library books had to be approved by Jed who forbid her to read novels. The books he selected on her behalf were of little interest to Laura. She yearned for stories and information about the world outside her vista. She could plainly see that the life she led was nothing like the characters she enjoyed most: strong women with lives of purpose.

This book-hiding could be a dangerous business. She had almost been caught several times. This led her to hide whatever book she was reading inside an empty box of Bisquick. On the rare occasion that Jed came home from church early, she had only to hear his car in the driveway or heavy footsteps on the back porch steps before quickly stashing whatever book she was reading inside the box.

Serendipities had become her escape. It was lovely to be inside the Serendipities shop with its gently-used furniture and bric-a-brac. She breathed in the comforting scent of old wood. Despite a lack of square footage and an overabundance of items arranged in tight but cozy groupings, the place was spotless and orderly, a testament to Marjorie's love for the business she had started on a shoestring. After divorcing in her late fifties, Marjorie had started Serendipities out of desperation, using her own household furniture and items as inventory those first months.

"I wasn't prepared to be anything other than a wife and mother," she said when Laura asked how she had known what to do. "I always dreamed of owning a place like Serendipities. It was hard, but I created a better life for myself."

Marjorie had once said—and Laura never forgot—that the success of Serendipities was proof that a dream could come true if you were willing to take chances and believe in that dream. It was a novel concept for Laura. A vision—little more than a daydream, really—could transform from idea to reality, like magic. This idea was vaguely troubling, since it didn't mesh with her understanding of scripture.

To Laura, the aroma of polished wood combined with the musty smell of upholstered fabric was as enticing as perfume. Her eyes roamed over the furniture she had admired on earlier visits: the enormous maple roll-top desk, a pedestal table with gold leaf trim, a dish cabinet with cut-glass doors. A few newer pieces on display included an oak treasure chest, a craftsman-style bench with a burgundy-colored brocade cushion, and a pale-yellow wicker bookshelf with a matching desk and chair. The paint was peeling in places. If it belonged to her, she would repaint it in a rustic ivory shade and replace the cushion with a floral print. She ran her fingers over the items, taking in every detail.

A year ago, Laura had accompanied Marjorie to a nearby estate sale to find new items for the store. There was so much to see—endless possibilities. Laura flitted from row to row, exclaiming over items she could envision in Serendipities and how they might be displayed.

"You have an eye for design," Marjorie had said. "When you like something, I know it will sell fast."

Laura had blushed at the compliment. No one had ever said she had an eye for anything. She felt self-satisfaction in the remark, but then remembered that pride went before a fall. Still, she carried the memory of Marjorie's praise like a dog-eared photo, retrieving it whenever she needed a lift.

Today had been one of those days. At breakfast, Jed sat at the kitchen table looking like a storm cloud gaining strength before unleashing a deluge. At lunch, he was in a foul mood, criticizing the homemade vegetable soup she ladled into his bowl.

"It doesn't taste the same," he complained. "What did you do to it?"

"I used fresh herbs, Jed," she said. "Oregano, basil, and thyme from the kitchen garden. They're healthy and good for you."

"I prefer soup from a can," he said in a gruff voice. "Did you finish ironing my blue shirt for Sunday service? Use a little more starch. It'll be in the nineties."

The minute he went back to church, she washed the dishes and hurried over to Serendipities. It was a diversion, yes. But more than that, the store had become a place of refuge for Laura, crammed full of reminders of what she imagined were vestiges of happier lives.

The store carried only a few valuable antiques, and those were consignment pieces. The trick to a successful shop like Serendipities was maintaining a balance of higher-end stock without having to make expensive purchases. People gave Marjorie their belongings to sell with the agreement they would receive a percentage of the purchase price. The majority of items for sale were great buys from estate sales—occasional tables, small chests of drawers, and affordable dining room sets. They were the treasures of people's lives, and in Laura's mind, that gave them inherent value.

As she fingered a queen-sized headboard covered in a faded green-and-rose fabric with raised silky petals and puffy leaves, she wondered who had slept in that bed. Had it belonged to an old married couple who held hands and tenderly kissed each other good night? She inspected a set of slightly chipped, silver-rimmed dishes in a delicate winterberry pattern that had graced someone's holiday table. By habit, she lowered herself into the hickory bentwood rocking chair. How many little ones had been soothed to sleep in this chair?

On most visits to Serendipities, Laura found odds and ends others discarded. She knew they could be turned into keepsakes. It didn't take much—a little elbow grease and scratch mender, fresh ribbon trim around a lampshade, or a bit of etching on a glass cabinet door—to turn a piece that was already lovely into something that would be treasured for generations. Her design skills were likely the one talent she possessed that Jed seemed to appreciate, although he made a point never to acknowledge her talents.

"It is sinful to take credit for something that came from God," Jed was quick to say when a church member complimented Laura on a set of hand-painted candlesticks at the church's flea market. Laura's face reddened at the demeaning words spoken in front of the other ladies. The house where she and Jed lived was as lovely as any home in the glossy cottage design magazines that she hastily peeked at in the grocery store.

As soon as Jed turned away, one of the women winked at Laura behind his back and whispered, "Don't you believe it, honey."

On top of an oak pedestal table at the back of the shop, Marjorie had arranged several items intended to evoke memories of Irish travel. Laura wistfully ran her fingers over a hand-tatted lace hankie like the one her Irish grandmother had always carried in her apron pocket. This handkerchief had yellowed to the color of chamomile tea. It was only two dollars, a small price for something so precious.

She sniffed the hankie in an attempt to conjure up sense memories of her maternal grandmother McGraw. But what came to mind, instead, was the Irish festival in Dublin, Ohio, near Columbus. She had taken Andrew to Ohio State for freshman orientation. It was a good thing that Jed hadn't wanted to go along. He hadn't approved of Andrew attending Ohio State and insisted that Laura handle orientation details.

She had relished one-on-one time in the car with her bright, amusing son, and enjoyed helping him decorate his half of the dorm room. Afterward, she had driven over to neighboring Dublin to enjoy an afternoon of lively music and cultural activities. It was her first experience attending the Irish festival. But it wouldn't be her last. She had a wonderful time, even if she had felt out of place in her drab dress and clunky black shoes. Other women going to the festival wore shorts and sundresses, cute sandals, and colorful jewelry. She caught a few of them glancing at her, and her cheeks reddened at the memory.

She had loosened her hair from its tight bun and allowed it to flow in waves down her back and shoulders. Feeling better about her appearance, she roamed for several hours, anonymous in the crowd. It felt great. With Andrew at Ohio State, she would have a reason to attend the festival each August for at least the next three years—maybe more if he followed his dream to earn a master's degree.

The small town of Dublin, Ohio was infinitely charming. Many of the sidewalks were brick. Stately homes mingled with businesses designed in a European style. Signage was tasteful, a testament to a thoughtful plan for the business district.

She parked Jed's car and walked the streets, enjoying the ambience of a well-tended town with an understanding and clear sense of its history. Indeed, Dublin, Ohio was founded by a man from Dublin, Ireland who recreated the town so that it resembled the Dublin of his childhood. She continued exploring until she arrived at the library, which beckoned her inside. A large sign on the outside wall announced a capital campaign to renovate the library.

Stepping inside, she sniffed the aroma of books as she made her way around the shelves containing fiction, nonfiction, and children's books. In the adult section, she saw a sign "The Irish Book Club of Dublin, Ohio welcomes new members."

How nice it would be to join a book club, especially one devoted to Irish literature. Laura smiled, imagining herself a member of such a group. She had wanted to be part of a book club in Parmenter, but Jed said novels chosen by anyone outside their faith were likely to be abominations of God's word. That was the end of the discussion.

After returning home to Parmenter, memories of Dublin stayed with her. They were like mini-vacations in her mind. She couldn't wait to go back there again. Andrew would be home for Thanksgiving break. She might be able to talk Jed into letting her attend Mother's Weekend.

Her thoughts returned to the present as she strolled around Serendipities. As the grandfather clock struck half-past one, Laura realized it was almost time to start dinner. She carried the lace handkerchief and a floral linen photo box containing an assortment of Irish postcards to the counter. The box was pretty enough to display on her mother's bedside table. The old woman would enjoy looking through the postcards. A few of them might even bring happy memories of her life in Ireland before her family emigrated.

"I had a feeling those would catch your eye," Marjorie said. If Laura hadn't seen the items first, Marjorie would have made her a gift of them.

Laura opened her straw purse and extracted a crumpled ten-dollar bill. She glanced up to meet Marjorie's eyes and then looked away, certain her friend could read her thoughts. It was becoming increasingly diffi-cult to hide her feelings about the situation at home. If Marjorie could tell something was the matter, could others? Laura had spent years culti-vating what she hoped was the model of a good wife and mother, a godly woman, a dutiful daughter, and supportive friend.

There were a few chinks in that persona, and she guessed Marjorie already knew what those were. They had once shared confidences about their respective marriages. Being divorced meant Marjorie was no lon-ger welcome at Sunday services. In their church, divorce was an abomi-nation. Although Marjorie's situation had been similar, divorce for Laura was out of the question.

Serendipities meant the world to her—not just because the store was a place of sanctuary, offering endless creative outlets. It was also because her friendship with Marjorie was a lifeline. Seeing Marjorie on a regular basis allowed Laura to know she was not alone.

"I couldn't pass these up," Laura responded after a moment, her eyes on the counter. "The handkerchief is just like the one Gran carried. It will remind my mother of her, I hope."

While Marjorie completed the sale, Laura fumbled anxiously with the tiny white-gold cross around her neck, a gift from Jed on their tenth anniversary. Feeling for the cross was less a measure of comfort than a compulsion. If she ever lost it, she'd never hear the end of it.

"I'm glad you came in today," Marjorie said, handing her the bag. "I wanted to talk with you about something."

"Oh?" Laura hoped it wouldn't take too long. She needed to get a roast beef in the oven.

"I could use some help in the store and wondered if you'd be inter-ested in working part-time. I know how busy you must be with all that your husband asks of you, but it would really only be a couple of after-noons a week, and I could be flexible with the hours."

Laura's cheeks flushed with pleasure. "I would love that," she said, a smile forming at the corners of her mouth. "I'll have to talk with Jed, of course."

"Of course. Let me know. I can't imagine anyone who knows the mer-chandise better than you do." Marjorie's chuckle was kind, understanding.

"I will. Thank you," Laura said.

Grasping the small package, she left the store on winged feet. As she walked the half-mile home, it was all she could do not to stop several times and wrap her arms around herself in a hug. She felt such a rush of bliss, she thought she might laugh or sing.

Entering the house by the back door, she caught sight of the clock on the kitchen wall. A little after two o'clock: time to start dinner. She gathered ingredients from the pantry and refrigerator, pulling out pots and pans. As she peeled potatoes, diced, and arranged them in a saucepan with cold, salted water, she imagined herself at the cash register ringing up her first sale. As she seasoned the small roast beef and tucked it in the oven, she imagined herself arranging items for display on shelves and tables. Savoring these happy thoughts made her glad for the routine of the same supper they ate every Wednesday at five o'clock. While her hands were busy, her thoughts were free to roam.

With a few minutes to spare, she mixed flour, shortening, water, and a pinch of salt for pie crust. A cherry pie with ice cream would put Jed in a good mood. She could use the extra dough to bake apple dumplings with a cinnamon-sugar sauce for his breakfast.

As she rolled out the pie crust, she considered her next steps. Marjorie's job offer was the answer to prayer, one she had never dared utter except in secret. The job might only be part-time, and it might not provide much money, but it felt as if she were about to embark on a real career. She leaned against the kitchen sink, lost in thought. How would she manage this discussion with Jed?

As she filled the pie tin with dough, crimping the edges, and spooned cherry filling into the crust, she practiced in her head what she would say. It needed to sound casual, as if the idea had just occurred to her. She tried a few times to get the right tone.

Perhaps the tact to take was a more practical one. With Andrew gone, she needed more to do. That might do the trick. Idle hands were the devil's playthings. She blew out a frustrated breath. No matter what words she used, Jed was likely to say no, and that would be the end of it.

Could she go to work without telling him? How would she explain checks from Serendipities? Jed would have to cash them for her. Could Marjorie pay her in cash under the table? No, she couldn't ask that of her. The safest thing to do was help out at the store without pay. She could tell him that she wanted to help someone in need. *Did she have to say anything at all?*

She frowned. Not being paid for doing work she loved? And why shouldn't she have a job? Lots of women had jobs. She was thirty-nine years old with a son in college. Childbearing days were over. This was supposed to be the second chapter of her life.

For as long as she could remember, she had dreamed of having her own business. She intended to start small by helping church friends. With any luck, her first clients would tell other friends, and the business would grow by word of mouth. She had learned these things through Marjorie who taught her a little at a time how she had built Serendipities from a thought—a wish, really—to a real business. Laura had seen an embroidered pillow recently that said, "A dream fulfilled was once a wish."

She chewed on her lip, thinking hard. Dinner might not be the ideal time to talk with Jed about her career aspirations. He'd simply belittle or worse, forbid them. She needed to plan this out, consider all the possible objections. One way or another, it was time to make change or spend the rest of her life with regrets.

CHAPTER TWO

JUST TWO WEEKS BEFORE HIS FRESHMAN YEAR of high school, Michael, their oldest son, drowned at church camp on an August afternoon. In the years that followed, Laura grieved—mostly in silence, unable to express the crushing emotions she felt, even to her husband. From unspeakable sadness to red-hot anger that left her breathless and faint, she grieved quietly, succumbing to sobs in the shower where the rush of water masked the strangled sounds coming from the depths of her soul.

Oddly, Jed never seemed to show the same level of grief. The tearfulness he exhibited when talking with members of the congregation seemed mostly for show. He rarely displayed an emotion that wasn't anger. It wasn't his way. Even so, he had been quick—too quick, she thought—to absolve the boys involved in the incident. Just two days after the funeral, he made a public statement about Christian forgiveness as Laura stood by, fingernails digging into her palms, eyes welling with frustrated, angry tears. She suspected that Jed found his bright, gentle son a black mark on his own beliefs about how males should behave.

Michael had always shown remarkable sensitivity, even as a toddler. In school, he was bullied for being different, for being more interested in music than baseball. Laura had taught him to play the piano, but Michael had progressed quickly on his own, composing songs with complicated chords by the time he was in fifth grade. He had a rich baritone voice. By the time he was thirteen, he was pianist and organist for Sunday services, saving the church money for a salary. His playing was flawless. Even Jed couldn't find fault.

Everything Michael did, he accomplished with great care and attention to detail. He was older than his years, frequently taking charge of his headstrong, wayward brother. In many respects, Laura realized she treated Michael as another adult in their family. It may not have been fair, but he was her staunchest ally.

He died on a Tuesday, hours after leaving for church camp—not enthusiastically, Laura recalled, but subdued, seeming to dread the day. She had kissed him good-bye and handed him his brown paper lunch sack. The sheriff showed up at their front door a little after three o'clock with the terrible news.

There were fleeting images in her mind: Michael's peaceful expression as he lay in the coffin, dressed in his best navy-blue suit, and Jed's tight-lipped remarks at the funeral, extolling God's mysterious ways and the sin of questioning. There were sympathetic comments from church members and a cursory investigation that resulted in no charges being filed against the three other boys in the boat. Michael drowned in just six feet of water not far from shore—a freak accident, according to the coroner. This was confusing for Laura because Michael had been an excellent swimmer.

In the final hour of his brother's life, Andrew was less than a mile away, leading a children's Bible scavenger hunt. When he learned of Michael's death, he was inconsolable and withdrew into silence. Andrew and Laura grieved quietly together, often behind closed doors.

With Ohio State two hours away from Parmenter, and seemingly a world away from his father, Andrew had his chance for a happier future. Bright and handsome, with a ready smile, he was the kind of kid who made friends easily and was sure to be a success in whatever work he chose.

Laura knew when he started drinking beer with other freshmen because he told her, certain she wouldn't share the information with Jed. This rowdy behavior wasn't unusual, according to the student services staff. A freshman from a small town, especially from a strict household, often took a walk on the wild side the first year away from home. But Andrew wouldn't last long in college if he didn't shape up.

"You know what will happen if you get expelled," she warned him. "Your father will insist on seminary."

Andrew had no idea what he wanted to do with his life. He did know, however, that he didn't want to be like his father. He heeded his mother's warning and curbed his behavior.

With Andrew away at school, Laura dared to think what life might look like at this stage of her life. She had thought so often of her own design business that she could envision every detail. The first time she mentioned it to Jed, he scoffed. "What do you know about business? Let's face it, Laura. You're not smart enough to make that work."

She needed something to occupy her time now that Andrew was away from home. She and Jed had no interests in common and never did anything or went anywhere together. There were no date nights to keep the romance alive, for there had never been any to begin with. Their almost non-existent courtship during her senior year in high school had been a disappointment for Laura, minus any of the silly romantic gestures other girls talked about: flowers and candy and stolen kisses.

He was her teacher. But more than that, Reverend Jed was a powerful man in their church community. As youth pastor, he was next in line to move up to the role of senior pastor in the church hierarchy. With Laura's father on the board of elders, there would be little question of a positive vote in Jed's favor. His future was set, and now his destiny was also hers.

Jed presented her with an engagement ring at her birthday dinner, her senior year of high school. Though she envisioned a sentimental proposal with Jed on one knee asking for her hand in marriage, there was no need since the engagement had already been arranged with her father. Jed sealed the deal by slipping a thin gold ring on her finger. The tiny diamond chip didn't sparkle the way she had imagined.

Dressed in a simple white gown, a lace veil covering her face, she made her vows on that early June Saturday to love, honor, and cherish Jed until death. Her bridegroom lifted the veil and kissed her chastely on the side of her mouth as the senior pastor pronounced them husband and wife. This was followed by an equally unmemorable ninety-minute reception with cake and punch in the church basement.

What she did remember was their honeymoon, a horrifying experience with none of the gentleness she hoped he might show her. He had taken her innocence, yes. But worse than that, over the years, he chipped away at her soul.

The beatings started within weeks of the wedding. The first time happened when she lost track of time at the library and showed up five minutes late for his Bible study class. She could see the white line around his lips, his simmering rage when she slipped into the classroom carrying her childish blue Bible.

"It was an act of disrespect that caused embarrassment for me, as your husband," he said on the drive home.

"I'm sorry," she said, genuinely sorry to have displeased him. Remembering the obligatory answer that he liked to hear from his students, she added, "It won't happen again."

As soon as they were inside the house, he slapped her hard enough to leave a red mark on her cheek. Then he twisted her arm, dislocating her elbow and leaving a large purple bruise. She lied to the family doctor about what had happened, feeling mortified for upsetting her new husband. Her purpose was to please him. As a member of their congregation, the doctor also served on the board of elders. No questions were asked.

She worked hard to avoid provoking Jed, and could recall in detail each time he struck her and the offense. In years to come, many of the beatings happened as a result of the harsh corporal punishment he inflicted on their sons, leaving welts on their backs and angry red marks on their bottoms. When she tried to defend them, or if she showed emotion or winced as they were punished, she was next. It was inevitable. What mother could stand by as her children were beaten and not react or intervene?

Before laying a hand on her, however, Jed sent the boys to their room. Laura knew better than to make a sound, even when he threw her against the wall in the kitchen and she slid to the floor in a bruised heap. It was for the boys' sake that she kept quiet. As they grew into strong teenage men, she knew that Michael and Andrew would come to her defense. That she could not allow.

FRIDAYS WERE LAURA'S DAY TO CLEAN the second floor of the house. As she ran the vacuum around the carpet in Michael's room, she paused for a moment to sit down on his twin bed. His room appeared exactly as it had that day he left for camp, a clean towel arranged over the rail at the bottom of his bed, as if he would use it again that night. His Bible and a few books were arranged in a neat stack on the chest of drawers.

Jed insisted they donate Michael's clothes to charity a week after his death. But Laura had kept one of the shirts she found on the floor of the closet. It wasn't like him not to put his dirty shirt in the laundry. She took it as a sign that she was meant to keep it. Was it possible that years later, the shirt still retained his clean soapy scent? She opened the top drawer, held the shirt to her nose, and breathed in, remembering how she had held him close that morning before he left for camp, kissing his freshly-washed hair.

Every time she made Michael's favorite dinner, roasted chicken and scalloped potatoes, she could hear his words of thanks, feel his hand on her shoulder, the appreciative kiss on her cheek, hear a snippet of songs he liked to play on the piano, sniff the aroma of the soap he favored.

A funeral wasn't closure—not really—not when she never had the chance to tell him good-bye. The boys in the boat claimed it was an accident, that Michael had bumped his head on the side of the boat when he dived off and resurfaced too close to the boat. But six feet of water was too shallow and the lake floor too rocky for sensible Michael to have dived in. More troubling, there was a gash on the back of his head. It could have been made when his head hit a rock. But now she wondered, could it have been made with the side of a paddle?

The boys insisted they had followed the required buddy system. But when Michael remained underwater after bumping his head, they reported not being able to locate him in the murky water, gave up, and went to shore for help. Andrew pointed out that Michael would have floated and the water wasn't deep. This comment got him in trouble with Jed who warned him never again to cast aspersions on the character of others.

Pushing the heavy Hoover vacuum down the hall, she made her way to the master bedroom. Dusting the furniture, blinds, and ceiling fan, she ran the sweeper over the circular woven rug, handmade by her mother as a wedding present. As she did so, her eyes fell on the wedding photo atop Jed's chest of drawers. She didn't look old enough to be a bride. In the photo, there were bluish circles beneath eyes that appeared lost. Her memory of that day was mostly about feeling out of control, as if fate had taken her by the arm and yanked her in a direction she wasn't sure she wanted to go.

She had understood from the moment Jed singled her out for special attention her senior year what her life would become. She would be a clergyman's wife and the mother of his children, a helpmate in her husband's ministry. Could she have refused him? Laura had wanted more out of life. But in a struggling Ohio town, what better future was possible beyond marrying the young minister next in line to be senior pastor at one of the largest Apostolic Pentecostal churches in the region?

Laura opened the top drawer that held her sensible underthings, neatly folded in squares, the old-fashioned bras arranged with the cups turned one inside the other—orderly, her way of managing at least this small detail of her life. On the underside of the drawer, fastened to the wood with duct tape, was an envelope. She removed it and sat down on the window seat. Inside was a two-inch stack of bills, a small portion of the money she had been saving for almost as long as she had been married.

By being frugal with their food budget, it was possible to save about four hundred dollars a year. Birthday money from her mother went in there, too. When the wad of cash became too heavy for the envelope inside the drawer, she moved some of it to the empty oatmeal container at the back of the pantry or a fake can of silver polish hidden in the basement cleaning cabinet. It was designed to deter burglars. She had another container under the sink with a false bottom that resembled a can of cleanser. She rarely considered why she was saving so much money. She only knew it was important to have cash to call her own.

"Pin money," her mother had once termed the money she stashed in her lingerie drawer. "Every woman needs a little money of her own," Eileen said in her lilting Irish brogue. "You'll be wanting to give your husband the occasional treat."

Of course, her mother had no idea that Laura had amassed so much. She never would have approved of a woman saving that much money without her husband's knowledge. When Laura's father died suddenly, her mother hadn't the slightest understanding of how to manage her finances. Laura wanted to learn and understand money management, but Jed resisted.

"You mind your business here at home," he told her. "I'll manage the money that I earn. You're lucky that I'm as generous as I am. You don't have to do any real work."

As Sunday service began at ten o'clock sharp, the organist played the first notes of the prelude. Laura winced as the woman hit a second wrong note. She thought of Michael who never made a mistake when he played. His creations and performances were flawless. However, Jed remarked on what he called inappropriate titles and insisted on religious names for his son's original scores. In this way, Michael's title, *Twilight Rhapsody*, became *Before the Crucifix*, and *Awakening Hope* became *Apostles, Ye Awaken*.

Laura sat in the front row with the same practiced, attentive half-smile on her face that she always did, watching Jed as he read Scripture.

He looked her way now and then, offering a benevolent expression that was part of his public persona. Her mind wandered as she looked out one of the open windows—a moment too long. He frowned. She put her finger against her nose as though stifling a sneeze.

Every Sunday was like the one before. Jed never took a Sunday off, even for a family vacation. "My flock depend on their shepherd," he always said.

She suspected that if the congregation ever took a shine to a guest pastor, Jed might not receive a contract the following year. Membership dwindled a little more each year, a trend Jed blamed on social media. Laura asked Andrew what this meant. He explained Facebook and Twitter to her, and showed her his clandestine accounts on a computer at the library. No one in the Fisher family had a cell phone.

Following church service, Laura sipped coffee with several other wives and watched her husband interact with parishioners in the base-ment social hall. He had already wolfed down three cookies and two brownies. This meant he wouldn't want a cooked lunch.

After arriving home, Laura changed out of her church dress into a long navy skirt and light-blue blouse. She fixed tuna salad sandwiches on white bread, sliced them into triangles, and arranged them on plates with cantaloupe slices and grapes. They ate their lunch in silence. As she rose to take their plates to the sink, Jed reached for her hand.

"Think we should go upstairs now, mother?" he asked. It wasn't a question. Her stomach lurched.

She had heard other women her age mention "empty nesting," that time when children left home, and they began relating to their husbands in an entirely new way, much as they had before the children came. Laura and Jed's relationship had never been a close one, their conversa-tions limited to what he wanted for supper or whether she had lined his trousers with the crease he preferred.

In lovemaking, there was no foreplay. She never actually considered what they did to be lovemaking. It was a marital requirement accepted by a dutiful wife. Pleasure for her was out of the equation.

"Let me wash the lunch dishes first. Nothing worse than the smell of old tuna salad." With her back turned to Jed, she ventured the next topic. "Now that Andrew is at school, I suppose things will be different now. I might need to find something constructive to do with my time." She hoped the discussion would put Jed out of the mood.

"I can't imagine anything more constructive than raising children. You will be forty on your next birthday. That is the age when women your age start having mental troubles, after their children leave home. I think it would be good for you to have another baby."

She whirled around to face him. "Oh, Jed. If it hasn't happened all these years since Andrew was born, maybe it can't happen anymore." She dared not use the term 'menopause.' "I'm approaching that age when . . ."

"Don't be silly. You're a young woman. Sarah gave birth to John the Baptist when she was in her nineties."

Laura bit her lip. "Such a beautiful miracle, Jed." She carefully added, "I doubt that I am worthy of such a blessing."

He rose from the table and took her arm, leading her toward the stairs. "Miracles require action. We'll keep trying until God grants us a miracle."

At that moment, Laura was consumed with such white-hot rage, her hands tightened into fists. She breathed in and out to contain her emotions as she followed him meekly up the stairs to their bedroom. An inner knowledge began to take shape. Somehow, some way, she would leave him.

Chapter Three

The next morning, Laura picked up the phone on the kitchen wall and dialed the number for Serendipities. She dreaded making the call, but Marjorie deserved a prompt response to her offer of a part-time job. There was an even more serious conversation Laura wanted to have with her, but that would have to wait. She needed to lay low and gather more information.

The next time she saw Marjorie in person, she would confide her plans to leave Jed. Marjorie would help her. She couldn't tell anyone else—not even her mother. She would find acceptance from Marjorie who had told her about the end of her marriage to an abusive alcoholic. A restraining order had been needed.

"Marjorie, hello. It's Laura," she began. "I want you to know how much I appreciate your offer of a job at the store. I would love to say yes, but . . ."

"But Jed doesn't like the idea," Marjorie finished for her in a flat tone.

"He doesn't like the idea of me working outside our home. He says I already have an important job as his wife, and that has to be my focus."

"I understand. I half-expected it," Marjorie said. "Hopefully, it didn't cause you any . . . difficulties."

Laura swallowed hard. The throbbing in her shoulder was a painful reminder of that difficulty. "I would love to work at Serendipities," she said, twisting the cord around her other hand. "I just thought I ought to tell you that I can't do it now. But," she faltered, "could you keep the job open for a little while? I'm working on this."

"Laura, is there anything else you want to tell me? Are you okay?"

"I'm fine," Laura said. A lump in her throat made it impossible to take a complete breath. She gently touched the sore spot on her shoulder at the neckline, where Jed had dug in his fingers, driving home his point. *You are never to bring up this subject again.*

"Laura?"

"Yes?" she answered in a near whisper.

"I care about your safety. I am always here for you," Marjorie said. "Promise you'll come to me if you ever need help. I mean that."

Despite her best efforts, a tear trickled down the side of Laura's nose. "Thank you. I'll stop by later this week." She took a deep breath. "I have to go now."

Jed's reaction to Laura's request to work part-time at Serendipities hadn't been a surprise to her. The moment she mentioned Marjorie's offer, his mouth formed that ugly white line she knew so well, and the vein at his temple throbbed. The redness in his cheeks, the result of uncontrolled rosacea, became a mottled purple a moment before he slammed his fist down on the kitchen table. The plates rattled, and a fork slid off the table onto the floor. As she bent over to pick it up, his long fingers latched onto the spot where her neck and shoulder met. He squeezed so hard, she cried out.

"You have more important things to do than play in that woman's store," he said. "She is no longer a member of my church. I allow you to shop there because I believe you are a good influence on her. But you are my wife and that is your full-time occupation. Am I making myself clear?"

"Yes." The pain in Laura's shoulder reached a crescendo as he squeezed harder on the tendons and bone. "Jed, please. I know my place. I won't ask again."

That night, to make his point, he took her by force. Afterward, as soon as she heard his first low snores, she wrapped herself in her robe and crept to the bathroom. With shaking hands, she reached behind the towels in the bathroom closet and removed the forbidden item she kept hidden there. Jed had asked her about it many years ago, seemingly satisfied with her explanation that it was a hygiene item for "that time of the month."

Filling the bag with warm water, she inserted the tube, wincing at the soreness of her tender flesh. Afterward, she ran warm water into the sink and washed away all evidence of Jed. "Deliver us from evil," she mouthed before she returned to their bed.

Jed lay on his back, one arm thrown across his eyes, his mouth open, snoring louder now. He hadn't heard a thing. She took a quiet breath and slipped beneath the sheets, raising them to her chin, positioning herself as far away from him as the full-size mattress allowed.

The bright light of the waxing moon shone through the slats of blinds in their west-facing room. Laura fixed her gaze on the shadows the moonlight projected onto the furniture and walls. A car made a swishing sound as it passed along the quiet street. Grateful for the peace that was possible only in the night when Jed's heavy sleep habits left him dead to the world, Laura used these hours to dream.

She envisioned a two-story house with a large front porch on a tree-lined street. The house had a spacious first floor with large rooms. One room featured tall built-in bookshelves. The other rooms contained beautiful furnishings, lamps, and collectibles. There were price tags on these items. It was a store, yes, but so comfortable and inviting, anyone who entered would feel right at home and want to stay a while.

The upstairs of the house offered a separate living space with a modern kitchen, two bedrooms, a large modern bathroom, and an open living room-dining room combination. In her mind's eye, she arranged furnishings in her new home in the sophisticated yet rustic farmhouse style she liked so much. After picturing this place over the course of a few years, she had begun to believe it actually existed.

The next morning, while Jed showered and shaved, Laura donned a blue housedress with a higher neckline to hide the purple marks his fingers had made. The bruises would predictably deepen in hue and then cycle from reddish-purple to blue-black, grayish-green, and finally yellow. Jed excelled at this kind of injury: a bruise that caused long-term discomfort. It was intended as a reminder not to upset him again.

She fried four strips of center-cut bacon and cooked his eggs over medium in the bacon grease, the way he liked them. Slicing an apple dumpling in half, she arranged it in a bowl with the cream pitcher next to it. Feeding him a big breakfast might mean he wouldn't be as grouchy when he came home for lunch. She buttered two pieces of white toast to the very edges of the crusts, cut the toast into triangles, and arranged the pieces on his plate with a sprig of parsley and a fan of fresh orange slices. She squeezed more oranges for his juice and set the glass on the table, along with his coffee cup and blood pressure medicines. Then she went to the bottom of the stairs to listen.

Even his sounds were predictable: the dresser drawer closing with a squeak, a thump-thump as two dress shoes dropped from a closet shelf to the floor, the first loud snort into a handkerchief, followed by the toilet flushing. She waited until she heard his footsteps on the stairs before pouring his coffee. It had to be the ideal temperature.

"Good morning," he said, entering the kitchen. He gave her a perfunctory kiss on the cheek. "Smells good."

"Would you like strawberry or boysenberry jelly on your toast today?" she asked, opening the refrigerator door.

"Don't you have any peach?"

"We ran out. But I'll get more peaches at the store and make you a nice fresh batch," she said. "I would have done it earlier, but the peaches weren't sweet the way you like them."

"I would enjoy that." He bit hard into a slice of toast, dabbing at the butter that dribbled down his chin. The cloth napkins they used were freshly washed and ironed.

"What are your plans for today?" he asked, raising his eyes to hers.

Laura drew in a deep breath. "I've got a few birthday gifts to buy for ladies in the Gethsemane Group," she said. "You know how they love to be remembered. Mildred Jackson turns ninety next week."

"Perhaps they'd enjoy some fresh peach preserves," he said, lowering his glasses and peering over them at her.

Laura swallowed hard. "What a nice idea," she said. "Economical, too."

He had read her thoughts. Of course, he would want her to stay away from Serendipities. It would be wise to avoid going there for at least a week or two. She felt disheartened.

"I'll pick up some peaches and make the jelly today," she said, forcing a smile. "Pork chops and cinnamon apples for supper sound good to you?"

"My, we are trying to make amends," he said with a smirk. She bit her tongue and lowered her eyes so he wouldn't see the anger she felt roiling up.

He handed her grocery money and left for the church a little before nine. As she watched him get into the Ford sedan, whistling "Onward Christian Solders," she closed the front door. There wasn't much time to get everything done before he came home for lunch.

She tucked the twenty-dollar bill into her purse, locked the front door behind her, and started off down the sidewalk. The grocery store was nearly a mile from their home. It was a sultry late September day. The back of her dress turned damp within minutes. She dabbed at the perspiration on her upper lip and quickened her pace.

The air conditioning at Save Mart felt heavenly as she pushed a small shopping cart around the produce section. She saw the bin of pink and gold peaches, perfectly ripe, and loaded enough of them into bags to make six jars of jam. Then she added two baking potatoes and a small bag of green beans for dinner. On her way to the front of the store, she selected two pork chops she found on sale.

She paid at the register, tucking the change into her purse, and picked up two of the grocery bags. She slid the plastic loops over her left arm. Then she lifted the other two bags and felt an instant jolt of red-hot pain shoot through her shoulder to her fingertips. She attempted to hook the bags over her wrist, but the effort left her feeling sick to her stomach.

The bags were too heavy. She'd never make it to the nearest stop sign, much less the whole way home. Her neck and shoulder hurt so much that tears formed at the corners of her eyes. She left the bags in her shopping cart, wondering if she dared push it home. She could call the store and let them know she'd return it later. Stopping at a bench outside the store, she contemplated her options. Then she wiped her wet eyes on her forearm and tried again to arrange the heaviest bags to her good arm.

"That looks like a heavy load. May I help you to your car?" It was a man she had seen in their neighborhood. She didn't know his name, but he lived in the yellow frame house a few blocks up the street. He was good-looking and dressed well. Today, he had on a pair of pressed khakis and a sky-blue golf shirt. She thought he was married, although she hadn't seen much of his pretty wife in recent years.

"I-I didn't drive. I walked," she said.

"You live over on Wells, right? I've seen you sweeping your porch," the man said. He smiled. "I'm John Conway."

"Pleased to meet you. I'm Laura Fisher." She could feel more beads of sweat forming on her upper lip, but this time it was from nervousness. Another feeling of nausea washed over her.

"Are you okay?" he asked. "Here, please sit down." He helped her onto the bench and sat beside her.

Laura was mortified. "I injured my shoulder yesterday," she said. "Stupid of me to think I could carry all these peaches. I promised my husband homemade jelly."

"I'll drive you," he said. "I insist."

"Oh, no!" she said quickly. "I mean, I couldn't impose on you like that."

His eyes widened. "It's no trouble at all. You live just down the street. We're neighbors. I promise; I'm safe."

Laura knew she couldn't make it the entire way home with such heavy bags. What choice did she have? Jed would be home for lunch around noon. Getting a ride home would save time.

"Thank you," she said, her cheeks reddening. "I don't know what I was thinking. I should have known I couldn't carry all those peaches."

"You were probably thinking how good that jelly would taste after you made it," he said easily. "You just skipped over the part about getting them home from the store. Your husband is a lucky man."

John Conway had a champagne-colored, late-model SUV with seats that sat up high. Laura felt silly and nervous as he loaded her bags of peaches into the back seat and held the front passenger door open for her. The inside of the vehicle smelled new. And when he turned on the air conditioning, Laura wished she could ride around all day with him.

"I'm glad I came along when I did," John said, offering her a quick smile. "No telling how much riper those peaches would have gotten in this heat."

It was a joke. She wasn't sure how to respond. Probably best to be polite. "I can't thank you enough. I don't know what I would have done," she said, afraid to look at him directly for more than a few seconds. "My husband has the car most days. I-I don't usually mind walking home from the store."

"What does your husband do?" he asked.

"He's senior pastor of our church. Full Faith Church of Love," she added.

John's face changed expression for just a moment. "Ah," he said. "The one-story red brick building over on Central? What denomination is it?"

Laura felt her cheeks grow warm. This was a sore point among many church members. Would he understand what it meant to be an Apostolic Pentecostal with all the variations in their denomination? Probably not. She considered whether such an answer might require more explanation than she was prepared to offer and decided to keep it simple. "It's Christian," she finally said.

Full Faith Church of Love was an independent version of another, much larger Apostolic Pentecostal congregation. A battle for power on the board twelve years earlier resulted in a lean year of contributions as offended members of the board, many of them wealthy, defected and started their own congregation. They became its first board of elders. Although similar in structure to the mother church, this newer congregation had taken an even more conservative approach, insisting among other things that women wear longer skirts and avoid shorter hair styles. Jed had been hired as the congregation's first senior pastor, a promotion for him from his previous role.

John smiled. "It's nice to know I have a minister nearby if I ever need one, though I fear I may be a lost cause."

Was this a joke, too? Laura turned slightly in her seat. She had never heard anyone make this kind of comment. "You are welcome to attend our church," she said.

John pulled up in front of Laura's house. "I've never known anyone who actually went there." He unbuckled his seatbelt. "Well, here we are. Let me help you take those peaches into the house."

"Oh, no, please. If you could just put them on the front porch steps, I can get them easily from there."

She was getting more nervous as the time approached eleven-thirty. What if Jed came home early? He wouldn't approve of her accepting a ride from a stranger, especially a man—even if that stranger had helped her get safely home—even if he might be a prospective church-goer.

John smiled. "I'd better get home myself. My wife isn't well."

Laura turned toward him. "Is there something I can do to help?"

"Jackie has A.L.S. They call it Lou Gehrig's disease. She's bedridden now."

"I'm sorry to hear that." No wonder she hadn't seen Mrs. Conway in so long. She would make an extra jar of peach jelly for John and his wife. This was in the realm of the duties of a pastor's wife. Surely, Jed wouldn't have a problem with that. "Thank you again," she said.

He stood by his car door. "Take care, Mrs. Fisher," he said.

"You, too, Mr. Conway." They looked at each other for a moment, just long enough for Laura to see the kindness in his eyes. He seemed to be studying her face with an expression she found disconcerting. "Well, good-bye," she stammered. "Please let your wife know I'll keep her in my prayers."

"I'll do that. So long," he said and got back into his car.

After retrieving the bags of peaches one at a time, Laura heated a pan of soup for Jed and made a bologna sandwich with a slice of American cheese. She filled two stockpots with water and put them on the stove to boil. The day was too warm to spend over a hot stove cooking and peeling hot peaches, but she had promised. More than anything, she needed to get back in Jed's good graces.

After a silent dinner, she washed and dried the dinner dishes, made a cup of tea for Jed, and placed it on the end table beside him, along with two Oreos. Then she mopped the kitchen floor twice. It would never do for Jed to notice stickiness on the linoleum. He would ask what she did all day. Her shoulder was a reminder not to give him any more reasons for complaint.

As she mopped, her thoughts turned to John Conway. What a gentleman he had been to offer help when she needed it most. How sad that his wife was so ill. The next time she went to the library, she'd ask the librarian to help her look up A.L.S. so she could better understand what John's wife was suffering.

"Jed, I'm going to take a shower," she said, heading upstairs. He didn't respond.

It was a little before eight-thirty. She felt drained and sick from working all day in the hot kitchen. Her shoulder throbbed like a bad toothache, and her arm was stiffening. Maybe a couple of Tylenol would take the edge off. She swallowed two with a cupful of water from the bathroom tap.

She turned on the water and adjusted it to cool before stepping into the shower. She could imagine herself under a tropical waterfall. Four minutes passed while she did her best to wash her long hair with one hand. She counted two more minutes under the cool water. Then she shut it off, conscious that she wasn't the one who paid the utility bills.

She towel-dried her hair with one arm, then finger-combed it to remove most of the tangles. She'd never be able to braid it tonight. She changed into a cotton nightgown and sank to her knees in prayer.

Jed was still downstairs reading scripture, preparing for Sunday's sermon. Perhaps tonight, she could have a reprieve from his attentions. If he pressed on her shoulder or arm, she wouldn't be able to stand the pain. He had seemed more tired than usual at dinner, offering her a nod when she served him the warm biscuits, butter, and peach jelly. After dinner, he went directly to his favorite chair, turned on the reading light, and opened his Bible.

Before turning in for the night, she tip-toed halfway down the stairs and leaned over the railing. She could see the top of his head, balding at the crown, as he sat in his chair. He always expected her to say good-night. But if she did, would he follow her upstairs? She weighed the risk and decided that when he finally came to bed, she would explain that she hadn't wanted to disturb him in his important work.

She turned down the lightweight blanket and sheets, and set the alarm for six o'clock. Lowering herself across the mattress at the bottom of the bed, she gingerly turned on her good side. Flinching in discomfort as she adjusted her body, she gazed out the windows at the tree tops on the darkened street. A fragrant breeze blew through the window, lifting the curtains. She savored the coolness, the sweet scent of freshly-mown grass. Crickets chirped their melodic cadence.

She lay for a while in solitude and silence, thinking about events of the past few days. "Please, Lord, help me to accept what is mine to bear," she implored in a soft voice. "Help me to be more grateful for my many blessings."

Feeling drowsy now, she closed her eyes. She awoke two hours later with a pounding heart. Where was Jed? She glanced at the clock on the bedside table. It was after eleven. He must still be working on his ser-mon. She went downstairs and noticed him asleep in his chair. His head tilted slightly to the right. She walked around to face him and saw that his eyes were closed, his mouth open. His skin was a weird bluish color.

"Jed?" She touched his forehead. His skin felt clammy to the touch, and she didn't think he was breathing.

With no idea of how long he might have been like this, she ran to the kitchen phone and dialed nine-one-one. "My husband isn't breathing," she said when the dispatcher answered.

"Does he have a heart condition?" the woman asked. "Have you per-formed CPR?"

"He's got high blood pressure. I just found him. I don't know how long he's been like this."

"An ambulance is on its way, ma'am," the woman said. "Is he on the floor? If not, try to get him on the floor. I'll talk you through the steps to see if you can get him breathing again."

"He's in his chair," she said. "I'll try to move him to the floor." She stretched the phone cord as close to the chair as possible, but it was no use. At this rate, using only gravity, she'd drop him face-down on the carpet. She ran to the hallway leading from the kitchen, and picked up the phone. "I can't move him," she said, trying hard to keep the hysteria from her voice. "I have a bad shoulder."

"The ambulance will be there soon, ma'am," the dispatcher said. "Try to remain calm."

It was probably only a matter of ten minutes, but seemed much longer before she heard sirens, and saw blue, white, and red lights flashing through the front windows of the house. She ran to the front door and flung it open, watching as first an ambulance, then a police car, and finally a fire truck parked in front of the house. The flurry of activity that followed produced nothing more than the pronounce-ment by one of the E.M.T.'s that Jed was gone, something Laura already understood.

The police officers asked her routine questions. Numb and dazed, Laura answered in a wooden voice, feeling vaguely guilty. She was glad they didn't ask the questions that paraded through her head. Could she have saved him if she had gone downstairs earlier? If she had ignored the pain in her shoulder and tried harder to move him to the floor? She looked at Jed's gray impassive face and covered her eyes with her hands.

One of the officers helped her to a chair and wrapped a comforter around her shoulders while the E.M.T.'s loaded Jed's lifeless form onto a stretcher. Though it was a warm, humid night, she felt so cold. This dead body was her husband. Though he was covered, one of his arms hung outside the sheet. She noticed his gold wedding band before the E.M.T. gently tucked in the arm, handling the body with respect as the new widow looked on. Still, Laura felt nothing. Nothing.

Where was Jed's spirit now? Hovering somewhere above, watching her? Was he judging her lack of reaction to his death? Should she have asked for his wedding ring?

"Ma'am, is there family you can call?" The young officer stood in front of her, holding a clipboard and pen.

"My son is at Ohio State," she answered. "My mother is in a nursing home."

"Friends, then?" the officer persisted. "You shouldn't be alone."

She looked at the young man and said in a plaintive voice, "I have no idea what to do."

"Why don't you follow the ambulance to the hospital? Someone will help you there."

"Yes, I'll do that," she said. "I need to change." She was still in her nightgown and robe, her feet bare. She lifted her arm, and her breath caught at the sharp pain in her shoulder.

"Mrs. Fisher, are you alright? Are you injured?" He looked at her intently.

"I hurt my shoulder."

"Let me have one of the medics take a look," he said.

"No," she said quickly, shaking her head. "I'm fine."

He gave her a look that spoke volumes. *He knew.* "Someone at the hospital should look at that shoulder. I can see the purple bruise above your neckline."

By holding onto the back of a chair, she was able to remain steady on her feet. "Thank you for your concern," she said. "I'll change my clothes."

Ten minutes later, fully dressed, she picked up her purse and car keys, and walked to Jed's car in the driveway. She unlocked the driver's side door, and tossed her purse on the passenger seat. Then she stood as if frozen, staring into the night sky where a sliver of moon shone and stars twinkled. Peace washed over her. Strange. It was the same peace she had experienced one time before, on the one-year anniversary of Michael's passing. She thought she felt him there.

"Mrs. Fisher, are you okay?"

She startled and whirled around, expecting to see another first responder, and instead came face-to-face with someone familiar, though she had trouble placing him, at first. Then her mind cleared. "Oh, Mr. Conway," she said, a memory of earlier that day replacing the fuzziness. "What are you doing here?"

"I heard sirens and saw lights. Then I realized it was your house. What happened?"

"My husband . . . I have to go to the hospital now."

"Is he alive?" John asked, more polite than curious. The ambulance had not flashed its lights or sped away into the night.

She shook her head. "It might have been a heart attack or stroke, I suppose. I-I was upstairs when it happened. I found him."

John walked over to Laura and stood just a few feet away from her, his eyes taking in her ghostly appearance. She was pale, her eyes large and lost. "I'm sorry for your loss. What can I do to help?"

"I need to go to the hospital," she repeated. She dropped the car keys on the driveway and bent to pick them up, but she couldn't reach the ground before taking in a sharp breath of pain.

He scooped up the keys for her. "You shouldn't drive yourself, not at a time like this. My wife is sleeping. I can leave her for a little while. Let me take you," he said. "I'd feel better if I could help."

"Thank you," she said, offering him a wan smile. What a kind man he was.

His eyes studied her as they had earlier in the day. She looked completely different than she had that morning, when she had worn her hair tightly fastened in a bun, her dress buttoned up to the neck. Now, with her brown hair long and free, a few strands blowing in the night breeze, she appeared otherworldly and so, so beautiful. Her blue eyes were vacant, her skin nearly white in the moonlight. The dress she wore barely disguised the ugly bruise snaking up her neck. Surely, whatever happened to her shoulder and neck hadn't been an accident.

Laura raised her eyes to meet his and saw compassion. He was unlike any man she had ever known, polite and caring, with no expectation of anything in return. And then, his arm was around her, gently leading her to the passenger side of his car, helping her in. He leaned across and fastened her seatbelt before shutting the door. She leaned against the headrest and stared straight ahead as he got in the car and started the engine.

"I have a friend, Marjorie. I can call her when I get to the hospital," she said.

"Don't you have a cell phone?"

"No. I can use a pay phone."

"You are welcome to use my cell phone," John said. "I won't be able to stay with you for very long, but I'll take your car back to your house and park it. I'll leave the keys under your front door mat. You shouldn't drive tonight."

"I believe you are right. Thank you."

He thought for a moment before speaking. "I'll give you my phone number, and you can call from the hospital if you need me to pick you up."

She glanced over at him. "I should call my son, Andrew. He's at Ohio State."

"Yes, he'll want to be with you, I'm sure. Were he and your husband very close?"

"No." She took in a deep breath and let it out. There was nothing more to say.

John glanced over and saw that her hands were clenched into fists at her sides. "I won't leave you until your friend gets there," he said and started the engine.

She had never imagined herself a widow, not even in her worst moments with Jed. There would be an autopsy to determine the cause of death. The emergency room doctor assured her that if his suspicions were correct, Jed had died quickly. She hadn't been certain whether the relief she felt at hearing this was for Jed or herself.

Laura agreed to have her shoulder x-rayed. There was nothing broken, but she saw the look that passed between the medical personnel. The bruise looked suspicious with its finger-like extensions.

One of the nurses gave her such a look of sympathy that Laura instantly felt ashamed. "God bless you, dear," the nurse said. "This injury won't take long to heal. But it would be good for you to see a counselor. It helps with all the experiences in life that cause us pain."

Looking back, the entire night seemed surreal. She had been given her freedom, although it was, no doubt, sinful to be grateful when the release came as a result of her husband's death. There would be no pregnancy to worry about, no need to arrange in secret to leave Jed. She would never have to tell Andrew what she had planned to do. There was no reason to talk with an attorney or prepare to file a restraining order. Part of her wanted to thank God for this unexpected deliverance. For indeed, it seemed like divine intervention. But wasn't it wrong to be thankful for something that meant someone else had to die?

John stayed with her at the hospital for over an hour before driving Jed's car back to her house. By then, Marjorie had arrived and taken over, acting as Laura's advocate. The next several weeks were a blur.

With Marjorie's assistance, Laura opened her own bank account and deposited all the cash she had hidden throughout the house, over four thousand dollars. She needed her own account right away since Jed had never put her name on the household checking account. She had funeral expenses to pay in addition to utility bills. She received a debit card, and Marjorie explained how to use it, as well as how to write checks and reconcile them on the ledger with the monthly statement.

"He must have believed he was immortal," Marjorie muttered. "What did he think you would do if something happened to him? Laura, your name should have been on that checking account," she said, clucking her tongue.

There also was no will, so it would take time for the estate to go through probate. Fortunately, with the debit card and money in her own account, Laura was able to put a down payment on a no-frills funeral. The money she had hidden away during their marriage would help until Jed's life insurance policy paid out. She remembered the policy was for a hundred thousand dollars. She would be able to live on that for a long while.

With her mother along for the ride, she drove to Columbus to pick up Andrew from school. Mother and son went through the motions of two public viewings at the funeral home. As church members filed one-by-one to the coffin where Jed lay in his best suit, Laura accepted their condolences. She comforted those who had supported Jed as elders and deacons, and played the role she had always played: the good pastor's wife. At the graveside, she and Andrew held hands while Jed's casket was lowered into the ground.

"It's over," Andrew murmured as they got into the car after the graveside service. Laura understood that he meant more than just the funeral.

It didn't come as a surprise that no one from the church asked about her plans for the future. A new minister would be appointed by the board of elders as soon as possible to fill Jed's role. That was their highest priority. There was no need for her to leave her home since she and Jed had owned it outright.

Throughout the next two days, Andrew remained by his mother's side. He seemed to understand what she was thinking without benefit of words, anticipating her needs. Laura noticed that Andrew hadn't shed a single tear, at least in her presence. She assumed he had feelings of some sort about his father, and encouraged him to seek counseling when he returned to Ohio State.

That Saturday evening, as they sat together watching the news, Andrew rose and went to his room. He returned with a jug of red wine and two juice glasses. Handing one to her, he poured his mother her first alcoholic drink.

"Andrew, where did you get this?" she asked.

"A neighbor brought it for you. I hid it in the closet thinking you'd throw it out," he said with his usual rakish grin. "Come on, Mom."

"Oh, I don't think . . ." she protested. "You know I don't drink alcohol."

"Why not?" he asked. "It's wine, Mom. Even Jesus drank wine."

She accepted the glass he handed her. It had an odd sweetish flavor—unaccustomed as she was to the taste of alcohol—but the warm feeling it produced as it slipped down her throat and into her chest allowed her to take her first complete breath in weeks.

"Dad is gone," Andrew began in a gentle voice. "You have choices now. What do you want?" A tear slipped down Laura's cheek. She wiped it away with one finger and took another cautious sip of wine.

"I need to work," she said. "I *want* to work," she corrected herself. She thought of Marjorie's offer of employment. "Marjorie offered me a part-time job. I couldn't accept it while your father was alive."

"You could move closer to me in Columbus. I would love that."

"I would, too. I need a little time to figure things out, son," Laura said.

"Grandma can come, too," he said. "Sell this house. Buy a new one. Get something that makes you happy, that doesn't remind you of him."

"Oh, Andrew," she answered, feeling exhaustion creep over her by degrees. "He was your father. We were married for over twenty-one years. Of course, I'll be reminded of him." What she didn't say was that when she thought of Jed, the guilty feelings that surfaced were entirely because she did not miss him. She felt free as a bird taking flight.

"Michael and I knew how he treated you. You deserved way better than him."

"He was your father," she said, but she spoke it as a matter of fact, without admonishment. "We won't speak ill of him," she added. She took another sip of wine. "I have thought about moving closer to you."

And she had, fleetingly. Little green shoots like tendrils of hopeful vines blossomed from this new plant that was taking root: her new life. She had already begun to think of what might come next.

CHAPTER FOUR

MARJORIE MADE GOOD ON HER OFFER of a part-time job at Serendipities. She trained her newest part-time employee to be assistant manager. What Laura lacked in self-confidence and job skills, she more than made up for in determination and enthusiasm. Under Marjorie's coaching, she learned the consignment business from inventory to bookkeeping, and even how to promote the business on a shoestring. She flourished under her mentor's patient instruction.

But Marjorie didn't stop there. She took Laura shopping for a new wardrobe and taught her how to apply a tasteful amount of make-up. "You'll have more confidence if you dress as other women do," she insisted. "You don't need mascara, but a little rose lipstick and blush will highlight your face. Make-up is intended to enhance, not advertise."

At first, Laura blanched at the slim pants Marjorie handed her to try on in the dressing room. Pants were what men wore. Yet she liked the way they looked, hugging her slender ankles. She frowned at herself in an above-the-knee navy pencil skirt and matching sky-blue knit top that showed off her curves. She had never before displayed her legs—or feet, for that matter—in public. These outfits were so different from anything she had ever worn. In these clothes, she was a different person.

"Give yourself time to get used to the new you. This is a good way to ease into dressing the part of a career woman," Marjorie said. "Many of our clients dress well, and as a matter of respect, we ought to mirror their style of dress." This, Laura understood. It was her duty to be acceptable to others.

The first thing Laura did after Jed's funeral was to move her mother out of the county nursing home and into Michael's old room—certain he would have wanted that. Her mother spent most days helping around the house and listening to the radio or watching game shows.

On Sundays, when they attended church, Laura continued to dress in the conservative manner expected of women. As Jed's widow, it was assumed she would continue attending church. The board of elders appointed an interim pastor. But without Jed at the pulpit, Laura felt she had no reason to be there. She worried that her faith was weakening or that she was thinking in a sinful manner.

Those old ways of looking—and being—had begun to shift as each day brought opportunities to learn about a world that, until recently, had been as foreign as another country. It was like learning a new language. She had a sense that every aspect of her past was being compartmentalized, the memories and experiences stored away in imaginary boxes, as her new life unfolded.

As days turned into weeks and three months passed, Laura marveled at the difference in her appearance and in the way she carried herself. She felt confident, even pretty. After seeing a television program about women who donated locks of hair to help other women who had lost theirs to chemotherapy or other conditions, Laura decided to cut her nearly waist-length hair.

Marjorie accompanied her to a salon where Laura's hair was cut into a becoming shoulder-length style that accentuated her valentine-shaped face. The new Laura bore little resemblance to the tired, careworn woman of former days. This Laura was downright gorgeous. She felt lighter in more ways than one, as unfettered as a bird taking flight.

She saw a therapist twice a month to help process all that had happened. From childhood through adolescence into adulthood, she had never believed her life had meaning or value beyond what others expected from her. At first, she had trouble speaking about how Jed had treated her. What did this sophisticated, educated woman with a doctoral degree know about being an abused spouse? As it turned out, the therapist had endured an abusive relationship before becoming a counselor—information she shared in a matter-of-fact manner that put Laura at ease.

"What happened to you is far more common than you might imagine," the counselor said.

Within a few months, as the therapist coaxed forth details with her gentle questions, Laura opened up more and more, sharing fleeting yet still painful memories, and beginning the process of letting go of shame and guilt. A little at a time, she peeled back layers of her life like an onion, discarding the skins, revealing what mattered most. She could have a better life.

As for Michael's tragic death, the counselor assured her that with time, she could find some measure of peace. She even suggested that Laura might come to a decision to pursue answers to her questions. That might be what she needed in order to achieve closure.

Laura worried that Andrew's experience growing up with an abusive father might mean he would have challenging relationships with women. How would he know how to have a healthy relationship free of violence? Andrew had been on the receiving end of many a beating, and knew how fast a cross word could turn into a punch.

As a boy, he was the brother whose mischief and antics often led to trouble, resulting in whippings with Jed's leather belt. It seemed to Laura that her youngest son relished the role of instigator, fearlessly facing his father in stare-downs. Even so, he took his punishment without protest or tears. Once spent, Jed's anger often dissipated. She later realized that Andrew's actions were heroic, intended to protect her.

"Mom, I'm different from him because I choose to be different," he said following one therapy session. "Michael and I used to hide under the bed when Dad had one of his fits. Michael said men who hit women and kids weren't real men." His expression turned sad. "Ironic, isn't it?"

"What's ironic, son?"

"That Michael was a better man than our father. He treated Michael like dirt because he didn't behave the way Dad thought a real man should. Remember how he teased Michael? He bullied him in front of everyone."

Expressed in that manner, Laura felt even worse about what Michael had endured. His own father had defended the three boys who likely caused his oldest son's death. Someday, perhaps she could talk with someone who understood how to reopen an investigation.

Laura spent more time visiting Andrew in Columbus. They attended several counseling sessions together. She loved the Columbus area and could imagine living in nearby Dublin. Each time she went to Dublin, she pictured herself strolling the streets of her new hometown.

She went to the Dublin library and even participated a few times as a guest in the Irish book club. The members were bright and funny, respectful of each other's opinions, and happy to welcome newcomers.

Some were teachers and writers. One was a nurse. A married couple attended together.

"Will you be moving here anytime soon?" Jan Armstrong, the librarian, asked Laura after her second visit.

"I'm beginning to think so," Laura said, a warm feeling enveloping her. "I feel right at home here."

Attending the book club that evening, Laura knew it was only a matter of time before she found a job in the Columbus area. There, she could find a new home. These thoughts invaded most of her waking moments, bringing feelings of such intense happiness, she felt certain something wonderful was about to happen.

With so many changes in her life, it was only natural that Laura would decide to leave the church. The interim pastor was hired a few Sundays into his probationary period. His young wife seemed not to want Laura around. There were murmurings about Laura's shorter hair, even though she still wore it pulled into a twist at church, and her different style of dress at Serendipities.

Even women who had been friends at church were unsure how to treat Laura now that Jed was gone. At first, their detachment hurt her feelings, but it also felt familiar in that they had treated her the same way after Michael's death. A woman who lost a child made others uncomfortable. A younger, attractive widow would never be accepted.

A month later, Laura stopped attending the church that had been a lifeline for much of her adult life. She chose another non-denominational church Marjorie attended, where differences mattered less than the intent of a person's heart and mind. In place of stern religious dogma, Laura was introduced to a loving, benevolent, merciful God. This God was a father-mother presence rather than an angry man with a long white beard, sitting on a throne, doling out rewards and harsh punishments. She was introduced to a God who created and loved everyone. Even more remarkable, women were valued for their talents and skills, and served as full members of the church's leadership and board.

It had been more than her new status as a widow that propelled her to try out new experiences. Laura was becoming the woman she had always wanted to be. Along with freedom to come and go as she pleased, she also found new intellectual freedom. She read the same books that the Irish book club members read. Every month, she commuted over to Dublin for monthly meetings. She made a circle of new friends.

Meanwhile, she continued to borrow stacks of books from Parmenter's public library each week. She devoured them, no longer worried about hiding her reading choices. Some of the books were romance novels. A few were undeniably steamy. She had avoided these kinds of books in the past because of the uncomfortable feelings they generated. Now, she was fascinated by what other women knew about love and sex.

What at first seemed scandalous and immoral behavior, coming from her strict background, became enticing. Even if she had no intention of acting out any of her desires, it didn't hurt to dream. She wondered what it would feel like to have a man touch her, kiss her, move his body with hers the way male characters in these stories did with their lovers. While her own sexual history had been wretched, maybe someday she would find someone who could awaken her passions.

When Laura wasn't working at Serendipities or spending time at home with her mother, she rearranged furniture in her house and displayed items that Jed had never liked. Down came the ornate cross over their bed, the one that depicted an agonizing, grotesque death on the face of Jesus. All these years, she had closed her eyes while dusting the dime store crucifix. In its place, she hung a simple white ceramic cross.

She paid for cable access and discovered a world of home decorating shows. She couldn't get enough of them. She devoured design magazines, cutting out photos of homes and furniture, pasting them into a scrapbook. Marjorie called what she was doing a "visioning tool." Laura especially liked the modern rustic look on so many home design shows and vowed to have a home decorated in that style someday.

"I'd like to see you established in a business of your own," Marjorie said one Saturday as they worked together arranging merchandise. "You could open a store just like this one. Dublin would be a great place, near your son."

"Oh, I don't know," Laura said. "I've thought about moving there, but I figured I'd just have to find a job. I don't have the first idea about starting a business."

"You don't have to do it yourself. I'll help you. Dublin is a real tourist destination. The shop couldn't help but do well, especially with your good taste and design talents."

Laura's forehead furrowed. "But I'm happy helping you here. I'm not sure I could run a place all by myself."

"You wouldn't—not at first, anyway," Marjorie said. "You need small business training and a mentor. I can help with that. There are classes available to help you learn more about running a business. That will help build your confidence."

"It seems too wonderful to believe," Laura said. She held her hand against her heart, certain it was about to leap out of her chest. For years, she had dreamed of having her own business. It had seemed an impossibility. Now Marjorie was offering her an opportunity to do just that.

"I'd want to call it Serendipities Two!" Laura exclaimed.

"Well, now, you couldn't have said anything that would please me more," Marjorie said, linking her arm through Laura's. "You're Irish. You can't help but be happy in a town named Dublin, even if it is in Ohio instead of Ireland." Her eyes twinkled.

"Let's celebrate," Laura said. She poured a cup of coffee for Marjorie and another for herself. Then she opened a packet of their favorite brown sugar cookies.

"Let's do it the way they toast in Ireland." Marjorie went to the kitchenette at the back of the store and retrieved a bottle of Jamison's Irish whiskey. She poured a little into both their cups and handed one to Laura. "Slainte."

IF SHE WAS GOING TO START A BUSINESS, it would require money and lots of it. A week later, Laura put her modest three-bedroom, one-bath house on the market. It sold in seven days for five thousand dollars more than the asking price. This was a shock, even to the realtor, since the home had no modern amenities. The buyers fell in love with Laura's design touches that evoked country charm.

Within the next few days, through a series of what could only be called serendipitous events, Laura and Marjorie learned through their estate sale connections that a two-story house zoned for retail in historic Dublin had just come on the market. It needed work, but the downstairs had spacious rooms perfect for displaying furniture and housewares. Even the kitchen could be turned into a display space for dishes and cookware. There was a library-den that Laura intended would remain as such. She envisioned shelves of books, comfortable stay-awhile furniture, and a coffee and tea bar complete with an assortment of cookies.

Best of all, there was a roomy two-bedroom apartment upstairs that was perfect for her and her mother. The stairs were a little narrow, but she would be downstairs working and could assist her mother, when needed. The place felt familiar. Could this be the house she had envisioned all these years during those stolen daydreaming moments? How was it possible that this house had every detail she had imagined? If imagination could help desires come true, what else could her daydreams create?

Laura took the proceeds from the sale of her home, along with the remaining insurance money from Jed's death, and put a sizeable down payment on the house in Dublin. The remaining mortgage was manageable, but she would have to establish her business quickly. There was no time for hesitation or second-guessing.

As she considered which pieces of furniture to move to Dublin and which to sell or give away, she realized that she no longer wanted any of these reminders of her life with Jed. In a flash of inspiration, she decided that the furniture and many of the decorative items she had placed so carefully around the house over the years could be the start of inventory for the new store.

"Bravo, Laura," Marjorie said, her eyes twinkling. "You're already thinking like a businesswoman."

Within a month, she closed on the new property and moved in. With instructions from a kind employee at the Home Depot, she mastered interior painting, reveling in the accomplishment. She had always believed these skills required years of training and mastery. Now she realized that learning-while-doing was an education in itself.

In celebration of her real estate purchase, she treated herself to a sectional living room set, coffee table, a craftsman-style dining room table with matching chairs, two queen-sized beds, end tables, and dressers for each of the two bedrooms. She decorated the apartment in the modern rustic style she admired in magazines and television design shows. Each day was joyful as she transformed the upstairs living space into a real home for her and her mother.

She polished the furniture she had lived with for over twenty years and put it on display in Serendipities Two. The old gray sofa was sad-looking, so she recovered it in a tasteful floral pattern and arranged colorful accent cushions in different sizes. The furniture was familiar . . . yet not. Arranged with other decorative items, she could almost imagine that her old sofa, dining room set, and bedroom furnishings could have a happier second life with new owners.

During the grand opening weekend of Serendipities Two, she surveyed her new business and felt such a feeling of accomplishment, she wrapped her arms tight around herself in a hug, scarcely able to believe her good fortune. For years, she had dreamed of a better, happier life. It had happened as if by magic. Marjorie was right. Anything was possible if you believed in your dreams.

Chapter Five

Two Years Later

"M OM, OVER HERE!"

Catching sight of Andrew in their favorite coffee shop, Laura removed her tortoise-shell sunglasses and side-stepped nearby tables to meet him. As usual, he sported several days' growth of beard. His dark-brown hair was a little on the longish side, but she liked it.

"Sorry I'm late," she said, sliding into the chair across from him. "I had to call in reinforcements because of a bus tour. Those are great for business."

Over the past two years, Laura had created a new life for herself—not without struggles, but with deliberation and careful planning. There had been ups and downs, marketing mishaps, and wild swings in revenue that resulted in fearful cash-flow moments. It was at times like these that she questioned her abilities. Marjorie's wise counsel continued to reassure her, and she was able to overcome these predictable events and persevere.

There had been other changes, too. Although she had loved living with her mother, the time had come for assisted living. Just a month earlier, Eileen had decided it was time to move into a retirement community in Dublin. She couldn't manage stairs and had gotten more forgetful.

It was lucky that Laura worked downstairs. She noticed water dripping through the ceiling and made a mad dash upstairs to contain the damage. Eileen didn't mean to walk away from the sink while it filled with dishwater. It could happen to anyone. Except Eileen knew it had happened several times in recent months. This had been the first time she couldn't contain the damage herself. She was embarrassed and apologetic.

"It's time," she said. "This is what I want."

Except for a few weeks after Jed's death, before Eileen joined her at the house in Parmenter, Laura had never lived alone. Without her mother providing the familiar grounding of a family meal and after-dinner viewing of Jeopardy and Wheel of Fortune, the evening hours stretched out endlessly. Instead of a meal with a tablecloth and cloth napkins at the dining room table, Laura ate her meals mindlessly at the kitchen counter, often right out of the saucepan.

When loneliness overcame her, she tamped down those feelings. This was just another phase of life. She'd get through it like everything else. Seeing Andrew on a regular basis and watching his relationship bloom with his fiancée, Emily, brought pride and joy.

Her life was full of happy experiences, too. She had close friends from the book club, enjoyed reading the books Jan selected, and was enthusiastic about her volunteer work for Dublin's annual Irish Festival. What else in life could she possibly need or desire?

"How are classes?" she asked Andrew as she arranged her sunglasses and purse on the adjoining chair atop his textbooks.

By taking classes year-round, he would soon complete his Bachelor's degree in marketing and computer science. He had already been hired by an I.T. company that would finance his Master's degree in international business. Andrew's determination to succeed was a source of pride to Laura.

In an act of good manners and respect, Andrew put his phone face-down on the table, something he always did when he was with her. "They're good," he said. "I like the one on entrepreneurship the best."

"Well, maybe you'll learn something that can help me out," Laura said, accepting her iced coffee from the server. "The shop is doing well, but I still think I should market more."

"You do a great job marketing," Andrew said. "You have good instincts. Word-of-mouth is strong advertising."

"I'm lucky that way. The location of the store is perfect. Anyone coming to the main street or eating at one of the restaurants can't help but see it. I've always thought the name Serendipities Two brings in people who are curious." Laura stirred her drink with a straw. "You know, don't you, that the word 'serendipity' means an unplanned discovery of something that makes you happy?"

"Plus, the store looks like someone's actual home," Andrew said. "If you walk by, you want to see inside."

"Well, it is my actual home," she pointed out. "I thought it might be nice to have an activity one evening a week to draw more people." She wrinkled her forehead. "Since the library has been closed for the last phase of construction, I've arranged to have the Irish book club meet at the store. It's only for a short time."

Andrew grinned. "That's brilliant. How many people can you handle?"

"About a dozen. We try to be open to newcomers, as space allows."

"You could meet a guy to go out with." Andrew gave her a knowing look. It wasn't the first time he had suggested she consider dating.

"Maybe someday," she said, waving off the idea with one hand. "Between the business and looking in on Grandma a few times a week, plus the library fundraising gala coming up in a couple of weeks, the Irish festival the first weekend in August, and now hosting the book club, it doesn't leave much time for a social life."

"Mom, all of those things you're doing . . ." He paused. "That's *how* you meet someone. You get busy with activities you like. That's how Em and I met—at a fraternity-sorority service project."

He had recently proposed to Emily. They planned to marry on Christmas Eve at Emily's church in Dublin. She was a wonderful girl, and Laura couldn't wait to watch them take their vows. They were perfect for each other.

It was also clear that they were on equal footing in their relationship. Laura felt wistful at the easy way the young couple related to each other, their delight in being together. They modeled the kind of relationship she had always wanted. Andrew said Emily possessed strengths he didn't have.

"She brings out all the qualities I want to improve in myself," he said.

But that kind of love, fresh and new, seemed beyond her grasp. How likely was it for someone in her early forties to meet a man, be instantly drawn to him, and have the relationship progress to marriage and happily-ever-after? What were the odds? And what if your history of love was troubled, and you couldn't trust easily?

Andrew smiled. "You could take classes, too. It doesn't have to be about business, either. You love to read. Take a literature class."

"Well, I never say 'never' anymore." She pushed her chin-length hair behind her ears.

"You look really pretty, Mom. That's a good color on you."

"Thanks, sweetheart," she said and reached out to stroke his cheek. Her beautiful boy.

Smoothing the skirt of the periwinkle-blue sleeveless dress over her knees, she glanced down at her sandaled feet sporting a fresh pedicure in a neutral rose hue. Pearl earrings and a gold bracelet watch completed the look.

"No one who saw you now would ever guess who you used to be." He grinned. "Dad must be rolling over in his grave. That short hair!"

She laughed and shook her head, joining in on the joke. "Are those *toes showing?*"

"You have a great personality. I mean it, Mom. Any man would be lucky to have you in his life."

This time, she decided not to dodge the subject. "Thanks for that. I suspect you're prejudiced." She laughed. "But seriously, after so many years of being under your dad's thumb, I feel free now to eat what I want, sleep when I want, and go where I want. No one is telling me what to do every minute of every day . . . or questioning whether I have a right to an opinion."

"Not all men are like Dad."

"Mercifully, that's true." They smiled at each other.

"Promise me you'll at least think about dating again." Andrew reached across the table and touched her hand.

"Okay, I will."

SERENDIPITIES TWO GREW SUCCESSFUL because of Laura's unshakeable vision for what she wanted to achieve. In her view, what she lacked in education and experience, she would make up for in hard work. Where once her dreams had been thwarted, now they had wings. Even baby steps got you to your goals, though the route might be circuitous and fraught with uncertainty.

Laura made one mistake after another those first two years, but she learned from them. Her biggest error was in not viewing everyone she met as a potential customer. It was only after a dozen people from the Irish Festival committee came to her store after a meeting that Laura understood the power of an elevator speech to market her business.

"Serendipities Two can help re-feather the nest you already love," she said, and realized it was the perfect way to get someone's attention.

In her first year of operating Serendipities Two, she did most of the work herself with just one part-time employee. Now she had a full-time employee, Cissy, and two part-timers, Judith and Marian. She felt a strong sense of responsibility to these women who relied on her for their income as she had once relied on Marjorie. Cissy was an Ohio State student and friend of Andrew's. Marian was an artist specializing in watercolors.

Judith was a retired shop owner. "Within six weeks, I was bored to tears," she told Laura. "Your store is the kind of place I wanted to spend time when I was working. So now, I can be retired, have fun, and feel useful."

Far from being intimidated by Judith's expertise, Laura jumped at the chance to have someone with retail and management experience assisting her. A corner of one room now featured handmade greeting cards and small gift finds that could be purchased to go with other items from the store. Judith took it upon herself to develop that area of the business. Marian's watercolors were displayed throughout the store for purchase.

Though she enjoyed spending time with her coworkers, Laura missed having Marjorie close by. The friends talked at least twice a week, but it wasn't the same as being there. Through the book club, Laura met someone who, from all outward appearances, was her total opposite. They were two single women who bonded over a love of Irish music and books.

Terri McDonald was a raven-haired pixie with waist-length hair she wore in a French braid. She preferred leather to fabric and often paired black leather pants with figure-hugging blouses and dramatic jewelry. She was a singer-songwriter with a popular regional band called Street. By popular demand, her band performed each year at the Irish Festival. She was generous and kind, always mentoring new talent. "All ships rise" was her motto.

Laura knew Terri had bigger dreams: to have Street open for a successful band on a national or international tour. It would cement her career as a musician. Although Street played gigs regularly around the region, it was necessary for Terri to give private music lessons to supplement her income. She took it all in stride, and was a popular vocal and violin teacher.

Although Laura and Terri could not have come from more different backgrounds, Terri had hinted at a past filled with heartache. Even so, she brushed off Laura's attempts to draw out the story. "It doesn't do any good to relive some tired old story over and over. It's done. It's in the past. Every time you tell the story, it brings all the characters back to life," Terri told her.

"I can't forget what happened," Laura protested. "It was over twenty years of my life."

"Of course, you can't forget," Terri said. "But Jed is six feet under. Don't dig him up every day and look at the corpse. Survive and be stronger. Find a better man. That's the best revenge."

"That ship may have sailed," Laura said, wrinkling her nose. "Besides, when would I find the time?"

"You have to *make* time for love," Terri said. "You don't even notice how many men look at you." Laura twisted her mouth, not quite believing her. "I'll help you set up an online profile."

"If it's going to happen, I'd rather meet someone the old-fashioned way," Laura insisted. "I'd be more comfortable being introduced by mutual friends or meeting a man when I'm out doing something I enjoy. Then he'd probably like the same activities that I do. Maybe at church. Then we'd have the same values."

"How likely is it that you'd get the kind of guy you really want?" Terri asked. "Deep down, you know what you want in a man. And you know the qualities you prefer because you already know what you *don't* want. Why not set the criteria on a dating website and get exactly what you're looking for?"

"You make it sound like placing an order online. How would I explain to people that I met someone on a dating site?"

"Who cares what people think?" Terri wrinkled her nose. "You might not meet Mr. Right. But you could meet a lot of Mr. Right Now's."

"You're different. I'm not as brave as you are, and I don't have much experience with men. You can handle yourself. I'm not sure I can," Laura said, nibbling on a cuticle.

"The only way to find out is to try," Terri said.

Laura considered her friend's words as she dusted a three-corner curio cabinet with cut-glass doors. It would be fun to go out to dinner and a movie, attend a concert, or see a play. It would be nice to cook for someone who appreciated her efforts.

A new man in her life would need to be patient and allow her time to get to know him. She would want to be his friend and know she was safe with him first before anything more could develop. Those were the ground rules.

She heard the familiar jangle of the brass bell she had installed on the front door of Serendipities Two. Turning, she saw Jan Armstrong, head librarian for the county's library system. It was Jan who led a group of avid readers she called the Irish Book Club of Dublin (Ohio). The group met once a month. While Dublin's library was undergoing renovation, Laura had jumped at the chance to host the book club at her store.

The group read the works of a wide variety of Irish writers from popular novelist Maeve Binchy to the classic works of James Joyce, W. B. Yeats, Jonathan Swift, George Bernard Shaw, and Oscar Wilde.

"Hi, Jan!" Laura called out. "Cissy, would you mind finishing the dusting over here?" she asked the petite redhead who readily accepted the Swiffer and got to work.

Jan reached out to give Laura a hug. "I meant to call you twice this week," she fretted, "but with the fundraiser coming up in a month, I lost all track of time."

"Did you get my sponsorship check, I hope?"

"Yes, thank you. Would you like your Serendipities signage to be in the area with appetizers or desserts?"

"Desserts, definitely. What did you want to talk with me about?"

"I had a call from someone wanting to join the book club, but we're at eleven people most weeks, and I didn't want to say yes without asking you first," Jan said. "He seemed very anxious to participate. His wife is in a nursing home, and I think he's lonely."

"Of course, it's fine," Laura said. "It's always nice to have a man's perspective, and we only have two men in the group now. I'm sure Jim and Frank will welcome another male perspective. By the way, what are we reading after *Dracula*?" She had been surprised that this horror classic had been written by an Irish writer named Bram Stoker.

"*Dubliners* by James Joyce," Jan said without missing a beat. "I've wanted to read it again, and this will be the incentive I need. I think you'll really like it."

"James Joyce's books sure are a workout," Laura said, shaking her head, "I was telling Andrew the other day that I have to read and re-read passages to get their full meaning. He agreed. But until he said it, I thought it was just me. I never had any college classes, you know. I graduated from high school one Saturday and got married a week later."

"They're a challenge for any serious reader. That's why they're worth reading." Jan smiled. "Reading is *how* we become educated, Laura. The more we read, the more we understand the world outside what we experience on such a limited basis. You're so bright. Just look at what you've accomplished without a degree."

"I learn a lot from books and articles," Laura agreed. "And even though the books we're reading were written during a different time and place, they're still familiar, somehow."

"Great literature is universal. We recognize ourselves and others—the way we think, the emotions we share, and realize we're more alike than different," Jan said. "James Joyce's stream-of-consciousness style of writing in *Portrait of the Artist as a Young Man* is exactly how a young child would think."

"I never read any of his books when I was in school," Laura said. "Joyce's books weren't on the approved list, I guess." She shrugged. "I missed so much."

Jan was quiet for a moment before speaking. "Laura, you are a different person than when I first met you. I came into your store one day and asked you a question about that trestle table I wanted to buy. You answered, but it came out sounding like a question. Now you speak with confidence. When I hear your thoughts or opinions, I'm always glad you took time to express them."

"It took a long time for me to learn how to talk to people." Laura thought back to those early days in Dublin. "I used to feel as if I was acting, pretending to be someone else. But after a year or two, I began to feel more like that person I wanted to be. In a way, I still feel like I'm making up my life one day at a time."

"Like writing your own story," Jan said, a twinkle in her eye. "Characters develop and grow over time. They overcome obstacles to achieve their dreams. If you were a character in a Maeve Binchy novel, how would she write your story?"

Laura considered the question. "I've already had one dream come true. This," she said, spreading her arms to survey the store, "is exactly how I pictured it."

"Imagine if you did the same thing for something else you've always wanted," Jan said. "I'm curious what the next chapter of your story will be."

Chapter Six

"Momma?" Laura rapped softly on the door to her mother's room. The elderly woman sat before an easel on a small round table, her back to the door, intent on a watercolor painting of the wildflowers and rippled pond outside her window. The painting was simple yet elegant, the images captured in deft, sure strokes. Laura hadn't known until recently that her mother possessed this level of talent.

Eileen waved her in, her back still turned, focused on the work in front of her. "What are you thinking? Perhaps a duck or two on the shoreline to give it some life?"

"It's very nice, as it is." Laura smiled, impressed. "Looks like something you could buy in an art gallery."

Her mother turned, the corners of her lips turning up in a shy smile. "Well, isn't that sweet of you to say?"

"You're a real artist, Momma," Laura said, setting a box of glazed pecans on a nearby table. Her mother had a sweet tooth.

Eileen had begun painting in earnest within a week of moving into her room at Glenview Gardens Retirement Community. A poster in the dining room had captured her attention. ART CLASSES. PAINT. DRAW. SCULPT.

Laura had taken one look at the expression of wonder on her face and said, "This looks like fun! Why don't you try it?"

Eileen's lips trembled as she answered, "Why, I believe I will."

Eileen attended art classes every day, producing such fine drawings and paintings that the instructor suggested she have her own exhibit in the dining room where other residents could enjoy her talents This was beyond anything her mother could have imagined. It was the perfect way to engage her mind and spirit. From day one, Laura saw the positive change in her mood and in her willingness to engage with others.

"Heavens," Laura said, nearly breathless, when she saw the first watercolor still life her mother painted of three green pears, one lying on its side. It was a remarkable picture, the light and shadows rendered with exquisite simplicity. "You never painted when I was growing up. Why not?"

Her mother shrugged. "When I was a girl, seems like I was always doodling with chalk or charcoal—whatever I could get my hands on. It got me in trouble a few times when I made pictures instead of copying my letters or doing arithmetic."

Laura couldn't imagine her mother as a girl. She had seemed old for as long as Laura could remember, dressed in the conservative attire of women in their church, her iron-gray hair swept up in a tight bun. The only jewelry she ever wore was a plain gold wedding band. Most of the women in the church looked at least fifteen years older than their actual age.

"It wasn't what we did in those days," Eileen continued. "We were married and concentrated on our husbands and children, our house-work and cookery. Besides, there wasn't money for art supplies," she explained.

"I wish I'd known this when you came to live with me." Laura was genuinely distressed to think how many years had gone by while her mother was denied an activity that would have brought her plea-sure "I could have made sure you had paints and paper, whatever you wanted."

Eileen held the paintbrush up as if poised to make a brushstroke in the air. "I suppose it never occurred to me until I saw that poster for art classes." She shook her head and smiled at the memory. "I wanted it more than I'd wanted anything in a long, long time."

"It seems that women put aside their own needs so they can take care of their husbands and children—always doing for others. They forget who they wanted to be when they were young," Laura said, set-tling into her mother's comfortable floral upholstered chair. Laura had furnished this room with as many familiar items as possible. She paused for a moment, thinking. "I'm not sure I ever knew who I was, or even what I enjoyed or preferred before I got married. I was just

Jed's wife, and Michael and Andrew's mother. Then I became Jed's widow."

"I didn't agree with your daddy that you should marry Jed," Eileen said, surprising Laura. "There was a meanness about him I didn't care for."

Laura's eyes widened. What had her mother noticed? She had never said a word.

"Yes, I saw it," Eileen continued. "You were a good wife." She looked directly at Laura, making a point. "You gave a whole lot more than you got from that man. Now you have a good life, and you made it for yourself. I'm proud of you."

"Thanks, Momma." Laura flushed at the praise. "My store is doing well. I can afford to do nice things for you. Please tell me if you need or want anything."

"I don't fancy anything else. I've got all I need and want. Thank you."

"You do seem happy here." Laura studied her mother's expression. There she saw contentment and peace.

"It's not as nice as your place," Eileen was quick to say. "But it's perfectly fine for my needs. I don't want you to feel like you put me out. I chose to come here. It was time. There are no steps to climb, and I don't have to worry about falling down 'em, neither."

"How's the food?" Laura asked. Meals were daily highlights in a nursing home. Residents measured time between breakfast, lunch, dinner, and an evening snack.

"Everything is good. You should try the minestrone soup we had today."

"I might do that," Laura said, her stomach rumbling. "I haven't had lunch yet."

As retirement communities went, Glenview Gardens was pleasant and well-maintained, with caring staff and plenty of amenities for its residents. It was considerably better than the county nursing home where her mother had lived for several years in Parmenter. It also was more expensive than Eileen could afford on her widow's railroad pension and Social Security, but Laura was happy to help with the remainder.

It had been a sad day when Eileen made the decision to move out of the apartment they shared, even as Laura acknowledged the truth about her mother's condition. Just as important, Eileen needed to be with people her own age. She was acutely lonely, having lost her friends one by one to death or dementia.

Fortunately, the transition to Glenview Gardens had been easy for her mother. She settled into her new room without complaint.

"I think I'll take you up on your suggestion about that soup," Laura said, looking at her watch. "It's been a long day. Can I bring you back anything?"

"You left me plenty of treats," her mother said. "I do love those Speculoos biscuits." She smiled.

"Those are the ones Granny loved. Remember?"

"I do," Eileen said, a look of delight crossing her features. "Now I'll enjoy them even more. I remember how my mother loved them."

"I'll bring you more when those run out. See you later this week." Laura kissed her forehead. "I love you."

She walked down the long corridor into the spacious dining area and delicatessen where residents and their guests could enjoy a meal or snacks. She greeted the hostess and took a seat at one of the café tables by the window, gazing out onto the walking trail that surrounded the lake.

"Mrs. Fisher? Laura?"

She turned quickly in her seat and could hardly believe her eyes. "John Conway?"

She would have known that smile anywhere. He wore a blue dress shirt and navy tie—office attire. A few more white hairs salted his wavy head, but otherwise, he looked the same as the last time she had seen him in Parmenter two years earlier. There he was, the man who had come to her aid on the day Jed died.

"My wife, Jackie, lives here now," he explained. "We moved to Columbus a year ago."

"It's good to see you," she said, rising to greet him. They embraced awkwardly. "My mother moved here a couple of months ago."

"I'm glad we ran into each other," he said. "May I join you?"

"Yes, of course." She was delighted. "I'm having a late lunch before I go back to work."

"Same here." He was silent for a moment. "I almost didn't recognize you." He paused, studying her features. "The last time I saw you . . . Well, your hair is shorter. You look . . . You look great, Laura."

Self-conscious and more than a little embarrassed, Laura wasn't sure how to respond. Memories of how she used to look came to mind. She cleared her throat. "How is your wife?"

He let out a long breath and raked his hand through his hair. "Not good. She's in the final stages of A.L.S. There isn't much more they can do to help her. To tell you the truth, she needed to be in full-time care when we lived in Parmenter. But there wasn't a place I thought was good enough for her."

"I know what you mean. My mother was in the county home there, and I worried all the time. I moved her in with me when Jed—my husband—passed away. She lived with me until recently."

"I remember the day you moved away. I thought about coming over to say good-bye, but when the moving truck left, I never saw you again."

Laura smiled. "The house sold fast. I bought the place where I have my business—Serendipities Two over in Dublin."

"I've been by it a few times." The server took their orders. "What kind of store is it? I'm afraid I don't have much time to browse."

"It's a specialty consignment store. I also do home design services. I named it after the store in Parmenter. You remember my friend, Marjorie? She helped me start this location."

"I do remember Marjorie. Wow, I'm impressed. So, you went from wife and mother, not working outside the home, to running your own business in just two years?" He shook his head in amazement.

"It's remarkable how quickly my life changed," Laura said. "I had a lot of help, believe me. Marjorie took me under her wing. I was lucky, too, that my mother was well enough to live with me. She did a lot of the cooking and housework while I built the business. She was with me until it became obvious that she needed more assistance—for her own safety. She needed to be on one level and away from dangers like the stove."

"Ah," John said. "We take these steps as we need to, I guess. I was hesitant to move Jackie from our house, but she was the one who insisted it was time. Fortunately, I was able to find this place, and Ohio State hired me right away."

"Do you teach?"

"I'm an attorney, a compliance officer. I miss the courtroom, but working for the university has been good. I enjoy the academic environment, the ebb and flow of the calendar. It's almost like being back in school. Every fall, I feel like buying school supplies." He grinned.

Laura chuckled. "I didn't know you were a lawyer. What kind of law did you practice before?"

"Criminal," he said. "I'll get back to it one of these days."

Time sped by as they updated each other on the changes in their lives. The server returned to refill their coffee cups. "Separate checks?" she asked.

"One, please," John said and waved off Laura's attempts to pay for her food. "Laura, I was raised to be a gentleman. Besides, I'm glad to see you."

"Thank you," she said, her cheeks coloring. Their eyes met, and for a moment, Laura lost all sense of time and place. He was as handsome as she remembered. She pushed those thoughts aside.

"Does your mom like it here?" he asked after several moments of silence.

"She does. She's even taken up art classes."

"It's strange that we haven't seen each other before today, although I tend to visit at off-hours," John said. He seemed to be weighing his words. "I can't get over the difference in you," he finally said. "I don't mean to make you uncomfortable by saying that. I think it's that you have such confidence about you now."

Laura's hand flew up to smooth her hair. She felt her face warming. "I'm sure I look completely different."

"In a good way," John said. "You look happy, at ease with yourself."

Laura bit her upper lip and flashed an embarrassed smile. "It took me a while to catch on to what the rest of the world knew about fashion."

"I think some women have a natural style without fancy clothes or a lot of make-up." He cleared his throat and looked away. "I've always said that about Jackie."

"It must be difficult, knowing she won't recover." Laura paused for a moment, considering her next words. "My mother is much older. It doesn't seem fair that Jackie should be so ill at such a young age."

John passed a hand wearily over his forehead. He took a sip of water before speaking. "I've had quite a few years to prepare for what will happen next. It's a progressive illness, and the stages are predictable and brutal. The hardest has been the breathing, swallowing, and eating challenges. She and I have talked a lot over the past several years about her death. She's ready—more than I am. That's selfish of me to say. She has suffered so much."

"I remember when we first met. You were such a caring husband," Laura said, and added, "I wasn't as lucky that way."

An expression crossed John's face that Laura registered as understanding. She guessed that he knew exactly what she was talking about, but was too polite to respond. "Do you have any children?" she asked.

He shook his head. "It was just the two of us. Jackie and I weren't able to have children. That was hard for her. And then, she got sick, and we decided we shouldn't even attempt to adopt. Her prognosis wasn't good from day one. We're closer than most couples, I guess, because we've had big hurdles that we had to handle together."

"I'm sorry for both of you, John," Laura said. "But I'm glad you and I reconnected. Please let me know if there is anything I can do to help."

"Definitely," John said. "I'm glad to know that you own Serendipities Two. Isn't that where the Irish book club meets on Wednesdays?"

"Yes, in my library room. How did you know about the book club?"

He cleared his throat. "I'm the newest member."

CHAPTER SEVEN

"**W**E NEED SOME GOOD PHOTOS OF YOU," Terri said as she navigated around the online dating site. As Laura's friend and self-proclaimed dating advisor, Terri took charge. "It can't just be a headshot. You ought to show yourself doing something active. Guys want to see whether you're in good shape."

Laura flexed the bicep in one arm. "Guess I could stand a little improvement."

"That means, they're checking out your boobs," Terri said, rolling her eyes. "You've got great legs, so let's find one that shows them off, too."

"Isn't that kind of shallow?" Laura wrinkled her nose.

"Face it, my friend. The dating pool is about two feet deep. Before you wade in, you've got to make sure your lipstick is on straight and your girls are perky." She put her hands on either side of her chest and pantomimed adjusting her push-up bra. "It's every woman for herself."

"I don't know, Terri," Laura said, unable to contain a laugh at her friend's antics. "I'd rather meet someone the usual way, you know, through friends."

"Friends don't always know what you want in a man. Only you know that. This dating site matches people based on algorithms. You tell the computer what you want. It finds someone else who could be a fit. Now, tell me, what do you want in a man?"

"I have no idea other than a nice, honest, reliable person who doesn't use me for a punching bag."

"Fair enough. You'll have a chance to email back-and-forth until you feel comfortable enough to talk on the phone. Take it in stages. Decide if you want to go for coffee—something safe. Drive yourself, of course."

Laura bit her lip. "I could say the wrong thing and embarrass myself. I'm not . . ." She paused to think of the right words. "You're a *personality*. You talk to an audience like you know them. I can be so awkward."

"Not true! You have a wonderful personality," Terri protested. "And being comfortable in front of an audience takes years of practice. I used to be nervous every time I got up on stage. I got better at it. And you are *not* awkward—just shy. When it counts, you know how to talk with people. Just be yourself. You're letting the universe know you're serious about finding someone."

"The universe. Do you mean God?" Laura raised her left eyebrow. She liked the term *universe*. It implied a non-gender specific benevolence. Fear of an old male God's disapproval had kept her in submission to Jed for what she believed were her sins. *His sins, not mine.*

Terri shrugged. "Call that higher power whatever you want. I find it easier to think in more spiritual terms—more personal," she added. "I think of it as larger arms around me like a safety net."

"I like that," Laura said. "Larger arms *protecting* me." She thought for a moment. "Okay, I have that photo from the business journal—the one that shows me standing with the Irish festival music committee."

"I'm in that photo. Seven other people are in that photo. This is not a group date." Terri let out a breath. "Okay, we can crop it."

"You probably have more photos of me on your phone than I do. I don't take selfies." Laura studied the photos of men onscreen. "Hmm, he looks nice."

Terri clicked on the photo. "I know him."

"You know him? How?"

"Every single woman in three counties knows him. I will not allow you to go out with him. Let me help you with this, buttercup, mm-kay?"

Laura was fascinated. "How am I supposed to know these things? I could go on a date with a serial killer!"

"You could. It's unlikely. But you could." Terri's eyes never left the screen as she typed in the information for Laura's profile. "You could also meet the man of your dreams. Unfortunately, you may have to kiss some horny toads first."

Laura grimaced. "Terri, I have never been on an actual date. My husband was a teacher at my school. We never went anywhere without a chaperone. I was never alone with him until our wedding night."

"And how did *that* go? Jeez," Terri said, looking up at Laura, her forehead furrowing. "You never even went to a school dance with a boy?"

"We weren't allowed to dance."

"Okay, so you haven't even entered the ramp to the dating highway." Terri sat back in her chair. "Lucky for you, I've dated enough for both of us. I can guide you. First, we will assess the possibilities. I will pre-screen 'em. How's that?"

"Do I get any say-so?"

"You can choose from the ones I pre-select. Let's face it, you lack the qualifications. If you like someone's photo and they seem to be a good match, according to the algorithms, I'll take a closer look. Now let's finish your profile. There are about a hundred questions to answer. Don't overthink this. What are your favorite activities?"

"Reading. Cooking." Laura thought for a moment. "I'm not very exciting, I guess."

"Sure, you are. We'll just put those items down the list a bit. You enjoy live music."

"I do! I always have fun whenever you're performing." Laura brightened up. "I love the Irish festival!"

"Concerts, movies, events, and theater," Terri suggested as she typed. "Sports? You don't have to play sports, but it helps to show an interest, at least."

"I don't really understand sports."

"You don't have to understand. That's where a man comes in. He can teach you. They love to teach us stuff."

Things were looking up. Laura stared intently over her friend's shoulder as she entered more information. There were questions about religious preferences, health, lifestyle, even political views.

"These days, politics can be a deal-breaker," Terri said. "I dated a guy who . . . well, never mind. Let's just say our votes cancelled each other's out. Plus, he was kind of creepy. The first phone conversation we had, he mentioned that he never went out with someone more than three times without having sex to make sure it was a good fit."

"A good fit?"

"Yeah. He said that. Unfortunate choice of words." Terri grinned wickedly.

"What did *you* say?" Laura's blue eyes widened. This was an aspect of dating she hadn't considered fully.

"I was polite. I said I didn't see it happening on his timeline. He said a few other things that activated my ick alarm. I turned off his access to my profile."

"I can't even imagine what I'd say to something like that. I'd probably run."

"Laura, when you meet the right guy, you will want sex—just probably not quite that fast."

An hour later, Laura's profile with three recent photos had been posted. No sooner did she enter her payment information and hit 'submit' than six photos of available men popped up. Her hand went to her heart. "Oh, my! It's like . . . it's like . . ."

"Like shopping on Amazon." Terri grinned. "Isn't the internet great?"

THE NEXT EVENING, LAURA CLOSED THE STORE promptly at six o'clock and set up the shop's library room for the Irish book club. She laid a lace tablecloth on the buffet and arranged dainty porcelain cups, saucers, and plates, along with flax-colored cloth napkins tied with sage-green silk ribbons. A three-tiered silver stand featured an artful display of assorted cookies—biscuits, they called them in Great Britain. She stepped back to survey the table with a critical eye.

Seating was the biggest concern. Furniture changed almost weekly in Serendipities Two as merchandise was added or sold. The library now contained a sage-green loveseat and yellow floral upholstered chair in addition to three small tables displaying knickknacks. She laid coasters with photos of Irish cottages on each table for her guests' teacups and saucers.

Although most of the seats were fold-up wood chairs, she had purchased tufted cushions in a green-and-white garden pattern to make them more comfortable and attractive. Then she purchased fabric chair covers from a wedding supplier and fastened them to the backs of the chairs with sage-green ribbons. The effect was so charming her guests couldn't help but think that they were in a real library on an Irish country estate.

She stood back to assess the furniture arrangement. The chairs were too close together but definitely cozy. If the book club got bigger, they'd have to return to the library for meetings. John Conway would probably be the last member they could take at her store.

Her thoughts turned to her unexpected encounter with John. It had to be fate. What was the likelihood that two people brought together during a chance encounter in a small town two hours away would meet up again later in a different place? She felt embarrassed that he had known her in Parmenter. Even so, she looked forward to seeing him tonight at book club. She had a new life. Perhaps he could forget the way they had met and who she had been then.

Hours after running into John so unexpectedly, she called Marjorie to share the twist of fate that had brought them together again. "I couldn't believe it," Laura said. "I recognized him immediately. And then, we talked and talked."

"The two of you might be kindred spirits," Marjorie said. "Look how he showed up to help you twice on one of the roughest days of your life. I'd say meeting him again is kismet."

"Here's the other interesting thing," Laura said. "He's a new member of the Irish book club. Can you believe it?"

Marjorie was silent for a moment before replying, "I think this reunion is meant to be. The two of you may become more significant to each other."

Laura had entertained a similar thought as she recalled details of her conversation with John earlier that day. But she shook her head, dismissing the notion. "That isn't possible," she said. "It would be wrong. His wife is still alive, and even after she passes, he will need time to grieve—at least a year or more. It's only proper. Anyway, they have been happily married all these years. What do I know about that?"

Marjorie paused before speaking again. "You have more knowledge about what makes a happy marriage than you think you do. You've experienced the worst kind. It's bound to be better the next time."

"To tell you the truth, I can't imagine it."

"Laura, you are a beautiful woman in your prime. I think you deserve romance—a happy marriage, even."

"Terri got me started with online dating," Laura told her. "It makes me nervous."

"Have fun. But be careful, Laura. There are a lot of men out there who are just plain mean, and you know that as well as I do. We've both had one of those apiece."

"I promise to keep my wits about me. Will you come for Irish festival again this year?" Laura asked. "It's going to be more fun than ever. Terri has invited several new bands to play, and we'll have more Irish dancers, too."

"You bet I will. I'm more tired than usual, kiddo. I could use a break."

As members of the Irish book club fixed themselves cups of tea and filled plates with cookies, Jan surveyed the group. "Our newest member hasn't arrived yet," she said. A slight frown creased her forehead. "I hope he didn't forget."

"He said he'd be here." Laura stirred sweetener into her tea.

Jan's eyebrows shot up. "You talked with him?"

"I know him," Laura said in a low voice. "We met when we lived on the same street in Parmenter. I ran into him yesterday after I visited my mom at Glenview Gardens. His wife is in the special care unit there."

"What a small world!" Jan squeezed Laura's arm. "Two people from Parmenter in this group. I'd say that's real serendipity."

As book club members found their seats and settled in with their refreshments, Jan began the discussion of *Dracula* by Bram Stoker. "This book continues to intrigue me," she said. "For one thing, the book had more sex and violence than you might expect for a book of its time. Remember, Stoker wrote in the Victorian age. It would have been shocking for people to read about sexually aggressive females. That would not have been considered 'proper' for the times," she explained. "He turned them into ugly vampires."

"I didn't care for the flowery Victorian language," Carol, a member and writer, commented. "These days, an editor would have cut that book in half. It got tiresome in places." Others agreed.

"I think Stoker approved of the good girl character, Mina, Jonathan's fiancée," Terri said. "She was the ideal woman. He portrayed Mina's friend, Lucy, as a sort of hysterical sleepwalker with questionable morality. Three men proposed to her in one day. Imagine! Then she became Dracula's first female victim. I get the impression he wanted to show readers that Lucy was just asking to be bitten and turned into a vampire. Be a good girl or else."

For a moment, Laura was glad for John's absence. What she was about to say would bring back a memory she'd rather he didn't hear. "I thought the same thing," she said. "She didn't deserve to be Dracula's victim. No one ever deserves to be hurt or killed by another person. There are real-life monsters."

"This theme of female sexuality and the way women are portrayed has become a theme in literary criticism of the book," Jan said. "It is why many people find this book difficult to read. But it was indicative of the times."

Laura realized that, in many ways, she had been born into a house-hold like those of the Victorian era, where women were expected to be submissive, to deny their human desires. She wondered if it would be possible for her, after so many years, to take a less conservative view of love. Could she forget the old days with Jed and enjoy passionate love-making with another man? As if on cue, her thoughts turned to John. Where was he?

"Jan, if you hadn't recommended that we read this book, I doubt I'd have waded in much past the first six chapters," Peg, another member, said. "I'm glad I finished it. It was way scarier than any vampire book I've ever read."

"True. There's an entire genre of vampire and slasher movies, television shows, books, and graphic novels that portray male vampires as more sensitive, romantic heroes. But," Jan emphasized, "Dracula *is* a monster. He couldn't be more dangerous. We know he needs to be destroyed for the good of humanity. The world depends on Dracula's destruction."

At half past seven, Laura heard the bell on the locked front door and rose to answer it. When she opened the door, John attempted a smile. But she could see exhaustion and strain on his face.

"Sorry to get here late," he said. "Jackie had a rough day. I had to leave work early to go over there."

"Is she any better now?" Laura assessed his appearance, noting that he looked not only tired but scared. What had happened?

"Unfortunately, this is the beginning of the end. It's only going to get worse. But, at least, she's sleeping comfortably now."

Laura nodded sympathetically and led him down the hallway toward the library. "I wish I had served something more substantial than tea and cookies. You probably haven't eaten any real food today."

"Not sure I can eat, but thanks."

He followed her into the library and took the only available seat across from her. Terri's eyes widened at the sight of him. Laura pretended not to notice.

Jan paused the discussion. "Glad you could make it, John. Everybody, this is John Conway. I'll try to remember to use names during the discussion so you can get familiar with who's who."

"Thank you for including me. I'm sorry to be late," John said. "Today didn't quite go according to plan." He opened his book and took a calming breath as if to clear his mind. Laura could sense that whatever had happened with his wife had caused intense fear.

Discussion of the book continued in typical lively fashion with members comparing Count Dracula in the Bram Stoker novel to other vampire books and movies. The discussion became even more spirited regarding the strength of female characters in vampire adventure shows. Laura had never seen the vampire television series most of them referenced. She did think, however, that the female characters in *Dracula* were written to be weak and unable to care for themselves without male oversight.

She felt a little preoccupied, watching John who listened attentively but didn't offer any comments. Occasionally, he frowned or nodded in agreement. She remembered her first few meetings of the book club, when she had hesitated to speak up because she wasn't sure her ideas had merit. Most of the members of this group were college-educated. Some had advanced degrees, taught classes at Ohio State, or were accomplished writers. Surely, John didn't have a problem being confident in his opinions. He was an educated man, an attorney.

It surprised her when, after the meeting, he said, "I felt like I didn't have anything worthwhile to say tonight. I'm not into vampire or slasher films or books. I read *Dracula* when I was a kid. When I re-read it this time, I was a little put off by it, frankly. I didn't think Stoker had a very favorable view of women."

"I thought the same thing," Laura said, impressed that he would make this comment.

Terri joined their conversation, sidling up beside Laura. "Hi, John. I'm Terri McDonald. Did you enjoy yourself tonight?"

"Nice to meet you, Terri," he said, shaking her hand. "I'm glad I came. Not only was the discussion interesting, but it's been great seeing Laura again. We lived in the same town."

"I'm from a small town in Western Pennsylvania called Walkers Corner," Terri said. "I've actually driven through Parmenter on gigs."

"What kind of work do you do?" John asked.

"I'm a singer. I've got a band called Street." She glanced at Laura before adding, "Laura should bring you the next time I play." Her face was pure innocence, but Laura knew better.

John took the remark in stride. "I'd like that," he said. "I wish I could stay and talk, but I probably need to get going. Thanks again for letting me join the group."

"I'll walk you to the door," Laura said, following him. She gave Terri a backward glance that could have French-fried her. Terri meant well, but she tended to be about as subtle as a Mack truck.

Laura and John stepped out onto the porch. A stiff breeze rustled leaves on the trees, promising heavy rain later. She tucked a strand of hair behind her ear and crossed her arms over her chest. "I'm glad you could make it tonight," she said. "I hope it took your mind off your worries for a little while."

"Earlier this afternoon, I didn't think I'd be able to get away." He grimaced.

"It sounds like it was pretty scary."

"She's giving up," John said, his expression pure misery. "I know she's suffering, and I can't blame her for wanting it to be over."

She reached out and laid one hand lightly on his arm. "What you're both going through is sad. I wish there was something I could do to help. You were there for me—twice—on the day Jed died. I realize it's not the same situation at all, but I'd like to be there for you, too, if there is anything you need."

"Running into you the other day was the best part of this week," he said. "It's nice to know you're close by." He shrugged. She could tell from his plaintive expression that he was sincere. "There are therapists available through hospice. I have support when I need it. What I could really use right now is a friend."

"We both could use a good friend," she said, handing him a business card from the table in the foyer of the store. "The Serendipities Two number is my mobile number. Call anytime."

"I promise to limit calls to after-business hours. I know how busy you must be. Thanks." He turned and went down two steps before stopping and looking back. "If you're going over to the nursing home, let me know. I'll probably be there a lot more now."

CHAPTER EIGHT

Over the next week, Laura carried on back-and-forth instant messenger chats with two men named Larry and Matt from the online dating site. She decided not to move to the in-person phase with Matt after a curious response he made to one of her messages. She revealed to him that she didn't have much dating experience, and he replied, "Let me be your first true love."

"Yikes. Too much, too soon," Terri said and made a retching sound.

Laura agreed. Matt's comment unsettled her. "I wanted to cancel the membership," she admitted.

"It was just one guy. This is called the screening process for a reason," Terri said. "Your vibes were spot-on. You're doing great."

Laura decided to meet Larry, the other potential match, for coffee. Terri reviewed the secure correspondence between them and gave Laura a thumbs-up. "He is very nice-looking and respectful in his communications. Plus, he can spell."

Laura chuckled. "I didn't realize that was important dating criteria."

"It might be anecdotal evidence, but in my experience, men who take the time to look up a word to make sure it's spelled correctly will be self-disciplined in other ways, too. Oh, and they also need to answer all the questions in the profile. If a question is left blank, it could mean they are hiding something."

Laura wore a pair of black dress slacks and a sleeveless white blouse topped with a periwinkle-blue summer cardigan on her first real date. Periwinkle was her favorite color and gave her confidence.

She walked to the coffee shop, arriving at half past seven, and looked around for Larry.

A tall man with salt-and-pepper hair, thinning at the crown, stood and waved. He had a slender build and was much nicer looking than his photo. Best of all, his smile was warm and sincere. He wore a golf shirt, pressed khaki slacks, and brown loafers. She liked what she saw.

When she reached the table, he reached out to shake her hand and said, "You must be Laura." He pulled out her chair for her.

"Thank you," she said. Her voice sounded squeaky even to her own ears, and her throat felt dry as dust.

"Your photos don't do you justice," he said. "You're way prettier in person."

Laura blushed and stammered, "Thank you, so are you," then mentally berated herself. That wasn't the right thing to say to a man. Sweat broke out on her upper lip, and she felt damp under her arms. With one finger, she wiped her upper lip and tried again. "It's nice to meet you."

"May I order you a coffee or tea?" Larry asked, glancing over at the server to get her attention.

"Iced tea, please. Thank you." Laura took a deep breath, certain that in this situation, she should say something else. But words failed her, so she waited for Larry to speak first. He was elegant in his mannerisms, seemingly quite comfortable meeting a woman for the first time.

For the next half-hour, they made small talk, avoiding anything too personal. Larry was divorced. She already knew that from his profile. Tonight, she learned that he had two grown sons. He expressed sympathy when she said she was a widow with one grown son, and that another son had died.

"I moved here to be near Andrew, my youngest son, and to start my business."

"I've been in your store. I liked it."

This was a safe topic. She explained how long she had been in business and how she got started. "I'd love to expand Serendipities someday, when the time is right."

"Have you dated much since your husband passed away?" he asked.

"This is my first date, ever," she said abruptly, and caught herself. She didn't want to provide embarrassing details about how she had married Jed with no real courtship. Too much information. "I mean, I'm just getting started."

"And how's it going so far?" he asked, a twinkle in his eyes.

"I don't have anything to compare it to."

Larry laughed out loud. Laura blushed fire engine red. "I'm sorry," she said, mortified.

"Maybe you'd be more comfortable if we take our conversation outside on a walk," he suggested. "Blind dates can be nerve-wracking."

"That's a good idea," she said, grateful for the suggestion. Surely, a walk would provide additional opportunities for discussion as they passed other businesses and landmarks. With any luck, she could avoid making any more gaffes.

The evening was warm and on the muggy side. Laura removed her sweater, carrying it over her left arm. What was she supposed to do with her other arm? Link it in his? Somehow, this seemed too familiar. She opted to keep her arms held tight to her body.

It was a perfect night in Dublin with the fragrance of summer flowers in the air. Here and there, people socialized on restaurant outdoor patios, talking and laughing. The ice cream shop had a line out the front door. As they strolled, Larry asked questions about Serendipities Two, and she answered in detail. It was the one topic she felt comfortable discussing.

Terri had advised her to ask questions of Larry, too—to learn more about his life, but also to show interest and keep the conversation moving. But Laura realized that when she did ask a question, she couldn't focus on his answers, and the flow of the conversation ended abruptly the moment he stopped speaking. Larry didn't try to fill these silences, although he did smile kindly and make eye contact a few times.

He probably thinks I'm a complete dolt. Laura felt a sharp pain between her shoulder blades. Dating was hard work.

It was nearing nine o'clock as the sun made its blazing descent in iridescent oranges and pinks behind the trees and storefront buildings. The streetlamps provided a magical glow, making old downtown Dublin look even more charming with its historic architecture and bricked sidewalks. They passed a popular bakery and a restaurant where customers waited for their names to be called. It was the perfect night for an evening stroll, but Laura began to feel desperate for the quiet and safety of her home.

"Beautiful sunset," Larry observed, pausing to gaze up at the sky.

"Yes, it is . . . beautiful." She kept walking, and he fell in step with her again.

Now they were a few doors from Serendipities Two. Would he expect her to invite him in for a glass of wine or a cup of coffee? They continued walking until they reached her front steps.

She turned to face him. "Well, this is where I live. It was very nice meeting you. Thank you."

"Oh, you live here, too?" He looked surprised.

"There is an apartment over the store," she explained. They had an uncomfortable moment of silence before she said, "Thank you again."

"Laura, I would like to see you again," Larry said, taking a step toward her. "However, I get the impression I have disappointed you in some way."

"Disappointed me? Oh, no!" Laura exclaimed, genuinely horrified. "You aren't a disappointment at all." She swallowed. "I am," she said. "I'm sure you have been on better first dates. I'm sorry."

"Perhaps you'd like to take a little time to get used to the idea of dating," Larry said. "It's perfectly understandable." The kindness in his voice told her he was sincere. He wasn't judging her.

She let out the breath she was holding. "That would be a good idea," she admitted, managing a smile. "I do need practice at this."

Larry chuckled. "I'll let you set the pace. Just tell me when—or if—you might like to go out again."

AFTER THE DATE, LAURA TOOK THE STEPS two at a time up to her apartment and texted Terri a distressed emoticon face. Terri texted back. "I'll be right over."

The moment she arrived, she folded Laura into a hug. "It's okay," she said in a soothing voice. "I'm sure it went better than you thought. Next time will be easier."

"I was awful," Laura groaned, covering her face with her hands. It was nearly ten o'clock when they settled onto the sofa with glasses of white wine. "I think he was just being polite when he said he'd wait to hear from me," Laura said, flinching at the memory. "He'll probably dodge my call, and I wouldn't blame him. Even I wouldn't date me."

"You're being too hard on yourself. Blind dates are stressful. No one actually enjoys them, unless it's love at first sight, I suppose. That's never happened to me."

"Then it definitely wasn't love at first sight." Laura let out a long sigh. "I had nothing to say to him, Terri. He's so nice. What is wrong with me?"

"There is nothing wrong with you. I'm sure you weren't *that* bad, and he did say he wanted to see you again. Bad first dates don't end like that." Terri rubbed Laura's back between her shoulder blades, loosening the knots. "It was your first date. You were honest and admitted it. The thing about you, Laura, is that you aren't a faker. You were uncomfortable, and it showed. At least, you didn't drink heavily beforehand to give yourself false confidence. Yes, yes," she said ruefully. "I've done that. When will you see him again?"

"I'll email him tomorrow to thank him for coffee and for being so understanding."

"And?" Terri paused in mid-rub.

"And what?" Laura turned to face her friend.

"And will you tell him that you want to go out again?" Terri resumed her gentle rubbing across Laura's aching shoulder blades.

"Um, well, yes. I just need to think this through a little more. I'll plan what to say next time."

"I wouldn't wait too long. He's a good-looking man, very eligible in this town. Heck, I'd go out with him." Terri raised her eyebrows as Laura whirled to face her again. "I'm kidding. Friends don't do that to each other."

Laura's cell phone rang. It was Andrew. She picked it up. "I guess you're calling to find out how my date went. To be mercifully brief, your mother is a dating dud."

Andrew let out an affectionate laugh. "My mother is one of the greatest women around."

"You're my son. You have to say that." She gave him a run-down of the date, finishing with "If I were Larry, I'd go right back online and find someone better."

"What does Terri think about this? I know she's got to be there," he said.

Terri took the phone from Laura. "Andrew, please tell your mother that a man does not think less of a woman for emailing after a date and saying that she would love to go out with him again." Terri held the phone out so Laura could hear Andrew's answer. "See? Don't let your son down. The boy needs a real father."

Laura burst out laughing. "Okay, okay. I'll email Larry tomorrow."

"SERENDIPITIES, MARJORIE SPEAKING."

"I sure could use your advice," Laura said without preamble.

"What's up?" Marjorie asked. "I've been hoping you'd call and tell me all about your coffee date."

"Argh. If you insist," Laura said morosely. "But first, before I forget, I have a question. Do you think it's worth buying enhanced exposure on social media as part of all the Irish festival promotions? I usually just advertise my business in the event program."

"Depends on where most of your customers are," Marjorie said. "To be honest, I've never been able to completely and accurately measure my investment on social media, although I certainly post on the page and pay attention to who likes it. The comments are usually good ones, and I can invite them to the store."

"I'm a sponsor for the library fundraiser in July and a sponsor for the Irish festival in August, so I automatically get ads in both programs. But I think I should do more to remind people I'm open during the entire weekend of the Irish festival."

"What about a giveaway from the store?" Marjorie suggested. "Something you can easily afford, of course. Start promoting it now on social media. When people stop by and fill out an entry form, get their email address and ask how they heard about the drawing. I'd do a post twice a week on social media before and during the festival. Make sure you remember to keep the list of emails for future sales and promotions. Sometimes I get busy and forget how valuable those can be."

"That's a great idea." Laura needed to finalize her ad in the festival program by the end of the week. "I should make more of an effort on social media. Andrew knows way more than I do."

"Ask him to help! I bet he'd love to do that for you." Marjorie waited. "Okay, so how did it go last night?" she asked again.

Laura told her friend about the date with Larry from start to finish. "I thought he had nice manners," she said.

Marjorie laughed good-naturedly. "That's not exactly a rousing endorsement. Was he good-looking? Did you have a good time? Are you anxious to see him again?"

"Yes. Not really. And I'm not sure." Laura scratched her nose. "Terri talks about having chemistry with someone. I don't think I felt anything like that with Larry. But maybe I was too busy trying not to say something stupid."

"You underestimate yourself. Have you ever felt chemistry with anyone before?"

Laura thought for a moment. "I have no idea what you're even talking about, so I guess not."

Marjorie laughed. "Trust me on this one. When you feel chemistry with a man, you'll understand."

"I enjoy being with John."

"The two of you have a history together. You come from the same place. It's natural that you would gravitate toward someone who is familiar—someone who was there for you. Chemistry is more than that. It's a strong pull to be with someone physically."

"I do think John is handsome." Laura scratched her nose. "If I were ever to want to be part of a couple again, it would be with someone as nice as John. But now is not the time." Laura told Marjorie about John's wife's deteriorating condition. "He's married, and his wife is dying. I don't want to seem improper."

Marjorie paused and cleared her throat. "Please, please, Laura, don't hold yourself back from showing him how much you care. He would benefit so much from the many ways you show kindness. You need his friendship, too."

Laura considered this. "But, Marjorie, I need to be careful not to give John—or others—the wrong impression. What would people say if they see us together? It doesn't seem right."

"What isn't right? First, it's no one's business, and no one else has the right to judge. What they will see, if they open their eyes and hearts, is two nice people whose loved ones are in the last stages of their lives and who are offering each other comfort. Your mother is in the same facility, and you're naturally going to see John while you're there."

Laura frowned. "What if he gets the wrong idea?"

"What wrong idea? That you care? I remember John from when he lived in Parmenter, and I certainly know you. The most important thing that could happen is that the two of you will show each other what true friendship can mean between a man and a woman. Friendship doesn't have to lead to anything more."

"That's true, I suppose."

Marjorie paused for a moment. "And if it does become more than friendship some day in the future, then you know you started on a firm foundation."

Laura intended to email Larry that evening to thank him for their coffee date, but as she logged onto the dating site, her phone rang. She saw from caller ID that it was John. Her heart fluttered, making it hard to breathe. "Hello, this is Laura."

"Laura, it's John. I hope I'm not disturbing you."

"Not at all. You can call anytime." But she knew from the sinking feeling in her stomach that something was wrong. "What is it, John?"

"Jackie passed away around noon today." In a voice that sounded gravelly with fatigue, he said, "She went into cardiac arrest as I was sitting with her. She had a Do-Not-Resuscitate order, so no one took any action. But I swear, it was all I could do not to beg them to try to bring her back."

"I'm so sorry," Laura said, her eyes filling with tears. "Where are you now?"

"I'm home, walking in circles from room to room. It's just been me here since we bought it. Jackie never lived here. But somehow, I feel her presence."

"Of course, you do. People who love each other are connected even when they're in different places."

"I knew this day was coming. She outlived the doctors' expectations. I should feel relief on her behalf that she is free, at peace."

"On some level, I'm sure you are relieved because she isn't suffering. But you're only human, and losing her hurts. I do know about grief and missing someone. Take it one day at a time," Laura said.

"There are so many details to handle. But first, I need to deal with her last wishes, which were to be cremated."

"When is the funeral?" Laura asked.

"There won't be one," John said.

"No funeral?" she asked, certain she hadn't heard right.

"Jackie's parents are gone. She was an only child, and there isn't really any close family. She didn't want any fuss made—her words, not mine. To be honest, she's been sick for so long, we didn't have any real close couple friends anymore, either. For all intents and purposes, we were alone together."

Laura gulped. "But no service? Are you sure?" She had never heard of such a thing.

"Laura, she was spiritual, not religious," John said. For a moment, he sounded distant, as if he regretted telling her.

"I see." Laura's voice trailed off. "Well, of course, you must do as she wished. But what about you? Don't you need closure?"

"I will take her ashes to the places she loved. That will be my closure."

"Is there anything I can do?"

"Could you help me go through her belongings? They should be given to those who can use and appreciate them."

"I would be honored." She decided now was the time to listen to what her heart wanted her to say. "John?"

"Yes?" His voice was barely audible.

"I didn't mean to sound as if I was judging that you aren't having a funeral for your wife. It's just . . ." She stopped, not sure how to express the thoughts cascading through her head in a confusing flood.

"I'm sure in your experience, that's unforgiveable." John let out a breath. "It's okay. I get it."

Her head cleared, and she knew what to say. "Unforgiveable? Oh, no." She thought for a moment. "There are many things I used to believe, John. Life has taught me far more than what my religion ever taught me. Life teaches us to be kinder."

Chapter Nine

If there was anything that could shake Laura's confidence, it was those times when she couldn't accomplish everything that was expected of her. Fear of failure kept her anxious and bound to the past. It had been drummed into her from childhood that responsibility and sin were inextricably linked. Disappoint someone, even unintentionally, and go straight to hell. It was that simple.

As a young wife, she learned that even perceived failure, in Jed's eyes, meant danger. Those old thought patterns were not easily broken. Sense memories were especially strong. A scent, a sound, even a taste could trigger an anxious moment.

She had always been a perfectionist and worrier. Like so many women, she played multiple roles. She had once heard the term *sandwich generation* to describe adults who tended parents and supported children while holding down full-time jobs. That certainly described her life. There were never enough hours in the day.

What had thrown everything out of balance was an incident at the nursing home. Her mother had lost her footing in the shower and fallen, resulting in a nasty bruise from hip to knee. It was fortunate that nothing was broken. For the elderly, broken hips often resulted in death from complications. Fortunately, the charge nurse called Laura, who took Eileen to the hospital to be checked over. Laura was so shaken by what had happened, she stayed overnight, dozing fitfully in a chair by her mother's bedside.

As if all of that wasn't enough, she was behind on her reading schedule. The book club was reading *Dubliners* by James Joyce. Jan had insisted it was important for lovers of Irish literature to appreciate the beauty of Joyce's prose, even the stream-of-consciousness style of writing. As host of the group, Laura was determined to finish the book.

"I got lost just a few pages into the first chapter," she remarked to John in a phone call that week. She had called to see if he needed anything, and told him about her mother's accident. Even through his own troubles, he offered a listening ear and words of comfort. He assured her that the staff at the nursing facility did a good job responding to incidents. It was an important change in her mother's condition, and Eileen would receive help showering from now on.

"I read *Dubliners* in college," he said. "It was required reading for English majors. I plan to re-read it again when I have trouble falling asleep." When Laura laughed, he added, "I didn't mean it that way. I'm not saying it's a snoozer. It's more difficult reading, and the effort makes me tired."

"Maybe I'll try the same thing," Laura said. "I could use a good night's sleep." She had a busy brain, but it was more than that. Even after several months, without her mother's gentle snore in the next room, every creak in the house, every night sound called her to attention. The security system didn't allay all of her fears.

With everything that had happened, Laura hadn't given another moment's thought to checking the online dating site. She had sent Larry a quick message after their date, thanking him for his time and for the coffee. She didn't say she wanted to go out again, and he didn't press her.

"The whole thing was just too awkward," she told Terri who asked each day if there was anything new to report.

"The better you know him, the less awkward it will feel," Terri pointed out. "Laura, you do know this is classic avoidance, right?"

Laura knew it was a lame excuse to say she was too busy to date. If you wanted to date, you had to make time. Now didn't feel like the time.

She had promised to help John give away Jackie's clothing and belongings, and that was a promise she intended to keep. When she noticed his refrigerator was nearly empty, she took a container of homemade soup. She checked in a few times a week and listened while he shared details of his "new normal."

"Without the routine of visiting Jackie every day, I'm adrift," he said. "I walk into a room and forget why I'm there. I can't seem to hold a thought for more than a few moments. Jackie was my anchor."

"It will get easier," Laura promised. "To be honest, after Jed died, there were so many things I didn't understand or even know how to do.

Things like managing bills and finances, credit, all of that stuff was new to me. I didn't live in the world the way most people do. My name wasn't even on the household checking account, so I didn't know how to write checks or reconcile the account."

"But you learned fast. Look at you now," he said. "You're a business owner with employees. You caught on fast."

When she delivered a foil-wrapped lasagna one afternoon, he invited her to stay for supper. "That smells incredible. Please stay. I'd welcome the company," he said.

"Thanks. I think I will," she said. They set the table together, and she dished out the lasagna onto plates. She also produced a colorful salad. Finding no salad dressing, she quickly mixed up a cider vinaigrette with ingredients she found in his pantry. They carried on an easy, lively conversation the entire time.

"After my husband died, I remember waking up each morning thinking that the house was too quiet. To be honest, I didn't miss the way Jed and I lived together. But I realized how much time he took up." When John laughed at this, she joined in. "I was used to feeding him at exact times, doing chores on the same days. My life revolved around his schedule. Then, without any warning, my time became my own. I could eat when I wanted, go wherever I chose." She cleared her throat. "Of course, my situation was very different from yours."

"Maybe not so different," John said as he set utensils on the table. "In many ways, my life was governed by Jackie's needs. Before we moved here, I began having troubles at work. I couldn't travel the way I needed to, and my billable hours went down. Eventually, the partners asked me to take a leave of absence. That was the end. I couldn't disagree with their decision. I put Jackie first, before my work."

"They asked you to go when your wife was so ill? That was heartless." They sat down at the table and began eating.

"You think I should have sued?" A quick smile made John's dimples pop.

Laura smiled back. "Did you try a lot of cases in court?"

"I handled criminal cases," John said. "The hours were long and unpredictable. When Jackie got so sick, I knew I couldn't keep it up. The decision was made for me."

Laura had never thought much about John's career as an attorney. This was an aspect of his life that intrigued her. An idea took root. "Do you miss trying criminal cases?"

"Yes and no. My work at the university is challenging enough. I get my criminal law fix by watching legal shows on television." John took a bite of lasagna and closed his eyes in bliss. "This is so good. Thanks for bringing over dinner. I've been living on peanut butter and saltines."

"It's the least I can do," she said. "Besides, you're right: it's no fun eating alone."

Their conversation felt relaxed and effortless with topics that segued easily into deeper discussions about music, art, movies, and of course, books. Laura realized that not once during dinner had she felt stressed or tired. Nor did it occur to her to leave for the quiet of her apartment. In fact, she hoped for more evenings like this.

As John spoke, she heard the depth of his comments and the sensitive manner in which he offered opinions or observations. It was at that moment she knew her feelings for him were deepening. The thought made her uneasy. Fate had pulled them together, and she felt powerless to fight the growing feelings. They finished their meal and washed and dried the dishes together.

He hung up the dish towel and grinned. "Hey, let me pour us a glass of wine. We can sit on the back porch. It's cooler outside tonight—not as muggy."

They went to the porch with their glasses of wine and sat on the glider. John set it into gentle motion with one foot. Neither spoke. As the sun began its descent and the streetlights came on, they watched the deepening hues of the night sky.

"Oh look, stars," Laura said, pointing to a cluster to the west. "It might be a constellation, but I never seem to recognize those."

"Me, either," John answered. Then he began reciting, "Silently, one by one, in the infinite meadows of heaven, Blossomed the lovely stars, the forget-me-nots of the angels." His voice sounded melodious as he recited the poem.

"That's beautiful."

"It isn't original. Longfellow wrote it. It's from *Evangeline: A Tale of Acadie*." He chuckled. "Having to listen to me throw out stuff like that is one of the hazards of hanging out with a recovering English major."

"It's lovely." She sipped her wine. "I think of my son as a star out there, somewhere. Sometimes I think I can even feel him near me."

"Maybe I'll think of Jackie that way, too—my shining star." He was quiet for a moment. "I can't imagine losing a child and not wanting some part of him to live on, especially when the death is so tragic."

Laura took a deep breath. "I'd like to ask you something." She shared the few details she had been told the day Michael died. "He drowned, yes, but there was evidence of a head wound. I just needed more information," she said, flinching at the thought. "It never made sense to me that there would be a gash like that from bumping his head."

"Was there an investigation?" John asked. "I vaguely remember some of the details. We only knew what we read in the paper. To my knowledge, none of the neighbors ever spoke with you or your husband."

That was true. Jed had insisted they keep to themselves in most matters. He certainly wasn't going to discuss the death of his son. "It happened at church camp," she began. "There were no witnesses other than the boys who were in the boat. Jed handled everything with the police." She rubbed the area between her eyebrows. "To tell you the truth, I wasn't in any condition."

"What did the other boys say?"

"That it was an accident, of course. I wanted to believe them, but I needed more details. I tried to ask questions, but Jed would get angry. He said it was important as Christians to forgive them. He made it sound like it was my fault for asking questions to help me understand." She thought for a moment. "With Jed, I didn't believe it was really about forgiveness. I just think he wanted the whole thing to go away so he wouldn't have to answer any more questions about Michael."

"I don't understand. If he were my son, I'd want to be sure of what happened, and I'd want the guilty parties punished, especially if I had any doubts that it was an accident." John stopped the glider. "Do you know the names of the other boys who were involved?"

"Oh, yes. I taught them in Sunday School. After Jed died, I saw them at his funeral. They couldn't even look at me."

"The guy who was police chief at the time of Michael's death wasn't known for being thorough in his work," John said. "I'm not saying he was negligent in this investigation, but I wouldn't find it hard to believe that he didn't dot all his i's and cross all his t's."

"It felt like no one cared what Michael went through. I heard all of these comments, 'Oh, the poor boys' and so on from people at church. 'How sad that they had to live with this memory the rest of their lives,' they said." She felt her hands shaking. "They *should* have to live with *some* kind of bad feeling. What about Michael? He was a good person, and no one said anything in *his* defense!"

John turned toward her. "Was your husband hard on your sons?"

"Jed was a strict father. He didn't believe in sparing the rod," Laura said. "He punished both boys for anything he didn't think was perfect behavior." She stopped for a moment to gather her thoughts. "Michael wasn't like other boys. He was gifted at playing the piano and organ, and he wrote his own music. He was a really good student. I have no doubt he would have been a success in life. He never gave us a moment's trouble—not like his younger brother." A quick smile crossed her face, thinking of Andrew. "And yet, Jed punished Michael more often for not behaving in ways Jed thought he should."

She remembered when Michael was six and announced to his father that his name was Michael, not Mike. Jed backhanded him across the cheek and warned Michael never to speak to him in that tone of voice. From that moment on, Jed made it a point to refer to his son as Mike. The memory made her sad.

John looked thoughtful. "Laura, do you think Michael's death could have been more than just an accident? Could it have been a hate crime?"

"If you mean, do I think those boys hated Michael for being different? I'd say they didn't like him." Laura took another sip of her wine. "Andrew says Michael got picked on a lot by those kids."

John was quiet again before speaking. "Laura, I have never wanted to embarrass you by mentioning what I observed the day we met."

"I can only imagine what you thought." Laura looked down at her lap. She felt warmth creep up her face at the memory.

"What I saw was a woman beaten down in more ways than one," John said. "When I saw that ugly bruise on your shoulder and neck later that night, I knew someone was responsible. I could guess who. Did it happen often?"

"I tried to be careful not to make him mad." Laura bit her lower lip. She wasn't sure how much she wanted John to know. "It happened when he got angry."

"I would have thought that a minister, of all people—someone who professed to be all about love and forgiveness, would behave in a more loving way," John said. He sounded angry now. "I'm sure that his behavior would not be condoned by anyone higher up." He pointed to the sky with his finger. Laura nodded. "So, he was a minister with an anger management problem who took out his rage on women and children. I'm glad he's . . . that you don't have to live like that anymore."

"So am I," Laura said. She cleared her throat. "I didn't feel free to say what I thought about Michael's death when it happened. No matter what, I should have spoken up," she said. "He was my son, too."

"You couldn't help what happened, and I doubt that speaking up would have changed the outcome." He started the glider moving again. "If you want advice about whether to pursue a request to reopen the investigation, I'd be glad to do some checking," John said. "It really bothers me that this happened, and all that you've had to endure thinking that Michael's death might not have been an accident. Whether or not the death was a premeditated act would be hard to prove, at this point, without someone's confession or testimony."

"Premeditated." The word made Laura's stomach lurch. Did she really believe that the boys she had known since they were babies had planned and carried out a murder?

"Let me know," John said. "You've been carrying a heavy load all these years. I can't promise anything will result from it, but we can try."

"Thank you," she said, her eyes filling with tears. She took a deep breath to regain control. He didn't need her grief on top of his own. She slowly rose to leave, handing him her empty wine glass. "Andrew should have a say in this, too. He doesn't talk about Michael much, but I know what happened still bothers him."

Chapter Ten

O N Saturday night, Dublin celebrated the opening of its new library with a lavish fundraising gala. Library patrons, business owners, civic leaders, and even a few local celebrities gathered at the library for an evening of regional restaurant samplings and live music. It was the first year for the gala, and the fundraising goal was steep. Jan Armstrong and her army of volunteers, including Laura, hoped to raise a quarter of a million dollars after expenses.

Laura, who was a patron of the library, jumped at the chance to participate. She provided a generous sponsorship from Serendipities Two. Dublin's library meant the world to her. It had been her first point of entry into life in the community, and it was the place where she met her first friends. The Irish book club was the cornerstone of her life in Dublin.

An hour before the gala, she stood in front of the floor-length mirror in her bedroom scrutinizing her appearance. She had treated herself to a blowout at the salon, giving her hair sexy lift and volume. The style of her navy-blue dress with its off-the-shoulder neckline and fitted waist managed to look alluring and demure at the same time. It had cost more than she felt comfortable spending, but it was easy to rationalize the expense since there was potential to meet new clients. She needed to look her best.

She and Terri shopped for their dresses together. "What do you think?" she asked, stepping outside the dressing room in her bare feet.

"Vava va voom. That's so perfect for you," Terri said, waggling her eyebrows. "Cocktails and *more.*"

Laura smiled at the memory, remembering her response. "It's the *more* part that gets tricky. Which dress are you getting?"

Terri had tried on three dresses in different lengths. With her long dark hair, she had looked ravishing in a black sequined dress with a shorter full skirt. Surely, that was the one she'd pick.

"This one," Terri said, surprising Laura. It was an emerald tealength dress with three-quarter inch sleeves and a fitted waist. The color matched Terri's eyes, and the slim waist showed off her trim figure.

"I thought you'd go for black and low-cut," Laura said with an indulgent smile.

"I'm not performing." Terri's response sounded almost curt.

"I didn't mean anything by that," Laura said quickly. "You'll look beautiful, like a princess. You could meet Prince Charming."

"A serious reader on a white horse?" Terri's ready smile returned. "It would be nice to meet a guy who doesn't assume that because I sing in a band, he can get laid on the first date." There was impatience in her voice. But Laura could hear disappointment and something else.

"How often does that happen?" Terri never talked about this aspect of her work.

"Regularly enough that I'm never surprised anymore."

"I have no idea what I'd do in that situation." Laura adjusted the neckline, realizing she would need to buy a strapless bra.

As Laura changed back into her regular clothes, troubling thoughts cascaded through her brain. At this age, she didn't think she had to save herself for marriage. But she definitely believed in waiting until she was in a committed relationship to sleep with a man. After all, this wasn't one of those four-chili pepper romance novels where head-over-heels attraction led to steamy sex by chapter three. This was real life.

She knew that Andrew and Emily regularly spent overnights at each other's apartments. Although they didn't flaunt this fact of their relationship, she had seen Emily's toiletries on his bathroom vanity often enough over the years to guess she wasn't sleeping on the sofa by herself. They had recently rented an apartment together. But, Laura reasoned, they had been together for quite a while and were planning to get married at Christmas.

What would it be like to have sex before marriage? She rolled her eyes. It would have to be better than her first time as a married woman. Predictably, she felt her thoughts drift toward John. "I sure hope I like sex better this time."

It was only when she heard Terri's laughter from the other side of the dressing room divider that she realized she had said it out loud.

Laura glanced at the clock on her chest of drawers. Five fifty-five. Cocktails started at six-thirty. She turned from side to side, assessing her appearance one last time. She wondered if the two-and-a half-inch pumps she had picked would prove to be a poor choice as the evening wore on, unaccustomed as she was to higher heels. Just in case, she tucked two band-aids into her black evening bag. A pair of pearl ear-rings and a simple gold bracelet completed the look. She applied a light coating of mascara to her naturally long lashes and smoothed on a matte rose lip color with staying power.

She drove across town to the library, which featured a new multi-level parking garage. Thinking of her feet, she took advantage of guest valet parking. She handed over the keys to her SUV and proceeded to the entrance where two older female volunteers greeted her. One of them, Betsy, was a member of the Irish book club.

"You look beautiful, Laura," Betsy said. "Have a wonderful time!"

Stepping inside the main door of the library, Laura paused to take in the sights. The new main floor was nothing short of spectacular. The word 'enchanting' came to mind.

The main level contained the children's area with sections for tweens and ready-for-kindergarten—a beginning reader's paradise. A white stone divider in the entryway had circle cutouts that contained peek-a-boo aquariums. Two bicycles perched atop a set of book shelves with a poster about bicycle safety and the importance of wearing a helmet. A panorama of low shelves filled with colorful books lined the entire space. The lower shelving meant parents could keep an eye on their children while they browsed. For a moment, Laura longed to be a young mother again, bringing her boys to find books to love for two weeks, then return them for new discoveries.

The fundraiser was sure to be a success, if the growing crowd on the main level was any indication. Guests milled about, dressed in their finest attire, migrating between noisy conversations normally discouraged in the library as they enjoyed cocktails and appetizers. Tonight, the Dublin library was *the* place to be. The campaign to create a bigger, better library had been generously supported by a record number of people and their businesses.

Dublin was a town on the move. With its growing population, expansion projects were underway to create new housing and commercial spaces. Dubliners were understandably proud of their town with its equal measure of historic laidback charm and modern chic. Most residents and business owners knew each other well and worked together to create a vibrant, thriving community. Those who had lived in Dublin for many years could spot a newcomer at a glance, but never failed to make visitors or new residents feel welcome. When she first moved to Dublin, Laura had received many helpful introductions and surprising kindnesses from townspeople who made it clear they wanted her to succeed.

Here in the children's section, appetizers from three local restaurants were arranged on long tables buffet-style. Adorning one of the tables was an ice sculpture of a child sitting cross-legged on the floor engrossed in a book. Laura couldn't resist reaching out to touch the intricate details carved into the ice.

Servers dressed in tuxedos hand-passed trays of drinks and tempting appetizers. Fresh strawberries rested at the bottom of flutes of bubbly Prosecco. Two bars placed strategically at either end of the main floor ensured no one would wait too long for a beverage. Lively Irish music featuring traditional and modern songs provided a toe-tapping vibe to put guests in the mood for fun.

Laura turned and saw a familiar face. Larry from the online dating site strode across the room toward one of the appetizer tables. He was accompanied by a stunning blonde wearing a black cocktail dress cut nearly to her waist in back. She looked to be in her thirties. Larry turned, saw Laura, and his eyes widened in surprise and pleasure. He grinned and waved. Laura smiled and waved back even as her face turned a deep shade of red, remembering their last encounter.

It had been several weeks since their coffee date and her last email to him. From the looks of things, he had meant what he said, that he was leaving the next move up to her. In the meantime, he had met someone who wasn't as shy, who accepted a date, and who clearly was having a nice time with him. She mentally berated herself. Had she been less restrained in her response to him, she might have been here tonight having fun with him, instead of feeling awkward and alone. She bit her lower lip, frustrated at her lack of courage.

Terri had been right when she said not to wait too long to show an interest in a nice guy like Larry. Laura had blown her chance. She could never reach out to him now—not when he had another girlfriend. Shyness was not reason enough to hide from life and the potential for joyful experiences. She wouldn't make that mistake again.

"Laura!" Jan Armstrong waved her over to join a group that included Anne, a regular customer at Serendipities Two. Laura felt relieved to see someone she knew at the party other than Jan. "Come join us. These folks are from Landsgate," Jan said.

Landsgate, headquartered in Dublin, was a large commercial real estate development company specializing in condominium complexes that included retail space and restaurants. In addition to Anne and her husband, there was an older couple and a handsome forty-something man who bore a remarkable resemblance to actor Hugh Jackman. He appeared to be alone and was so good-looking that Laura couldn't take her eyes off him. She tried not to stare as Jan made introductions, starting with Laura.

"This is Laura Fisher, another of our sponsors," Jan told them. "She owns Serendipities Two. It's my favorite place to get quality collectibles and gifts."

"Mine, too," Anne chimed in "Laura's taste is exquisite."

"Thanks, you two," Laura said with a grin, turning to Anne. "I'll have to remember to quote you in my next advertisement." She was relieved. Discussions about the store were always easier than other topics. "You'll have to stop by next week when I set out new pieces from an estate sale. I know how much you like hand-blown glass. There is a gorgeous bowl that resembles an ocean spray."

"I can't wait to see it," Anne said. She smiled at her husband. "Todd indulges me in my little second-hand obsession." Todd laughed and winked conspiratorially at Laura.

"Let me introduce our other guests," Anne said, indicating the other couple, Sally and Ben, and the man who had captured Laura's attention. "This is Greg Waters. He moved here a few weeks ago."

"From where?" Laura asked. Hollywood came to mind first.

Greg's shock of wavy dark-brown hair fell just slightly over his forehead, and he had chocolate-brown eyes and an expressive mouth above a strong chin. She felt a flutter that began in her stomach and traveled down.

"Philadelphia," Greg answered, his eyes never leaving hers. "I'm the new Vice President of Finance for Landsgate."

"Welcome to Dublin," she said automatically, wondering if the strange feeling in her lower abdomen could be hunger or something more worrisome.

"It's nice to meet you," he said with a smile that showed movie-star perfect teeth. "May I get you something from the bar?"

Laura's cheeks flooded with color. "Yes, thank you. A Chardonnay?"

"You've got it." She watched him walk toward the crowded bar, his stride confident. He glanced back at her as if expecting that she would be watching him.

Jan grinned and linked her arm through Laura's. "Have you been downstairs to the dessert area on the lower level? I think you'll love it."

"I haven't investigated the food yet. I just got here," Laura answered, still watching Greg as he stood in line at the bar. "I'm sure it's wonderful. Thanks again for allowing me to sponsor the desserts. I promise I won't stand there obnoxiously handing out business cards."

Jan laughed. "I don't care if you do," she said. "This is an event benefiting the library, but it's also a gathering for the community. A library is a place for everyone to come. No matter who you are or what interests you, you can find a resource from the library. And you, Laura, are a true community treasure."

Laura felt a warmth in her chest, happy that someone as respected as Jan recognized that her work had value, not just for what it brought in income, but for what she was able to do for others. She spent considerable time with customers, learning their tastes and preferences, remembering what pieces they loved and researching historical information about items for them. There were many evenings she searched the internet for furniture or collectibles, knowing these would bring joy and pleasure to her customers. Leave it to Jan to say the words she needed most to boost her confidence.

Greg returned with a glass of Chardonnay and handed it to her with a flourish. "I asked for their oldest vintage. It's three," he said. His friends laughed.

"Thank you," she said, joining in. "A three-year-old is okay. Two-year-olds are just plain trouble." When the group laughed again, she realized she had made a witty remark. Pleased, she allowed her eyes to meet Greg's.

Jan excused herself to greet other guests, and Greg's colleagues migrated toward other groups. It was clear that the executive team of Landsgate was there to network. Laura wished for a moment that Greg could stay with her.

"I'll see you later," he said, lightly touching her arm.

"It was nice meeting you," she said. Her skin tingled where he had touched her.

After Greg walked away to join his colleagues, Laura scanned the first floor for Terri who was nowhere in sight. Maybe she would find her upstairs where the main buffet items were located.

Food was now high on Laura's priority list. She needed to eat something, or she'd be tipsy from the Chardonnay. Drinking her way out of social discomfort wasn't a good idea.

The elevator stopped on the second floor, which featured adult fiction and non-fiction, and where dinner offerings included pasta primavera, lemon chicken, smoked salmon, and beef tenderloin. She saw two more bars set up on either side of the room. A jazz quartet with a female singer performed easy-listening favorites. The music was just loud enough to permit conversation. People milled about in groups, nibbling from small plates or grazing as they stood at tall boy tables.

Realizing that she hadn't eaten anything except a bagel since early morning, Laura filled a plate with lemon chicken, salmon, and pasta, and made her way to an empty table near the elevator. Hopefully, Terri would show up soon. She felt conspicuous on her own. Most people attending were couples.

She thought of Greg and was grateful she had been able to keep up her end of the conversation. Surely, a man that good-looking could have any girl he wanted. With any luck, he'd look for her later and they could get better acquainted. She would force herself to be more outgoing.

Since Terri was still nowhere in sight, Laura finished her dinner and walked downstairs to the new café on the lower level. There, sumptuous desserts filled tables arranged with spectacular hues of summer flowers. In addition to the café, this level also featured meeting rooms. She saw a sign in gold script *Sponsored by Serendipities Two*.

The dessert bar was resplendent with decadent treats, as appealing to the eye as to the taste buds. No one could possibly resist the temptation to sample the beautiful pastries, cupcakes, profiteroles, pastel-colored petit fours, and macarons of various colors and flavors. She filled a small plate with a profiterole, lemon bar, lavender macaron, and a cupcake swirled high with pink frosting and silvery sugar sparkles.

There was a coffee bar in one of the smaller meeting rooms along with a table of self-serve liqueurs and a bowl of whipped cream. What would a Dublin coffee bar be without Irish coffee? Another room contained café tables and chairs where groups visited over coffee and dessert.

As she poured coffee from an urn, she felt a hand on her elbow. Startled, she almost dropped her cup. It was Terri, looking elegant and sophisticated in the forest-green dress that was so becoming on her.

Her dark hair was braided and arranged around the crown of her head. This Terri McDonald appeared very different from the woman who performed on stage in black leather, her long raven hair swinging freely as she sang and played her fiddle.

"Terri, you look stunning. Really beautiful."

Terri held a flute of Prosecco with a large strawberry resting on the bottom. Bubbles rose languidly to the surface. "Thanks. So do you. I couldn't find you upstairs. Are you having fun?"

"Sort of. I hate coming to things by myself," Laura said.

Terri whistled under her breath. "There are some good-looking men here tonight. Unfortunately, most of them appear to be married."

"Not all of them. I saw Larry, the guy I had coffee with. He's with a date. Do you suppose it's serious?"

"How could it be serious?" Terri sniffed. "He's recently been active on a dating site. Anyway, right now, Larry isn't married or engaged. He's just here with a date."

"I was planning to email him again. Now, I don't know . . ." Laura's voice trailed off.

"If he talks with you tonight, you should definitely show interest—well, not if his date is right there, obviously. That would be rude."

"But if this woman really likes him, I don't want to stand in her way," Laura persisted. "He might have just met her and found his true love."

"Spoken like a true sister-friend," Terri said, grinning. She took Laura's cup and poured Irish whiskey into it, then spooned a dollop of whipped cream on top. "Here you go. Liquid courage," she said. "Maybe his date invited him to attend the event with her."

"You mean she asked *him* out?"

"Women do that now." Terri fixed an Irish coffee for herself, and they touched their glass mugs together. "Whoa," Terri said, her eyes riveted to the door where Greg had just made his entrance. "Will you look at that hunka-hunka burning love?"

"His name is Greg," Laura said, nearly snorting at Terri's description. "You *know* him?"

"I met him downstairs a little while ago. He just moved to town from Philadelphia. He's Vice President of Finance for Landsgate." She took a gulp of fortified coffee. "He got me a glass of wine. Then he said something funny, and I said something back." She took another sip. "I did okay."

"Well, hallelujah," Terri said. "You just had your first serious flirtation. Oh, and look, he's coming this way. Judging from the look on his face, I'd say it won't be your last chance to practice your flirting skills tonight."

Laura smoothed the front of her dress and took another gulp of the strong drink. "Any last-minute advice?"

"Hey, you just landed the dreamboat of the night. I stand humbled before you."

Laura laughed and squeezed Terri's elbow. "Thanks for helping me." Then she made direct eye contact with Greg who headed toward her. "I think I understand now what you mean by chemistry."

CHAPTER ELEVEN

As she skipped up the steps to her apartment, Laura sang the chorus of a new pop song she had heard on the car radio. She felt weightless, floating on air, no longer aware of her tired, achy feet. She had never felt this alive.

Kicking off her high heels, she padded in stocking feet to the full-length mirror where just hours earlier, she had dressed for the gala, unaware of the surprising turn the evening would take. *I look different.* She moved closer to the mirror, inspecting her features. Her complexion had a rosier glow than usual. Even her eyes were a more vibrant blue.

She mentally reviewed all the business connections she had made. They paled in comparison to the one who now consumed her thoughts: Greg Waters. After he rejoined her, Terri excused herself. Laura and Greg spent another forty-five minutes talking until the blinking overhead lights let everyone know the event was over. When he walked her to the front entrance of the library, he waited with her while the parking attendant fetched her car. As Laura stepped to the driver's side, Greg handed the valet a ten-dollar bill.

"Thank you," Laura said, impressed at the gallant gesture. "It was nice to meet you."

"Truthfully, meeting you made the entire night worthwhile," Greg said. "Until that point, it was just another networking event with better food and drinks." He laughed and she joined in.

"Your coworkers seem really nice," she said. "I hope you'll like your new job and be happy living here."

"Well, after tonight, things are definitely looking up." Greg held the car door open as Laura placed her evening bag on the passenger seat. "I wondered if you'd like to have dinner with me on Tuesday."

This, too, was unexpected. Laura did a quick mental review of her schedule. "I'd love to," she said.

"Great." Greg leaned in and gave her the lightest of kisses on her cheek, daringly close to her mouth. His lips felt smooth as butterfly wings. Laura shivered. "I'll pick you up at seven," he said.

THE NEXT THREE DAYS PASSED IN A FLURRY of blissful anticipation interspersed with equal moments of acute anxiety. What would she wear? What topics of conversation could she initiate? She obsessed over every possibility, even wondering if Greg might change his mind. This went on until Terri suggested they shop for a new outfit to give her confidence.

"This color would look beautiful with your eyes," Terri said, handing her a dress in a blue-and-white seersucker. "It's a cool summer fabric and will look nice with those strappy white sandals you have." They picked out a slim gold bracelet inlaid with blue stones and matching earrings that brought out the color in Laura's peaches-and-cream complexion.

On Tuesday, Laura had such difficulty concentrating on work that Cissy, who had taken over several tasks, finally said, "Earth to Laura."

Laura reluctantly left her daydream date with Greg—the one where he was kissing her at the front door. Although she had no experience with the kind of passionate yet gently restrained kisses that came with budding romance, she had seen enough romance movies to know what she wanted her first kiss to feel like. "Sorry, what were you saying?"

"I said we just got a call that the furniture from last weekend's estate sale will be coming later this afternoon. I don't see those pieces on the spreadsheet."

Laura shook her head ruefully. "That's because I didn't put those in the system yet. Sorry, I've been a little preoccupied."

"Everything okay?" Cissy asked. She had been Laura's first employee and had shown herself to be so trustworthy and dependable, Laura often relied on her to manage the store and deliver the day's deposit to the bank.

"Everything is fine. I just have too much on my mind. What time is the delivery?"

"Four-thirty. I can stay, if you want."

Laura grimaced, realizing that the delivery might be delayed, which wouldn't allow her the time she needed to get ready for her date with Greg. She had an appointment to get her hair trimmed and styled. She had already pressed and hung her new summer frock on the dress form in her bedroom. "Could you? That would be great. I have plans for this evening, and I'll need plenty of time to get ready."

Cissy's eyes twinkled with mischief. "As distracted as you've been lately, I hope these plans are *fun* plans, as in *man* plans."

"Why, yes, they are," Laura said, her cheeks coloring. "I have my first date in . . . well, let's just say in longer than anyone can imagine."

"Have fun, and don't worry about the furniture delivery. I've got this. I have one condition, though."

"If you stay past closing time, I'll pay you more," Laura assured her.

"That's not the condition. You have to promise to tell me all about your date," Cissy said, throwing her arms around her boss in a hug. "If anyone deserves to find her true love—the handsome prince on the white horse—it's you."

The handsome prince parked his silver Mercedes convertible and rang the doorbell of Laura's apartment promptly at seven, his arms full of vibrant summer flowers.

"Oh my! They're gorgeous," Laura said, a blush creeping up her face. Finding a large enough vase to display the profusion of blossoms and greens necessitated a trip upstairs. She hadn't planned to let him come upstairs to her apartment on their first date, but the flowers would wilt without water.

He followed her up the steps and waited in the living room while Laura scurried to the kitchen to find a vase. She nervously arranged the blooms in a large crystal rectangular-shaped vase and set it on the dining room table. She could see him studying the artwork in her living room. She closed the bedroom door on her way to join him.

"Thank you again," she said. "I love all the gerbera daisies. The colors you chose are my favorites."

"You can thank the florist for the selections. I told her they had to be just right."

Laura swallowed, not trusting herself to speak. "They are . . . just right."

He walked toward the front windows to check the street view. While he had his back turned, she caught a glimpse of herself in the mirror over the dining room buffet. She noted that the dress, nipped at the waist with a slightly fuller skirt, still looked crisp from its recent pressing. Lord, she was nervous.

Greg turned around, flashing his one-hundred-watt smile. His teeth were so perfect and white; he could have appeared in a toothpaste commercial. He was exceptionally handsome tonight in a teal golf shirt with a Pebble Beach Golf Club insignia, pressed khakis, and polished dress loafers. The look was casual. Yet, Laura registered that every detail of his appearance demonstrated expensive taste and money to afford whatever he liked.

"Your place is nice—exactly what I'd expect of someone who handles high-quality furnishings and design," Greg said. "Think you could make some improvements to the house I just bought?" He grinned and sauntered toward her.

She took a step back involuntarily. It unnerved her that they were alone together in her apartment, an occurrence she hadn't taken into consideration. "If you want me to do a design consultation, I'd be glad to schedule something next week," she said, falling into business-speak to hide her nervousness. "How old is your house?"

"It's only a couple of years old. It was move-in ready, which was a plus. But I think it lacks character. I could use a few pieces of furniture, maybe an area rug or two. I haven't been sure what to buy."

"After I see what you have, I'll know what you need," she said automatically. A self-conscious smile followed. This phrase had become her professional credo. She cleared her throat and explained. "It's a thing I do. I look at what you have and repurpose it. Then if you need something new, it's obvious what that should be."

"To you, maybe. Can't wait to see you work your magic." He glanced at his watch. "I made reservations at Tucci's. It's the perfect night to sit outside on their patio, and we can walk over. Shall we?" He held out his arm to her. She linked her hand over the crook of his elbow.

The next three hours were everything Laura could have imagined on a first date. Greg's career in finance and economics had led to a wealth of interesting business experiences. He was well-traveled, and not only for business. He had been to several countries that Laura dreamed about visiting, including Ireland and Italy. He also was a good listener, asking insightful questions that drew her out of her shell. Best of all, he made her laugh.

"Are you divorced?" he asked as they finished their salads.

"Widowed," she said. "My husband died three years ago."

"I'm sorry," he said, his face registering something that she decided was sympathy, though it could just as easily been uneasiness. "That must have been very difficult."

"Yes, just not in the ways you might expect." She weighed her response. She didn't want or need his pity. She intended that he would view her as a strong woman able to manage anything that came her way.

"We didn't exactly have the best marriage. He, uh, had a temper."

Greg's eyes widened. "Surely, you don't mean . . .?

She cleared her throat and started to speak, swallowed, and tried again. "I worked very hard not to give him any reason for anger."

He let out a long breath, studying her features. "I hate to ask this, but were you relieved when he was gone?"

She leaned back in her chair, unsure of how much she wanted to admit to this near-stranger. "There was nothing easy or uncomplicated about the emotions I felt. After a little while, I moved here to be closer to my youngest son, and I started my business."

"Wow. In just a couple of years, you went from what sounds like a really bad marriage to being a widow and dealing with all of that . . . to being a business owner in a different city. Laura, that is remarkable. I'm not sure I have your strength." Greg held up his glass of red wine. "A toast? To endurance." They clinked glasses.

"Do you have children?" she asked.

"I have a daughter, Emma." She watched him cut his salad into smaller bites, buying time. "I'm divorced from her mother," he finally said. He took a sip of wine. "To be honest, Emma and I aren't exactly on the best of terms. She was angry when her mother and I separated."

"How long has it been?"

"A little over two years since the divorce. Much longer since we separated."

It seemed an awfully long time for a parent-child estrangement. "Maybe your daughter just needs time to adjust to the changes," Laura suggested. "How old is she?"

"Twenty. She's a junior at Villanova. I'm afraid she views me as the reason for the divorce. It's a long story." His lips formed a thin line. He didn't seem anxious to share more details.

Laura let the subject drop. Families and relationships were complicated. Perhaps he would share more later. Her gut told her this was an important piece of his history.

Their conversation turned to his new house and what he hoped to do with it. Greg had purchased his home in an affluent area of Columbus still under development. Even modest homes in that area cost upwards of five hundred thousand dollars. "It's nice, but it doesn't feel homey," he said. "It could use a decorator's touch."

"I'd be glad to take a look and let you know what I think," Laura said, sipping her red wine.

At a little after nine o'clock, they left Tucci's and walked back to Laura's place. "Would you like a cup of coffee?" she asked. "We could sit on the front porch and people-watch."

Greg hesitated a moment. "No coffee for me, thanks. I wouldn't turn down a glass of wine, though."

"Red or white?" she asked.

"Let's stick with red," he said.

There was an awkward moment when Laura unlocked the front door. His hand was light on her lower back. When she stepped inside, he was on her heels, following her upstairs. She had hoped he would sit on the cushioned wicker furniture on the front porch while she got their wine. He followed her into the kitchen while she opened a bottle of pinot noir and poured two glasses. She handed him his glass, which he promptly set down on the counter. Then he took her glass and did the same. He reached around her waist and gently pulled her close in an embrace. She thought she felt his heartbeat through the golf shirt, though it might have been her own heart thumping so wildly.

Laura raised her face to look into his eyes, and he kissed her. It was tender yet passionate, a promise of more. She felt his tongue and involuntarily stiffened, but Greg's kiss was nothing like Jed's forced kisses that had frightened her over the years. She wanted Greg's kiss to last forever. He held her in a way that was protective yet passionate. They kissed for a minute or so, and then he released her. She was surprised that she wanted more.

"I have wanted to kiss you since we met at the library. You made that cute comment about the age of the wine," he said. "You're adorable."

Laura let out a relieved laugh, remembering. "I didn't know what to say. Greg, to be honest, I'm not very experienced with men. I hope you don't find me dull."

"Dull? You are anything but dull, Laura Fisher. You're entrancing, captivating, and gorgeous." He kissed her again, just a peck on the lips this time. Then he picked up their glasses of wine. "After you," he said as they made their way downstairs to the front porch.

The next morning, Laura inserted a coffee pod into the Keurig at the same instant her phone rang. Dublin Library appeared on the screen. "This is Laura."

"Got time for lunch?" Jan Armstrong asked the moment she heard Laura's voice. "I'd like to get your impressions of the event. After expenses, I think we'll make a little over two hundred and sixty-five thousand dollars."

"Oh my gosh, you went over your goal! I'm so glad. Everything was wonderful," Laura said. "There wasn't a single glitch. And I met so many people."

"Did you have a good time?"

"Oh, yes." Laura smiled. "I'm glad you called. I was going to call you later, anyway, because I may need some tips on getting through *Dubliners*. I'm struggling."

Jan chuckled. "That book has as many layers as an onion. It's one of my favorites, but I have to work at it, too." She paused and then cut to the chase. "I saw you and Greg Waters leave together."

"We didn't exactly leave together. He walked with me to get my car. But I did have dinner with him last night," Laura said.

"How did it go?" Jan pressed. "He's gorgeous—quite the catch."

Laura sighed with happiness. "Yes, he is gorgeous. I had a great time, and I think he did, too."

"Is he a reader?"

Laura laughed. "That's the first thing a librarian always wants to know." She thought back to their discussion. "He likes non-fiction—mostly management books," Laura said. "In other words, he isn't likely to join the Irish book club."

"Opposites attract. Enjoy yourself," Jan said. "As long as I've known you, I've never seen you with a man other than your son. It's time for a chapter like this one in the story of *your* life."

"Like one of those true romance novels?" Laura chuckled. "I never knew what people meant when they used the term chemistry. Now I do. I definitely do."

Jan let out a hearty laugh. "Your friends will live vicariously through you, myself included. I love my husband with all my heart, but his idea of a romantic gesture is taking out the trash without waiting for me to ask him. Not that I don't appreciate that," she added. "Relationships have seasons, and it's fun to watch someone in the springtime phase."

"He brought me flowers." Laura smiled and bit her lower lip. "Would you believe getting flowers from a man is also a first for me? I stayed up late last night marveling at them."

"Oh, Laura," Jan said, her voice catching with emotion. "I hope Greg is the one. If he isn't, there will be someone even better. For someone as full of love as you are, it's inevitable."

Chapter Twelve

"**T**HIS CLOSET IS FULL OF JACKIE'S summer clothes," John said, opening the double doors to a massive walk-in closet in the guest room of his house. "The rest of her stuff is in the master bedroom." He shook his head. "She had a lot of clothes."

"Her taste was exquisite." Laura caught a tantalizing whiff of jasmine cologne as if someone wearing it had just passed by. She saw John take in a deep breath as if catching it, too.

He touched the sleeve of a pearl-white jacket, fingering the fine brocade fabric. Laura remained silent, allowing him time to process what needed to be done. Going through a loved one's belongings and letting those reminders go was difficult but important in the grieving process. She winced, remembering how easily she had given away everything of Jed's, without a moment's hesitation. But, oh, how she had suffered donating Michael's clothes.

John handed her a sky-blue silk frock with a tiny, fitted waist. Laura peeked at the tag. Jackie had been a petite size six. From the wedding photo of Jackie and John perched atop a cherry chest of drawers, Laura could see that a twenty-something Jackie had worn her brown hair shoulder-length, curling about her heart-shaped face.

She turned and caught John watching her as she studied the photo. "She was so pretty. How did the two of you meet?"

"At a fraternity-sorority party. She was the prettiest girl I'd ever seen." He smiled. "She had this hilarious laugh—contagious, you know? Just hearing that laugh coming straight from her belly made me laugh, too."

Laura's eyes scanned the room, taking in the queen-sized four-poster bed where Jackie and John had slept together, loved each other. How wonderful that they had been so close while sharing the responsibilities of marriage and the trials of serious illness. What was it like to experience that kind of enduring love?

Jackie had owned several pieces of expensive jewelry—gifts from John and her parents, which he intended to sell. With the proceeds, he planned to set up a scholarship fund at Ohio State in Jackie's name. "Education meant a lot to her."

"What did she study in college?"

"Elementary ed. She was a kindergarten teacher," John said. "She loved children, and they loved her." A shadow crossed his face. "We weren't able to have kids. Just when we started considering our options, we learned about her A.L.S. It was one of the saddest moments in her life when she realized that if we had children, she might not be able to care for them, to see them grow up. She made the decision not to pursue fertility treatments and to just enjoy the kids she saw every day. But it was hard, you know? She stopped to peer into every baby carriage."

"How sad for her—for both of you," Laura said, her heart aching at the image. "Even though our boys didn't have the ideal childhood, I was young and healthy enough to enjoy them. I consider them my greatest accomplishment."

"I remember seeing your boys in the neighborhood," John said. "Your older son always walked like an adult, keeping a close eye on his little brother. I thought he looked so serious for a kid."

"He had a lot to deal with," Laura admitted. "His father was hard on him. If there is any comfort to be had, it's that Michael is at peace now."

John squeezed her elbow. "You understand what I'm going through in a way most other people don't. That's how I feel about Jackie. I will always miss her, but I wouldn't want her to continue living as she did. I need to grieve the loss of her and then find a way to celebrate everything that she meant, not just to me but to others, too."

"That should be a goal of mine, too," Laura said after a moment. "I'd like to find my own peace with what happened to Michael so I can do something as a way of honoring his life."

They worked for almost two hours packing Jackie's clothing, shoes, and handbags. Together, they carried them out to Laura's SUV. She planned to take everything to a clothing consignment store. The money from their sale also would help support the scholarship fund.

After the last armload of clothing had been loaded into the back of the vehicle, John stood to the side while Laura closed the rear gate. "We don't have to deal with this today, but I could use your help with some furniture, too," he said. "I'd like you to have them for your store." They went inside, and he showed her a set of bedroom furniture, a pedestal table, and a massive armoire. "I might have other things later," he said.

"I'll bring by the consignment paperwork tomorrow," Laura said. "This furniture will sell fast. Oh, and I'm not taking a commission."

"Of course, you should. I don't want any money from the sale of these," John said. "They were inherited from Jackie's parents."

"But, John, I don't think you understand. This table will sell for at least four hundred dollars, maybe more," Laura said, running her hand along its smooth surface. It was a beautiful pedestal table inlaid around the perimeter with opalescent mother-of-pearl. "This is in perfect condition. Are you sure you want to part with these pieces?"

"Very sure. It's *because* Jackie loved them that I can't see them every day," he said. "There are too many memories. I need for whatever is around me now to be emotionally neutral. Otherwise, I can't let go of her. Does that make sense?" Laura nodded. He passed his hand over his eyes. "That wardrobe?" He pointed to the massive armoire. "The bedroom furniture? They were in our first apartment."

"I understand." And she did. She would figure out how to use the money in some special way to honor Jackie.

John swallowed hard. "Now all I have to do is figure out what to do with the house."

"May I offer a little piece of advice from personal experience?" Laura leaned against the doorframe between the master bedroom and the hallway.

"Please."

"Don't feel that you have to take care of everything all at once," Laura said. "When Jed . . . when my husband passed away, I didn't let go of the house right away. Oh, I wanted to, believe me. I wanted to get away from everything that house represented, but it was too overwhelming. I needed to take baby steps. Marjorie helped a lot. The opportunity to open Serendipities Two brought everything into focus, and it was easy to take care of those last details. The sale of the house happened almost without any effort. By then, I knew what I wanted and where I was going."

"That's a good point," John said. "This house is in a good location, close to campus. It will sell easily, when I'm ready. Thanks again for doing all of this."

Laura picked up her handbag. "You're welcome. I'll call to make arrangements to pick up the furniture."

"Can I at least buy you lunch for all your hard work?"

"That's nice of you, but my helper this afternoon has to leave at one-thirty. I need to get going." She started for the front door, admiring the oriental runner in the foyer.

"Another time then." He was a few steps behind her. "Laura?" She turned to face him. "I couldn't have gotten through the past two weeks without you. Thanks for being there—for sending over such wonderful meals and for helping me today."

"I'm glad to help. Will you be at the book club meeting this week?"

"Can I show up even if I haven't finished the book?" he asked, looking sheepish.

"Of course, you can. I finally finished it—not sure how much I actually understood," Laura admitted with a shrug. "If that makes me sound thick, I guess I am."

"Thick? It makes you sound real." John let out a quick laugh. "That's a quality I greatly admire."

MEMBERS OF THE IRISH BOOK CLUB agreed that reading James Joyce's critically-acclaimed book of short stories, *Dubliners*, had been worth the effort. Each reader managed to decipher deeper meanings in the author's carefully-chosen prose. Laura found much to ponder in the stories. The characters sparked memories of people and situations that felt all too familiar, though the stories were set in Ireland a little more than a hundred years earlier. Her Irish grandparents had lived in Ireland when Joyce was writing the book.

The stories were about disappointments in life and love, the deaths of unremarkable people, and the touching remembrances of those people by others. Characters led difficult, often poverty-stricken lives. The city of Dublin in these stories appeared dreary and gray, in her mind's eye, as if color had not yet arrived there. This, too, was familiar. When she thought of Parmenter, she pictured the places of her former life in shades of black-and-white. In contrast, her life A.J. (after Jed) bore little resemblance to the monochromatic life of hardship, heartbreak, and abuse she had endured during her marriage.

"Which story was your favorite, Laura?" Jan asked during a lull in the discussion.

"The Dead," Laura answered without hesitation. She gathered her thoughts for a moment before explaining. "I didn't expect to like it when the story began. At first, I couldn't figure out why James Joyce gave it that title." She paused. "What I took from the story was that memories of people we have loved and lost are always with us. But what struck me most was that the young husband, Gabriel, never realized that his wife, Gretta, had memories of her own—that she was apart and distinct from him."

"Go on," Jan said. "You're getting at something very important."

"Gabriel assumed that the world revolved around his thoughts, his experiences, what he wanted. His wife had lost a young love—a boy who cared so much about her that he risked his life to see her, and he died for it. No one knows what kind of pain or guilt Gretta went through, least of all Gabriel. She moved on with her life and married him. But she kept the memory of that boy to herself. Gabriel was angry that he didn't know this about her. It was as if she had no right to her own life, her own memories."

Jim, whose wife Carol had brought him into the book club, said, "Maybe he thought he should know about it—that his wife ought to have shared that with him. What I'm saying is he might feel hurt that she kept that incident to herself."

"Fair enough," Jan said.

Terri sat forward in her chair, frowning. "When women of that time married, they gave up who they were as daughters in their father's household and became their husband's property. They owned nothing of their own. They really were extensions of their husbands. My first instinct when I read this was that what Gabriel thought about, he naturally assumed Gretta thought, too. If he didn't have an experience like that, why would she?"

Laura remembered her sheltered girlhood, living under her strict father's roof, followed by young married life with Jed. She was certain this type of experience would seem foreign to the members of this group. She cleared her throat. "This story may have been written a long time ago, but people still live that way."

Several women in the book group nodded, though Laura believed it was more out of politeness. These women were well-educated and affluent. Three had been married for decades. Carol attended the book group with Jim who clearly treated her as his intellectual equal.

Laura glanced over at John. "Thank goodness, not every man believes his wife is an extension of himself."

He met her eyes before speaking, choosing his words with care. "I was probably just as guilty of assuming my wife wanted whatever I wanted." He raked his fingers through his thick wavy dark hair. "Even so, I never believed she didn't have her own thoughts. That's what made her interesting." He shrugged and offered a smile. "I can't imagine anything more boring than a woman who thinks like me."

Waves of gentle laughter circulated around the room. In his words, Laura heard sincerity. She thought of Andrew and the way he listened attentively to everything Emily said. Pride welled in her chest. Her son would be a good husband and partner.

Jan removed her reading glasses. "Joyce chose the title 'The Dead' deliberately, just as he chose every word of his prose. I think of him choosing his words the way a painter dabs color onto canvas to bring out the fullest details of a leaf. Short stories require that each word be powerful, and this is one of the strongest short stories ever written. The title refers to the people we have loved and lost. Memories of people stay with us, good or bad."

Members of the book club remained after the ninety-minute session, gobbling up double-fudge brownies and lemon bars Laura had baked the evening before. As John got up to leave, he gave her a friendly peck on the cheek before heading to the front door. Terri watched, biting her lower lip, saying nothing.

"In the mood for a movie and some sangria?" Laura asked her as they moved furniture back into place for the next day's shoppers. "I'm not sleepy yet."

"Sure." Terri followed her upstairs and plopped onto the overstuffed sofa. Laura microwaved a bag of buttered popcorn and fixed a pitcher of red sangria with sliced oranges, limes, lemons, and apples. The friends settled in front of the big screen television, the huge bowl of popcorn and pitcher of sangria on the coffee table within easy reach.

"This is just what we need tonight," Terri said. "Wait, don't turn on the movie yet. I haven't heard every single detail about your date with Greg." She raised her eyebrows suggestively.

"It was wonderful," Laura said. "Well, not the way you think, maybe. We walked over to Tucci's. I can't remember exactly what I ate, only that it was good. I enjoyed the conversation, too. I wasn't even nervous." She thought happily of the evening. "We don't have a lot in common, but everything he says is fascinating."

"Yep, that's chemistry. Did he kiss you?"

"He did—right away," Laura said. "I didn't expect that. Then he kissed me again before he left. I couldn't ask for a better first date."

"I'll say." Terri slurped her sangria. "It would be better if you had more in common, though."

"Do you think this is a mistake?" Laura asked, suddenly worried.

"Not a mistake. Call it fun and enjoy it for what it is. It wouldn't be the worst thing, you know, if this is one of those things that starts out like fireworks and then fizzles on its own. As long as you don't get hurt, that is."

Laura took a sip of sangria and nibbled on an apple slice. "I'm hoping it's the kind of love that lasts forever. While we're getting to know each other, we can make some memories together. Wouldn't that give us more in common?"

Terri munched on a handful of popcorn while she considered the question. "I think for a relationship to go the distance, you need to have interests in common and shared values. It seems like you have way more in common with your friend, John." She leaned back against the sofa. "Watching you tonight with him makes me think it will be hard for the two of you to be friends if you're dating Greg."

"Why do you say that?"

"The two of you are fonder of each other than you realize. That is bound to become an issue sooner or later."

Laura's eyes flew open. "Terri, it isn't possible for John and me to have anything other than friendship. His wife just died. He said he's thinking about selling his house and going back into a law practice, maybe even back to Parmenter. There's a lot going on in his life."

"I didn't say either of you is ready for anything more than friendship. I just observed deeper feelings. Friendships can have deep feelings, too. So, there's no reason for you not to have fun and see where things go with Greg."

"True." Laura topped off their glasses from the pitcher. "To be honest, I didn't expect to be so attracted to Greg. He could be the one."

"Oh, no you don't," Terri said, setting her sweating glass onto a coaster on the coffee table. "Don't you dare entertain those kinds of thoughts this soon. Get to know him first. Let's face it: you pretty much had an arranged marriage. Now you have a chance to find out whether or not this guy is right for you."

"Do you think he'll want to sleep with me?"

"Only if you're lucky." Terri rolled her eyes. Seeing the concerned look that flashed on Laura's face, she quickly added, "Listen, you don't have to do anything you're not ready for. But trust me, with the kind of chemistry you say you have, you'd better be prepared."

Chapter Thirteen

As the first weekend of August drew near, preparations for Dublin, Ohio's acclaimed annual Irish festival took on a heightened fever. Porta-potties sprang up like mushrooms in the late summer humidity. White, orange, and green signs in the colors of the Irish flag dotted the landscape around town, offering an assortment of goods and services—urgent care, dental implants, and even hair transplants—as though they were part of the Irish festival experience.

Anyone doing business in Dublin took the festival personally. Everyone, it seemed, claimed Irish ancestry, welcoming out-of-town visitors into their stores and businesses, and offering luck-of-the-Irish discounts. Laura got in on the action, offering a stained-glass floor lamp as a store raffle item. The fact that Laura was, in fact, Irish by lineage only made the festival more special for her.

On Tuesday, she attended a final meeting of the festival organizing committees, where volunteers and city leaders shared eleventh-hour updates. The event was a well-oiled machine, and even the city government played a major role in its success. For one glorious long weekend, all eyes were on the small town in Ohio known as Dublin.

Although she enjoyed all the bands and individual singers who performed, Laura particularly loved the Irish step dancers. She often wished she had been allowed to learn the challenging steps in the days when she possessed a younger, nimbler body. But dancing was forbidden in her church.

She also looked forward to cultural workshops, Irish folk tales and myths, and stages featuring Celtic sports and, especially, the popular Celtic canines. In addition to better-known breeds such as Irish Setters and Irish Wolfhounds, there was the Irish Glen of Imall Terrier, Irish Soft Coated Wheaten Terrier, Kerry Beagle, Kerry Blue Terrier, Irish Terrier, Irish Water Spaniel, and the Irish Red and White Setter. Bred to be working dogs, Laura found all of them irresistible.

Her volunteer role during the festival was to act as a host for one of the big stages where she was assigned. This meant communicating with audio-visual people to make sure the sound system worked properly, offering bottled water to musicians and dancers, and relaying messages. It was her job to make sure everyone inside the tent, whether on stage or in the audience, had a good time.

Receiving an invitation to join the entertainment committee had been a stroke of Irish luck. After meeting Terri through the Irish book club, moving to Dublin, and getting to know her better, Laura learned that Terri chaired the committee. It had been the perfect introduction to life in Dublin. Laura loved the process of reviewing prospective performers and helping to decide which groups got the nod. Some singers and musicians were annual crowd favorites.

"This is one event you don't want to miss," she told Greg on their fourth date. They had gone to the movies and then out for a drink on the patio of another restaurant. Live music could be heard just about any evening on one of the outdoor patios.

"It's no fun going by myself," he said. "I'd rather stay with you."

"You don't want to just sit in one tent. You want to explore everything. We can walk around together when I'm not volunteering. I promise you won't be bored. When I'm done volunteering, we can have a Guinness and take in some live music," she promised. The old familiar need kicked in to reassure and soothe a man expressing his displeasure. She reminded herself that it was safe now to assert her own preferences. "Almost all the bands have been here before, and we know they're popular. Make sure you download the festival app so you know times and stage locations."

She had forgotten to tell him that Marjorie would be here for the festival and planned to stay in Laura's guest room. "My friend Marjorie has offered to help out at the store over the festival weekend so I can spend more time volunteering."

Greg looked grouchy. "Why would you want to volunteer and have to work so hard? Aren't there other people who can lend a hand?"

"We have at least twelve hundred volunteers. But it's a big festival that goes on from late Friday afternoon through Sunday evening. We need a lot of people. This festival is important to the community." She looked into his eyes. "Don't worry, we'll still have plenty of time together." She took a drink of water, her throat constricting.

Terri was right. It took practice to speak up. What if he decided he didn't want to date her because she was too busy?

"Then he isn't the right guy," Terri had said when Laura voiced that concern. "For someone who didn't know if she even wanted to date anyone, why are you letting this guy influence decisions you've made—things you love to do—before he ever came on the scene?"

"You're right," Laura said. "But I really like him. I don't want to drive him away by not being . . ."

"What, his beck-and-call girl?" Terri interjected, raising one eyebrow.

"Stop. What if he decides someone else is more available?"

"You *are* available, just not on his exact time table. It's called having a life."

"Okay, I know what you're saying. I don't want to be a doormat, but I also want to show him that I *want* to be with him."

Terri's eyes filled with compassion. "You are not a doormat. You never were. You were a woman in a desperate situation trying to remain safe and protect her kids." She took Laura's hand and looked into her eyes. "That is over now. This is now, and every choice is yours."

"But how do I know . . .?"

"You don't know—not for sure. No one ever knows for sure. But if you listen to your gut, you'll know. You're smart. Now you get to be the one to decide who, what, when, where, and how someone is allowed into your most personal space . . . which is not what you think, by the way. It's your heart."

"I thought you meant . . ."

Terri squeezed Laura's fingers. "I know what you thought I was going to say. And may I remind you that other personal spaces in your body are your own, too." She grinned.

Laura let out a long breath. "I already made this commitment to volunteer. It isn't right for me to back out."

"You've had exactly four dates with Greg. It's way too early for him to be expressing displeasure at how you choose to spend your time. If I were you, I'd give that guy Larry a call and see if he'd like to go out."

"Two men at the same time?" Laura was aghast.

"Three, if you count John."

LAURA ALSO ENCOURAGED JOHN TO ATTEND the Irish festival. "There are so many great bands that travel here for the weekend," she said, naming a few of them.

"I'll let you know if I think I can get there." His response was unusually abrupt.

His reluctance surely stemmed from all the to-dos on his list. The day before, she had sent a truck over to his house to pick up the furniture he wanted her to sell, and had supervised the packing and loading of each piece. He left the university and met her at his house, but seemed distracted and distant.

"Before they start loading, are you sure this is what you want to do?" Laura asked, wondering if his detached demeanor meant he was having second thoughts about parting with the furniture.

"No second thoughts," he assured her. "This is the right next step. I'm talking with a realtor about what changes I ought to make to the house, in case I decide to sell it."

"I don't think there is much you'd have to do. Your kitchen and bathrooms are updated. The hardwood floors look great." Another thought came. "Will you stay in this area?"

"I took the job at Ohio State because I thought Jackie should be at Glenview Gardens. Now that she's gone, I may decide to go back to trying criminal cases. I've been thinking more and more about returning to Parmenter. Real estate is less expensive there."

"Oh." Laura frowned. Parmenter held few good memories for her. "Is living there what you really want?"

"While Jackie was so sick, I concentrated on what was best for her. Glenview Gardens is expensive, and long-term care for someone as sick as Jackie costs a fortune. But I'm sure you know that. I don't have the financial reserves I used to have."

"I understand. Mom's care isn't completely covered by her income, so I help out." The truth was that she had begun drawing down on her own savings more lately. She bit the inside of her mouth. "I may need to do something to build more business for myself."

"So, I guess these and other topics are fodder for more life conversations," John had said, his tone lightening. "I know you're busy this weekend with the festival. Would you like to meet for coffee next week after your life gets back to normal?"

"I don't know what normal looks like, but I'd love that," she said.

MARJORIE ARRIVED ON THURSDAY EVENING, looking weary and more than a little pale. She had difficulty carrying her overnight bag up the front porch steps. Laura quickly grabbed it from her hands and carried it the rest of the way up to her apartment. Marjorie was usually the epitome of boundless energy. What was the matter?

"Your usual room awaits you," Laura said with a flourish. "I've put clean towels and some toiletries in a basket over there." She led her into the guest room. Fresh flowers adorned the nightstand, along with a lavender candle.

"It's as lovely as always. Thank you," Marjorie said, lowering herself onto the bottom of the bed. She stifled a yawn. "I might just close my eyes for a few minutes, if you don't mind."

"Not at all. You rest while I fix supper." Laura knew that Marjorie still routinely worked ten- to twelve-hour days, as Laura often did. "I'm not sure you ought to be working in the store this weekend while I'm at the festival, especially when you're this tired," Laura said. "I can run over and close early, or ask Cissy or Judith to work a few extra hours."

"I can handle a half-day tomorrow and Saturday. Don't you worry about me," Marjorie replied. "If you have a nice comfy chair near the cash register, I'll be fine."

"Are you coming down with something?" Laura asked. "I've never seen you look this tired."

"I have Lyme Disease. Didn't I tell you? It takes longer to recover at my age, even with the medication I was given. I've been closing up earlier than usual the past month, trying to get a little more rest."

"Lyme Disease is serious, and no, you didn't mention it. If you need a nap while you're at the store, just take one. Whoever else is working can handle things for that long."

While Marjorie took a half-hour nap, Laura brewed a pitcher of iced tea and set the table for dinner. She was glad to have her friend all to herself tonight. There was so much to talk about. No matter what the subject, Marjorie's advice and insights were always spot-on.

She checked the bubbling Irish stew and sliced freshly-baked soda bread. Hearing a step behind her, she turned to find Marjorie in the doorway. "Feel better, I hope? Dinner is ready."

"Everything smells wonderful."

"It's not fancy, but I thought Irish stew was appropriate. During Irish Fest, it's practically illegal not to eat Irish favorites."

"I'm glad we stayed in tonight. The drive tuckered me out." Marjorie smoothed the front of her blouse. "So, how are things progressing with that new man of yours?"

"He's not exactly *my* man. But I have to admit, I'm having a good time." Laura turned to face Marjorie. "I don't know what to do or how to manage this, but I'm trying not to be afraid of love."

"With your experience, that is heroic, I'd say." They sat down, and Marjorie unfolded her napkin in her lap.

Laura ladled stew from the tureen into their bowls. "I think John has been a big factor in helping me understand that not all men are like Jed. I know from John and Jackie what a good marriage can be like. His friendship feels safe, and we talk as if we've known each other all our lives. That helped me have confidence talking with Greg."

"John is a good man. The way he handled his wife's illness, the sacrifices he made to be sure she had the best care . . . Well, not everyone has that kind of devotion or character in dealing with such a difficult situation. And now that she's gone, he has to figure out what to do with the rest of his life." Marjorie took a spoonful of stew and tasted it, giving Laura the thumbs up.

"Figuring out what to do after being married a long time is a slow process. Even years later, old memories get stirred up. At least, that's how it has been for me."

"You've grown so much, in so many ways. It's time for the next adventure, and every adventure needs a love interest." Marjorie chuckled.

"I really like Greg." Laura looked plaintively at Marjorie who appeared thoughtful.

"What do you like about him?" she asked.

Laura considered her question. "I like that he challenges me. I'm learning so much about things I've never experienced. He's been to France and Italy and China and loads of other places. When we go out, I feel like . . . someone other than myself. I feel like a normal woman out with a normal man."

"What in the world do you mean by that?" Marjorie sat forward. "You *are* a normal woman."

"I'm not. Normal women my age have had more life experiences. Normal women date their husbands before marriage. I never did that. I watch other women, and I wonder how they manage to make dating look so natural." She thought of the attractive woman Larry had brought to the library gala.

"Well, now, *that's* normal, especially after what you've been through. Listen to your intuition," Marjorie advised. "If something seems off, or if you're uncomfortable with something he says or does, listen to your gut. If he seems to be pushing too hard for intimacy, speak up and let him know you need more time."

"What if he gets impatient?"

"Oh, he probably will. But if he cares for you, he will understand your need to move cautiously. How honest have you been with him about what happened with Jed?"

"I told him that Jed had a temper."

"You didn't say he beat you so badly, you required emergency care more than once."

"We're just getting to know each other. I don't want to turn him off." Laura bit her upper lip. "I don't want him to see me as a damsel in distress."

"No one who knows you now would see a damsel in distress. But I understand that you want to be careful about over-sharing." Marjorie accepted the basket of soda bread Laura handed her and took a slice, slathering it with a generous amount of Kerry Gold Irish butter. She licked her thumb. "Make sure he is emotionally available. Otherwise, you'll be giving more to him without ever receiving what you want or need in return. That's my advice."

Laura took a spoonful of soup and chewed, savoring the mix of flavors, before speaking. That term 'emotionally available' wasn't something she had ever heard before. "I think I know what you mean. If I'm going through a difficult time, it's important that he is willing to be there for me." She paused as the next words came to her. "The way John has been."

"John is a good teacher for you." Marjorie finished her bread and wiped buttery fingers on her napkin. "That may be the sum total of his role in your life. He is teaching you about the kind of man you want in your life."

"That makes sense." Laura felt brighter.

Marjorie took another taste of the stew after it had time to cool. She closed her eyes in bliss. "Oh, this is really good."

"One of my customers brought me a bag of produce from her garden. The carrots and potatoes are home-grown."

"It's delicious," Marjorie said, savoring another spoonful. "I miss having time to make a nice meal for myself."

"I try to cook pots of soup or casseroles to get me through the week. Lately, I've been cooking more often so I can send food over to John." Her forehead furrowed, looking at the dark circles under Marjorie's eyes. "It's important that you to take care of yourself while you're recovering. If you need help at your store, I'd be glad to come to Parmenter for a few days."

"I can't ask that of you." Marjorie said, tutting.

"I want to. I'll check my schedule and arrange for Cissy and Judith to cover here."

"But you have so much happening right now. Are you sure?"

"Very," Laura said, laying her hand over Marjorie's. "The original Serendipities will always be a special place to me. Let me see what I can work out."

CHAPTER FOURTEEN

"ALL ABOARD!" BELLOWED A JOLLY WHITE-HAIRED MAN with a fake white beard attached with loops to his ears. Laura and thirty of her fellow Irish festival volunteers clambered onto the luxury tour bus. The bus driver wore green from head to toe and had adorned himself with multiple strands of shiny green beads and a leprechaun hat. He had festooned the interior of the bus with green, orange, and gold beads; Irish flags; and signs proclaiming, "Kiss me, I'm Irish" and "Irish Beer Drinkers Make Better Lovers!"

The tour bus was part of a fleet that picked up volunteers and festival-goers from a remote parking lot a few miles away from the festival grounds and dropped them off at points along the festival park route. Buses ran continuously during festival hours at no charge to riders. It was an easy way to avoid parking headaches, but the truth was that Laura loved riding the buses. Before her first ride several years earlier, she had never been aboard one of these luxury vehicles. Now she'd never consider going to the festival any other way. It was part of the fun.

On their last date, she invited Greg to join her on the shuttle bus, but he declined with a disbelieving laugh. "Thanks, I'll do Uber," he said, shaking his head. "Why would you want to ride on one of those slow crowded buses?"

"It's part of the experience," she replied without a moment's hesitation. "There's a lot of excitement on the bus. We sing Irish songs."

"How about if I just find you later." He didn't look pleased, and his reaction tempered her enthusiasm.

"Sounds good," she said. His tone left her off-kilter. "I'll have my cell phone turned on."

The bus dropped Laura and half the volunteers off at the north gate of the park. She disembarked, breathing in the tempting smells of popcorn, pizza, barbeque, skewered chicken, and funnel cakes. A long line had formed to buy Dublin drink tokens. Volunteers at beer tents expertly topped off pint-sized cups of Guinness at warp speed for thirsty customers. What was an Irish festival without a Guinness or two?

At seven-thirty, as Laura surreptitiously checked her phone for a missed call or text message from Greg, she looked up and saw him approaching. He carried a Guinness. The grin on his face said it all. "TGIF," he said, and leaned in for the quick kiss she offered.

"Good day today?" she asked.

He shrugged. "I'm ready for the weekend."

"You're getting here at the perfect time. The next show starts soon." She pointed across the tent. "See that table over there? Would you snag that for us?"

"Sure," he said amiably. "Let's sit down and catch up."

"Can't sit just yet—soon, though," she said, holding onto the fingers of his free hand. "I'm on the job till nine. Actually, would you save two seats? Marjorie, my friend, is here this weekend."

"Marjorie. Is that the one who sings?"

"Terri is the singer. She's around here somewhere, too. Her band is playing later. Maybe save three seats, if you can?"

"Have I met Marjorie? Where is she staying?" His tone was curious but measured.

"You haven't met her yet," Laura said, adding, "You'll really like her. She's not just my friend; she's my mentor, the person most responsible for my success." She knew that she was rambling but couldn't help herself. "She's helping at my store while I volunteer this weekend."

Greg took a long swallow of his beer. "That's nice of her. But you haven't answered my question. Is she staying at your place?"

"Of course. I wouldn't let her stay anywhere else." Laura cleared her throat of the lump that had formed. "She's one of my closest friends."

"I'm sure I'll enjoy meeting her," he said in a bland tone that was impossible to read. He squeezed her hand and let it go. Her heart skipped an uncomfortable beat as she turned to greet the performers trooping up the stairs to the stage.

Marjorie arrived about a half-hour into the show. Her face was flushed from heat and summer humidity. From her place to the right of the stage, Laura was grateful to see that Greg stood up to greet her and held out a chair for her. Then he brought her a bottled water. From time to time, Laura glanced over. She was glad to see them engaged in what appeared to be a pleasant conversation. Marjorie's opinion about Greg mattered a great deal. If Marjorie had concerns, Laura would heed them.

When her shift ended, she joined them at the table. Greg brought Laura a Guinness, although Marjorie declined. "I'm about done in," Marjorie said. "I think I'll head out. You two have fun without me. I'm going to turn in early."

Laura hugged her friend, concerned at the redness of her face and neck. "I put more bottled water in the fridge at home. You look worn out from this heat." She leaned in and murmured, "I won't be late. Please don't wait up for me. And call or text if you need anything."

She watched Marjorie make her way slowly through the crowd on her way to the north gate where the bus would pick her up. She met Greg's eyes. "I hope this wasn't too much for her."

"She's a nice lady," Greg said. "She doesn't look healthy."

"She has Lyme Disease," Laura explained. "Thanks for looking after her back there while I was working."

"No problem," he said. "She told me how the two of you became friends."

Laura flinched. "What did she say?"

"That you met at her store, that you are the best person she knows, and you give a hundred percent of yourself to everyone and everything. I don't find that hard to believe." The expression on his face spoke of an underlying message.

"I do the best I can for anyone who needs me," she answered after a moment. "I never thought I'd have the opportunity to live the way I do now. She's a big reason why. I'm grateful."

"Well, life seems to agree with you," he said. He patted her bare knee, resting his hand there.

An unfamiliar sensation surged through Laura that was so strong, she shivered. *Desire*. Though unfamiliar, the feeling was exquisite. Every time this man touched her, she wanted what she had never experienced before: unbridled passion. It was unnerving. When they met, the attraction to him had been instantaneous.

"One of these weekends, I'm going to whisk you away for some R and R—to a place where no one needs you and where you can concentrate on having a good time," Greg said, leaning in and nuzzling her neck. "Just you and me."

Her stomach lurched, that gut feeling she was learning not to ignore. It was important that she wait for lovemaking until she felt confident that Greg was more than someone she would date for a short time. She wanted to make love with someone she believed could be significant in her life. But this feeling spoke of something more.

"Let's walk around a little," she suggested.

"Where are the whiskey tastings?" he asked, peering at the app on his phone.

"At the other end of the park."

They set off in search of the whiskey-tasting tent. Along the way, they passed the pizza booth where Terri stood, munching on an enormous slice of thin crust pizza. She wiped the grease from her lips when she saw them. "Thought I'd grab dinner before my set."

"That looks good," Greg said, eying Terri's pizza. "You want a slice?" he asked Laura.

"Sure. Thank you."

A text message pinged on her phone. She glanced at it and saw that it was from Andrew. *Emily and I are at the Celtic Rock tent. Where R U?* She walked away from the pizza line as she texted back *Near the pizza booth.* She smiled at his next message. *Are you with Greg?*

Ah ha, the plot thickened. Andrew wanted to meet Greg. She texted her response *Yes* and turned to find Greg near the front of the pizza line, talking intently to Terri. Terri had a quizzical expression on her face. She looked annoyed. Abruptly, she turned away from Greg and walked toward Laura, Greg's eyes following her. He didn't look happy, either.

"Hey," she said, squeezing Laura's forearm. "I didn't want to take off without saying good-bye. I need to start getting ready to play. I'm opening tonight for Gaelic Rush."

"What just happened?" Laura asked.

"Nothing," Terri said.

Laura didn't believe her. "Really?"

"If it turns into something, I'll let you know."

This wasn't reassuring. "We'll be over to hear you perform after we eat," Laura said. "Andrew wants to meet Greg. Do you think it's too soon to introduce them?"

"How can you avoid it? Anyway, it's not as if you're announcing your impending marriage," Terri said, looking as if she'd like to say more. "It's a good idea to get your son's perspective."

Laura was more curious than ever about what had happened between Terri and Greg. But this wasn't the time to pursue a line of questioning. If Terri said it was nothing, it was probably nothing. "I'm anxious for Andrew and Greg to meet. I'm sure they'll get along great."

"You'll know soon enough," Terri said. "Gotta go. Wish me luck."

Laura hugged her hard. "You always have my best wishes. You know that. You'll be amazing!"

She returned to Greg and accepted the slice of pizza he handed her with a small stack of napkins. After wolfing down their pizza, Greg took Laura's hand, and they headed across the festival grounds. At the whiskey tent, Greg knocked back two shots of the finest Irish blend they offered, and accepted a third. He handed it first to Laura, who deflected. "No, thank you. One beer was enough."

"Come on. One won't hurt," Greg said.

She shook her head. "No, thanks."

He downed the shot and took her arm. "Come on, let's get out of here."

"Street is playing over there in a few minutes," Laura said, pointing toward Celtic Rock. "You don't want to miss them. Terri is such a fantastic singer, and she plays the violin like nobody's business." She watched as his expression changed. "It looked like the two of you were having an interesting discussion."

"She's quite a character," he said, shaking his head.

"What do you mean?" she asked. They started walking again. She waited for his response.

Finally, he said, "She has an edge to her. That's all."

"An edge? I think it takes a little while to get to know her," Laura said in defense. "She knows everyone, and everyone likes her."

"I think she has an overactive imagination. Surely, you've noticed that she exaggerates things."

Laura had no idea what he meant, but wanted to keep the mood light. This was supposed to be a fun evening. It didn't feel as fun as it usually did. She felt that familiar tension as she worked to keep the mood light and their conversation on an even keel.

She took in a long breath and let it out. It was true that Terri's sense of humor could result in her comments being misconstrued. Terri was known for being quick on the draw. Clearly, she had made a remark that Greg took the wrong way. She would have to get to the bottom of this.

At the Celtic Rock tent, Laura spotted Andrew and Emily sitting at one of the back tables. She waved and scurried over to them, hand-in-hand with Greg. "Hey, you two!"

Andrew stood to embrace his mother, kissing her on the cheek. She hugged her son and then Emily. "I'm glad we could get together tonight," she said, turning to Greg. "This is my son, Andrew, and his fiancée, Emily. This is Greg."

Greg extended his hand to Andrew who shook it. "Nice to meet you."

Emily looked curiously at Greg and reached over the table to shake his hand. "It's nice to meet you, Greg," she said. "What do you think of the famous Dublin Irish Festival?"

"It has a lot to live up to," Greg said with a quick grin. "I've only been hearing about it every day since I met this girl. She's a one-woman marketing campaign."

Laura laughed and sat down beside Andrew. She patted the seat beside her, and Greg sat down. "We did a quick whiskey-tasting. Well, Greg did. You know me. One Guinness Mom."

Emily gave her a glance that spoke volumes. Her first impression of Greg seemed to be a good one, but Laura knew Emily would have more to say later.

Andrew, on the other hand, appeared wary. He remained aloof, barely speaking, and not smiling. But wasn't this to be expected? For the past several years, her son had been the only man in her life. No doubt, he had to size up this new guy, make sure he passed muster.

Though he was friendly, it was clear that Greg wasn't trying to impress the son and daughter-in-law-to-be of the woman he was dating. He simply assumed his place in Laura's life. She wished he would try a little harder to ask more questions of Andrew, to draw him out. Instead, Greg turned on the charm with Emily.

Thunderous applause arose as Terri walked on stage, fiddle in hand. She looked every bit the part of a celebrity musician with her silky black hair flowing nearly to her waist, a low-cut green halter top shirt, signature black leather pants, and high-heeled ankle boots.

Street, Terri's band of ten years, was an annual crowd favorite at Dublin's Irish Festival. Members of the band, a drum player and bass guitarist, followed her onto the stage to even more applause. Terri adjusted her microphone and introduced her band members, letting festival-goers know that this was the seventh year Street had played on this stage. Laura was so proud of Terri, she felt as if her chest would burst.

"We're going to start tonight with an all-time favorite from an Irish lad you all know, I'm sure. His name is Colin, and he hails from Galway Bay." Terri raised her fiddle, swinging her long hair back-and-forth in a move that signaled her band to start. The fiddle, bass guitar, and drums began on cue in a thunderous sound of high and low tones that sent shivers down Laura's back. Terri was in her element on stage. The song was a crowd favorite and had people tapping their toes. It was the strongest start possible to her show.

Laura glanced over at Greg, gauging his reaction. "Isn't she great?"

"Surprisingly so." He stood up. "I'm getting another beer. Can I get you anything?"

"A water would be great. Thank you."

"Can I get either of you anything?" Greg asked Andrew and Emily.

"No thanks," Andrew said, his back to Greg.

"No thank you," Emily said and met Laura's eyes. Andrew wasn't himself tonight, though he had seemed fine earlier. What was going through his head?

Greg returned ten minutes later with a Guinness and Laura's bottled water. He handed it to her but didn't sit down. "Sorry, long line," he said. Before she could respond, he added, "I'm heading to the restroom."

"Okay." It was easier to talk without him. "I think his consumption of liquids finally got the best of him," she said to Emily.

"He's really handsome," Emily said. "He looks like someone famous."

"Hugh Jackman," Laura produced. "That's what I thought the first time I saw him. Andrew, what do you think?"

"He seems fine, Mom. If you're having fun, I'm happy for you." He kept his eyes fixed on the stage, not making eye contact.

Emily reached across the table and Laura took her hand. Winking, Emily glanced at Andrew and mouthed the words, "He's being overprotective."

When Greg returned, Laura sat back in her chair and felt his arm around her shoulders, his legs touching hers. She was conscious of every movement he made, every breath. He began stroking her upper arm with the tips of his fingers. She had a difficult time concentrating on the music. She was conscious only of his touch.

After the second set, the audience rose to its feet, applauding and whistling, a request for an encore. Street did one more song. Laura stood up to dance in place to the rollicking favorite. She held her arms up in the air, clapping where Terri could see her. Greg did not rise from his seat. He checked the schedule app on his phone.

When the song was over and people began leaving the tent, Laura sat down again. "That was so great. I wish she'd play a few more songs."

"I don't know about you, but I've had enough loud music for one night."

"She's really good, isn't she?"

"They're pretty good for a local band," he said. It didn't sound entirely complimentary.

Andrew and Emily followed them out of the tent. Andrew shook hands with Greg and gave his mother a hug. Emily hugged Greg and Laura, in turn.

"I'm glad you could meet Greg," Laura murmured to Andrew. "What you think of him matters to me, you know."

He frowned. "I think your friend has had too much to drink. Did you drive yourself here, I hope? If not, we can take you home."

So that was the problem. "No need," she said, smiling. She kissed him on the cheek. "I took the festival bus. I'll be fine."

Greg put his arm around Laura's waist as they walked off the park grounds and onto a residential side street. When they got to the nearest intersection, he pulled out his phone and tapped a rideshare app on his phone.

They waited until the driver arrived in a black luxury SUV. "Hope you had fun," she said. "I'll talk with you tomorrow."

He kissed her, holding her tight against him. "You've never been to my house before. It's time for you to see Casa Waters." He bowed slightly at the waist. "Your chariot awaits."

"Not tonight. Marjorie is at my place, remember?" Involuntarily, she put a little distance between them with one foot. Andrew was right. Greg had been drinking heavily all evening, and she could guess what the result might be of going to his home without transportation of her own.

An old fear seized her, a memory of Jed grabbing her and yanking her by the hair to the bedroom. She shook off the thought. Greg wasn't Jed. Even so, this wasn't the right time to go home with Greg. She had daydreamed for weeks about a romantic evening with him beginning with a candlelight dinner followed by slow dancing, and then a mutual agreement to make love.

She would buy a beautiful piece of lingerie—something to mark the occasion, something unlike anything she had ever worn. He would lead her into the bedroom where he would show her how wonderful lovemaking could be. She wanted her first time with him to be memorable for all the right reasons.

Greg pulled her closer and kissed her again, more urgently this time. The rideshare driver looked away. "Marjorie is probably sound asleep. It's time for us to get to know each other better," he said in a hoarse voice.

"Marjorie is my guest, and I need to get home and check on her," she said in as firm a voice as she could manage. The look he gave her said it all.

"When do you think you'll be ready for us to have a real relationship?" he asked in a low voice. It didn't escape her notice that, despite the thin line formed by his mouth, he sounded disappointed, wounded. Had she hurt his feelings?

She cleared her throat, finding her voice. "We've known each other less than three weeks."

He pulled away from her and opened the back door of the rideshare. "It's just that I want you so much. I thought you wanted me."

"I do," she said quietly. "But it can't be tonight. I'm not prepared for this."

He reached for her hand. His face was contrite. "Sorry, babe. I guess I let the whiskey do the talking for me. You're worth waiting for."

Relief flooded through Laura. "Sleep well," she said, standing farther from the curb as he pulled the car door shut.

She walked up the street to the north gate and boarded the tour bus to satellite parking. As she took her seat near the back of the bus, her mind replayed everything Greg had said, certain that her responses to him had been all wrong. He sounded frustrated with her, even angry. She blamed herself. Surely, she had given off the wrong signals for him to have behaved that way.

Settling into her seat on the bus, she stared out the window. What a fool she had been to think she could date someone like Greg. He soon would grow tired of her.

Memories flooded her mind of Jed preaching against sins of the flesh. How could she ever have a healthy, loving relationship with anyone with those kind of thoughts in her head? She sighed deeply. Her life with Jed could never be unremembered. She had to face the facts: she was damaged goods.

CHAPTER FIFTEEN

"I'M IN THE KITCHEN!" MARJORIE CALLED when she heard Laura's steps in the front hallway. "There is a pot of lavender-chamomile tea brewing and some cookies."

"What are you still doing up?" Laura asked. "It's really late. You need your sleep."

"I'm not wasting precious time sleeping when we have so much to catch up on," Marjorie answered. She wore a set of blue-striped summer pajamas and a light matching robe. Her gray curly hair was damp from a shower. "Did you and Greg have a good time?"

Laura considered her response. The evening hadn't been quite as enjoyable as she had hoped. "I mostly had a good time . . . well, until he tried to convince me to go home with him to see his house."

"As in, 'Stay the night,' I presume?" Marjorie poured a cup of tea for Laura and passed the plate of cookies across the table.

"I think we can assume that's what he had in mind." Laura took in a deep breath and let it out slowly. "I'm sure I would have had a hard time getting away if I'd gone to his house. I wouldn't have had my car, for one thing. But the truth is, I might not have had any willpower to resist him. That makes me nervous."

"You're the one who decides on this matter," Marjorie said emphatically. "I can imagine that being as attracted to him as you are, it would be tempting to succumb to his charms. But what you want, dear, is love-making, not just sex, and that doesn't work long-term when one person puts pressure on another." Marjorie took a sip of her tea. "You've already had a man who didn't respect boundaries."

Laura remembered the careless way Jed had treated her body—roughly, as if she was a possession he didn't particularly appreciate. He had even said that it was her duty as a woman to submit to him whenever he chose, and that she had no say in the matter if she wanted to remain in God's favor. Telling your husband "not tonight" was a sin, he said. Looking back on several nightmarish experiences with Jed, she recognized it now for what it was: marital rape.

"Since Jed died, I haven't thought very much about sex, not in a real-life way," she admitted. "I watch movies and read steamy books about love and romance, but it doesn't seem real. Surely, love will be better with a man who is, well, better than Jed. I know it isn't supposed to be the way it was with Jed."

"Past experiences leave deep impressions." Marjorie added two heaping spoons of sugar to her tea, and stirred thoughtfully. "Time does heal, Laura. Take things slowly until the fear lessens. By the way, I thought Greg was very pleasant. He has wonderful manners, and we had a nice conversation. But if I was you, I'd continue to stand my ground until all doubts are removed."

"He might get impatient and say 'Forget her,'" Laura said. "I may not be ready to sleep with him for a while yet. I can't expect him to wait."

"Then you know he doesn't respect your feelings. If he doesn't respect what you want, he won't respect other things about you, either. You'll end up with another controlling man."

"True." Laura took a bite of a cookie. "Something happened tonight between him and Terri. I'm not sure what it was, but it didn't sit right with either of them."

"Did you ask him?"

"Yes. He said Terri has an edge and that she exaggerates. I need to ask her what happened."

"I would." Marjorie bit her upper lip, considering the matter. "Terri is a dear friend, and she won't hold anything back. It might have been nothing. Their personalities may not have jived."

"Maybe." Laura sipped her tea. "So, enough about my dating woes. How are you feeling? You looked so tired and miserable before you left tonight. Promise me you'll take things easy until you're well."

"It may take months to get back to feeling normal, or so I'm told. I'm not a spring chicken anymore." Marjorie let out a long breath. "The truth is, Laura, I'm thinking about the future and what I want to do with Serendipities. I'm considering retirement."

Laura's eyes flew open. "Retirement! Oh, but Marjorie . . ."

"I know, I know. My life has been about my business. What will I do without the work I've loved, the routines, the customers who have become friends?" Tears formed at the corners of her eyes. "Frankly, I don't want to close the store. It has a great reputation, and it's doing well. But I have to think about what comes next. I don't know if this is the right time to say this, but I'd like you to take over Serendipities. You can run both places, as long as you have good help."

"Me, manage both stores? Oh, Marjorie, I don't know." Laura felt her stomach tighten. "I appreciate your confidence, but I don't think I'm in any position to buy the store from you."

"I wouldn't expect you to buy it outright," Marjorie said. "We could do a lease-purchase arrangement over time. I don't need money from a sale of the business to be okay financially. I've got social security and retirement accounts that will keep me in the manner to which I've become accustomed." She let out a little laugh. "Fortunately, my creature comforts aren't lavish."

"But spending regular time in Parmenter . . ." Laura shook her head. "There are so many memories. Most of them aren't good." She chewed the inside of her cheek. "I'm not saying no. I just have to think about it."

Marjorie smiled. "Nothing has to be decided now. Why don't you plan to drive over some weekend soon, like we talked about before, and we can continue this discussion. I'm not in a rush. I would just like to begin the process." Marjorie stifled a yawn.

"I think we should sleep on this," Laura said, though she doubted she'd sleep a wink tonight—not after this discussion.

"I'm entirely serious when I say this can happen over time. There's no need for worry."

Laura smiled. "I can come next Friday evening and stay the weekend. Maybe by then, I will have had enough time to process the idea. I don't want you to close Serendipities. And I really don't want a stranger buying it since my business has the same name. Another owner might turn that name into a liability."

"Laura, you are so astute," Marjorie said, smiling proudly at her. "I mean that. You are one of the most naturally talented business people I've ever known. You're smart and savvy."

"*Possessive* may be a better word for how I feel about this. It makes sense for me to take over the business. Aside from you, no one cares about that store more than I do. I guess I just didn't expect you to ask now." She smiled, feeling humble. "Thanks for having faith in me."

"I've always had faith in you. You've been one of my heroes for years, Laura Fisher."

Laura's face flushed with pleasure at the unexpected compliment. "I never thought of myself as being worthy of being anyone's hero," she answered. "It hasn't been that long since I was that sad, dowdy preacher's wife who sneaked over to your store as often as possible, who prayed for a better life." A look of dawning crossed her features. "I used to dream about the career I have now. I could picture every detail, every piece of furniture, how I would decorate the store. It felt like a fantasy, and then suddenly, it became real."

"Funny how that happens, isn't it? When you want something, when you want it so much that you can envision and experience it with all your senses—feel joy just thinking about it—why, it comes to you on wings of angels." Marjorie rose from her chair and walked around the table. She kissed Laura on the top of her head. "I couldn't believe in anyone else the way I believe in you. You're a winner."

Laura reached for Marjorie's hand and held fast. "Until we became friends, my life was just something that happened to me . . . something I had to get through every day. I just kept breathing, but I wasn't really alive. I don't know where I'd be if it weren't for you."

"Oh, sweetie. I'm the lucky one—to have you," Marjorie replied. "You're the only one I can imagine trusting with Serendipities. You have accomplished so much, and I want you to understand the power you have to make things happen. I just helped get you started. You don't really need me. But," she smiled. "I'm glad you think you do."

Laura's eyes clouded over. "The whole envisioning thing . . .?" She shook her head. "On the night Jed died, I was upstairs wishing I could be free of him. I went downstairs, and he was dead. I was free, but I didn't mean for him to die."

"You didn't cause his death," Marjorie said, pulling out the chair beside her and sitting down again. "You aren't the kind of person who would ever wish harm on another being, even if he was the meanest snake in the bag. It just happened."

"I didn't try to save him."

"He was already gone. You were injured. You never could have moved him." Marjorie bit her upper lip before speaking again. "He never did take care of himself. You told me that often enough. And that temper?" She whistled. "I imagine that teeny-tiny heart in his body finally gave out from lack of use. You were due for a happier life. That's what I think."

As she brushed her teeth and removed her make-up, Laura thought about everything Marjorie had just said. Healing took time. Memories were like old tapes, replaying themselves with the whiff of a familiar scent or a few bars of a song. Yet wasn't it also possible that those bad experiences could be considered in a different way—as events that helped transition her to new growth?

It was true that the bad stuff didn't last forever, and even negative emotions like anger or sadness were like changes in weather. A dark, stormy day could blow over and reveal blue skies. The trick was to remain faithful and believe that nothing bad could possibly last forever. The darkest night ended with the dawn of a new morning. Good always won over bad.

MARJORIE LEFT FOR PARMENTER early Monday morning. As Laura cleaned up their breakfast dishes, she wondered about John. She hadn't seen him at the Irish festival. If he had been there, it was odd that he hadn't called or texted so they could connect. She decided to call him on the pretense of asking whether he planned to attend the book club on Wednesday evening.

The phone rang twice before he picked up. "Laura, how are you?"

"Fine. How are you?"

"Good, good. Glad you called."

"We haven't had a chance to talk since last week. I just wondered if you'd be at the book club tomorrow night."

"Indeed, I have completed the assignment and am prepared to participate fully," he said, sounding light-hearted. "I meant to let you know that I visited with your mother on Friday afternoon."

"You went to see my mother? I'm sure she was thrilled to have a visitor."

"I was over that way on business and decided to have lunch at Glenview Gardens, for old times' sake. While I was there, I thought I'd check on a few people—see how they're doing. I peeked in the art room and saw your mom. She was painting, of course. She's quite good."

"I think so, too. As a kid, I never knew she had that kind of talent. It's sad, really, that she didn't get to pursue art until so late in her life."

"Looks to me like she's making up for lost time. Anyway, I noticed something and thought I should mention it." He paused. "I wouldn't get overly concerned, but you might want to have the nursing staff follow up."

"What is it?" Alarm bells triggered in her head. "I haven't been over since last Thursday. Between the Irish Festival and Marjorie staying with me, I've been lax." She felt a stab of guilt.

"Your mom seemed short of breath. Maybe it's nothing."

"It isn't nothing. She has congestive heart failure, and that's a sign that it may be worsening. Thanks for telling me."

"I'm sorry for the delay. I should have called you right away, but I got busy and it slipped my mind until you called. In my spare time, I've been setting up my law practice here at the house. I've got a room near the back with a separate entrance."

"Do you have a timeline for going full-time?"

"I'm transitioning gradually, working from my home office in the evenings and on weekends. I have one client lined up and a few more possibilities. I'll have to leave the university before I hang out my shingle. And, at some point, it will make more sense to rent an office."

"Sounds exciting," Laura said. "Fortunately, I don't know any criminals, so I'm not in a position to refer anyone."

There was a moment of silence before she heard him chuckle. "I think we can be grateful for that," he said finally. "You're funny."

She felt a flush of pleasure. While being with Greg had given her more confidence, John was still the man whose approval meant the most. "Are you still thinking about selling your house?"

"Not now. You were right about taking it slow. I have money from Jackie's life insurance. Fortunately, she took out that policy when she was in her mid-twenties, before she was diagnosed with A.L.S. It's enough to live on for about two years, if I'm careful."

They talked for another few minutes. "I was hoping you'd make it to the Irish festival. You need something other than work in your life," Laura said.

"I did go—for a little while," he said. "I don't like going to things by myself."

"I didn't see you. You should have texted or called me. When were you there?"

"Friday night."

"Oh." Thoughts swelled in her head like a giant wave about to crash.

"I saw you from afar. Looked like you were on a hot date. Far be it from me to thwart romance."

There it was. She had no idea why it bothered her so much that he had seen her with Greg. "Um, I just started dating again."

"I'm happy for you. He's a lucky man."

"John . . ." What could she say? "It would have been fine if you had spoken with me. Honest."

"I wouldn't dream of such a thing. No third wheels allowed."

She thought of all the times she had accompanied couples to special events, or the times she had been invited to dinner and found herself the only single woman at the table. "I understand what you mean."

"You deserve a nice guy," he said. "I'll look forward to meeting him sometime."

Another thought occurred to her. "It would be nice for the book club to go out some night to hear Terri and her band. That would be easier for you, right? It's a gang."

"It would. Actually, that sounds like fun. Thanks for checking in with me," he said. "See you tomorrow night."

CHAPTER SIXTEEN

ON WEDNESDAY, THE IRISH BOOK CLUB met at Laura's store to discuss *Circle of Friends* by the late Twentieth Century Irish author Maeve Binchy. The acclaimed novel with its interconnected stories turned out to be a nice change of pace from the heavier themes of the *Dubliners* stories or the dark disturbing Gothic tale of *Dracula*.

In contrast, *Circle of Friends* was a heartwarming story about a group of young friends in Dublin, Ireland whose lives interact as they move into the complexities of adulthood. Laura had seen the movie version of the story and loved it. The book was even more satisfying than the movie.

She had managed to read the entire novel in just a few evenings, propped up on pillows in her four-poster bed, a cup of chamomile tea on the bedside table. Reading provided a peaceful transition between work and sleep. Without a good book, she often woke numerous times in the night, her busy brain already racing to the day ahead.

Though she had grown up in a small, close-knit community in Parmenter, Laura had never enjoyed the sort of young adult friendships Binchy wrote about. But now, thanks to the Irish book club, she had a cherished circle of friends, each of whom brought special qualities to her life.

Terri, so close in age, was like the sister Laura never had. They spent as much time together as possible. No one could make Laura laugh the way Terri could. Laura admired Terri's tenacity and often tried to emulate her easy social skills.

Jan's expertise in library science could be intellectually intimidating to Laura, at times, though she knew that was never Jan's intention. Jan was a supportive friend who encouraged Laura to believe in herself. She also was generous in sharing information or insights on any topic. Most of all, Jan seemed to have an innate sense of when Laura could benefit most from praise or a compliment.

Yet, it was Marjorie who was, and always would be, Laura's first and best friend, the one who had initiated Laura's wider circle of friends. It mattered not at all that Marjorie was decades older. They were in perfect sync, sharing not only difficult experiences, but keen interests in antiques and interior design.

It was Marjorie's unwavering support to Laura during her darkest days that had cemented their friendship. Both had survived unhappy, dangerous marriages to deeply troubled men and endured oppression as members of a religious denomination that devalued them as people based on their gender. With determination and grit, they had created new lives for themselves by making deliberate choices and taking brave actions. Laura would remain forever devoted to Marjorie for her many kindnesses.

As the years passed, Laura avoided seeing the changes that age brought to her friend. She couldn't bear the thought of losing her. Taking over Marjorie's Serendipities business was the start of what Laura recognized was the march of time. Someday, she would have to live without Marjorie. That was the hardest thing to bear.

But even the best friendships occasionally had to withstand conflict. Laura was hesitant to talk with Terri about the exchange she had witnessed between her and Greg at the Irish festival. It had been almost a week, and Terri had been uncharacteristically distant. Marjorie encouraged Laura to get the issue out into the open. Even so, it was with difficulty that Laura broached the subject. She invited Terri over to watch a movie, as they so often did on weekday evenings.

"It looked like you and Greg had some sort of disagreement at the festival. I couldn't help but wonder what it was about," she said as they sat down on the sofa with wine and popcorn. "You can tell me."

"He had the impression that I was someone else," Terri said dismissively, munching on a handful of popcorn. "Sometimes people assume something, and it turns out to be wrong."

"You mean he mistook you for another person?"

"In a way." Terri crossed her arms over her chest, looking uncomfortable. "He thought he could say something to me. He was mistaken."

"What did he say?" Laura felt her heart skip several anxious beats.

"It doesn't matter who said what. What matters is that you're careful with this man."

"Terri, if he said or did something wrong, I want to know about it."

"Look, you've just started dating him. You aren't a couple—yet. Have you considered that he may be dating other people?"

"He says he isn't. He says . . ."

"He may say a lot of things, but you don't know him well enough to know if what he says is true."

"I have no reason not to believe him," Laura said, trying not to sound defensive. "He hasn't said anything bad to me."

"You barely know him, Laura. Before you make a decision to give your heart to him, make sure you're both on the same page about expectations. You may want happily-ever- after, and he may be thinking happily-right-now. It's a bigger deal to you than it is to him."

This thought pained Laura. "We're really attracted to each other. There is something about him that draws me in. I don't know why. It's as if I've known him before."

"Well, maybe you did. Maybe you were lovers in a past life, and he's coming back for another round." Terri believed in reincarnation.

Laura didn't know what to believe but didn't discount the idea outright. Much couldn't be explained in black-and-white terms. "I do wonder why I was attracted so quickly."

"It also could be that obsessive phase of a new relationship, when your common sense takes leave of you," Terri continued. "You can't get him off your mind. Everything he says, everything he does has some kind of meaning, and you try to read too much into it. Once you move past that phase, you will wake up to who he really is, and you may find out that he isn't compatible with who you are."

Laura felt a sinking feeling in her midsection. "That means when you meet someone, you can't trust that your feelings are valid. I thought chemistry was a good thing, like a sign."

"Chemistry has its place, but no, you shouldn't make snap judgments about people. Over time, you'll learn what you need to know. Believe me, I have been where you are," Terri said. "I have fallen for someone, and it was a disaster."

"Terri, I'm sorry." Laura was tearful. "You always seem invincible."

"I'm not as tough as you think I am. Just make sure Greg knows what you expect from him. And you ought to know what he expects from you—because right now, the two of you are worlds apart." She peered intently at Laura.

"We really like each other. Yes, he wants more from me. We've discussed that. I've been clear about needing more time before I go to that next level."

Terri bit her upper lip and paused. "You just asked me what happened. Did you ask him?"

"I did." Laura didn't want to proceed further with this line of questioning, remembering how Greg had answered. She didn't want to hurt her friend.

"What did he say?" Terri lowered her eyebrows. "Trust me, nothing you say will surprise me."

Laura bit her lip before speaking. "He said you have an edge and that you exaggerate."

"I'll bet he did," Terri said bitterly. "For the record, I do have an edge. I do exaggerate sometimes. But I don't take crap off of men who think it's funny to make personal comments when they don't know someone."

"What did he say? You still aren't telling me, and I'm imagining the worst."

"He said it surprised him that we're friends because we're so different. He said you're sweet and sort of innocent. The comparison was that I'm the opposite. I said yes, you are sweet, and he'd better be nice to you or else." She picked at a thumb-nail, her eyes downcast. "It was just a comment. I didn't mean to start anything."

"Terri, he is nice to me. What you said probably sounded like you assumed he'd end up hurting me. You don't have to be responsible for me."

"I didn't make a terroristic threat, Laura." Terri's foot began a nervous tap. "I was just making conversation. I also might have said something to the effect that you're getting your feet wet in the dating pool after many years. Sorry if that embarrasses you. I shouldn't have said it, but I thought he seemed sort of . . . cavalier. He laughed and said, 'Not like some people who have taken quite a few laps in that pool, eh? I bet you have some strokes you can teach her.'"

"That was so rude of him! But it sounds like he was offended by what you said and struck back." Laura felt her knees quivering. "He had a couple of beers. He wasn't thinking clearly. He's usually such a gentleman. He should apologize."

"I won't hold my breath for that," Terri said. "I'm going to say it again: don't rush into anything with this man. You don't come from the same place."

"I know that. He's so different from any man I've ever known. He's already taught me so much."

"I don't doubt he can teach you things. I'd worry what those things might be. They could involve an STD."

"Wow." Laura felt angry now. "That was beneath you."

"Forgive my *edge*." Terri stressed the last word. Then she passed a hand over her eyes. "Okay, I'm sorry, I shouldn't have said that."

"I don't want us to fight over him," Laura said.

Terri let out a small guffaw. "Oh, trust me. We aren't fighting over *him*. I'm fighting *for* you. I'm trying to help guide *you* to a place where you can make a decision about a man you barely know."

"A decision about . . .?"

"Sleeping with him, first off," Terri said. "For the record, you definitely should wait on that."

"I know you want me to date other people. But I'm not like you. I can't handle more than one." As soon as the words were out of her mouth, Laura saw the hurt in Terri's dark eyes. "I'm sorry. That came out wrong." She reached out to touch Terri, who recoiled. It was as if Laura had struck her. "I meant you're more experienced with dating, and I don't know what you know."

"I know you didn't mean it." Terri licked her lips and took a breath. "I'll admit, I haven't exactly been a paragon of virtue. All that matters to me is for you to be happy. Greg wants more from you than you are ready to give, and he won't be patient."

"I told him I need more time, and he seemed okay with that."

"For now, he seems okay with it. Before you take that next step, make sure you know what you really want long-term," Terri said. "In my opinion, he isn't good enough for you."

A sob erupted from somewhere deep inside Laura. "Oh, no. I don't think I'm good enough for him," she said, tears filling her eyes. She shook her head. "I think it's too late for me to find love. I don't even know what it looks like."

Terri leaned forward and took Laura in her arms. "Yes, you do, my friend. You are the most loving person I know."

AS MEMBERS OF THE BOOK CLUB assembled in Laura's library room over cups of tea and coffee, Jan welcomed them. "The characters in Binchy's

Circle of Friends share an Irish heritage, yet each comes from a very different background. The story takes place as they attend college in Dublin. As they embark on their adult lives, they are still young enough that their characters are still forming. I don't mean their story characters. I mean the individual characteristics that define who they will be later in life. And they also are learning that choices have consequences. As readers, we wonder how their friendships will stand the test of trials. And, after all, isn't that the mark of true friendship?"

Laura smiled at Terri who smiled back. Their first serious disagreement had shaken Laura to the core. She had spent her entire life being careful to avoid upsetting others. If she disagreed with a friend, would she lose that friend? But that hadn't happened. She and Terri had weathered the experience and were stronger for it.

She knew Terri had her best interests at heart. In a way, Laura identified with the character of Benny in the novel, a young woman from an overprotective household whose parents want to control her every move. Benny falls in love with handsome, popular Jack, a relationship her school friends Nan and Eve believe has no future. Even worse, Benny's parents don't approve of Jack.

Laura knew her parents never would have approved of Greg. He was not a church-goer. He was divorced. Even now, she wondered whether it was a good idea to introduce him to her mother. Even if Eileen could accept a man who was divorced, she would never understand why Greg was estranged from his only child. To be honest, Laura had trouble with that, too.

"Benny's friends think the relationship between Benny and Jack can't go the distance because of how they view her. It's their perception of Benny's limitations that color their judgment," Terri said. "They don't see the real Benny. But they also have their own agendas."

"But weren't those friends right about Jack?" Jan asked. "After all, he cheats on Benny—with Nan."

"Even Jack doesn't think Benny is good enough for him," John said. "He takes her for granted, and when she isn't available for him whenever he likes, he betrays her. So, yes, her friends do see more about him than Benny can see."

"But she's in love for the first time in her life," Laura said. "It's all new to her. How could she know any better?"

"There are signs she doesn't want to see," Betsy said. A spry woman in her eighties, Betsy frequently offered deeper insights. "If I had paid attention to signs that I had before I married my first husband, I'd have sent him packing early. Thank goodness, number two is a lamb."

Laura smiled at her. "I also think Benny has responsibilities the others don't have," she pointed out. "Unlike her friends, she has to go home, rather than living at school. Her parents have expectations of her, and she does what they ask of her. After all, they are paying for her education. When her father dies and she has to work for his business, she does what she has to do," Laura said. "She fulfills her responsibilities."

"Unfortunately, while she is being the good daughter, Jack is doing whatever he wants," Carol said. "So, Benny's friends were right about him."

"But her friends weren't the kind of friends you'd want for Benny. I didn't like Nan," Mary Ellen remarked. She was a nurse who always crocheted during their discussions. "She may have had a tough home life, but she isn't exactly showing good judgment in her actions. She isn't seeking true love. She's looking for a leg up in the world with someone who turns out not to be worth it."

"They all have a lot to learn. It made me mad that none of them think Benny has much on the ball," Terri said. "But she has better values and more strength than any of her friends. We get to watch her learn and grow. She even solves a crime. I'm not so sure the rest of them will do as well in life as Benny will."

"Benny's very first love is shaken by heartbreak," Jan said. "She is betrayed at a particularly vulnerable time in her life. She has a choice to make about whether to forgive and resume that relationship." She paused. "Does Jack really love Benny?"

Everyone was quiet, thinking. Terri was the first to speak. "I think he liked many of her good qualities, and being with her made him feel like a better man." She shrugged. "Or maybe he thought that being with her came with economic advantages. Sorry, but I guess I'm a cynic. I don't think he really loves her."

John leaned forward in his chair. "I think Jack loves her in his own way. Unfortunately, his way isn't good enough for someone like Benny. She deserves someone who really appreciates her. The most important thing is that Benny has to realize she deserves better. Until that happens, the right guy doesn't stand a chance."

As members of the book club continued their lively discussion, Laura glanced surreptitiously over at John every now and then. The third time, he smiled at her. She felt her face grow warm. He looked handsome tonight in a gray fisherman's sweater and dark navy jeans. She had wanted to sit beside him, but someone else had beat her to it. Maybe he would stay afterward, and they could talk.

HER THOUGHTS DRIFTED PREDICTABLY TO GREG. They had gone out to dinner the evening before at a new Italian restaurant. Their dinner began with wine and Caesar salads prepared tableside, then progressed to their main courses and a dessert of delectable creamy cannoli with shaved chocolate and cups of strong, rich coffee. Greg urged her to have a digestif of Amaretto. The almond-flavored liqueur smelled so nice, and the glass was so tiny, Laura drank it straight down. Immediately, she began coughing.

Greg smiled. "Just sip it," he said, and ordered her another.

Their conversation was unhurried, a summary of the past few days, including insights into Greg's work as a chief financial officer and the personalities of a few of his colleagues. Unfamiliar as she was with corporate life, the matter-of-fact accounts of his days sounded vitally important, beyond the scope of what most people could manage. Greg knew so much about everything. How could she ever hope to keep up her end of conversations and hold his attention? Her life seemed small and meaningless, by comparison.

"I understand how to keep my inventory and business accounts, but I could never do what you do," she said.

He smiled. "Not to toot my own horn, but this is what I do for a living, and I've gotten quite good at it. Perhaps you might want to begin some classes toward an MBA."

"Oh, no," she said, coloring. "I don't even have a regular college degree."

"Well, now you have me. I'm glad to help you with matters of finance," he replied in a smooth tone. He reached across the table, and she placed her smaller hand in his. He was so worldly and sophisticated, so unlike anyone she had ever known before.

Tonight, he looked even more dashing than usual in his impeccable gray suit, clearly the finest quality. While reviewing his menu in the dim light of the restaurant, he had donned a pair of stylish glasses, giving him a studious appearance. She was proud to be seen with him.

"I'd be glad to look over your business accounts any time," he continued. "For that matter, I can guide you with your personal banking and investments, too."

Laura considered how lucky she was to have such an experienced man willing to guide her. Like Marjorie, Greg seemed to have her best interests at heart. "Thank you," she said, and felt something so strong, so warm, she wondered if it was the start of true love.

As they parted at her front door, he invited her to a performance of the symphony orchestra that Friday evening. Greg was a lover of symphony and opera. Laura wanted to accept his invitation, but remembered her promise to Marjorie.

"I need to go to Parmenter this weekend. I have some matters to attend to."

"Why don't I drive you there?" Greg asked. "We can get separate hotel rooms, if that makes you more comfortable."

"That's sweet of you. I'm staying at Marjorie's house. I'll be working there. It's actually a business trip."

"I promise not to try any monkey business," he said in a teasing voice.

"It's nice of you to offer, and I appreciate it. But not this time, okay? I'll be back Sunday evening. But I'll call you while I'm there." She tilted her face up, and he kissed her. With his hand on the small of her back as he drew her in, she felt desire so strong, it was nearly impossible to pull away. But finally, she took a step back, putting the slightest distance between them.

"One of these weekends, I am going to whisk you away. I mean that," he said. "We should have more time together. You can't always be this busy."

Her throat tightened at the tone in his voice. She had to make him understand. "Marjorie wants to talk with me about taking over her store. It's the right thing to do. No one cares about the original Serendipities as much as I do, or has more reasons to want it to be successful. I hope you can understand."

He let out a long breath, sounding a trifle impatient. "I understand business. What I don't understand is why you seem to want to do everything by yourself. I'm offering to drive you there and help you. Finance is my thing."

"I know it is! And I appreciate the offer. Really, I do. I will definitely ask your advice after I hear more details. I'll be working in the store all weekend, so there won't be time for fun, anyway."

"Guess I'll be left to my own devices. I'll do my best to stay out of trouble." He squeezed her hand and turned to go, leaving her wondering what he meant.

Chapter Seventeen

"Just this small suitcase—oh, and this little bag, too," Laura said as John opened the rear of his SUV.

"You pack light for a girl," he said, laughing. "I brought more than you did."

John had convinced her to allow him to drive her to Parmenter and back. "I've been meaning to go for over a month," he said. "I have some things to take care of involving Jackie, and I want to get together with a friend, too."

They had made their plans after the book club meeting on Wednesday evening. As everyone left Serendipities Two, John lagged behind the others. She decided to seize the moment.

"I was hoping we'd have a chance to catch up," she said to him. "Can you stay a little while?"

"Sure," he said.

Laura was relieved that Terri hadn't wanted to join them, although she had invited her, too. "Not tonight, thanks," Terri had said, hugging her. "I'm tired. I want to get to bed early." She squeezed Laura's fingers and whispered in her ear, "Three's a crowd."

John and Laura went upstairs to her apartment. She lit a scented candle on the coffee table and went to the kitchen. John made himself comfortable on the sofa, paging through a design magazine while she poured glasses of white wine and arranged an assortment of cheeses and crackers on a plate. "I thought the book discussion was good tonight," she said, joining him. "It wasn't as heavy as the last two books we've read."

"That was my first time reading a Maeve Binchy novel," John said. "Jackie was a huge fan of her books, so there are still probably some on the bookshelves in the living room. Do you want them?"

"I'd love to have them," she said. "I like the way the author styles little stories within the bigger story. Then everything ties together."

They sat companionably together on the sofa discussing the book and then local politics. Laura tucked her legs underneath her and reached for her wineglass. All the stressors of the week dissipated as they talked. There was something about John that made her feel at home with him, as if they'd known each other forever.

It was a surprise when the conversation took a decidedly uncomfortable turn. "So, we haven't discussed your new friend, Greg. How did you meet him?" he asked.

Laura wasn't prepared for the question. She gulped, wondering how much to tell him. "We met at the library fundraiser. We've gone out a handful of times," she said, trying to sound casual.

"What do you like most about him?" He seemed to really want to know. There wasn't a hint of anything resembling jealousy in his voice.

She cleared her throat. "He's interesting and smart. He has traveled all over the world. I like hearing about places I've never been. He knows so many things I don't know."

"So, he's intellectually stimulating. That's good." His brow furrowed. "What else?"

She thought for a moment. "He treats me well."

"I like hearing that." He looked serious. "You deserve to be treated well."

"I don't have a lot of experience dating, John," she blurted out. "I'm sure he's frustrated with me, at times."

"Like when?"

Laura's face warmed. She couldn't tell John that Greg wanted to sleep with her. What would he think?

"I watch other women—how they behave with a man—and I know that I'm not like them. I'm not educated or experienced the way other people are. Before I moved here, my life was this big." She held her fingers apart a few inches.

"I think you handle yourself very well. You're a smart person, Laura, and a college education isn't an indicator of intelligence. You can learn just as much by reading or doing things that interest you. You learned a lot through the school of hard knocks." He set his glass down on the table and turned to her. "Please don't try to be someone you're not. Who you are is perfect."

"See, that's the whole point. I'm not sure I know who I am. What could I possibly bring to Greg's life that he couldn't have with anyone else?"

"Maybe you're exactly what he's looking for. You have a lot to offer."

She shook her head slowly. "Oh, I don't know about that."

"Are you kidding me?" He looked pained. "As your friend, let me tell you a few qualities I've observed. First, you are one of the kindest people I've ever met. You're sincere and honest. It would never occur to you to cheat or lie to someone. You'll do anything to help a friend. I say that from experience." He looked into her eyes. "You have value for who you already are. Hey, I value everything about you. And I care about your happiness."

"Thank you, John." She was deeply touched. They looked into each other's eyes. Laura held her breath. She wanted more than anything to take his hand. Did he feel the same way?

"Do you want things to get more serious with him?"

She focused again on Greg. "If he's the right one. Sometimes I wonder." She tried again to explain. "I don't move fast. He wants more from me than I'm ready to give."

"Ah, I get it," he said, nodding.

"I'm not very experienced at any of this, John." This discussion was becoming more intense by the moment. "I'm afraid of being pushed into something and regretting it."

"I'd say you're being cautious and wise. If you're not ready, that's a sign to wait. It's okay. The right guy will understand."

"I can't believe we're talking about this—you know, sex," she said, blushing. She let out an embarrassed laugh.

"That's what friends do," he said, chuckling. "Someday, I may need to have this same discussion about whether or not I'm ready. Hopefully, you'll give me great advice."

She let out an embarrassed laugh. "I would say the same thing: wait for the right person."

"Right."

"Did I tell you I'm going to Parmenter this weekend?" She explained the plans to assume ownership of Serendipities. "I promised Marjorie that I'd give her a hand. But I also want to observe things."

"You mentioned it briefly. That's terrific. I'd imagine it's a huge weight off her shoulders knowing you're willing to run her store the way she would."

"We'll need to structure a lease-purchase arrangement. Marjorie said she'll have her attorney start looking into how best to do that." She thought of Greg's offer to review financial documents and assist with the purchase. It seemed premature to ask a man she barely knew to review her business and personal investment accounts.

"You'll need someone to look after your legal interests, too," he said. "If I can help, I'd be glad to. In my role with the university, I handle contracts, too."

She wondered how this could be different than accepting Greg's help. But for some reason, she didn't feel the same level of discomfort with John. "Thank you. I really appreciate that. Taking over Marjorie's store is a lot to think about, considering I never thought about owning two stores."

"You're turning into a regular business tycoon," he said. "I can say I knew you way back when." He was quiet for a moment. "I have put off going back to Parmenter. There is one very important thing I need to do. Why don't we go together?"

Her heart swelled with happiness at the thought of driving with John. This was an unexpected benefit to the trip. And, after all, why shouldn't they go there together? John had ties to Parmenter that were just as strong as hers.

She remembered Greg's offer to drive her there and felt torn and a little guilty. Should she tell him about the change in plans? If she didn't, was she being dishonest? With John, there were not the same concerns that she would have to face traveling with Greg. John would drop her off at Marjorie's house, and they would connect again for the drive home. It was easier all around.

Still, her conscience nagged at her. There was nothing between her and John other than friendship. She and Greg were not a couple. Words of love or commitment had not been spoken yet. In a tone nearly brittle with disapproval, Terri had reminded Laura recently that this early in their relationship, Greg had no right to have expectations, to think she should alter her life just to suit him.

Grinning, she made her decision. "I'd love to go together. I've been anxious about driving there on my own. I visit the cemetery every fall to plant tulip bulbs around Michael's grave. But I never actually go into town. It's easier to stay completely away from familiar places."

"That's understandable. You don't have good memories of living there. But, Laura, you're a different person now, and there is no one there who can hurt you anymore."

"You're right. It's only the memories that scare me," she said. "I can work through those, but it will be easier with you there, too."

"Going together will be easier for both of us. I've been procrastinating. Now I know why. I didn't want to go by myself." He glanced at his watch. "Jeez, look at the time: almost eleven. I should get going." He stood up and stretched. Studying her for a moment, he smiled. "Thanks for the wine and such interesting conversation."

He stepped forward and took her into his arms in a hug, holding her close as she relaxed into his embrace. As they stood together, Laura's face against his chest, she breathed in the clean scent of his soap, heard the beat of his heart, and felt safe. Being with John felt different than being with Greg. She had no idea which direction to go with Greg. But right now, John felt like her true north.

"Heck, no, you shouldn't tell Greg that you're going to Parmenter with John," Terri said the next morning when Laura called her. "First, there is no purpose to be served except to make Greg jealous. Are you trying to make him jealous?"

"Of course not. That never occurred to me," Laura said. "I don't want to be dishonest with him."

"You're not being dishonest. You and John are friends, and both of you are from Parmenter. It's fuel-efficient. Think of your carbon footprint. These arrangements with John came together after you had already told Greg no. You didn't choose John over Greg. And besides, you would have had to think about Greg the entire weekend, when you really need to focus on Marjorie and your new business plan."

"You're right. Thanks." Instantly, Laura felt better.

"You haven't told me any details about last night," Terri said. "So, how long did he stay?"

"Long enough," Laura said with a chuckle. "Everything was going great until he asked about Greg. It's nice that John is such a good friend. He cares about my happiness."

Terri snorted. "He's a good friend who wants to be more than a friend. If you ask me, he's keeping tabs on the competition."

On the two-hour drive from Dublin to Parmenter on Friday afternoon, Laura and John fell into easy conversation, punctuated by periods of companionable silence. John played smooth jazz on satellite radio. Laura passed him bottled water and handfuls of pretzels, grapes, and peanut M&Ms as he drove. She felt lighthearted and happy, as if they were on a mini-vacation.

On longer drives with Jed and the boys, Laura sat stiffly in the front passenger seat willing the boys not to get into a spat that might cause Jed to turn mean. By the time they were in school, they knew better. With John, she felt comfortable, able to speak whatever was on her mind.

It wasn't until they hit the outskirts of Parmenter that her mood shifted. It was easy to forget about her hometown when she lived over a hundred miles away. Time had dulled the sharp edges of those memories. It was an entirely different matter to keep those memories at bay when she saw familiar streets, passed businesses she had frequented, and saw faces she recognized.

"Are you okay?" he asked, glancing at her as they sat at a stop light. "I can pull over for a minute. You look pale."

"No, keep going. I'm fine." Her voice sounded breathy as she worked to control the strong emotions overtaking her in sickening waves.

"Just breathe. Let me know if you want to stop."

At the next intersection, they turned the corner onto Marjorie's street, and John parked in the driveway. He glanced over, smiled reassuringly, and shut off the ignition. Walking around to her side of the car, he opened her door, and went to retrieve her bags from the back of the SUV.

"I've got this," he said, carrying the small suitcase and carry-on bag to Marjorie's front porch. They stood together, waiting for Marjorie to answer the door.

"Thanks," Laura said, feeling suddenly self-conscious. "What time should I be ready to leave on Sunday?"

"I'll pick you up a little before four o'clock, okay?" His eyes lingered on her.

She nodded. "I hope you have a relaxing weekend with your friend."

"I will. You, too."

When Marjorie saw them on her doorstep, her eyes lit up. They exchanged hugs, and John followed Laura inside, placing her bags in the foyer.

"Will you stay for dinner, John?" Marjorie asked. "Nothing fancy, but there's plenty. Cherry pie a la mode for dessert."

"Thank you. It's hard to pass up that offer, but I'm meeting one of my friends for dinner. I'd like to check in to the hotel first and change clothes." He turned to Laura. "Hey," he began, appearing to choose his words with care, "On Sunday, I'd like to take Jackie's ashes to the lake and sprinkle them over one of her favorite spots. Would you mind stopping with me on the way out of town? If you'd rather not, I understand. You didn't know her."

"I didn't know her, but I wish I had. Anyway, I know you, so I'd be honored," she said. "Of course, I will. See you Sunday."

"What a wonderful man he is," Marjorie said when John got into his car. "I hope you had a nice time driving over. I imagine he's got such an interesting perspective on life."

"Funny, but we don't even need to talk to communicate. Our experiences and thoughts seem to be in sync. We like the same music, the same activities—especially reading. It's nice to feel this kind of companionship with a man."

She realized that she and John were similar in other important ways, too. Each understood grief in the wake of tragedy. Each had lost their spouse, though their marriages had been very different. Each was learning to live as a single person.

Marjorie placed an arm around Laura's shoulders. "He is a rare find."

Chapter Eighteen

ON Saturday morning, Laura and Marjorie unlocked the front door of Serendipities to a steady stream of customers. It felt wonderful to be back in the old store. Regular shoppers remembered Laura and expressed warm welcomes, inquiring about her whereabouts the past two years. As she shared details of her life in Dublin, it seemed no one recalled that she had been a very different Laura when last they knew her.

Sales were brisk on Saturdays, especially during August when people took advantage of summer sales. Serendipities was one of the few older businesses still doing well, thanks to its reputation for high-quality merchandise and fair prices. There were less than ten thousand residents of Parmenter, but loyal shoppers came from surrounding communities. While thrift shopping was a popular, trendy activity, it was also a reality that those on tight budgets often relied on second-hand stores.

The store still smelled of old wood, musty fabric, and lemon furniture polish. Laura sniffed the air and knew she was at home here, too. Though a charming antique, the cash register Marjorie used was outdated by at least three decades. Laura made a mental note to upgrade to the newest technology. She needed to be able to manage sales receipts from Dublin. She looked around with a loving yet critical eye. Serendipities definitely could use a few updates.

In Laura's eyes, it seemed all of the businesses in Parmenter required face lifts. They appeared as tired as the townspeople, their signage faded or missing letters, the parking lots riddled with deep potholes. The display mannequins posing in the front windows of the men's store wore newer clothing styles, but retained their nineteen-fifties hairstyles. One mannequin was left with only parts of his nose and two fingers.

The lacquer-haired mannequin reminded Laura of her childhood Barbie doll's golden-haired boyfriend, Ken. Even then, she understood Ken's role in Barbie's life. There would be a wedding. They couldn't live together in the Barbie dream house, otherwise.

She hadn't yet learned how children came to a marriage and had asked Santa Claus for a baby for Barbie and Ken. She smiled at the memory. Her father thought the dolls immoral because of Barbie's large breasts encased in the snug swimsuit and tight-fitting clothing. Her mother insisted that in childhood, at least, Laura ought to have the same toys as other girls her age.

Much had changed in Parmenter since Laura was a girl. Few manufacturing businesses were left standing, and those that remained were scaled back. The only stable business in town was the hospital, since the majority of Parmenter's residents were older. In a town that relied on the healthcare industry to survive, those who were not currently being treated for a condition were summarily assigned an illness that needed to be monitored routinely.

Yet, much was the same. People who stayed tended to have few options. Younger people left for college or the military after graduation. Most didn't return. Laura didn't doubt that had fate not intervened, she would have died in Parmenter much as she lived. Each day seemed the same as the one before. In a struggling small town, she would have always wished for more.

The brass bell on the front door of Serendipities jangled again. Laura looked up from a table display she was arranging and saw a young woman dressed in the same conservative style of dress that Laura had once worn. The young woman's blonde hair was pulled into a tight bun secured with hairpins. She recognized her as Ruth, a student in the youth Sunday School class she taught for many years. Ruth's eyes widened when she saw Laura, and then she quickly looked away.

Laura decided that Ruth must be about twenty-four now, the same age Michael would have been. They had been classmates from kindergarten through high school. Ruth was married now, judging by the thin gold band on the third finger of her left hand—not a surprise. Most girls in the church married by the time they were eighteen. Her wide blue eyes had that anxious look Laura knew so well. Ruth studied Laura out of the corner of her eye while she browsed the shop.

"Ruth, how are you?" Laura asked, walking toward her. There seemed little point pretending they didn't know each other. "It's been so long since I last saw you. You're all grown up now."

"Yes, ma'am. Married with two boys, three and almost two," Ruth said.

"I bet they're darling." Laura smiled. "Is there something I can help you find? That daybed is nice. Did you notice that it's a trundle? The lower bed pulls out . . . like this." She demonstrated by pulling out the bed and patting the mattress. "If you put your littlest guy in the lower bed, you don't have to worry about him falling out."

"He has nightmares and rolls out," Ruth said with a sigh. "I was just lookin.' It's more than I can afford."

"I understand," Laura said, smiling. "Keep checking back." She whispered, "It's about time for it to go on sale."

"You're dressed real pretty," Ruth blurted out. Her face reddened.

"Thank you, sweetheart," Laura said, swallowing the lump in her throat. She smiled. "I'm glad you stopped by today. I hope you're doing well."

Ruth's face clouded over. "I'm fine, but I have to get home now. My husband likes his supper at four-thirty. I better not be late."

As Laura and Marjorie closed up shop for the day, she heard the ping, a text message from Greg. *Can you talk?* She tapped back a quick reply. *Still at the store. I'll call you later. Hope you're having a fun weekend!* He did not respond.

That evening as Laura settled down with tea and a slice of crumb cake to watch the nightly news, she thought of Ruth and an involuntary shiver ran up and down her spine. Marjorie sat across from her, doing needlepoint. She often framed these small pieces and sold them in the store. That was another potential avenue of business to investigate. Perhaps quilters and other needlecrafters would want to sell what they made.

Laura hesitated to interrupt the comfortable silence, but a thought had taken hold, and she couldn't shake it loose. "Today, while I was working, I saw Ruth, one of the girls in the Sunday School class I taught. She's married now with two little boys. It reminded me that Michael would be that age now. Maybe he'd be married with a family of his own."

"Or maybe he'd be living the life he was destined to live, to be the person he really was," Marjorie stressed in a gentle tone. "You always knew the real Michael, even if Jed didn't want to see who he was. Michael might still have been married with a family. It's just that his family might have had two daddies."

"You're right," Laura said softly. "When I began to understand that he wasn't like . . . didn't behave the way . . ." She sighed. "I didn't talk with him about it. I wish I had told him I understood and loved him, no matter what."

"I'm sure he knew how you felt, and that you loved him unconditionally." Marjorie set aside her craft. "Ruth reminds me of you, the way you used to come into the store and study every item with such wistful eyes." She let out a long breath. "I don't believe she's safe at home."

Laura felt an ache around her heart. "I sensed that. I wish I could help her—the way you helped me."

"That's a decision every woman has to make for herself. You can offer help, but she has to accept it and be ready to take steps to get out. I don't know that Ruth is as brave as you are."

"I wasn't that brave, Marjorie. I wanted to leave Jed, but the fact is, I was set free by his death."

"Ruth's husband has one of those businesses where he repossesses cars and motorcycles. He has no compassion, from what I hear. Not everybody is a deadbeat. In a town like this, where so many people have lost their jobs and couldn't make payments, he isn't popular."

"Do I know her husband?"

"Ruth married Luke Forrest."

And then she felt Marjorie's hand on her back, guiding her head down between her knees. Her voice sounded strangled. "Oh, God, no."

Luke Forrest had been one of the last people to see her son alive. He was one of the meanest boys she had ever encountered. He also was one of the boys in the boat the day Michael drowned.

GREG TEXTED HER AT NINE-THIRTY THAT NIGHT, as she was dressing for bed, to ask how things were going. She texted back a quick *Fine, but I'm exhausted. Heading to bed now.* She didn't want to talk with him or exchange a thread of text messages. After the shock of hearing Luke's name, what she needed now was sleep.

As she settled under the covers, she tried hard to push the memories of Michael's death out of her mind. It had been nearly eight years since that terrible day. Returning to Parmenter, seeing Ruth again, and finding out who she had married brought on a flood of strong emotions and conflicting thoughts.

Even worse, after talking with Marjorie and having her say the words Laura had never quite been able to say, that Michael had been gay, brought another much darker layer to the feelings she had tried to push to the background. Even John had asked if Michael's death had been a hate crime. Had she ignored the obvious? Had he been killed because he was gay? Until this time, she had chalked the incident up to bullying. Now she knew it had been far, far worse.

Michael was gone, and nothing could bring him back. The other boys surely bore some measure of blame for his death—had gone on with their lives as though nothing had happened. Where once she had wondered about the details of what happened that day, now she had to know. She would never rest fully until she learned the whole truth. Was it too late?

She felt certain Ruth knew the truth. How could she convince her to talk? She needed to convince Ruth to share what she knew.

The next morning, she borrowed Marjorie's car and drove to the church where she had attended nearly her entire life. She had no intention of going inside. It had been over two years since the last time she had been there. She was dressed for work, not church.

She parked and watched as parishioners entered. The sign in front proclaimed the sermon that day. "God sees all, hears all, knows all. How will He judge you?"

Though the day was sunny and warm, she shivered and drew her sweater about her shoulders more tightly. This world of sin and judgement was all too familiar. From childhood, she had been warned about an angry God who would sentence her to the fires of hell. One didn't just walk away from that kind of thinking overnight.

After joining a church that was non-denominational, she had adopted a stronger sense of spirituality, and made time each morning for readings that helped ground her for the day. These moments of peaceful study helped with those old feelings of unworthiness and guilt. She understood now that she hadn't deserved to be abused. In fact, she no longer believed that her life with Jed was anything more than an unfortunate experience from which she had been released. Bad times didn't last forever. She was free now to live a happier life. Yet how easy it was to slip back into old ways of thinking when she was around those who thought and believed that way. So why was she at the church now?

What compelled her next was something she would have been hard-pressed to explain. Heart pounding, she got out of the car and headed for the front door. It was as if her feet propelled themselves. She went up the steps and into the vestibule.

The familiar smell of cleaning solution, musty carpet, and stale coffee brought back a rush of emotional scenes starting from her earliest recollections. It was her childhood church, after all. This was God's house. She belonged here, too, though it felt like a place from another life.

She heard the organist's prelude and accepted an Order of Worship program from the elderly female greeter. "So nice to see you, Laura," the old woman said, pressing her cheek to Laura's. "It's been too long."

"Thank you, Louise. It's nice to see you looking so well," she said in a low voice, smiling in the way she always had with parishioners—a practiced rising of the corners of her mouth that made her cheeks hurt. She let that forced smile go and offered Louise a smile that showed how much she appreciated the woman's sincerity.

Steeling herself before she lost her nerve, she proceeded into the sanctuary as more sense memories washed over her, coming in like waves with a dangerous undertow. Her entire life until just a few years ago had revolved around this church. She remembered sitting as a child on the carpeted steps with her Sunday School class while the minister told his children's Bible story. She took her first communion at age eight, dressed in a white caftan symbolic of purity. As a teenager, she sang soprano in the choir. She married Jed at that same altar and endured Michael's and then Jed's funerals in this church.

It had not been a good idea for her to come here today. Whatever the motivation had been, it was a mistake. Dabbing at perspiration on her upper lip, feeling more and more anxious as parishioners turned to stare at her, she kept her eyes to the front, that semi-smile pasted on her face.

In the front pew, where she had spent every Sunday morning for over twenty years, she saw the back of an ash-blonde head—the new pastor's wife. The pastor sat on a bench behind the podium, reading his Bible. He was a younger man, overweight with a florid face, prematurely bald in front.

Automatically, she glanced toward the stained-glass window on the right side of the sanctuary. The image of Mary holding the dead body of

Jesus across her lap had been a comforting sight to Laura—until Michael's death. After that, she could not bear the sight of Mary's stricken face raised heavenward in emotional agony, searching in faith for her God, seeking strength at a time when surely, it was her motherly right to question why her beloved son had been sacrificed.

Laura swallowed hard and licked her dry lips. Mary's faith surely had been stronger, less likely to waiver. After all, Mary had borne the son of God. The sainted Mary never would have experienced the same angry, hopeless thoughts that still plagued Laura. Mary would have accepted her loss with grace, understanding that God had a bigger purpose for claiming his son from Earth. A woman's loss was of little consequence in the bigger picture, wasn't it?

As the pastor's wife, Laura had dared not speak her feelings openly in those months following Michael's death. Suffering in silence, her tear-stained face raised each Sunday to the rays of sunlight filtering through the stained-glass windows, she prayed for grace, for strength, for forgiveness for believing that Michael's death had been anything other than a crime, a terrible mistake by a God who perhaps hadn't been paying attention that afternoon.

As parishioners continued entering the sanctuary, they headed straight to their familiar pews, where they sat quietly, praying, reading their Bibles, or chatting in low voices. Rarely did anyone change seats. It was considered a near offense for a newcomer to sit in a pew where a long-time parishioner normally sat. Faces would pull in disapproval, and as if by cue, the guest would move to the back. Laura glanced around and decided to sit in one of the empty pews in back. If she sat in the last one, perhaps no one would notice her. She slid across the pew to the very farthest corner.

She picked up a new burgundy-colored hymnal bearing the words *Songs of the Lord Most High*. On the back of the pew in front of her, she saw the Communion cup holders. Fingering the wood inserts with three holes big enough to hold the tiny glasses, she thought of the too-sweet grape juice, the blood of Jesus. Religion and its rituals could be so comforting. But for Laura, this place was the opposite of comforting.

In a flash of intuition, she knew why she had come inside. It was Ruth who seemed to call to her. Laura was certain that seeing Ruth yesterday had been the compulsion that propelled her inside today. She wouldn't be able to talk with her, not with her husband sitting there beside her. But there was something so vulnerable about Ruth that Laura felt a sense of responsibility—perhaps as Marjorie once had felt for her.

Peering around the head of the tall man in front of her, she caught sight of Ruth in a pew about ten rows ahead and to the right. Ruth's head was bowed as if in prayer as she sat beside her husband. The collar on Luke Forrest's white dress shirt was too tight, and he tried repeatedly to loosen it. Even looking at his adult back, Laura would have known him anywhere, even after all these years.

He had been a beefy-looking boy with fair skin and dark auburn hair he wore in a buzz cut. He was the kind of kid who ran with a pack like a young wolf looking for prey. He was nasty, too—quick to punch or kick with no provocation. And, oh, he'd had a smart-alecky mouth. She had never liked him, even as a toddler. But perhaps it was because he had bullied Michael so mercilessly, even as far back as nursery school.

She opened her hymnal and marked the first song with her program, pretending to be studying the week's congregational calendar. Women's Bible Study, Tuesday at seven. A church spaghetti supper next Saturday.

Although she had dressed in a plain light-blue cotton dress, the full-skirt fell just to the knee. It was too short. Surreptitiously, she tugged it lower. Even the peep-toe dress flats she wore were considered too revealing. At least, she wasn't wearing much make-up. Still, she knew her clothing was raising eyebrows among the other women with their long skirts and long-sleeved blouses, their hair fastened into tight buns. *The way I used to look.*

She realized that she no longer bore any resemblance to the old Laura who had attended here as a child, a teenager, a young woman—the pastor's wife. She wasn't like these people—perhaps had never been. She had always questioned their ways, though she had never dared do so publicly.

Now she viewed their rules as backward, even illogical. She was different. She had changed and could never change back. How else could she have had the courage, the audacity, to walk into this church on a Sunday morning dressed in modern attire, her hair cut into a chin-length bob, flagrantly turning a blind eye to their rules? And rather than feeling embarrassed or self-conscious, she felt strong, independent, free to be herself.

She sensed rather than saw that she was being watched. Looking up from the hymnal, she noticed that Ruth had turned around. Her eye contact was direct, almost pleading.

Laura smiled before mouthing the word "Hi."

And then, she saw it: the look of pure fear that crossed Ruth's face. The young woman was frightened to see her there. Luke glanced backward at Laura. She could tell from the rage-filled expression on his face that he was furious. It would be safer for Ruth if Laura did not approach them.

In that moment, Laura knew that her suspicions were correct. Luke was guilty in Michael's death. She set her jaw and made the decision to pursue the truth, no matter what it cost her.

The Forrests' toddler boys sat quietly between their parents, making no sound. Children were expected to be seen and not heard during the church service, which often went beyond an hour. Punishment was swift for those who fussed or caused problems. A "board of education," a wood paddle board drilled with holes, had been a fixture in a closet at the back of the church for decades, ensuring good behavior in the sanctuary for even the smallest children. Only infants up to eighteen months went to the nursery.

Luke looked her way again and narrowed his eyes. As the pastor talked about judgment day, when sins would be counted and punishment dealt, Laura wondered whether Luke ever experienced moments of guilt over his treatment of Michael. How could a God-fearing man take part in an incident that led to another boy's death and feel no remorse?

It was Luke who likely had been the ringleader in the boat that day. It would have been just like him to get an idea into his head and force the others to go along with whatever misdeed he planned. The sheriff had ruled it an accidental drowning based on what the not-exactly-impartial eye witnesses had said. Had one of the boys hit Michael with the canoe paddle, injuring him so severely that lost consciousness? For this, she knew had to be the truth. Michael had been a strong swimmer.

Seeing Luke today, she wanted more than ever to know the truth, even if it brought more pain. Husbands shared details of their actions with the women in their lives, believing they would be loyal and protect their secrets. Luke had been the kind of kid who liked to brag about his exploits. It was inconceivable to Laura that Ruth wouldn't have known at least some of the details of what happened that day.

Besides, the church congregation was tightly-knit, the town far too small to keep big secrets. Laura resolved to get time alone with Ruth. But how? When might she see her alone? She would have to figure out a way.

At the end of the service, as the congregation sang the closing hymn, Laura slipped out of the pew and made her way toward the lobby. She desperately wanted to avoid the receiving line of parishioners waiting to shake hands with the pastor and his wife. Attending the coffee hour after church was out of the question. She felt a rivulet of sweat trickle down the center of her back.

She walked briskly to her car and got in, turning the air conditioner to full blast. She had a moment of nausea, but as cool air flooded the car, she felt herself relax. Her dress was damp, and she felt exhausted by the mental energy needed to remain there through the service. No matter what, she would never set foot in that place again.

She watched as a few people drifted out of the church, stopping to say good-bye to each other. Most people stayed after service for coffee and cookies. She glanced at her watch. It was time to go to Serendipities. She needed to be there by noon, when the store opened on Sundays. There would be a part-time employee who would close the shop at five o'clock.

Laura turned the key in the ignition and glanced in the rear-view mirror, preparing to pull out onto the street. It was then that she caught sight of Ruth and her family leaving the church. Ruth and Luke's little boys were replicas of their small, pretty mother with her blonde hair and blue eyes, their features delicate like hers. The little boys trailed behind the grownups, holding napkin-wrapped cookies and kicking at pebbles on the sidewalk.

Luke turned to them, his face red and stern. He barked, "Get a move on!"

The youngest dropped his cookie and stopped to retrieve it. Luke walked toward him, raising his hand to the child, who started to cry, moving as fast as his small legs could carry him. Luke crossed the street to an enormous red 4X4 truck parked two vehicles in front of Laura's car and got in. Before starting the engine, he yelled to his frightened family, "Get in!"

Laura partially rolled down her window and abruptly stopped. She knew better than to call out to Ruth. Luke would be watching his wife's every move—watching Laura now, too, in his rear-view mirror. Breathing slowly, filled with despair, desperate to stop what she saw happening, Laura nevertheless resisted the urge to get out of her car. And do what? She wasn't in any position to help Ruth—not now. She had to be careful not to put Ruth in an even more dangerous position. She prayed that Luke would not hurt her or their sons.

"Get in the truck!" he yelled at Ruth.

Laura registered the unbridled anger in his voice and flinched as sense memories flooded over her. Ruth scurried to put her boys in the back seat. There was no time to buckle them into car seats—not with Luke yelling at her and gunning the engine. She opened the door to the passenger side and clambered into her seat. As she reached out to close the door, the truck sped off.

Laura held her breath, frightened for Ruth as the young mother struggled to close the passenger door while the truck gained speed. Then another thought came to her. What she had done today was thoughtless, careless. In her determination to get at the truth for Michael, she had unwittingly caused a dangerous situation for Ruth. She felt sick to her stomach, knowing the kind of day Ruth would have.

Laura's sudden appearance at church had unsettled Luke to the point of rage. Though it wasn't her fault, she had to face the fact that seeing her had been the unfortunate catalyst for whatever might happen to Ruth or her children today. Tears dropped from Laura's face into her lap, leaving wet spots on the fabric of her skirt.

How often had she done something to displease Jed, only to suffer from his angry silence or, worse, a beating as a reminder of her misbehavior? For an abused wife, Sunday was no different than any other day, with no respite from fear. She had to make it up to Ruth.

The day passed so quickly that Laura had no time to call Greg or even think of him. Hearing a ping on her phone, she glanced at it. It was Greg. *What time do you get back?*

Not sure, she texted back. *Planning to leave around four o'clock, but have a stop to make on the way back. I'll let you know when I get closer.*

Laura walked through the shop, passing the trundle beds Ruth had admired. She stopped and studied the price tag. Dare she make a gift of them? It would have to be anonymous. She made a split decision to buy the trundle beds and put them on hold in the store. Marjorie could call Ruth and let her know that the beds hadn't sold and would Ruth kindly take them off her hands? New inventory required floor space. She wrote a check for the beds and put it in the cash register with a note.

A little before three o'clock, Laura returned to Marjorie's house to change into slacks and a sleeveless blouse for the drive home. She applied a little more make-up. It was likely Greg would want to take her out for dinner when she got home.

John would be here soon, but she craved more time with Marjorie. A plate of warm snickerdoodles graced the dining room table, along with a pitcher of freshly-brewed iced tea.

Laura squeezed a lemon slice into her tea and smiled at her friend. "I bought that trundle bed at the store."

"Oh? How will you get it to Dublin?"

"It's not for me." She explained her plan to make a gift of the beds to Ruth.

"That man of hers might not allow it. Charity, you know."

"It's the only thing I could think to do. I want to help her." Laura nibbled on a cookie. "She seemed awfully scared when she saw me at church this morning."

"I thought you wanted to get an early start at the store. You went to church?" Marjorie sounded incredulous. "How did it feel walking in there?"

"My original plan was to get to the store extra early. I drove by the church on the way, parked in front, just looking, remembering. All of a sudden, my feet were taking me inside." She shook her head. "It was strange being there. I saw Ruth. She was with him, with Luke." The man's name tasted bitter in her mouth. "He saw me. Afterward, he was really mean to her and the kids. I feel like I put her in danger."

Marjorie sucked air through her teeth. "Could be. I don't think you should have gone there."

"You may be right. It was an impulse."

"It's nice that you want to help Ruth. It must be like watching a rerun of your life."

"I can't deny that seeing her makes me think of that part of my life. But I realized while I sat there that I am not like those people anymore. It's more than looking different. I don't believe as they do."

"You have always been so much smarter and stronger than you realized when you were married to Jed," Marjorie said. "I always knew it was simply a matter of time before you made big changes to your life."

"You were the one who helped me see who I could be," Laura said. "You gave me my start."

"No, my dear. It was self-interest to hire you. You were the best qualified person for the job. Oh, I may have given you a few little pushes. But you were the one who took the leap off the branch and flew. You are a smart, capable woman who can do anything she puts her mind to."

Laura swallowed the lump in her throat. "Thank you. Maybe some-day, I can do for Ruth what you did for me: help her figure out how to make a better life for herself and her kids."

"Not everyone has your strength and willpower, Laura. She may not be willing to leave. She may not *want* to leave."

"Maybe not," Laura agreed. "But I have to try. The trundle beds are not a big deal to me, but I saw how much she wanted them."

"You needn't have paid for them, you know," Marjorie said.

"I wanted to. This is a gift. Even if she doesn't know it, it's from me to her, one mother to another."

Marjorie bit her upper lip. "Okay. I'll call Ruth and make the arrange-ments to offer those beds to her. I do think I should put a small price on it so it doesn't look like charity. They have their pride."

"Of course, you're right. Her self-esteem is low enough already."

"Now," Marjorie said, spooning sugar in her tea glass, "let's talk shop. After two days, what do you think about taking over the store? Any sec-ond thoughts or concerns?" Her voice was gentle. She folded her arms on the table. "I know it's a lot to think about. You'd want to make changes, I'm sure, and those would cost money. Don't worry that I'll think every-thing should remain the way it is now. My way doesn't have to be your way. It will be your store."

"First, I have to arrange a loan so I can buy the store. You still haven't told me how much you want for the business and the building." She hoped she could afford the purchase price.

"I'm not naïve enough to think the store would survive without you at the helm," Marjorie began, letting out a breath. "It's doubtful that any-one else would keep Serendipities going. That's what matters most to me, you know. A buyer might close the store and use the building for some other purpose. It would be the end of my dreams and hard work. I can't bear that—not while I'm still alive."

"I will take good care of your store," Laura promised. She waited before posing the question. "Have you thought about a selling price?" She knew that real estate prices in Parmenter had never recovered after the last recession. Still, she wanted Marjorie to be happy with the outcome.

"Perhaps we could consider a lease-purchase plan where you pay me each month toward the purchase price. I'll have Social Security and investment income. It would be helpful if I could have an additional seven hundred and fifty a month." She pursed her lips before speaking again. "Does twenty-five thousand sound like a fair price to you?"

Laura's eyes flew open in disbelief. "For everything? The store and the building? Oh, no!" She tried again. "Marjorie," she said in a firm voice. "That's not enough. On the market, you could get at least fifty thousand dollars for the building alone."

"That is debatable in this town," Marjorie said. "The building will need a new roof, and there are other deferred maintenance costs. It isn't exactly a prime piece of property."

"Are you sure you don't need more money to live on—to maybe do some traveling?"

"I'll be fine on my savings and Social Security. Laura, I have given this matter considerable thought. You may need to put more money into the store to modernize it. I'd like to see that. You can put the rest of your money into investments. Someday, you will want to retire, too."

"But what about your son? Shouldn't you give him a chance to buy it?" Laura saw the flicker of pain that flashed across Marjorie's face. This was a sensitive subject, but the question had to be asked.

"My son stopped talking to me after I left his father. That man turned my only child against me. You know that, although you've been kind enough over the years not to ask me questions, for which I am beyond grateful." Marjorie looked intently at Laura. "I consider you more than a friend. You are a daughter to me."

Laura's eyes filled with tears. She reached across the table and took Marjorie's hand. "That is the most wonderful thing you've ever said to me."

"Then we're set. This store belongs to you now." Marjorie rapped hard on the table with her other hand as if bringing down the gavel on a hard-won judgement. When she spoke again, her voice sounded pained. "When you have a child, you think you will always have that child's love. I seem to have lost my son's love. I know you will always make sure I am loved."

Chapter Nineteen

"**T**HANKS AGAIN FOR COMING WITH ME," John said as he inserted the key into the ignition.

"I'm honored that you asked." Laura fastened her seat belt and considered whether it had been such a good idea for her to come along. After all, it was the lake.

"I promise this won't take long. No big emotional scenes." He was quiet for a moment before adding, "At least, I hope not."

"Whatever you need to do is fine with me. This shouldn't be something you rush through on my account. It's too important."

He rounded a corner, taking them through Parmenter's main business district. They passed Serendipities. "Everything go okay this weekend?" he asked.

"Yes, although I'm still reeling from what Marjorie just said." She told John about the low sale price for Serendipities. He whistled. "I don't have to worry about a big loan to buy the business. It's the perfect situation."

"Wow." John's fingers tightened on the steering wheel. "It will make her proud when you turn that store into an even bigger success."

"I hope so. I couldn't bear to let her down."

Laura stared out the window as they passed the sights of Parmenter. They were familiar and not in a good way. She tried to view them through fresh eyes. She wasn't the same woman who had left Parmenter in her rearview mirror. Yes, she would be part of this town again, if only through her business. Fate had handed her an unexpected gift, and she would make the most of it.

John drove through a rural area for about seven miles before turning onto a roughly-paved road out of town. As she took in the sights, she felt a jolt in the area of her heart. Her mouth became dry. Just like that, another flashback was happening, and she was powerless to stop it.

In the next instant, Laura was overcome by her strongest sense memory yet. The scene was as vivid in her mind's eye as if it had been yesterday. It was the one-year anniversary of Michael's death. Jed had admonished her to stick to routines and avoid emotional displays.

"It won't bring him back," he had said in a stern voice. "We have to set a good example, show others to trust in God's will, no matter how we feel."

Andrew was furious hearing this. At breakfast, he announced that he would spend the day in the woods where he and Michael used to play. "I'm spending the day remembering my brother," he said, a stubborn set to his jaw.

"You'd be wise not to take that tone with me," Jed said. But he let it go. He had a meeting of the board of elders that morning at eight o'clock.

After Jed left the house, letting the back screen door close with a hard thwack, Laura wrapped her arms around Andrew from behind and kissed his hair. Moving woodenly, grateful for routines that required no real thought, she fixed French toast, his favorite. "It's important for us to do what we need to do," she said. "That is what I am planning today."

Andrew sat at the kitchen table, silent, fighting tears. He picked at his breakfast before finally giving up. Laura felt his suffering and wanted to help him, but her own heart, already broken, had little left to give. She did the best she could to offer comfort, her words sounding hollow even to her own ears.

She would go to the lake today. What she would do there was less a thought than simply being in that place. She needed to be where Michael had spent his last hours on earth. She washed the breakfast dishes and assembled a tuna casserole and salad for dinner. There would be little time to cook this afternoon.

When Jed came home for lunch, Laura asked in a nonchalant tone if she could borrow the car for the afternoon. "We need more groceries than I can carry. I can pick you up at the church at four-thirty."

If all went well, she could allow herself almost three hours to carry out her plan. If she was careful, he'd never know where she had gone today. Jed had said he couldn't allow himself the luxury of sadness—that he understood God's mysterious ways better than most.

When they arrived at the church, he put the car in park and stepped out. Laura unbuckled her seat belt and got out of the car, walking from the passenger side around to the driver's side. As she reached Jed's side, a parishioner who served as president of the board, emerged from his car and greeted them with a tip of his hat. "Pastor, Missus."

"Have a good afternoon," Jed said, kissing her on the cheek. In a lower voice, he added, "Don't get carried away and forget the time."

Bile rose in her throat. Getting into the car, she shut the door quickly and drove away, headed to the lake. She took enough money to replace the gas needed to get there and back. It was important to go by herself— to be alone with memories of her son. But she dared not slip up and make a careless mistake.

That afternoon had been a turning point for Laura—the beginning of the rest of her life. She stood for a few moments on the shoreline, staring at the murky brownish water, imagining what must have happened that day. What had Michael's last moments been like? Had he struggled, been afraid? As red-hot anger seized her at the injustice of it all, as it so often did, Laura cursed this place, those boys, and the shoddy investigation into Michael's death. It may have been bullying, but it had turned deadly.

She dared not speak her opinions, especially a year later, when no one wanted to remember that dreadful day. Jed could force her to behave in certain ways, warn her not to speak in public about her suspicions, and admonish her not to air her feelings to others. But he couldn't control her thoughts. They were unseen, unspoken. They belonged only to her.

The water drew her in, though she was not a swimmer. The most she had ever done was wade at the shoreline in her skirt while her boys splashed happily not far from shore. Kicking off her shoes, she entered the water, flinching at the cold. Despite the summer heat, this lake was always frigid, fed by streams originating in Lake Erie. Underwater detritus clung to her ankles as she moved farther from the shore. Her skin adjusted to the water temperature quickly, making it easy to keep going. Chest-deep now, her dress and undergarments soaked through, she felt the stony, sandy bottom. The water was deeper now, nearly to her neck, and it was more difficult to keep her feet planted on the bottom. Yet, strangely, she felt no fear.

With her next step, the bottom gave way, and she was free-floating, arms and legs moving of their own accord. She had reached the spot where the lake deepened to six or seven feet. She could have screamed— could have flailed her arms and legs in a struggle to stay afloat. These basic biological impulses to survive never crossed her mind. The motion of the water itself was powerful, propelling her forward even as her head slipped beneath the surface. Bubbles floated around her as the air escaped her lungs.

She would never speak of that day—or what happened next—to anyone, not ever. The experience was too other-worldly, too personal. If she told someone, even her mother, she risked being labeled crazy or worse, a heretic. Mystical events were deemed evil. Jed would have her committed. But she knew what happened that day was real. Michael had saved her life.

From her underwater vantage point, her hair floating freely around her, she noticed rays of light shining down through the water. Her heartbeat slowed as a feeling of warmth and peace overcame her. In the next instant, she felt as if she were being pulled upward by larger arms. She had no power to resist the disembodied force that lifted her up and out of the water toward the sky before gently depositing her on the beach.

She noticed that her clothing was dry. Had she hallucinated? It was then that her knees buckled and she dropped to the sand. She couldn't comprehend what had just happened, but she knew whatever it was, it was meant to help.

Michael was with her. Though she could not see him, she felt her son's strong arms encircle her from behind, supporting her. She smelled the sweet aroma of his scent, listened to his words of comfort and love.

But how could this be? Had she drowned and joined him? She laid her head back against his chest. She had never felt so safe, so loved.

Laura believed in an after-life—was convinced that Michael had gone to that place everyone called Heaven. And yet, here he was, holding her. She let him know how much she missed him, how very much he was loved. Her words, held in check so long, spilled out, and she spoke freely, uninhibited by guilt, fear, or shame. For once, she felt heard. She told Michael everything that was in her heart as the feelings of peace intensified.

It was as if there was no time—no past, present, or future. Time, if it existed at all, happened not on a continuum but in all directions at the same time. She felt whole in a way that she never had before.

Coming back to an awareness of her surroundings, she assessed the area around them. Not another soul was in sight. But how was that possible? It was a hot August afternoon, and this was a public beach. She was still in the flesh, still existing. Michael had come from another world, unseen yet close enough that he had known she needed him.

She felt the energy shift, heard him urge her to go home. He reminded her that his brother still needed her, that it was nearly time to serve dinner. And then he was gone. Even this many years later, she could remember how it felt to be with him, understood that an invisible veil could never keep them apart. What she had felt as the loss of him was grounded by something more powerful than grief: an inner sense of him with her.

Michael would always live in her heart. And this deeply-held under-standing was what allowed her to go on with her life. That day she had experienced Michael's presence beside her on the shore had been a promise that he would always be as near as her memories of him. She closed her eyes and wished John the same acknowledgment of Jackie's presence—as near as his next thought.

Chapter Twenty

John spoke very little as they made their way through a wooded area outside of town, past farmland and park campgrounds. It was fortunate he hadn't spoken during the time Laura was experiencing the flashback. If he had, she might have had to explain. Then he would have felt the need to comfort her. That she couldn't allow. What was about to happen was not about her. It was about him.

Laura understood that his silence meant he was lost in thought, mentally preparing for what surely would be an emotionally draining task ahead. Saying good-bye was the most difficult part of loving someone.

He turned onto a bumpy rural route and drove another mile until the lake came into view. Parking along the side of the road, he shut off the engine. Then he reached between the front seats into the back of the car and retrieved a small, padded bag. Laura watched him unzip it and remove a brass container. *Jackie.*

He said nothing, merely nodded for Laura to follow as they walked carefully across the uneven, grassy field. She saw the makeshift dock where Michael and the other boys had gotten into the boat that day. She took in deep breaths willing herself not to cry.

She stopped at the juncture between grass and sand, needing to take a breath. He turned and gave her a questioning look. She offered an encouraging smile.

"Are you sure you don't want to be alone to honor her?" she asked. "I can wait in the car."

His eyes widened in recognition. "I just realized this must be the place . . . I shouldn't have asked you to come."

"I've already made my peace here. It's okay. I can stay."

"I promise I won't be long." He took slow, deliberate steps toward the water's edge as gentle waves lapped at his canvas deck shoes and soaked the hem of his jeans. A breeze picked up, stirring the leaves on nearby trees as he lifted the lid of the urn.

Laura heard his voice, a word here and there, carried on the breeze. The words he spoke to Jackie were private, between lovers. Laura stepped back, clasping her hands in front of her. Every move he made was deliberate in carrying out his wife's last wishes.

She wondered if he could sense Jackie's presence here the way she had experienced Michael. She heard him chuckle, as if he and Jackie were sharing one last joke, before he turned the urn on its side and sprinkled ashes into the water, letting the tide carry them away. He stood for several minutes, a hand shading his eyes, watching until the ashes drifted out of sight on the ebbing flow of the waves.

The sun shone its glittering rays of gold on the water. The sunlight was almost blinding. Laura said a little prayer for his healing and happiness.

When she opened her eyes, John was walking toward her. "And so, it begins," he said, putting his hands in his pockets.

"What is that?" she asked gently, her head tilted slightly.

"My life without her," he said. "I know she would want me to be happy."

They stood together at the water's edge, watching as the sun began its late afternoon descent. She longed to stay, to witness the vivid streaks of rose, coral, and yellow as they intensified. The most stunning shades were hours away, toward twilight. John showed no sign of wanting to leave. She couldn't be sure how long they stood there. Nor could she know his thoughts. She was aware only of a feeling of absolute serenity.

Later, headed west on the interstate, a stream of questions ran through her head. But she waited for him to speak first. When he finally glanced over at her, flexing his hand on the wheel, she could see the peace in his expression. "Thank you," he said. "There isn't a lot I can say right now, but I was grateful not to be alone."

They were silent for a few moments. Then, testing his mood, she said, "I'm guessing this weekend was about other things, too. Did you have a nice time with your friend?"

"We did. We went to a steak place for dinner and had a couple of beers. I don't know how long it's been since he and I did that—long before Jackie got so sick, I guess."

She persisted, gently. "Did he talk with you about moving back to Parmenter?"

John was quiet for a moment. "He did." Signaling, he changed lanes. "I'm still weighing my options."

"Would you be happier in Parmenter than Columbus?"

"Why do you ask?" His eyes never left the road.

"Just wondering, I guess."

"Real estate is a heck of a lot cheaper in Parmenter. I could sell the house in Columbus and purchase a small house in Parmenter and maybe another building for my law practice."

"You could. Or you could rent business space." Laura decided to speak what was on her mind. "Unless you need an entire building, you could rent space on the second floor of the Serendipities building for your office. There are four rooms on that second floor including a bathroom and a little kitchenette. You'd want to do a bit of remodeling. I could help with that."

"There are worse things, I suppose, than having you for my landlord," he said in a teasing tone. "That's an interesting proposal. I'll think about it."

"I've seen from experience that friends *can* do business together. I'm sure we can come to an equitable arrangement. The details just need to be clarified."

"Are you saying that you'll need an attorney to write up a contract?" He glanced sideways.

"There are worse things, I suppose, than having you for an attorney," she answered.

He laughed. "Touché."

"Actually, I do need a good attorney."

"I'll give you the friend discount." She saw the corners of his mouth turn up.

It was time to say the words that had been on her mind all weekend. "John, I want to hire you for another reason, too—even more important than the business. I want to find out the truth about Michael's death. I want justice for my son."

His response was deliberate, measured. "I'm not surprised that being in Parmenter would get you thinking more seriously about that. It would require reopening the case. That won't be easy." His cheeks puffed out before he let out the air. "We'll have to look for someone willing to talk about what happened that day."

"I know where to start." Laura told him about meeting Ruth. "She is married to one of the boys, Luke, who was there the day Michael died. I have always believed Luke was guilty, maybe even the ringleader. She has to know something."

"Chances are, you're correct. Wives know things that husbands wish they didn't."

"What's the next step?" She turned to watch his profile as he drove.

"Let me do some digging. I'll talk with my former law partner and see what he thinks."

"My concern is that if I bring Ruth into this, her whole world could explode. She's an abused wife. It could put her and her kids in danger. And I doubt she is prepared to support herself and her little boys if her husband goes to prison."

"It's only natural that you'd care what happens to her. You're going to have to keep those empathetic emotions separate from the facts of the case."

"I understand that. But after seeing the way that man treats her and their sons . . . If what I believe is true, and it turns out Luke is responsible for Michael's death, she and the boys are better off without him."

"That's easy for you to say. Just playing devil's advocate here."

"When Jed died, my life turned upside down. It was hard to learn how to live in a world that had passed me by in every way. But his death also forced me to take action. I had to make a living for myself. My life is so much better now. Andrew's life is better, too."

"You had the courage and the willpower to take on that challenge. Ruth might not be as strong."

"It wasn't me doing all of that by myself, not completely. Marjorie was there for me. It's because she cared about me that I am where I am now. I could be the same kind of mentor for Ruth."

"That would still have to be her choice." He paused before speaking again. "You'll never be dependent on anyone ever again, Laura. You're much stronger now. You always were. You just didn't know it."

"Ruth can find her strength, too."

"If we find a lead to reopen the investigation, she's going to need strength for what comes next."

"I know I'm right that Michael didn't drown by accident. I have always known that. It was just this weekend, though, that I came to the understanding that his death wasn't just the result of bullying. You mentioned a hate crime. I believe Michael was killed for who he was. That's what I have to know for sure. And I want whoever was responsible punished."

"If there is one thing I've learned in this line of work, it's that there is always someone who knows something," John said. "We just have to get that someone to talk."

They exited the interstate, driving through Columbus into the outskirts of Dublin. As John turned onto the street where Serendipities Two was located, she saw a male figure sitting in one of the wicker chairs on her front porch. Her stomach did a back flip. "It's Greg," she said.

"Were you expecting him?"

"I was going to call him when I got here," Laura said. "He didn't know you and I were driving together."

He looked at her sideways. "Does that matter?"

"He wanted to drive me there himself, but I said not this time. It was before you and I found out we were both going to Parmenter separately this weekend."

"If I saw the girl I was dating get out of the car with a strange guy, I'd hope for an explanation—not that there is anything for you to feel guilty about," he said.

They emerged from the car. Laura flashed a broad smile at Greg and waved. "Let me get my bag!"

John popped the trunk and put her suitcase on the curb. Greg descended the steps to meet them.

"You must be Greg," John said, extending his hand. "I'm John. Laura and I were neighbors in Parmenter."

"Did something happen to your car?" Greg looked at Laura. Her SUV was parked in front of Serendipities Two.

"My car is fine," she said. "We found out at book club on Wednesday that we were both going to Parmenter this weekend and decided at the last minute to carpool." John was right. She had no reason to defend her decision, but the look on Greg's face said otherwise. She leaned her head up for the quick kiss he planted on her lips. "I have a lot to tell you."

"I'm looking forward to it," Greg said. He put his arm low around Laura's waist. "I've missed you."

"I've missed you, too," Laura said, embarrassed to say this in front of John. Greg's statement should have delighted her. Instead, she felt uncomfortable. She looked at John and smiled. "Thank you again," she said. She stepped out of his embrace and leaned in to give John a quick good-bye hug.

John looked pained. "It's I who should thank you," he said. "I couldn't have gotten through today without you."

"I was honored that you asked me," she said, sounding more formal than she intended. "It was good for me to be there, too."

Greg frowned. "Let me get that bag," he said and snatched it from the curb. "I thought we could grab dinner, if you're not too tired."

"Dinner sounds good," she said. She and John exchanged glances. She wished she could read the expression on his face.

He finally spoke. "I'll call you later this week."

"Oh, yes, please do," she said. "I'm anxious to hear what you find out."

"About what?" Greg asked with a short laugh. "This all sounds very mysterious."

"I'll tell you everything at dinner," she said.

The two men eyed each other in a way that made Laura feel even more anxious. Sweat broke out on her upper lip as an old memory surfaced. It had been at least fifteen years since it happened, but she could never forget.

These memories seemed to be coming more frequently of late. Was it because she was spending time in Parmenter again? The thing about memories from the past was that they left emotional scars long after the actual injuries healed. Senses were the trigger: sights, sounds, smells, *the taste of blood*.

She and a male member of the congregation had exchanged pleasantries while Laura served up strawberry shortcake at a church social. Jed had seen them talking and laughing, had grilled her when they got home before throwing her against a wall in the dining room. That brief, innocent encounter had resulted in Laura suffering a bloody nose and a split lip.

Greg is not Jed. Oddly, this thought gave her no comfort. What did she know about how any man viewed the attentions of other men? From the looks of it, John and Greg didn't like each other.

John laid his hand on the trunk of his car. "Well, I'd better go and let you two get on with your evening," he said.

"Thanks again," she said. For Greg's benefit, she added, "See you at book club."

John got into his car and drove off. Laura watched until his car reached the next block.

Taking Greg's hand, she moved toward the porch. "Would you like a drink before we go to dinner?"

"Sure," he said in an even voice. "I'm anxious to hear about your weekend. Sounds like it took a slightly different turn than you thought."

"It did," she admitted as they started upstairs to her apartment. "So much happened that I didn't expect. I haven't been back there since I moved away. To tell you the truth, it was a lot to take in."

He put her suitcase in the foyer. "You had a friend to help you through it."

She blinked. His tone was even and controlled, but she sensed a simmering displeasure. "John *is* a friend," she stressed. "We go way back. He was very helpful to me one day when I was married and having troubles with my husband." She blew out a long breath, feeling weary. "I had a shoulder injury and groceries too heavy to carry. He gave me a ride home from the grocery store. I wouldn't have made it, otherwise."

"A shoulder injury? How did that happen?"

"Greg, there are things about that time of my life I'd rather forget. But just so you understand, John also drove me to the hospital the night my husband died and stayed with me until Marjorie got there."

Greg ran a hand through his hair. "I'm glad you told me. I don't understand, though, why you didn't mention that the two of you were driving together."

"I just found out the other day that he had plans to go there, too, and . . ." She paused. "His wife just died. He had things to take care of in Parmenter."

She hoped he would accept this explanation without further comment. It was the truth, after all. His expression altered, but she couldn't decipher the look. It wasn't sympathy—more along the lines of suspicion.

"We went to the lake in Parmenter so he could scatter her ashes." She leaned against a kitchen counter. "It's the lake where my son drowned."

"I had no idea," Greg said, drawing her into his arms. "You don't have to tell me anymore." The message was clear. He wanted her to stop this unpleasant talk.

"But I need you to understand," Laura said after a moment. This was important. "I'll be going back and forth between here and there. I'm going to take over Marjorie's Serendipities store and . . ." She hesitated. It might not be the ideal time to mention plans to reopen the investigation into her son's death. What if nothing came of it? "There's another situation I may need to deal with, too."

He shifted, putting a little distance between them, before placing his hands on her shoulders. He looked intently into her eyes. "I can tell it's serious. But whatever it is, I know you can handle it." He took in a breath. "Now, what do you say we walk over to Tucci's? Let's have a nice dinner and catch up."

"That sounds great," she said. Perhaps she could broach the subject at dinner. She picked up her purse and keys. "I'm ready."

They walked up the street toward the restaurant, holding hands. "I hope you didn't have to wait too long for me," she said.

"About fifteen minutes. If you give me a key to your place, I won't have to wait outside in the future," he said.

She was saved from having to answer as they entered the restaurant and Greg greeted two men he knew at the bar. She sensed their appraising looks, enjoying the feeling of being with Greg, of being someone special to him.

Their server motioned them to follow her. Greg's hand rested low on her back in that proprietary way he had of guiding her into a room. They sat across from each other in the booth. Greg accepted the menu from the server and reviewed the specials while Laura studied his face. He was the kind of man who could turn a woman's head. He had singled her out for attention. Still, there were things about him that made her uneasy. No doubt, it was her inexperience with men.

"Here, babe," he said, handing her the special menu. "The specials look good tonight. I think I'll have the salmon."

She blinked, her heart beating rapidly. *Babe*. He had called her babe, the same term of endearment Andrew and Emily frequently used with each other. Surely, this meant he cared for her. It was this kind of love language she yearned to have in her life.

In her mind's eye, she saw herself in the kitchen making his favorite meal. They sat together on the sofa after dinner, a soft blanket covering their legs, watching the evening news. Then, he'd take her hand and they'd walk together to the bedroom.

He was speaking to her. She snapped back to attention. "So, this guy John is fresh off the death of his spouse. Sad. It's likely to take years to recover from that."

She took another sip of water. "They were very close. I didn't have that kind of marriage."

He smiled at her, brightening up. "Neither did I. You and I have a lot to explore together. Now," he said, "Chardonnay or Merlot?"

"Chardonnay, please." She waited until he ordered wine for her and a dirty martini for himself. "I'm sorry for not telling you John and I drove together," she said after a few minutes. "I wouldn't want you to think . . ."

"It just seems odd that you didn't mention it."

Her stomach tightened. She had every right to go there with John. Yet she hadn't been entirely honest. "You're right. I should have mentioned it. It's just that he's a friend and I didn't think there was any real reason to bring it up. We lived in the same town. We were both driving there."

He shook his head. "Don't you think that the time you spend with him, you know, helping him sprinkle his wife's ashes . . ." He made a motion with his hands to illustrate. "Well, it might make it tougher for him to move on. You may have to distance yourself, for his sake."

Laura thought for a moment. Was this really what was best for John? How could it be right for friends to distance themselves at a time when they most needed support?

Greg took a deep swig of his martini and set it down. He smiled broadly. "About this new business venture of yours . . . I can get you a good rate on a business loan—through connections I have."

She smiled. "That's nice of you. But I don't think a loan will even be necessary—well, at least not for the purchase of the business. Marjorie and I are going to have a lease-purchase arrangement."

"Oh?" His left eyebrow shot up. "Might that be her way to retain control? She still owns the store until you purchase it outright. What if you want to sell it?"

This much was true. But Laura knew this was not Marjorie's objective. It wouldn't be her objective, either. Hadn't Greg ever had a business dealing that was based on a gut instinct of trust? Or maybe businessmen as successful and important as Greg knew better. "She wants to retire, but she also wants to make this as easy as possible for me. The purchase price is very reasonable." She explained the terms to him. "Marjorie is like family to me, Greg. I can trust her the way she trusts me."

Greg took a quick gulp of his martini. "Look, you don't have all the experience I have in business. I'm a chief financial officer. I have seen deals like this, and they don't turn out well. Business arrangements with family and friends are difficult, at best." He shook his head and made direct eye contact. Taking her hand across the table, he continued. "You're very trusting, Laura—too trusting. Look at your friend, John. It's plain to see that he wants you as more than a friend. Another man can recognize that, babe."

Laura's eyes opened wide. "He just lost his wife. What is between us is strictly friendship."

Greg reached across the table for her hand. "Well, if that's truly the case, he won't have a problem backing away so that you and I can grow our relationship."

Laura's gut flip-flopped. It was a feeling she had learned to heed. For years, she had missed out on words of love, had longed to hear words of endearment from a man. Yet, there was something in Greg's message that didn't feel quite right. There was something familiar in this sensation of walking on eggshells, choosing her words with caution.

He continued, "I'd feel better if you agree to limit the amount of time you spend with him. Think of this from my perspective. You won't go away with me for the weekend, but you took a weekend drive to another town with him. How do I know what he has in mind? Look, I'm just a normal guy who cares for a beautiful woman. If I seem a little jealous, maybe I am."

Laura's heart soared at his words. He cared for her! At the same time, she felt unsettled and a bit confused at his admission of jealousy. In her experience, jealousy could turn dangerous. And yet, hadn't she observed John behaving in much the same fashion? The two men had faced off earlier in a way that told her they didn't like each other. This was a two-way street. Of course, Greg would feel threatened by John. Confusion settled over her, clouding her judgment.

For the moment, there would be no discussion about John's help in reopening an investigation into Michael's death. That would only add fuel to the fire. "You don't need to feel jealous," she said after a moment. She squeezed his fingers. "John is a friend. He'll understand."

Chapter Twenty-One

"During his brief life—just forty-six years—Oscar Wilde was one of the wittiest and most charismatic writers alive or dead—not just in Ireland, but in the entire British empire," Jan said, introducing *The Picture of Dorian Gray*, the story she had assigned her book club readers. "Coming from an aristocratic family, Wilde naturally had the finest education. He wrote wonderful plays—highly satirical—about society. You've heard of *The Importance of Being Ernest*. It was, and still is, hilarious." She continued, more seriously, "After his homosexuality became known—which was a criminal offense at the time—Wilde was sent to jail for a couple of years. After his release from prison, he fled to France. Presumably, he felt safer there."

"France has always been less uptight than other countries. That seems like a good place for him to land," Terri remarked. "Was he successful writing while he lived in France?"

"No. Sadly, he died without a cent to his name." Jan sat back in her chair, surveying the group. "I wonder whether the experience of prison broke him or whether the fact that he had been in prison prevented any further success of his work."

"It's sad that anyone would be punished for being who they were, who they were born to be." The words were out of Laura's mouth before she realized she had uttered them. Her throat constricted, briefly shutting off her air supply. She coughed into her fist, steeling herself before continuing. "Worse things than jail time happen to people who are gay. It can be a death sentence."

She felt John's encouraging eyes on her as she spoke. But to say more would have required that she talk about Michael with this group of people, some of whom were more fond acquaintances than close friends. The experience of Michael's death might be a stronger way to make her point, but it was more than she was prepared to acknowledge now.

Aside from Terri, John, and Jan, no one else in the book group knew anything about Laura's background. She wanted to keep it that way. Maybe someday, she could share more.

Terri smiled her support at Laura. "I liked the book, but I agree with Laura. It's troubling that so many people still find reason to judge those who aren't like them. If you think about it, no one is exactly like anyone else. That leaves a lot of room for judgement."

Laura watched as Terri nibbled a lemon bar, dropping powdered sugar on her dark jeans, and swiping at it with her napkin. Her own dessert lay untouched, though she noticed John had devoured both of his cookies.

"Wilde was judged harshly for the characters in this story," Jan said. "It may have been the impetus for his prosecution."

"Persecution, you mean," Terri said. She looked around at the others, now silent, their eyes downcast. A pall settled over the group. Licking sugar off her thumb, she glanced over at Laura who was looking at her watch, clearly anxious for the discussion to be over. It was nearly eight-thirty.

Jan took the cue and closed her notebook. "We're reading something a little lighter for next time," she said with a smile. "*Gulliver's Travels* by Jonathan Swift."

"Anyone else want to go out for a drink and Irish music?" Terri was on her feet. "We could celebrate the life and works of Oscar Wilde. One of my favorite Irish bands is playing. Come on," she urged.

It was a short walk to the Irish pub known for its generous pours and craft brews. With all twelve members of the group going out, three booths were needed. Recalling her earlier conversation with Greg, Laura waited until John scooted into a booth before she moved to another booth next to Jan. Although she would rather have sat with John, it was good for him to get to know other people.

She caught Terri's raised eyebrows. "Go sit with John," her friend mouthed.

She shook her head. It was too late to make a different decision. She would explain her reason later. Between songs, she strained to hear the conversation at his table, smiling at the easy laughter. Nursing a glass of wine, she nibbled at appetizers on the table, pretending to have a good time.

Guilt frayed the edges of her already taut nerves. It didn't feel right to distance herself from John. But surely, Greg had a point, even if it might be misguided. It was a wonder that either man bothered with her. *This is the talk of low self-esteem.* She bit the inside of her lower lip, reminding herself that she and John had good reasons to remain in close touch, and that perhaps her guilt was misplaced.

Hours later, as members of the group said their good-byes, she turned and found him waiting for her.

"I thought you'd sit with us," he said. "There was plenty of room."

"Next time," she said. "I needed a little time with Jan. Talk to you tomorrow?"

His expression was indecipherable. "Sure."

"YOU'RE REPEATING THE ONLY PATTERN that's familiar to you," Terri said as she followed Laura upstairs to her apartment. It was nearly ten-thirty, but neither was tired. Stepping inside the living room, Laura flicked on the lamp.

Terri sat on the sofa, crossed her legs, and laced her fingers around her knee. "You're allowing Greg to control who you spend time with and what you do. It's a slippery slope. Surely, you see that."

"I think it's only natural that Greg doesn't want me to be too friendly with a man who might seem to have feelings for me," Laura retorted. "I don't want to hurt John, so I'm making it clear to him that we are just friends."

"Are you?"

"What do you mean? Of course, we're just friends. Greg is my boyfriend."

"Greg is the guy you've just started dating. I think 'boyfriend' might be a tad premature." Terri leaned back against the sofa, crossing her arms over her chest. "Look, I get it. You like him and want to please him. Unfortunately, he seems to think he has the right to say whatever he wants and whatever he expects from you."

"I'm glad I know what he thinks. It's safer that way." Laura walked into the kitchen and opened the refrigerator, pulling out a bottle of watermelon-infused water. She opened it with a quick twist and drank deeply. The water was ice cold. She pinched two fingers to the area on her forehead to stop the intense ache.

"Did you just hear what you said? *It's safer that way?* Communication works two ways. Are you able to ask him to stop seeing other women?" There was no emotion in the question or the expression on Terri's face. For that reason, it was all the more devastating.

Laura pivoted toward her. "Have you seen him with other women?"

"No, but I don't care for the comment he made at the Irish Fest the night I met him. I know a player when I see one."

"Isn't that opinion based on your own past experience with men?"

Terri looked as if she had just been slapped. Her cheeks reddened. Licking her lips, she took a deep breath, considering her response before answering, "Yes and no. Yes, I have had an unfortunate conversation with Greg. Yes, I have experienced that type of man before—the kind who will date several women, and none of them will know about the others. But no, that opinion is based on my concern for your happiness."

Laura softened. This was Terri, outspoken Terri who loved her. She had to clarify the issue for her. "It was a misunderstanding. Greg said so. I wish you'd give him another chance." She handed Terri a bottled water. "It would mean a lot to me if you'd give me some credit. I may not have a lot of experience dating, but I know something important about him. He respects the work I do, and he listens to my opinions." She looked directly at Terri. "He doesn't hit me."

"Not every kind of abuse causes bruises." Terri opened the water bottle, took a thoughtful sip, and replaced the cap. "There are other kinds of abuse, you know. Words can hurt, too. I believe what Greg is doing is manipulative, and that is emotional abuse."

Laura sagged onto the sofa. "Okay, I'll admit, I'm over my head with Greg. I know he wants me to have sex with him. I'm dealing with that. In the meantime, I'm trying to . . ." She bit the inside of her cheek until it bled.

"Placate him?"

"Yes, I guess that's the word. I need time to figure out some things."

Terri moved closer. "Tell that to Greg. If he's as great as you think he is, he will understand. A man who understands everything in your past and still expects you to do what he wants, when *he* wants it . . . is just another Jed in an expensive suit."

GREG PICKED UP LAURA FOR DINNER the next evening, holding the passenger door of the convertible for her and waiting until she was safely buckled in. "Top down?" he asked.

"That sounds like fun," Laura said. "It's such a nice night." She waited until he had the top lowered and secured. He buckled his seatbelt and reached over, placing his hand over her knee.

She reached for his hand and took it. "I wonder if we could talk first, before dinner."

"Is something the matter?" His jaw was squared tight. "Do you not want to go out tonight?" She heard impatience in the tone.

"Actually, I want to share something important with you." Laura turned in her seat to face him. "There is a reason why I move so slowly, why I'm so cautious . . . about us."

"You told me already. Your husband had a temper."

"It was more than a temper, Greg. He beat me and our sons. I was injured severely enough to need medical care."

"Laura, I would never hurt you." Greg's eyes met hers. "You have to believe me. I am not the kind of guy who hits a woman. I don't have to do that. I'm man enough to know better."

She smiled. "I know that about you. I do. But I still need to move slowly, to know that what we have is real before I go any further in this relationship. Could we just take our time with the physical part?"

She watched his jaw relax just a little. "You sound like you think I'm going to force myself on you." He pushed the button on the ignition and pulled away from the curb. "When we make love, I want you to be there because you want to be."

Make love. Laura's heart soared. These were caring, loving words. It felt right to venture further. "I need to say one more thing. John really is a friend, nothing more."

"Okay. If you say so, I believe you." Greg released her fingers and stroked her leg. As he did so, he pushed her skirt higher, his hand moving inches higher on her inner thigh. She forced herself not to jump.

He grinned. "You're hard to resist, babe. Can't blame a guy for trying."

Chapter Twenty-Two

Laura woke at four in the morning, heart racing, her mouth dry as cotton balls. Thoughts of the night before with Greg jangled with memories of time with John, ensuring she wouldn't sleep. She punched her pillow a few times in frustration before deciding the night was over. Padding into the kitchen, she poured a glass of water and drank it down, then poured another.

Her mind raced with thoughts of Greg's hands on her body, the exhilarating sensations she had experienced. Never before had she desired a man so much that she was willing to let caution fly to the winds. She leaned against the counter, considering what had almost happened. Thank goodness, Greg had the good sense to stop because Laura knew what had happened between them had been more than she could resist. Now all she felt was embarrassment.

She shook her head, not at all sure who had been acting in her place. Certainly, the woman of last night was not the usual Laura. This Laura had welcomed Greg's kisses, had been willing to go further, had actually encouraged a state of undress.

After a leisurely dinner, Greg topped off her glass with more wine from the bottle and suggested a three-day trip to Chicago the following weekend. "It's a beautiful city with lots of water views, historic bridges, great restaurants, and all the shopping you could ever want. There are even a few day trips we could take on the train. Lake Michigan is massive. It looks like an ocean. You'll love it." He quickly added, "I'll get us two rooms."

Although her brain sent out caution signals, her heart was a goner. It had been such a wonderful dinner with him, and if she was being honest, she wanted more. Taking in a deep breath and letting it out, she smiled. "I'd love to. Will we drive?"

"We'll fly. I'll make all the reservations." In a teasing tone, he added, "What we do with the second room is up to you." He was already searching for flights on his smart phone.

She had no other plans to rearrange. It was just a weekend trip. People went on weekend trips all the time. He had promised two rooms. What more was there to consider?

Greg paid their dinner check, and they headed back to her house, holding hands. Turning the key in the lock of Serendipities Two, she shut off the alarm system. He was behind her, his hand low on her back, propelling her inside. As they reached the stairwell to her apartment, he pulled her into an embrace. As she whirled to face him, she threw her arms around his neck to steady herself. He pulled her closer, leaning into her. But it was Laura who initiated the kiss. She felt daring, a woman of the world.

His hands were on either side of her face as he returned the kiss, covering her mouth and then her neck in kisses, evoking that oh-too-familiar flutter in her lower abdomen. The kiss deepened, his tongue exploring hers as his fingers roamed over the jersey fabric of her blouse. He pulled her shirt from the waistband of her skirt, putting his hands on the sensitive skin of her sides. She shivered.

To Laura, it felt as if they floated up the stairs, his hand never leaving her lower back, guiding her forward. She barely remembered how they ended up in her bedroom. Events were hazy on that score, and she didn't think it had to do with the three glasses of wine she had consumed. Oh, she had been intoxicated; of that, she had no doubt. But she also had been drunk with desire, with the unfamiliar sensations he was creating in her body. A wanting for Greg had thoroughly overcome her.

Once in her room, his hands were on her breasts, the fastener on her lacy bra giving way easily to his experienced hands. In one quick move, he raised her top over her head and tossed the shirt and her bra onto the floor, pressing her against him as his hands moved lower. His mouth was on her breasts, teasing her with his teeth. It was as if her body was acting of its own accord.

He half-lifted her onto the bed and covered her body with his. She felt the crispness of his dress shirt on her skin, the feeling as unfamiliar as it was exquisite. She was shaking uncontrollably now, but not from fear. This was entirely different. She wanted him, could feel how much he wanted her.

He rose from the bed and began unbuttoning his shirt. "Are you on the pill?"

She had an appointment to see her doctor to discuss birth control options—had thought she would have more time to prepare for this moment. "Um . . . I'm not yet," she admitted. "I wasn't ready for this to happen tonight."

It was as if a wall came down between them. He shook his head. "You took me by surprise," he said, as if this had all been her doing. "I'm not prepared to face fatherhood again at this age." She could tell he was displeased—blaming her. "Let's take care of that before we go on our trip together."

She was mortified, embarrassed to find herself in this half-dressed state. Greg stood before the mirror on her closet door, checking his appearance, fixing his mussed hair. Even his eyes were controlled, the look of a man about to exit.

She rolled to the side of the bed and scampered into the bathroom, yanking her robe off the hook on the back of the door. What had she been thinking? This was not the way things were supposed to happen—not their first time together. She had imagined it differently. What had just happened would pollute the anticipation of the next time.

She clutched her robe shut with her hands and moved to face him. "Greg, I'm sorry. I didn't mean to let things go so far. What you must be thinking . . ."

He let out a deep sigh. "I thought you'd had a change of heart. I thought you were prepared. Good thing I was able to stop in time."

"Maybe I had too much wine. We started kissing, and things got out of hand."

"Next time," he said. He offered her a chaste kiss on the cheek. "I'll let myself out."

She had crawled back into bed, pulling the comforter over her face, desperate to forget what had just happened. Only hours later, when sleep evaded her, did the thought occur to her that birth control should have been on his mind, too. Why had he accepted her apology without offering one of his own?

She had no doubt he would regret inviting her to go with him to Chicago. Would he call later today? If not, it would be the sign she needed. He was tiring of her reluctance, tired of wanting her to act different, be different. Maybe it was for the best.

She put on a nightshirt and wrapped herself in a light blanket. Curling up on the sofa, she watched the navy-blue sky lighten in stages, moving through a range of blues so visually stunning, Laura understood why her mother felt the need to paint pictures. When something so beautiful struck your emotions this way, it was only natural to want to preserve the scene forever in a way that could be enjoyed again and again. Marveling at this thought, she stayed awake, watching the sun rise before making a pot of coffee. She would have to remember to share this experience with her mother when she dropped by later.

"WHY, IF IT ISN'T THE PRODIGAL SON," she joked when Andrew dropped by the shop early that afternoon. She hadn't seen him since Irish festival. They had exchanged text messages and talked twice, but it wasn't the same as being with him.

He flashed a quick grin before embracing her. "I thought I'd see if you'd like to join me for coffee."

She checked her watch. "I was planning to slip out later to visit Grandma, but sure, I can take a quick break now." She went to find Cissy to let her know she was going for coffee. "I'll bring you back a cinnamon latte," she promised.

Andrew looked particularly handsome in a dress shirt, tie, and navy slacks. "Are you working in an office today?" she asked. "You look very professional."

"I had a class presentation. Thought you might like to see me in something other than ripped jeans and a tee-shirt." They left the shop and walked down the block. "Actually, I wanted to talk with you about something," he said. "We haven't really talked in weeks, and I think it's my fault. I didn't know what to say."

"About what?" They gave their coffee orders to the clerk at the counter and went to sit at their favorite table.

"Emily says I owe you an apology." He twisted his mouth. "I think she's right, as usual."

"I don't understand." She studied his eyes, as blue as her own. "What did you do?"

"I wasn't very nice to your friend when we met him at the festival. Emily said I acted like a brat." He flashed that signature grin again. "Sorry if I embarrassed you."

"Well, you're a cute brat." Laura accepted her coffee from the server who brought them their drinks. "It's possible that you were being protective of me. In that case, I forgive you."

"I *was* being protective. But it was more than that. There was something about him I didn't like. I know I said you should date again, and this is your life. But not him, Mom."

"Andrew, what about him makes you feel that way? I'm not . . . well, I'm not experienced with men like Greg, and I might not be seeing everything about him. Help me understand."

"It's a guy thing." Andrew blew on his coffee before taking a cautious sip. "Guys recognize stuff about other guys. He's got this way about him, this sort of 'I know everything and you don't' thing going on. He's arrogant. A guy like that will take what he wants. I worry that he'll try to take advantage of you."

"He does know a lot," Laura said. "That's one of the things I admire about him. He's intelligent and sophisticated in ways that I'm not. I've never been to business school. I just run a small secondhand store."

"You're selling yourself short, Mom. You're every bit as smart as he is. But I wonder if he can fully appreciate everything about you—what you've accomplished, how far you've come. There is far more to you than meets the eye."

She smiled. "Thank you, son." Needing him to understand, she chose her next words with care. "He appreciates that I own a business and that I have design talents. Of course, he has no idea of who I used to be . . . before I moved here and became who I am now. He knows the improved Laura, not the sad, fearful Laura. I like that. I don't want to be reminded that I used to be a doormat to an abusive man. I like that Greg sees me as someone worthy of his time."

"You're more than worthy, Mom. Is he worthy of you?"

She cleared her throat. "He asked me to go to Chicago with him." At the stormy look that appeared on Andrew's face, she hastened to add, "Two hotel rooms, of course." It was important he understand it was her decision. "I thought it might be nice to go somewhere I've never been, experience the world beyond Ohio. Chicago is one of the biggest cities in the world. I also thought it would give me a chance to know him better." Her expression grew more serious. "I might not like the Greg I get to know. How can I explain that he makes me feel different? More special than I ever felt with your father?"

"Mom, it wouldn't take much to improve on how Dad treated you.

The simple fact of not hitting a woman still doesn't make a guy a prince." He finished his coffee and set the cup on the table. "Greg thinks with his little head, not his big head."

Laura was quiet, registering the comment. "Oh, Andrew," she said, stifling an embarrassed laugh. "I'm a grown woman. I promise I'll be careful."

"When are you leaving for Chicago?"

"We're flying out Friday. I've never even been on a plane. This is a big adventure."

"I'm your son. I can't tell you what to do. But as your son, I can promise you one thing. If I find out he has done anything to hurt you, I'll hunt him down."

"Andrew." She covered his hand with hers. "I love you, and I appreciate your concern. But if I ever hope to have real love in my life, I have to take chances. I have to learn how to live the way you and Emily do."

"Emily is the kind of person you can trust completely. That's the difference. I never have to worry about her motives or whether she has my best interests at heart. I have to work at this relationship because I never learned from my father the right way to treat a woman."

"How *did* you learn?" This was something she needed to understand. "Your father certainly didn't teach you."

"Emily taught me. The right man will help you be the best version of yourself. You'll grow together in the relationship, Mom."

"How did you get so smart?" Tears clouded her vision. She cleared her throat and squeezed his hand. "Change of subject?" He nodded. "I told you I'm buying Marjorie's store in Parmenter. Well, I have a friend from Parmenter who is going to help me. He's an attorney, and I trust him."

"Mom, I think that's so great. You can handle both stores. But are you sure you want to be back there?" He looked doubtful. "I'm not even sure I *ever* want to go there again."

"A lot of memories got dredged up as I saw things that reminded me of what life used to be. But I didn't have to do it alone. I stayed with Marjorie at her house, which helped. I also drove over with my friend, John. Do you remember the man who lived up the street in the big yellow house, the one whose wife was so ill? He and I ran into each other at Glenview Gardens one day and have become good friends. His wife was there until she died earlier this summer. He's part of the Irish book club."

"I don't remember you talking about him. Were you keeping him a secret for some reason?" Andrew's teasing tone was back, lightening the moment.

Laura thought for a moment. "To be honest, I'm not sure. Maybe it's because his wife just died, and I didn't want anyone to get the wrong impression. We're just good friends. He might rent out the space over Serendipities for his law office. He's also a criminal attorney."

"You need more decent guy friends. I don't think there's anything wrong with that. I sort of remember him." He looked away. "When Michael and I used to walk to and from school, he'd talk to us sometimes. He seemed like a nice guy."

"There's one more thing, Andrew." She looked into his eyes. "I've asked John to help me find out what happened to Michael. You and I know there wasn't a real investigation. I want to know what really happened, and I hope it's not too late for that. If something more happened than an accident, I want justice."

"We know who did it, Mom. It was that rat bastard, Luke, and his friends, Jason and Dan."

"Yes, we know they were there that day. We don't know details. We have to figure out how to get one of those boys to confess to what really happened. I believe one of them hit Michael with the oar and caused him to lose consciousness and drown."

"And John is going to help you with that? You're not going to confront those losers on your own, right?" He looked worried.

"Actually, my goal is to learn just enough that the investigation can be reopened. I'm telling you this because it's important for both of us to have closure."

"When Dad made that holy forgiveness scene, I knew I could never do it—forgive the ones who did this to my brother. But I also didn't think I could ever forgive Dad. One day a couple of months after he died, I went to the cemetery. I wanted to yell at him, call him out on all the stuff he did to us—to you. I really went off on him, cursing him, calling him the most awful names I could think of. And then something really strange happened."

"What was it?" For a few moments, Laura forgot to breathe.

"I felt Michael there. I didn't see him, but I felt him. It was as if he was assuring me that I could get past this—that I had to let go of the rage at Dad. It would do more harm to me in the long run than to Dad who was dead. It certainly wasn't going to bring Michael back."

"I do know what you mean. I had a similar experience at the lake on the anniversary of Michael's death." Laura said. "I was so angry and sad; I thought I might just walk into the water and join Michael in Heaven."

"You thought about killing yourself, Mom?" Andrew's eyes widened.

"It wasn't the plan, but once I got there, it seemed so much easier to die than to keep living with that pain. But then, I felt him there. He was with me, saving me. I knew he was fine, and that I was supposed to carry on." She brushed his face with her fingers. "I'm glad you told me what you experienced."

"But you still haven't forgiven the ones who killed him, right?" Andrew looked like a lost little boy. "I can't do that."

"I haven't really forgiven anyone, Andrew." Laura's eyes filled with tears. "I know it's important not to carry bitterness around in my heart, but until I know the truth about how it happened, I can't forgive anyone who was involved. That includes your father. But where he's concerned, I suppose it's time I tried forgiveness. It might be the only way to get rid of him. He still lives rent-free in my head."

As Laura worked on payroll that afternoon, she heard the ping of a text message. It was from Greg. *I need your birthdate in order to purchase your plane ticket.*

She texted back. *I'll reimburse you for the price of my ticket.*

In seconds, she had his response. *It was my idea to go and my decision for us to fly. Trust me, Laura, you can make it up to me.* He added an emoji of a smiley face that looked more like a leer than a smile. At least, he still wanted to go with her.

She took several deep breaths to quell the butterflies in her stomach. Hopefully, this would not turn out to be a mistake. Terri disliked him. Andrew disliked him, too. Even John seemed to have strong negative feelings about him, as evidenced by his behavior when the two men met in front of Serendipities. At what point might she have to admit that whatever chemistry she had with Greg might not be the ideal basis for a lasting relationship?

Chapter Twenty-Three

"**M**OMMA, I'M TAKING A TRIP TO CHICAGO this weekend with a friend," Laura announced as she and her mother ate dinner together in the dining room at Glenview Gardens. It would be irresponsible for her to leave town without letting her mother know. "I've never been to Chicago. I've never flown anywhere, actually. It'll be an adventure."

She decided not to mention that she was going with Greg. Though her mother had gotten more progressive as years went by, Laura felt certain this wouldn't extend to a weekend trip with a man who wasn't Laura's husband.

"Your father and I went to Chicago once," her mother mused. "Such a beautiful lake, and so much to see and do. We were there because Uncle Pat died, but we stayed for an extra day." She smiled at the memory. "If you take some photos, maybe I could paint a picture for you."

Laura's face brightened. "I meant to tell you that I saw the most beautiful sky the other day! I'm not an artist like you, but I thought how amazing it is that you can turn beautiful scenes into paintings. I wish I could do that, too."

"Now, don't be saying that. You're very creative. Just look at your beautiful store. Everything is arranged so nicely. Each area of the store is set up like the scene in a painting."

Laura smiled her thanks. "I'll have even more space to arrange pretty things, Momma. I'm buying the Serendipities store in Parmenter—the one Marjorie owns. I'll have two stores. Can you imagine?"

"More work, Laura?" Eileen didn't sound approving. "Doesn't the store here keep you busy enough?"

"It does, but the first Serendipities has always had a place in my heart. Marjorie can't stand the idea of selling it to anyone else. Neither can I."

"You always had a special something about you," her mother said, reaching over to stroke Laura's hair. "Had times been different, you could have gone to college, maybe. But that wasn't how our family did things, was it?"

"No." Laura's expression turned sad. "Did we waste our early years, Momma? Could we have had the dreams we had, the things we love, even sooner?"

"Regrets are a waste of time, Laura Rose," her mother said. She tasted a spoonful of her chicken noodle soup. "All those might-haves and should-haves don't mean a thing in the end. When life handed you lemons, you turned them into lemonade. Just look at you now, the owner of two stores. I'm proud of you, my girl."

"My lemonade is that much sweeter now," Laura said with a smile. "And you're right about regrets. I guess the bad stuff only matters if we don't learn from those experiences. Now I want to do all the things I couldn't do before."

"By chance, does that friend you're going to Chicago with . . . does he happen to be your nice young man, the one who visits me?"

Laura nearly choked on her soup. "My nice young man?"

"Why, yes. John. He's such a good person—so fond of you. He stops by at least once a week, and we talk. Sometimes we take short walks."

"What do you talk about?" Laura hadn't known that John was a regular visitor.

Eileen didn't answer the question, merely continued on. "He volunteers here. Sometimes he brings around the reading cart or delivers snacks. You didn't know that? Oh, he's a fine man."

Laura shook her head. John had never mentioned he was a regular volunteer at Glenview Gardens. "I guess it's not surprising. John is a good person."

"He comes in and plays cards with people, and he visits those who don't have family or many friends. He stops at my door to say hello, watches me paint sometimes. We talk a little bit about you—nothing you need to be concerned about."

Laura attempted an easy laugh. "I'm not that interesting, am I?"

"He seems to think so."

"Oh?" Laura's face turned scarlet.

"I believe he's been lonely, not just since his wife died, but for many years. Oh, sure, he had his routine, coming over here twice a day. It was all he knew: thinking about her, doing for her. All those years." She tut-tutted. "Now that his wife is gone, he has to figure out what is next."

"John is a lawyer with Ohio State. Did he tell you? He's got plans to go back into his law practice. That will keep him plenty busy."

"Work only gets you so far, I tell him. I say, 'Laura is like you that way. All she does is work.'" Eileen buttered her roll, glancing up to meet Laura's eyes, making her point. "If my opinion counts for anything, I think the two of you have lived long enough *for* other people. Now it's time to live for yourselves. What are you waiting for?"

"Oh, Momma. He's recently widowed. You aren't suggesting . . ."

Eileen smiled and held up her hand. "I'm not finished. When I say don't live your life for other people, it also means don't mind so much what other people think or say. People will always talk. Most of it isn't worth listening to."

"That is not how you raised me." Laura let out a short laugh.

"Oh, don't I know that." She shook her head. "Maybe I've learned a thing or two. I raised you to sacrifice yourself for others. It's what I did, and it's all I knew. But that doesn't mean I was always right. This life is about joy, not constant struggle. If you and John decide you want to be together, I say don't waste much more time. Neither of you is getting any younger, you know."

"Momma, it's not John I'm going to Chicago with."

"I guessed that." Eileen wiped the corners of her mouth with her napkin. "There has been enough judgment in this family. But I'm still your mother. Keep your wits about you in that big city, and don't forget the most important thing a woman needs to remember to protect."

"Her virtue." Laura put down her soup spoon.

Eileen let out a hearty laugh. "Virtue? I've got news for you. You've lived the virtuous life and look what it got you: Jed. Be particular about who you give your heart to. Make sure to pick a man who will always put your needs first."

"Thank you, Momma. I love you."

"I love you, too."

ON WEDNESDAY MORNING, LAURA PACKED and re-packed her small suitcase for the trip to Chicago. Greg had said they would dress up for dinner every night, but that she should bring several pair of comfortable walking shoes. When it came time to pack nightclothes, she chose a pale pink silk nightgown with spaghetti straps and a matching robe. It was entirely within the realm of her imagination that she and Greg would sleep together. Best to be prepared.

Being prepared extended to the other matter Greg had mentioned for the second time. After talking with her doctor, she decided to go with a new form of birth control, inserted under the skin of her arm. It was her first experience asking for birth control, never having used anything other than the rhythm method. She could tell by the raised eyebrow that the doctor was surprised, but at least, she hadn't said anything.

In fact, her doctor was matter-of-fact about contraception, insisting that Laura also use a back-up method for a period of weeks. She guided her through the process of inserting and removing the diaphragm until she felt confident. "You're at that age when accidental pregnancies happen because women think that part of their life is over . . . until they find out it's not," the doctor said. "Best to be safe. I've delivered enough 'whoopsie babies.'"

Laura texted Terri to tell her she had finally gotten birth control, but didn't receive a reply. Terri had been noticeably quiet the past two days after Laura shared that she and Greg were going to Chicago. She yearned to share the excitement and nervousness she was feeling with her best girlfriend. But that friend had made it clear she didn't approve of Greg.

"I hope Terri is okay," Laura said to Greg at dinner that evening. "I haven't heard back from her, and it's not like her. We talk every day, about everything."

Greg frowned. "Isn't it obvious? She's jealous of what we have." He cut his burger in half and then into quarters—his way of limiting the amount of food he ate. He took a bite, chewed slowly, and made direct eye contact. "Women do that, you know—not women like you, Laura. You're a generous person. I've seen it before with other women. They're the best of friends until one gets the guy. Then the friendship changes."

"Not Terri," Laura insisted. "She's my best friend. She was the one who suggested I open myself up to dating."

"It's part of maturing, babe. Face it: you're outgrowing Terri."

THE CALL THAT WOULD ALTER LAURA'S LIFE FOREVER happened at six-fifteen Thursday morning. She had just stepped out of the shower and was towel-drying her hair. She picked up the phone on the third ring. "This is Laura."

"Laura, this is Amanda Walker, head nurse at Glenview Gardens."

"Hello, Amanda. Is anything the matter?" Laura had never received a call from the head nurse. When her mother had fallen, the call had come from the charge nurse on that shift.

"I am so sorry, dear. Your mother passed away in her sleep. One of our nurses found her a little while ago when she took medication to her room."

"I just saw her Tuesday evening. We had dinner. She seemed fine." Laura stared into space. How was this possible? Her mother had been so full of life at dinner. She would never forget their last conversation. Her mother had understood far more than Laura ever realized.

"At her age, with her conditions, it can happen suddenly. We share your grief. Eileen was a wonderful woman, such a sweet soul. We loved caring for her. Such a marvelous way she had with her art. I do believe her days painting were happy ones." The nurse paused. "I'm so glad you were able to visit with her." Amanda spoke calmly in that way that nurses do when comforting family members. "I am certain she went peacefully."

"I don't know what to do." Laura felt the same as she had the day of Michael's death, with no idea how to take the next step, the next breath.

"We will need for you to come by today so that arrangements can be made to transport her to whichever funeral home you choose."

"Yes, of course. Her arrangements have already been made." Eileen had wanted to be cremated. "Let me finish dressing and I'll be right over."

She texted Terri. "My mom just died. Heading over there now."

Within a few seconds, she received her response. "I'm coming with you."

The next several days were a blur as Laura moved automatically through her day, answering questions and tending to the details of her mother's unexpected death. Since Eileen had been cremated, and there were no family members other than Laura and Andrew, the decision was made not to have a formal visitation. In the end, Laura and Andrew decided to keep things simple and welcome friends with an open house at Laura's home.

Eileen's ashes had been given to Laura in a small box. The thought had occurred to her, when Eileen shared her last wishes years earlier, that she would take her mother's ashes to her birthplace in Kenmare,

Ireland and scatter them there. It was a fitting tribute to the woman who had loved her homeland but had never returned.

On the day she learned of her mother's passing, Laura texted John with the news. It wasn't more than forty-five minutes later that he arrived at her doorstep with an arrangement of flowers and a sympathy card. "How can I help?" he asked. "Put me to work."

"I can't think right now," she said, exhaustion taking over as tears filled her eyes.

He pulled her to him, patting her back as she cried. "I understand," he said.

The next day, Marjorie came from Parmenter to help run the store and kept Laura focused on matters at hand. "You gave your mother the most wonderful gift, having her stay here, then helping her transition to another place when it was time," she said. "You allowed her dignity and grace."

Terri stayed with Laura, too, camped out on the living room sofa so that Marjorie could have the guest bedroom. Andrew and Emily appeared every few hours, always there just when Laura needed a hand. She assigned them tasks that seemed beyond her physical limits: picking up items at the grocery store for the open house and helping to pack boxes containing her mother's personal effects. Laura donated her mother's furniture, knowing they would only bring sadness when she saw them. She understood why John hadn't wanted furnishings as reminders of Jackie. Her mother's worldly possessions fit into six boxes, which were stored in Laura's guest room closet. These mementos of her mother's life would be sorted later when Laura felt better able to face them.

Greg's reaction to hearing the news had resulted in a particularly distressing moment for Laura. Their trip to Chicago had to be postponed. She thought he would drop everything to be with her. That had not happened.

"I'm sorry for your loss," he said, sounding so formal that Laura's fragile heart, already decimated by grief, shriveled like a balloon losing all its air. "I'm sure she was a nice lady. I'll take care of cancelling the plane tickets and the hotel." He paused. "Maybe we can go some other time. Let me know if there is anything I can do."

Be with me. "Thank you." She waited for him to say more, perhaps an acknowledgment of the depth of her loss. But that didn't seem to be his way.

It was she who broke the silence. "Please come by on Sunday for the open house." Hearing nothing, she finished, "It would mean a lot to me."

IT WASN'T A SURPRISE THAT EVERY MEMBER of the Irish book club came to the open house. A few brought appetizers and desserts. Others brought casseroles, containers of soup, a tray of cookies, or homemade pie. Jan had been the one to communicate the news to the members. "Everyone in the group loves you so much, Laura," she said.

Many of Laura's customers appreciated being invited upstairs to her home. Some spoke of the feelings of welcome and comfort they received in the store, which now seemed an extension of Laura's living space. Laura felt the same. Upstairs or downstairs, Serendipities Two was home.

Greg's absence at the open house spoke volumes. Even more painful was the wall she felt go up between them during the week following her mother's death. As two, then three days passed without hearing from him, she began to consider the possibility that Greg might have flaws she hadn't recognized before. There were signs she had tried to ignore, namely his lack of emotional response and the awkwardness she witnessed when he interacted with her family and friends. But perhaps she expected too much too soon.

From her previous role as a pastor's wife, Laura knew all too well that some people weren't good at handling death. They coped by distancing themselves. Greg likely was one of those people. She would be patient and wait for his call or text message.

Later that week, as Laura arranged a cherished collection of used books in the library room, she heard bells jangle on the shop's front door. A few moments later, she saw Anne, the customer whose husband worked with Greg at Lionsgate Corporation. "Anne, how nice to see you!" she said, hurrying to greet her.

"Laura, I saw in the newspaper that your mother passed away. I am so sorry for your loss." They exchanged hugs. "I came to see if you'd like to come to a barbeque at our house on Sunday. Feel free to bring someone, if you like."

"Thank you! I could ask Greg Waters. I've been seeing him since we met at the library gala."

The look of surprise and discomfort that crossed Anne's face was definitely not Laura's imagination. "Oh." Anne's cheeks flushed with high color. "I don't know quite how to say this. Greg is bringing someone else."

"Oh, my gosh," Laura said, covering her face with her hands. "I didn't know he . . ." She couldn't finish. The pain in her chest felt as sharp as the sting of humiliation. "I shouldn't have assumed we were exclusive. But we were planning a weekend trip together . . . until my mother died. Then I couldn't go." She knew she was rambling. Her voice trailed off.

Anne's expression was full of compassion. She touched Laura's arm. "You're still welcome, of course, but under the circumstances, you might not want to come."

"No, I guess I'd better not. Thank you for inviting me, though."

"Some other time." Anne moved toward the door as she spoke. Laura could tell she was anxious to get away. "I'm sorry about having to tell you about Greg. Really, I had no idea you were dating him. If it's any consolation, he is a bit of a player, as they say. There was no way you could have known."

"Don't be sorry. I'm glad to know the truth. It would have been awful if I had shown up, only to see him there with another woman."

Her first dating experience had been a disaster. She would be more cautious next time, if there was a next time. In the meantime, she played the details in her head over and over, thinking of the many mistakes she had made.

"Shake it off," Terri advised. She had rushed over as soon as Laura texted her the news. "There are good men out there. He just wasn't one of them."

"You tried to tell me. I wouldn't listen," Laura said. "How could I have been so stupid? All the signs were there. I guess I wanted things to be different."

"You wouldn't be the first woman to give a man the benefit of the doubt only to find out that he's a heel. Don't beat yourself up over it. Just move on."

"I don't think I want to," Laura said. "I don't have the heart for it."

Chapter Twenty-Four

O VER THE NEXT MONTH, LAURA TOOK STEPS toward assuming ownership of the original Serendipities store. Since she and Marjorie were in agreement on every point of the sale, it was a relatively easy matter for John to draw up paperwork.

"How often will you be in Parmenter?" he asked, handing her a small stack of papers to sign. "I imagine you'll want to keep a close eye on things for a while."

"I'll go as often as I need to, at least for the first year. Actually, I'm going over Friday. I want to be at Ruth's house when the boys' beds are delivered." She signed one of the documents where John had marked it with a yellow sticker, *Sign here*. "Marjorie will arrange to have the truck deliver it, but I want Ruth to know that I'm her friend."

"Does she know that you bought the beds for her? Does her husband know about the beds?" John sounded uneasy.

"I don't know. Marjorie said she accepted twenty-five dollars from Ruth just so there was an exchange of money—in case her husband was suspicious."

"If you're going to their house, you ought to have someone with you," he said. "Marjorie should go, too."

"All I'm going to do is stop by and make sure it gets set up the way she wants it."

"When?"

"The truck will be there by eleven o'clock. I don't think it will take long."

"Are you planning to ask her any questions about the case? If so, I'd recommend easing into the subject. Start out by saying you remember her from when Michael was in school with her. Ask her what she remembers about Michael."

"That's a good idea. Mother to mother. It might be naïve of me to think she'd actually tell me anything she knows about what her husband did."

"She can't be forced to testify against her husband, you know. What we need is enough information to get the case reopened," John said. "It won't be easy."

"I know the odds are against me. But I have to try. It isn't just about justice for my son anymore. I also want to help Ruth."

"She may not want your help." John leaned back in his chair. "Laura, not everyone is like you."

She smiled. "I appreciate that you believe I'm strong. I wasn't always." She bit her lip. "She may not think anyone *can* help. I know what that's like. I didn't think I had options. If I had tried to leave Jed, he would have followed me. I would have needed a restraining order."

John's expression was grim. "If she talks to you about anything she knows, she could put herself in danger."

"I know." Laura chewed on the inside of her lower lip. "If she can just give me something to go on, some little hint, I can figure out another way without putting her at risk. There has to be another way, John. There just has to be."

John glanced at his watch. "It's almost five-thirty. Do you have dinner plans?"

"I could whip up something." She grinned. "I'll admit, though, a burger and fries would taste way better."

"I agree. A burger joint." He stood up and slid into the sleeves of his suit jacket. "Oh, wait. This won't cause problems for you, will it? I mean, if you and I have dinner together?"

"I think Greg and I are officially over." Laura frowned. "You're my friend." She crossed her arms over her chest. "I do as I please."

John raised one eyebrow and smiled. "Spoken like a woman who knows her own mind."

HER CELL PHONE RANG THE NEXT MORNING as she dressed for work. Greg's caller ID appeared on the screen. Laura's heart leaped into her throat as she considered whether to let the call go to voicemail. She didn't feel ready to talk with him. Now that she knew he was seeing another woman, Greg was probably calling to tell her he didn't want to date her anymore. It would be easier to let him end the relationship.

"This is Laura," she answered in a formal tone.

"Hi, babe. Just wondering how you're doing," he said.

She registered the word *babe*. "I'm fine, thank you. And you?"

"I'm good, actually. I'm sure you're wondering why I've been out of touch recently. I want to apologize." He paused.

Laura listened. Was it possible that he had a reasonable excuse for his absence? No phone call or even a text message in over a week—the week after her mother died?

"Work has been brutal lately—long hours and an unexpected trip out of town for a couple of days last week. I knew you had a lot going on with your mother dying and so forth. It just seemed like a good time to give you the space you needed."

"The space I needed?" Surely, he wasn't serious. "Yes, it was a difficult time, and there were many details. But it would have been nice to at least hear from you. I thought we meant more to each other."

"My bad. I don't deal very well with death."

"I don't know anyone who does." Disgust tainted her words. "You go through it one moment at a time supported by the people who care about you."

"Look, I can tell you're mad. I just wanted to reach out and see if we can have a do-over. I still have your plane ticket to Chicago. How does next weekend look for you?"

Laura was shocked. Anger roiled up in her stomach. He was seeing another woman and yet still expected that she would go on a weekend trip with him. It was the first time in her life she could remember feeling this kind of clarity, certain of exactly what to say and do. She would be the one to end this relationship. "I think you should get a refund on that ticket and take your other girlfriend."

"What are you talking about?" She heard the inflection of hurt in his voice that she now recognized as false and manipulative.

"You don't have to pretend any longer, Greg. I ran into a friend who knows you, and learned that you are seeing someone else."

"We never agreed to be exclusive, Laura," he wheedled.

"The thing is, Greg, I'm not the kind of woman who can go off on a weekend trip with a man knowing we are not exclusive. I want more from a relationship."

"If that's the way you view this, I guess there's nothing more to say. You're a terrific person, and I hope we can stay friends."

This was not the kind of friendship she could imagine, either. "Thank you for the enjoyable times we've shared. Good-bye, Greg."

SHE DOVE INTO HER WORK, intent on improvements to the store in Parmenter. Although she and John had discussed the idea of him renting the second floor above the store for his law practice, Laura decided to turn that space into a second-hand bookstore and coffee shop.

"I think it's a stroke of brilliance," John said when she shared the news.

Andrew agreed, saying, "Mom, that is such a great idea!" His beaming smile brought instant pleasure. Andrew's opinions meant the world to her. "Parmenter needs a cool place like that."

She laid her hand on his cheek. "I'm planning to do online sales, too," she said. "Will you be my consultant on the website and help me with all those pesky marketing and sales details?"

Andrew grinned. "I'm starting my own consulting firm. You can be my first client."

AFTER GREG, IT JUST SEEMED A GOOD IDEA to remain unattached. Dating had been more stressful than fun. And, after all, she had Andrew and Emily and all her friends. The book club offered its own social structure. She had a good life without a man. Perhaps love wasn't in the cards for her.

Most nights, she stayed up late reading. The Irish book club had a new assignment for the December meeting, *Angela's Ashes*, by Frank McCourt. Laura had read the acclaimed bestseller some twenty years earlier—in secret, for Jed hadn't approved.

She had borrowed the book from the Parmenter library when she took Andrew and Michael on their weekly visit. It was such a satisfying book; she had lost all track of time while reading it. So engrossed was she in the heartaches and antics of the McCourt family that she had nearly been caught red-handed—reading the novel while standing over the kitchen sink.

Fortunately, hearing Jed whistling a hymn as he made his way up the back walkway, she managed to stuff the novel inside a near-empty Bisquick box on the counter. Jed never suspected a thing. From then on, all of her library books went into the Bisquick box. As time went on, it became a recurring act of willful disobedience. She didn't agree that books were dangerous. Small-minded, mean-spirited people were the real dangers.

Now she could read whatever she liked, whenever she wanted. While she dated Greg, she had fallen behind on her reading. Curling up with her books felt comforting and safe. "I don't think I'm cut out for romance," she told Terri.

"You just need time to recover," Terri assured her. "Greg wasn't good enough for you. It was a hard lesson, but it could have been much so worse. Imagine if you had slept with him while he was involved with someone else."

"How will I know when I'm over this?" Laura asked, her voice quavering.

"When the time is right, and when the man is the right one, you'll know." Terri handed her a gift-wrapped box. "Here, I saw this and thought of you." It was a fabric-covered journal with a matching pen.

"A diary! It's so pretty. Would you believe I've never had one before?"

"It's amazing what stuff comes out of your head when you write things down—very therapeutic. Later on, you'll read your entries and see how much you've grown and changed in your attitudes or in the things you want." Terri's look was rueful. "I started journaling during the most difficult year of my life. My husband and I had just split up. Then I had a series of rebound relationships. Then a guy stalked me."

"You've never told me that!" Laura was surprised that Terri had never shared such a terrible story with her. "Why didn't you ever say anything?"

"If you keep talking about a past experience, all you're doing is keeping it alive. That's in the past. If I continue talking about it and thinking about what happened, I have to live through it all over again."

"I've heard you say that before. But it's hard to let things go."

"I don't know why bad memories seem stronger than good ones. Maybe it's a self-defense mechanism. For a couple of years, I kept all of my notebooks from that time. I wrote what I was feeling every day to help me process what was happening. At first, I thought I contributed to the problem, when really, all I did was be polite and nice to him. He followed Street, so wherever we performed, he'd be there. When I look back on it, I see how it all unfolded. Finally, I stopped blaming myself."

"I do blame myself for what happened with Greg. I should have listened to you."

"Shoulds are a waste of time. It's what you do with the lesson learned from it that counts."

As she drove into Parmenter that Friday, Laura noted the businesses in the two-block radius near Serendipities. The library was across town, so a used book store on the second floor of her building was likely to have good foot traffic. With a coffee shop offering coffees, teas, and baked items, along with sandwiches and soups, Serendipities should see a nice uptick in customers. There was no elevator, so a chair lift would ensure compliance for those with disabilities.

Marjorie was enthusiastic when Laura told her of the plans. "What a marvelous idea! It would have been too much for me to handle, but I can visualize what you're thinking."

"I'd like to keep our suppliers local. That way, I can make sure we're getting the best possible products. That will be a shot in the arm for other local businesses, too. That's the biggest thing I learned in Dublin: that all ships rise when we buy and shop local."

Taking over the management of the original Serendipities store had been easier than Laura expected. She had already started a second Serendipities location from scratch, learning by doing. This time, she knew all the potential pitfalls as well as the opportunities. Taking risks was part of being an entrepreneur. Walking around the Parmenter store each time she visited, she felt a sense of accomplishment, of competence. She felt confident she could make Serendipities even more successful.

Lately, she had begun to think more about how her self-confidence had grown over the past two years. Everyone she knew thought she was smart, interesting, and successful. From Marjorie, who had believed in her first, to Terri and Jan, Andrew, Emily, and now John, each one had let her know how they viewed her. So, why then, was it still hard for her to see herself the same way?

She had to acknowledge that it was only memories of the past that kept her fettered to an old opinion of herself. As a member of the Dublin downtown business community, she was well aware that every year, new businesses started and sometimes failed. She had been at risk to be one of those business failures. And yet, she had managed to make her store a success.

Remembering something Jed had said to her, she bit her lip. She had mentioned to him that she might like to have her own business. Like a shot, he had retorted that she wasn't smart enough. But that wasn't true. She now owned two successful stores. Jed had been wrong about her. He had been wrong about so many things.

She arrived at Serendipities at nine-thirty Friday morning and did a quick review of accounts payable and receivable. Marjorie was still at the store a few hours each day, easing into retirement. Laura smiled as she reviewed the ledgers. Lucky for her, Marjorie was meticulous about records and bookkeeping.

As she set her purse under the counter, her cell phone rang. It was Marjorie. "I'm heading over to the store to keep an eye on things while you're gone," she said. "I still don't like the idea of you going over to Ruth's house. Be careful."

"I will. And it won't take long. I just want to have a friendly conversation that opens the door for the future," Laura replied. "With any luck, maybe I can convince her I'm not the enemy."

Chapter Twenty-Five

Ruth and Luke Forrest lived in a neighborhood of compact houses originally built for returning World War Two servicemen and their families. The simple two-story homes featured brick and frame exteriors. Over the years, many of the homes had been updated and enlarged. Ruth and Luke's home was well-tended with a profusion of colorful chrysanthemums in front and a vegetable garden on one side. Someone had a green thumb.

As she waited in her car for Serendipities' delivery driver to arrive, Laura surveyed the house and yard. She saw two metal lawn chairs with green-and-white webbing arranged side-by-side on the porch. A red tricycle and small blue bike with training wheels were parked beside the front steps of the porch. From all appearances, this was a happy family with young children.

Laura had promised Marjorie that she would remain in her car until the truck from Serendipities arrived. She looked in her sideview mirror and saw the white box truck turn the corner onto the street. She waited until it came to a full stop before she exited her car. The driver whose name was Ed had been a delivery driver for Serendipities since Marjorie opened the store.

"Hi, Ed!" Laura greeted him with a hug. "It's great to see you!"

"I hear you're the new boss," Ed said enthusiastically, sporting his characteristic grin. He was not an employee of Serendipities, but Marjorie treated him as if he was.

"I feel as if I've come full circle," Laura said. "I never expected to actually own Serendipities. Marjorie gave me my start, you know."

"She knew exactly what she was doing," he said. "You're the best person to take over the store."

"That's sweet of you to say." She smiled, taking in his words. Ed wasn't the kind of man to dole out compliments easily. "Hey, this delivery should be pretty quick. I'll greet Mrs. Forrest and signal when she's ready for you to bring in those beds."

"Sounds good," he said, and headed to the back of the truck to begin unloading the trundle bed frames and mattresses.

Now that the moment had arrived to see Ruth, Laura was relieved Ed was there. With a sense of mounting trepidation, she walked across the front yard and up the four concrete steps to the front porch. Opening the screen door, she rapped lightly on the door. From inside, she heard the strains of the theme song from "Sesame Street" and Ruth's voice admonishing her sons to sit still and watch their show.

The door opened slowly. Laura noticed Ruth's face before any greeting could be spoken. A purple bruise covered the left side of the young woman's face beginning just below the eye and extending to the hairline. Her lip was cut and swollen, still oozing blood.

"I didn't know you'd be here, too," Ruth said with difficulty. Her swollen mouth prevented easy speech.

"Oh, Ruth." Laura couldn't take her eyes off the young woman's ravaged face. She recoiled, hand over her heart. "Oh my God. When did he do this to you?"

"It was just a stupid fall down the stairs," Ruth said, evading Laura's eyes. "I was carrying a laundry basket."

The monotone voice, so practiced at this type of excuse, couldn't fool Laura. How many times had she made a similar statement, a studied look of silly-me contrition on her face? *Thou shalt not lie.* Those excuses for Jed's abuse had all been lies. Yet, Jed had approved of those lies.

She turned slowly and gestured to Ed. It would be nice to prepare him for what he was about to see. Ed made his way up the front walkway, carrying the headboard protected by a quilted cover.

"Ma'am, where would you like this?" he started to say and then stopped speaking, as Laura had done, when he saw Ruth's face. He looked questioningly at Laura, who nodded.

"This way." Ruth opened the door wide and walked through the front hallway.

Laura and Ed followed her inside. Two little boys sat motionless, quiet in a way that little boys rarely are, watching with eyes too large for their small faces. They were neatly dressed in matching outfits.

"Hi, boys," Laura said, smiling. "Are you excited to be getting new big boy beds?"

Ruth stared at Laura. "Will this take long?"

"We'll be as quick as we can," Laura said, moving down the short hallway toward the kitchen. "Ruth, let's get out of the way and let the driver finish up."

They stepped into the spotless kitchen that still smelled of breakfast bacon and toast—so familiar, it turned Laura's stomach for a second. Four strips of center-cut bacon, two eggs over medium, white toast— Jed's daily breakfast.

She was careful to keep her voice low. "Ruth, I can see what has happened to you. You don't have to make an excuse, not to me. I know. My husband used to hurt me, too."

"Not Pastor Jed." Ruth winced as she tried to form the words without moving her upper lip.

"Yes, Pastor Jed. I can't tell you the number of times he did the same thing to me. I want to help you."

"I don't need your help. I'm fine. We're fine." Ruth looked fearfully around, glancing at the back door. "You shouldn't have come."

"I own the Serendipities store now, Ruth. I wanted to make sure . . ."

"You shouldn't have come. My husband won't like it that you're here."

"I understand." Laura made direct eye contact. "Just know that if you need help, there are people who care—who understand. I didn't know that when the same thing was happening to me."

Ruth started to speak and put a hand over her sore mouth. Laura waited, listening to the sounds of a Muppet song coming from the living room. She knew Ruth didn't want her children to hear their conversation. "Best we go outside," Ruth said into her hand.

They walked down the front porch steps and out into the yard. Ruth stopped, looking up with a mixture Laura recognized as fear and helplessness. The young woman's lip had started bleeding again.

Laura reached into her handbag for a tissue and handed it to her. She spoke in a low, gentle voice. "I came today for two reasons. For the beds, yes. But I also hoped we could get better acquainted. Do you remember when you were in my Sunday School class? I've known you since you were tiny. I don't like what I see."

Ruth's fingers touched the bruise under her eye. "I told you, it's nothing. I've had worse."

Laura sighed. How often had she explained away unusual bruises to members of the congregation, to the children's librarian who had once pulled her aside during story time to ask if she needed help? To her doctor who had asked during a routine exam whether she was safe?

"I remember every single one of my injuries, even though they happened over more than twenty years. It stopped when my husband died."

Ruth looked disbelieving. "He was a minister, a man of God! He couldn't have done such a thing."

"Ruth, my husband beat me so often, I was scared to death of him. Every time he hurt me, he said I deserved it."

"Did you? Seems like husbands have reasons to be mad at their wives when we don't listen or move fast enough."

Laura's eyes widened in horror. "What exactly does 'fast enough' even mean? Has Luke ever hit you for something you had no control over? For things you didn't know he would get mad about? When he was simply in a bad mood?" This was a point any abused woman could comprehend. "There is never a good reason to hurt someone, especially someone in your family, someone you promised to love."

"Why did you come back to Parmenter? Look at you," Ruth said, her expression a mixture of derision and wistfulness. "You with your expensive outfits and your stylish hair and makeup and stuff. You don't belong here anymore."

"Ruth, I do belong here." Laura's gaze was direct, firm yet gentle. "I just bought the Serendipities shop from Marjorie. I also own a second Serendipities store over in the Columbus area. It's my business. I'll be here a lot more now."

"My husband doesn't want me talking to you." Ruth glanced around, clearly anxious.

Laura remembered the petite girl with a tangle of golden ringlets whose plain hand-me-down dresses were always at least a size too big for her. She had grown into a young beauty, and Luke had claimed her for his own.

Now she appeared colorless, her once lustrous blonde hair lackluster, tied back in a low bun. She wore a shapeless blue dress that hung on her too-thin frame. In that moment, Laura saw Ruth as a frightened child. She wanted to take the girl in her arms but dared not.

"Ruth, standing here, seeing how afraid you are, my only wish is to erase those bruises I see, make the pain from that split lip go away. At this moment, all I care about is you. It's like looking at myself not so long ago. I want to help, if I can."

"You can't help. No one can." Ruth's expression of pure misery spoke volumes about the utter hopelessness she felt. Laura understood that feeling only too well. "I can't leave him—not with the boys still so little." Ruth shifted from one foot to the other. "Anyway, I got nowhere to go and nothing I know how to do, other than be a wife and mom."

"That's what I thought, too. But I was always arranging things to make homes look pretty. I used to shop at Serendipities. Then I started working there with Marjorie. Now I own the store. Dreams have a way of working out. I hear you're a wonderful baker."

Ruth's dull eyes brightened a little. "I had a part-time job in the bakery at Bob's Shop Rite. They even let me make wedding cakes." She shrugged. "Luke didn't like watching the boys, changing diapers. He said I needed to be home for him and the kids."

"My husband didn't allow me to work, either. But life has a funny way of making things happen that we could never have expected. Someday, things could be different for you. Who knows? You could end up with your own little business. I used to dream about my own store, and now look. I own Serendipities."

"I was afraid you were here for another reason."

"What would that be?" Laura's heart began beating wildly.

"Luke says you're here to make trouble for him."

"I believe your husband had something to do with my son's death," Laura answered abruptly. "He was in that boat when Michael died."

Ruth said nothing, and her expression gave nothing away. "Michael was nice. I'm sorry it happened."

"Do you know what happened?" Laura asked. She couldn't stop herself. "I never understood how or what happened. I've never been able to recover from it. It would help so much if I could understand the truth."

"Luke hates people like Michael," Ruth said, shaking her head. "It would kill him if either of our sons . . ." She stopped, coloring to the roots of her blonde hair. "I'm sorry, but in our church, that's a sin."

"What is?" Laura needed her to say it.

"Luke says your son was a sinner."

"My son was an innocent boy, a good boy. He didn't deserve to die," Laura said, struggling to maintain her composure. She felt her hands ball into fists.

"That's not what Luke thinks."

"Ruth, your husband isn't right about many things. It isn't right to hurt you and mistreat your children." The anger she felt was nearly at a boiling point, but she had to remain calm.

They heard Ed's cheerful whistle, clearly intended to let them know of his presence, as he emerged from the house and met up with them on the sidewalk. "I'm all done here," he said. "Hope the little ones like their new beds." He started to hand the clipboard to Ruth. "Ma'am, could you just sign here?"

Laura intercepted the clipboard with a smile. "I'll take care of finishing up. You can get on to the next stop. Thanks so much, Ed."

The driver tipped his cap at them. Ruth signed for the delivery as Ed got into his truck and pulled away from the curb. Laura accepted the pen and clipboard from Ruth, exchanging them for a business card. "Keep this handy—in a safe place," she advised her. "You never know when you might need help."

Ruth tucked the card in her dress pocket and nodded. "You'd best get out of here," she said. "My husband . . ."

"Did you tell her?" A male voice boomed, and Luke emerged from the back of the house, his beefy face purple with rage.

"She already knows," Ruth said, backing away fearfully, even as Laura unconsciously stepped in front of her like a shield.

"Get in the house," he barked at Ruth who scampered up the front steps and into the house like a frightened child. She slammed the front door. Laura hoped she would take the children upstairs and shut them safely away from their father. It was already too late to protect Ruth—or herself.

Luke stomped across the grass until he stood inches from Laura's face. "You don't know nothing about what happened!" he said.

"Oh, I do know." She made direct eye contact. "I know all about what you did." She didn't need to state that Ruth's battered face was evidence enough of what he had done. "What you did is wrong."

"Your son was unnatural! It's a sin to be like he was!"

Laura felt her knees shaking but planted her feet firmly, forcing herself not to move. What was he saying? Luke was a man with anger management issues. When angry, men like Luke could be their own worst enemy. It was vital at this moment that she keep him talking and remember everything he said. She forced a dismissive laugh that even to her own ears sounded strangled. She was so scared, she fought vertigo. "You're wrong."

"I'm not wrong." The look on his face turned murderous. "At least, I won't have to see your son in hell because I know that's where he went. I'll be in heaven."

"I sincerely doubt that." She could smell his hot, sour breath in her face.

He spit out his next words. "Someone had to do something about guys like him who aren't real men. You're as bad as he is, owning a business, acting like a man. You'd better shut up before I shut you up." He jabbed his finger hard into her shoulder blade, emphasizing his words. "Like I did him."

She winced from his forceful touch but didn't move. Would this admission alone be enough? She forced herself to remain calm and shook her head as if not believing him, expressing doubt about what he could do. This was a dangerous tactic. She knew better than anyone what could happen next. What if he struck her? From somewhere inside came a strength she hadn't known she possessed. She had to be brave.

"Luke, I know who you really are. You're not man enough to do anything like that to me. I bet you weren't even the one responsible that day. Some other boy with more courage killed my son. You were just a weak boy, a boy with silly notions about what was right and wrong."

He shoved her backward with one hand, causing her to stumble. But she righted herself. "Now you've gone too far, bitch. Of course, I did it. I killed him, and there's nothing you can do about it. You can't prove anything."

"There's something I can do about it." At that moment, John stepped out from behind the bushes from the other side of the house. "Don't lay another finger on her—or your wife and kids."

Luke's face registered shock and something more. It was the realization that there were two witnesses to what he had just said. "Who the hell are you?"

"I'm an attorney and someone who just heard you confess to the murder of this woman's son. Someone who just saw you accost her. Someone who also saw your wife's injuries and heard her say you made them." John stepped forward.

"You can't prove anything. He's been dead and buried for years. I'll deny everything," Luke said.

He moved toward John just as they heard a siren approaching. A police cruiser, lights flashing, stopped in front of the house, and two officers emerged, guns drawn. They approached Luke. One of the officers said, "Luke Forrest! Face down on the ground and don't move."

"I didn't do nothing. These two are causing trouble for me and my family," Luke protested. "You should arrest them!" But he complied with the officer's order to get on the ground.

"Luke Forrest, you're under arrest."

Chapter Twenty-Six

"Thank goodness, you called the police," Laura said to John as he reached her side, guiding her away from the flurry of actions the police were taking. Luke's hands were cuffed, and he was read his rights. "He could have attacked both of us."

"I didn't call the police, Laura. A neighbor must have done it. Are you okay?" he asked, his arm around her waist, partially holding her up.

Laura's heart pounded in her chest. Her breathing was shallow and rapid. Sweat trickled down her back. The adrenaline that had kept her upright throughout the ordeal was gone now, and she felt shaky and light-headed. Despite her efforts to appear calm, she had been terrified. Luke had believed her to be alone and defenseless, and had unleashed what she recognized as lethal anger. She already knew he had no qualms about hurting a woman.

"I'm fine—just a little shaken up," she said to John, giving him a weak smile. "I sure am glad you showed up. Speaking of that, how did you know . . .?"

"When we talked the other day, you mentioned what time you'd be here." He paused and grinned. "I figured I'd better get here, too. I'm your attorney, you know." He grinned.

"Thanks," she said. "You're more than my attorney. You're actually more like my hero. How is it that you seem to show up at the most opportune times?" Hadn't he been there twice for her on the day Jed died?

"Fate, I guess." He studied her for a moment. "You're white as a sheet."

"I'm fine," she insisted. Thoughts began falling into place as her head cleared. "Thank goodness, Luke didn't see you until after he confessed. John, he actually admitted to killing Michael! I can hardly believe it."

"Two of us heard him say it. He can't deny it."

"Ma'am, do you need medical attention?" one of the police officers asked. His partner had Luke stowed in the back seat of the police cruiser.

"I'm okay, just a little shaken up," she said. She glanced anxiously toward the house. The front door remained shut.

"Don't go anywhere yet," the officer said to her and John as he returned to the car and got on the radio, communicating with the dispatcher.

"I have to make sure Ruth is okay," Laura told John. "Poor thing is probably scared out of her mind."

Feeling steadier, Laura made her way to the front door. It would be a normal reaction for a wife to come to her husband's defense after seeing him arrested. But the door remained shut. Laura knocked and waited. She knocked again, but no one answered. Turning the knob, the door opened with a creak made even louder by the silence inside the house. As frightened as Ruth must have been, she had known better than to lock her husband out of the house.

"Ruth!" she called up the stairs. "It's Laura. The police are here. You're safe."

She moved from room to room, checking under beds and in closets. She called Ruth's name again at the entrance to the cellar door before realizing that she and the children were gone.

Laura went downstairs, through the kitchen, and outside to the back yard. A driveway behind the house led to an alley. She walked toward the alley and found a worn stuffed rabbit on the gravel driveway. She looked to the left and right, wondering which direction Ruth might have taken. In an instant, it hit her. *She took his truck!*

She hurried around to the front yard. "She's not here. I think she took his truck."

"She's already at the police station," one of the officers said. "She showed up there with the kids and told the desk sergeant what was happening. She was afraid of what her husband would do to you." He indicated Luke with a nod of his head. "That's why we're here. We need to ask you a few questions, ma'am. You, too, sir."

In response to the officer's questions, Laura recounted briefly what had happened when she and her driver delivered the trundle beds. She described her horror at seeing Ruth's injuries. "I tried to help her. I knew the danger she was in. I saw her face and . . ."

"She's receiving medical treatment now," the officer said.

Laura took in a deep breath and let it out slowly. "I always believed Luke was responsible for my son's death," she said. "Today, he admitted it—to me, and John heard it. But there were others in the boat, too, that day."

"Mr. Forrest will be questioned. What happens after that is up to him," one of the officers said. "Of course, you and Mr. Conway will need to talk with our detectives. We'll need you to think hard about all the details as far back as you remember."

"I'll never forget anything about what happened." Laura flinched, remembering the shock at hearing her son was dead, the intense grief, the anger that she had never quite been able to tamp down.

The officers headed toward their vehicle. "You can follow us to the station."

"You okay to drive?" John asked, taking her by the elbow. She allowed him to guide her toward her car while troubling thoughts paraded through her head. Though they were safe now, and Luke was in custody, Ruth's troubles weren't over—not by a long shot.

"What Ruth did—going to the police and reporting what she knew— took so much courage," Laura said, letting out a deep breath. "I hope she follows through with pressing charges against him for the latest beating. He can't deny that, either." Her face clouded over, and she put a hand over her heart.

"What are you thinking?" John asked.

"Luke could get out on bail, right?"

"I would think with these charges, bail would be pretty steep. But, yes, he could." John took her hand, warming it between his. "I know you won't rest while you think she's in danger. But you have to understand it's her choice, her life."

"If she's living in the house and he gets out, her life will be even more miserable." Laura felt sick to her stomach. "She's the reason he got caught." She swallowed hard. "*I'm* the reason she turned him in. She was helping me. I can't let her face this by herself, John."

"I'm sure you'll do everything you can to help her. By the way, you did an amazing job today," he said, letting out a low, appreciative whistle. "A criminal investigator couldn't have set that confession up any better than you did."

"I was desperate to keep him away from Ruth. Then things took a different turn. I just reacted and tried not to pass out." She sat down in the driver's seat of her car.

"What you said to him, not correcting his misperception? He thought you were talking about the beating." He chuckled and shook his head. "Then, when you questioned his manhood . . ." He took in a deep breath and shook his head. "No detective could have done a better job. But I really thought he was going to punch you."

"So did I."

"You are really something, Laura Fisher." He slapped the roof of her car. "See you in a few minutes." He went to his car.

Laura pulled down the driver's side visor and checked her face. She was beginning to get a little color in her complexion. She started the engine and followed John downtown. He pulled into a diagonal parking space in front of Parmenter's police station and she took the space beside his.

They met on the sidewalk in front of the police station. "Well, this is it," she said. "I'm sure this will be an ordeal in itself, but I have faith that justice will finally be served."

"You can do it. You've got the strength of ten people," John said. "It hasn't been that long since you were in Ruth's position. Given everything you've been through, your willingness to put yourself in harm's way for her sake . . . Well, it makes me admire you even more."

Laura blushed. "I'm just glad you were there."

"We make a pretty good team," he said. "Are you ready?"

"As ready as I'll ever be."

They walked through the double glass doors into the lobby of the police station and approached the front desk. Over the next two hours, they related their accounts of what had happened at the Forrests' house, and then waited another two hours while files were pulled from the day of Michael's death.

Laura had been right. There had been very little done in the way of an investigation. Her son's death had been ruled an accidental drowning, based on the statements given by the other boys. Jed sat with the other boys at the police station, praising them for their efforts to get help. They were released to their parents. For Laura, Jed's refusal to stand with his own son was the ultimate betrayal. She'd had no voice then. Things were different now.

LUKE WAS ARRAIGNED THE NEXT MORNING on homicide charges in the death of Michael Fisher. The two other men, Jason and Dan, who had been in the boat that day, said Luke had been the one to strike Michael with the side of a canoe paddle while the boy's back was turned to him. After Michael was in the water, Jason and Dan claimed to have had a change of heart and wanted to help him, but Luke had threatened them if they tried to rescue the unconscious boy.

Three days after his arrest, Luke's father and two uncles posted bail, and Luke went home to Ruth and the children. Although Jason and Dan had been involved in the incident, there was a statute of limitations since they were accessories to the crime. They were released.

Luke also was charged with domestic abuse and child abuse. The evidence on Ruth's face, the history of broken bones and lacerations requiring x-rays and stitches, were too obvious to ignore. When questioned by an officer, in the presence of a child psychologist, their four-year-old said, "Daddy hits Mommy. He hits me and my brother, too."

Though Ruth had shown strength of character in going to the police and pressing charges against her husband, she had never taken steps to leave him. It was hard to imagine that Ruth wasn't going through an even worse hell now that Luke was home.

Laura understood that in a situation such as Ruth was facing, she would never be truly free. Although she continued to worry about Ruth's safety, a part of her knew it would be pure stupidity on Luke's part to do anything more to her or the children—especially not when he was awaiting trial for murder. Another attack on his wife would send him back to jail.

But Luke wasn't known for his ability to be rational or reasonable. Laura could imagine the tension in the house after Luke returned. How long would Ruth have to endure living with such a volatile man before his case went to trial?

John had assured her that Luke wouldn't escape punishment. But how long would a judge sentence him to prison? Given the circumstances and the time that had passed since the crime, it was conceivable that he might be out in seven to ten years. Whether Ruth remained married or left Luke, she would need to plan for a future on her own with the children. An idea began forming in Laura's mind.

Chapter Twenty-Seven

Little by little, life began a slow return to a semblance of near-normal, though Laura still felt unsettled by the turn of events, particularly what was still happening in the legal system. There was so much she didn't understand about process and procedures. John was always there to explain and offer reassurances.

"The district attorney knows his business, Laura. There is nothing more you can say or do," John said.

The arrest of Luke Forrest had fallen into place so unexpectedly—as though helped by an unseen hand. It was as if the scale of justice, so long off-balance, had finally righted itself. Deep down, Laura believed that Michael had also been with her on the day she was confronted by Luke.

In keeping with her annual practice of visiting the cemetery every year, she went there on her way back to Dublin that Monday morning. The cemetery was located about five miles away from Parmenter in a neighboring town. On her arm, she carried a basket of tulip bulbs and her gardening tools. This was her autumn ritual, her way of continuing to care for her boy.

The old church cemetery sat on two acres of rolling hills. Many of the names on the headstones were as familiar to her as family, for she had known these souls for generations. She walked up a slight hill from the dirt path and located the gray granite headstone that bore her son's name, Michael James Fisher, and the span of his life cut so tragically short. She knelt on the ground in front of his headstone and began digging in the grassy soil.

"I'm back," she told him. "I came here to tell you something important, although I'm guessing you already know." She began depositing tulip bulbs in the dirt. They would produce a profusion of color next spring. As a toddler, Michael had often picked his mother's tulips, presenting them to her in his chubby fists as a bouquet. They were the only flowers anyone had ever given her in those days, and Michael's adoring innocence made them that much more precious.

As she covered the bulbs with soil, she shared with him all that had transpired since her last visit. She even told him about her awful experience dating Greg and how embarrassed she still felt at being so naïve. She felt certain he was aware of his grandmother's death. "I'm sure you were there to welcome her," she said, chuckling at a memory. "Grandma always promised she'd look you up first thing."

She rose from her kneeling position and swiped the dirt from her hands. Gathering her gardening tools, she paused. Before leaving, there was something else she needed to say. Tears ran down her cheeks as she spoke to him.

"Sweetie, you must have had such a hard life. I'm not sure I fully understood what you must have endured. For that, I am truly sorry." She felt the sadness begin to lift as if Michael was there comforting her. "I couldn't allow Luke to get away with what he did to you," she said. "I'm just sorry it took so long."

She glanced over at Jed's grave two feet away. Faded plastic flowers from the dollar store were stuck into the ground haphazardly. As his widow, she had never made much of an attempt to tend his grave—had done the bare minimum to keep the church ladies from gossiping.

Just two weeks earlier, she had been going through documents in her desk at home. She pulled a file from the bottom drawer and glanced inside. She had placed anything related to Jed's death inside that folder. Opening it, she saw three extra copies of his death certificate and the paperwork that had accompanied the insurance check. There were other documents in there, and she quickly reviewed them. A sealed envelope inside the folder caught her attention. Glancing at the return address, she saw that it was from the medical examiner's office. She remembered signing for an autopsy.

What was this? Why was the envelope sealed? Curious, she slit it open and unfolded the letter from the medical examiner's office. Attached was a typed form detailing the results of Jed's autopsy.

"Cause of death: aortic aneurysm." She mouthed the words, not quite believing her eyes. She had been told by the medics the night of Jed's death that it looked like a heart attack or massive stroke. No one had said anything else to her.

After Jed's death, she had felt guilty because she hadn't done more to try to save him. Her arm had been too badly injured to be able to move his dead weight from the chair. He was already gone when she found him. That she knew.

Now she also understood that there was nothing she could have done that night to save him. An aortic aneurysm took a life quickly as the person bled out internally. She tried to remember details of the weeks following Jed's death. She had been so overcome with stress over the funeral and worry as she dealt with finances and started working for the first time.

Even so, why hadn't she opened this envelope previously? She glanced at the date on the letter and realized that it had been during a particularly difficult time when she was in counseling, healing emotionally from Jed's abuse. Her therapist had suggested she put aside all matters except her own recovery and wellbeing.

She had not allowed Jed to die. Nothing about that night had been her fault. Although she had not grieved him in the manner that someone typically grieved the loss of a spouse, she had not been completely without a sense of his loss. Jed had been her husband for over twenty years. He was the father of her children. Happy or not, she had shared a life with him and had done her best to be a good wife and mother.

There was a saying she had heard once, that the opposite of love was not hate. To feel hate for someone, although negative, still demonstrated strong emotions. No, the opposite of love, Laura knew, was apathy. Jed had treated her with indifference, not love. And what about her? She had accommodated him in every way, done the best she could. No, she had not hated him. But neither had she truly loved him.

She considered this for a moment. Jed had given her two wonderful sons. Despite his lack of loving attention as a husband and the physical abuse she had endured for two decades, he had provided a roof over her head and meals. But it was she who had created a home for their family, had done everything he expected of her as his wife and the mother of his sons.

The headstone that bore his name had been purchased by the church elders. It was far more ornate and—truth be told—more ostentatious than Laura's budget had permitted, featuring a large cross and inlaid white marble flowers. She studied his name, Rev. Jedediah Michael Fisher, and wondered, as she had so often, how a father who had given his middle name to his firstborn son could have been so completely lacking in love toward that son. Jed and Michael had been as different as dark and light.

Under Jed's name, the words "Beloved Husband and Father" had been chiseled into the stone. The sight of this false sentiment turned Laura's stomach, as it did each time she saw it. She vowed never to join him here. She could never rest in peace beside him.

For the next few moments, she remained, enjoying the early autumn breeze on her face, the sound of leaves rustling, the smell of freshly-mown grass. She steeled herself, her back straight as an arrow, as she spoke the first words she had uttered to him since the day he died. "You may have hurt me, but you did not break me."

ON MONDAY, WHEN LAURA RETURNED TO DUBLIN, it felt like a new beginning. She decided it was the first day of the rest of her life. This was a new chapter. She was particularly anxious to see Andrew and Emily who had invited her for dinner. She had so much to tell them.

She spent the afternoon at Serendipities Two before heading to Emily and Andrew's apartment. Their cozy apartment was furnished with furniture castoffs from Emily's parents' house with a few carefully-chosen items from Laura's store. Here and there, she admired well-designed, simple Swedish-style pieces from a favorite box store. This eclectic combination of furnishings, often described as shabby chic, looked charming.

Laura often gifted them with one-of-a-kind home accessories—items she now saw lovingly displayed throughout the apartment. Beaming with pleasure, she noticed that Emily had taken each of her design suggestions and created her own inviting, stylish home.

"I hope you approve," Emily said. "I always try to imagine how you might arrange things."

"I more than approve," Laura said, hugging her tight. "If you ask me, this place has your unique stamp on it, Emily. What a wonderful place for you to share your lives."

Over plates of Andrew's savory grilled shrimp and vegetables, they discussed all that had happened the previous week. Andrew had been predictably outraged when first told of Luke's behavior toward Laura the day of his arrest. "I'd like nothing more than to kick his ass from here to kingdom come," he had fumed over the phone. "What kind of moral degenerate kills an innocent boy and then attacks the victim's mother?"

"Let it go, son," Laura said, fearful of what Andrew might do if he ever saw him. "Luke will be punished. This is our chance to finally heal."

Over one of Emily's lattice-topped cherry pies, Laura concentrated on happier news. She told them of her progress at the original Serendipities store, including the expansion plans upstairs. "I could imagine a place where visitors could enjoy a cup of coffee or tea and have a baked treat or light lunch. Quality used books will be available for purchase. I might add some magazines, too."

"I thought your friend John was going to lease that space," Andrew said. "Isn't he moving back to Parmenter?"

"John has decided to stay in Columbus. There is more business for his law practice there," she said. "But he'll still help me with anything legal relating to the store in Parmenter. I don't know what I'd do without him."

"I'm glad you broke up with that jerk, Greg," Andrew interjected with feeling. "He didn't deserve you."

"Greg was a learning experience for me, Andrew," she said with a rueful look. "I had never dated before I met him. I made a few mistakes, but it's easier to know what you *do* want in a man once you know what you *don't* want." She took a sip of Chardonnay. "What I would really like in a romantic relationship is what I see in yours: a solid friendship based on mutual interests and history. I have never experienced that with anyone."

"Yet," Emily stressed. "You don't know what the future may bring *yet*. Something tells me you *will* find the love of your life." A look of pure mischief crossed her face. "In fact, you may already know the perfect man."

The expression on Emily's face caused Laura to laugh out loud. "You never know," Laura mused. "Life has been full of surprises lately."

THE IRISH BOOK CLUB MET THAT WEDNESDAY to begin a series of discussions about the works of Twentieth Century Irish poets, including several female poets. Jan believed the works of these writers, many of them acclaimed nationally and internationally, were destined for inclusion among the greatest poems of all times. Laura found the poems deeply meaningful, many written about day-to-day Irish life and the female experience. She thought about all that her mother had endured as a girl in Ireland. Laura knew life in the United States had often presented a different set of hardships for Irish immigrants. But her mother had rarely complained.

"Life is about getting on with things," Eileen said in her lilting brogue. "We never felt sorry for ourselves. Life was hard in Ireland, yes. But it was hard in this country, too. Irish people weren't always treated nicely. We did the best we could and were thankful for a day's wages."

As book club members arrived at Serendipities Two that evening, Laura offered them an array of scones, biscuits, jams, and whipped cream, along with pots of strong Irish tea. She had enjoyed the poems, many of which dealt with human suffering, even death, yet were comforting in the beauty of the words so carefully chosen. In just a few words, so much could be expressed. Laura was beginning to discover how much she enjoyed poetry, especially the works of Eaavan Boland, an acclaimed female poet whose work resonated with her own life.

As she waited for Jan to start the discussion, Laura remembered one of Michael's piano compositions, the haunting lyrics her son had written, seemingly foreshadowing peace from earthly suffering. In a flash of sudden, horrific insight, she realized that there was a message in his lyrics. He likely had contemplated taking his own life.

With members of the book club now seated comfortably, enjoying their tea and refreshments, Terri tapped the side of her teacup with a spoon to get everyone's attention. "Jan, excuse me. Before we start the discussion, I think we should listen to the amazing adventures of Laura Fisher and John Conway. Those two captured a killer last week." Seeing the look of surprise that crossed Laura's face, Terri said, "Laura, don't you dare say I'm being overly dramatic. It's an amazing story. Go on."

All attention focused on Laura who sat beside John on the floral chintz-covered loveseat. They exchanged glances before John said, "Hey, all I did was show up. She had the bad guy cornered and had already tricked him into confessing. It's definitely her story to tell."

Surprised intakes of breath came from the book club members. "You make it sound like an episode of 'Chicago PD,'" Laura said, unable to contain a laugh. "The truth is the man we're talking about has always been a troublemaker. He was well-known for being violent. When I realized that he was abusing his wife and kids, I was more certain than ever that he had done far worse to my son." She took a sip of tea. "He was the one who killed my son, Michael."

As book club members expressed shock and horror, she continued. "With John's help, we were planning to have the investigation reopened."

She told them about the day Michael died and her frustration that the perpetrators evaded punishment. "Although I wanted justice for Michael, I thought it might be too late. I asked for John's help when I learned he was an attorney who had worked on criminal cases."

"The problem was that the crime had happened over a decade earlier, and there had not been a real investigation," John interjected. "We needed someone to talk about what they knew."

Laura explained that she had just purchased the original Serendipities store in Parmenter where she had gotten her start in business. "While I was working in the store, I saw Ruth, the wife of the man I believed had been involved in killing Michael." She flinched. "Seeing her, how she was dressed, the way she carried herself as if she had to apologize for taking up space, was like looking at an image of myself from when I was married."

Seeing the confused looks that crossed the faces of several club members, she continued. "I saw her husband's behavior that weekend and realized she and the children were likely being abused. I know something about that," she said in a wry voice. "I was an abused wife. You don't forget, no matter how hard you try." She cleared her throat. "Anyhow, I had hoped she would share information that could help us reopen the case. But then . . ." She trailed off for a moment, "I began to really care about her situation, and I wanted to help her the way a friend helped me."

After relating how she came to be at Ruth and Luke's house that day, delivering beds for the children, Laura said, "She was bruised and bleeding. I offered to help and let her know she had options. Then her husband showed up. He was angry that I was there. He started saying terrible things, and he shoved me. I have no doubt what would have happened if John hadn't suddenly appeared."

Laura and John finished the story, taking turns sharing their accounts of what each had seen, heard, and experienced. John ended the account by saying, "I heard everything."

"So, Luke *accidentally* confessed to the murder?" Jan asked in amazement.

"It was unbelievable," Laura finished. "He was proud of what he did! He threatened me, and as it was happening, the police showed up."

"Get this," John interrupted. "Ruth, his wife, drove herself and the kids to the station and told them Laura was in danger. She told them everything she knew!"

"But, John, I don't understand. How did you know she was in trouble? What made you go there, too?" Jan asked.

"I followed her," John admitted. "I'm her attorney. I had to make sure she didn't get in trouble or get hurt."

As members of the book club exchanged knowing glances, Terri said, "You're more than her attorney. Face it: you guys have a history of being there for each other."

"This is actually the second time John saved me," Laura explained, and recounted their first meeting the day of Jed's death and how he had helped her again that night.

"So, meeting up again was meant to be, even though it was by happenstance," Carol piped in. "If you ask me, that's the perfect definition of serendipity. It's the perfect name for your stores."

Laura smiled. "You're right, it's a lovely word. Meeting up again with John at the retirement home where his wife and my mother lived at that time . . . Yes, I'd say that a lot of serendipitous events came into play."

They spent a half-hour reviewing the poetry Jan had asked them to read. As the grandfather clock at the back of the store chimed half-past eight, Jan closed the volume of poetry open on her lap. "We didn't get through many of the poems I wanted us to review tonight. But what we heard was so much better. I don't know about the rest of you, but I think Laura's story would make a great novel."

ON FRIDAY NIGHT, TERRI AND HER BAND, Street, played at the Irish pub. It was their twice-monthly gig and always drew a crowd. The pub was Terri's favorite place to perform and where she had gotten her start performing in Dublin. Tonight, she planned to debut an original song.

Laura was more than ready for a night of fun. It had been an unusually busy week at Serendipities Two. In addition to a couple of bus tours of Dublin, part-timer Cissy hadn't been able to work as much that week because of exams in her master's program.

Laura called Andrew and Emily. "I really need a night on the town. Why don't you guys join me?"

"Why don't you invite your friend, John?" Andrew suggested. "I'd like to thank him in person for helping you—I mean, us."

The thought had already occurred to her to ask John. But she had hesitated, unsure of how he might read such an invitation. This was not an after-book club outing at the pub. If she asked him to join her, would he think she was asking him out on a date? Now, with Andrew and Emily joining them, and with Andrew's suggestion that she call him, she could easily make the call.

John accepted with enthusiasm. "I'd really like to go," he said. "I haven't seen Andrew since he was little."

Laura arrived at the pub at seven-thirty, dressed casually in black knit slacks and a periwinkle blue sweater that matched her eyes. She felt oddly nervous—had, in fact, looked forward to tonight more than she would have thought possible. Over the past several weeks, her relationship with John had evolved naturally from friendship into the possibility of something more, it seemed. But it was still too early for romance.

They hadn't discussed this. Neither had ever brought up the subject of dating. Yet, there was something between them that felt loving and familiar. The best word she could think of was companionship—the kind of compatibility that felt as comforting as your favorite fleecy robe. They were able to pick up a conversation after several days and continue in mid-stream as if there had been no lapse. Did he feel it, too?

Tonight, watching him walk through the door of the pub, she thought he had never looked more handsome. He wore dark navy jeans that hugged his lean physique and a navy cable-knit sweater. His face lit up when he saw her.

She stood to greet him, and they met in an easy hug. "John, this tall young man is Andrew, that little boy you remember. And this is his fiancée, Emily."

"Great to see you again. I want to thank you," Andrew said as the two men shook hands. "For protecting my mom and helping her last Friday. You helped me, too. We've needed this kind of closure. And I feel a whole lot better knowing we have someone like you on our side."

"It was quite an experience," John said, flashing a grin. "You had to be there to get the full effect of Laura Fisher on a mission to get her man."

They laughed. Laura felt her face flush. The potential double entendre didn't escape her attention.

"The county's criminal prosecutor will handle the case. He's good," John said. "I'd love to work on this one with him, but I can't. I'm a witness to the events that happened the day the defendant confessed. But I can certainly offer my thoughts."

John turned to Emily. "You may be marrying this guy. But you probably can't imagine him as a little kid, always getting into trouble. If there was a puddle, he jumped in it. His brother couldn't do much to stop him."

"He has managed to mature a little bit," Emily replied with a straight face.

"Something tells me John has more stories that he will be only too glad to share for your entertainment," Andrew said, rolling his eyes.

John nodded conspiratorially at Laura, who laughed, remembering Andrew's antics and how a contrite Michael would have to explain how an innocent walk home from school with his younger brother turned into more laundry for his mother. Laura was grateful for the gentle way John included Michael in the scene he recounted—a sensitivity that allowed for a pleasant memory rather than a painful one. That was the most poignant part of remembering loved ones: a memory that included someone who was no longer there could bring that person back to life, if only for a moment. She smiled her appreciation at John.

Andrew ordered a round of Guinness draughts, and they sat back to enjoy the show. Terri introduced her band members and kicked off the first set with an audience favorite, "Cotton-Eyed Joe." This classic tune usually resulted in at least a handful of customers in the corner demonstrating their best line dancing or Irish step-dancing. Terri's silky long dark hair swung from side to side as she played her fiddle.

When it was time for Terri to introduce the song that she had composed, she became tearful at the microphone. "Love is always around us if we recognize it for what it is. The words we choose, the actions we take, are all part of showing someone we love them. Hope you like this ballad of love."

Laura was enthralled, listening to the sweet sounds of Terri's fiddle as she played. When she lowered her instrument and stepped to the microphone to sing, her lyrics were the story of love lost and new love found, of hope and courage to love again.

Laura watched Andrew lean over and say something in Emily's ear. She turned toward him, her eyes bright with happiness. She touched his cheek with the palm of her hand, a caress so tender, it brought tears to Laura's eyes. Laura caught John watching her reaction.

"I know," he said. "They make a great couple. I predict a long, happy marriage." She smiled at him in silent agreement as a tear dribbled down her cheek. John reached over and smoothed it away with his thumb. "Don't cry. All the credit for how he has turned out goes to you."

At that moment, John's cell phone vibrated, skittering across the table. He caught it and glanced at caller I.D. Eyebrows raised, he offered a meaningful look to Laura and answered. "Hey, what's up?"

Laura watched as his eyes widened by degrees. "When?" he asked. "Where did it happen?" As he listened, his eyes focused on Laura. Her stomach seized up, and she swallowed several times, fighting nausea. Her gut told her whatever had happened, it concerned Ruth. Andrew and Emily were listening now, too. "Do you know who did it? . . . Wow." He was silent for a few moments before ending the call. "Yes, of course. I'll let her know. Thanks for calling."

"What happened?" Laura asked.

"Luke Forrest is dead."

CHAPTER TWENTY-EIGHT

"I CAN'T BELIEVE IT. WHO JUST CALLED?" Laura leaned back in her chair, feeling as if the wind had been knocked out of her. Andrew and Emily clutched each other for support.

"That was my friend in the district attorney's office. Luke was assaulted and left for dead by the side of the road. It was on one of the county roads—not much traffic out that way. But someone driving by saw a body lying next to a truck and called 911. Luke was able to tell the cops what happened, but he didn't last very long after they got him to the hospital. Massive internal injuries. Those guys meant business."

"Was it . . .?"

"Jason and Dan, his two so-called friends."

"I don't understand. Why would they kill him? I thought you said it was too late for them to face charges."

"My guess is they were settling a score," John said. "Stupid on their part. Because of the statute of limitations, they couldn't be convicted just by being in the boat the day that Michael died. Now it's a homicide."

Laura pressed her fingers against her eyes, envisioning the scene. Then she stood up. "I have to see Ruth."

Andrew had been silent, listening to every word John said. His eyes snapped with sparks of anger as he raked his fingers through his hair. "I'm glad he's dead," he said, his mouth forming a hard line. "But not like this! I wanted him to stand trial for what he did. I wanted him to suffer."

"There will be a trial—just a different one than what we expected." John said. "If you think about it, Andrew, justice is being served. Three people were involved in an ugly act that went unpunished for over a decade. One guy paid the ultimate price with his own life. At least now, those other two don't get off scot-free."

Laura watched her son's face go through a range of expressions. It was clear that Andrew was fighting a war in his head. Emily took his hand, kneading his fingers between hers. "It's over," she said in a soft voice. "You and your mom can finally have peace."

Andrew nodded. He looked at Laura. "So, what happens next?"

"I'm going to Parmenter to see Ruth tomorrow," Laura announced. "Tomorrow is my day to work at the store here, but the other employees can manage. They can close up early, if need be."

Emily exchanged glances with Andrew who nodded. "We can lend a hand."

After a restless night of tossing and turning, Laura gave up on the notion of sleep and packed an overnight bag, intending to be in Parmenter before the store opened at ten. She called Marjorie from the interstate to tell her about Luke's death.

"There was nothing on the news last night, and I haven't seen the paper yet this morning," Marjorie said. While they talked, she picked up *The Parmenter Herald* and glanced over the headlines. "Nope, nothing in the paper yet. Boy, when this hits the media, all heck is going to break loose. Those men have good jobs. One of 'em, Dan, is a deacon at the church." She whistled under her breath.

"They wouldn't have ever seen a day of jail time, John says. That is, until they decided to get even with Luke." Laura slurped the rest of her large Dunkin' Donut's coffee. She was going on caffeine and willpower now.

"This week sure has been a roller coaster," Marjorie stated. "How are you holding up, love?"

"I'm stunned. I wanted Luke punished. Now he's dead. Shouldn't that be the end?" She searched for words to express what she could not yet fully explain. "Andrew and I feel the same way. We wanted the truth to come out during the trial about what really happened. We wanted others to know the truth."

"As soon as the details hit the media, everybody will know what happened," Marjorie pointed out. "This is the biggest thing to happen in this town since the mayor got arrested for horse-stealing."

Laura turned onto Main Street, noticing that the new Serendipities sign had been installed. The colorful, whimsical signage had better curb appeal. "Don't you love the new sign?" she asked.

"Everyone comments on it," Marjorie said. "I love what you've done so far. Your plans for the upstairs are fantastic."

"I'll head over to see Ruth after I check on things here at the store. I want to see how the workmen are progressing."

"You'll be impressed." Marjorie was silent for a moment before adding, "Tell Ruth I said hello, will you? I'm glad she's safe now. Poor little thing. But she'll need counseling—lots of it."

"You're right. This all takes me back to the night Jed died," Laura said as she pulled into the parking lot behind the store. "At first, I was completely numb. Then I felt guilty for feeling nothing. Then I had to face the money worries, figure out how to pay bills, and take care of Andrew's tuition. You showed me what to do, step by step. I can help Ruth the way you helped me."

"The way I was helped, too," Marjorie said. "Women have to be there for each other."

To Laura's delight, the café kitchen had been mostly installed, except for the large refrigerator-freezer that was on back order. Laura was pleased to see plenty of room for the six café tables she had ordered. There was even a small alcove for a cushioned window seat and comfortable wingback chairs. Other chairs and tables would be arranged around the perimeter. With any luck, she'd soon have all the permits she needed to open.

She unlocked the front door of Serendipities to a steady stream of customers that morning. A circular sent to area homes had included a coupon offering ten percent off purchases of fifty dollars or more. No one could resist a bargain, it seemed. If business continued like this, she'd need another part-timer on the weekend. After checking inventory, she did payroll, checked receipts against bank deposits, and found everything in order.

By two o'clock, it was time to leave. She quickly finished a container of yogurt in her car, and headed over to Ruth's house. But first, she made a quick stop at the grocery store to fill a basket of food and treats. She also tucked a gift card inside, in case Ruth was short on grocery money.

When she parked at the curb in front of the house, an involuntary shiver ran up and down her spine. Had it really been just a week ago that events had taken such an unimaginable turn? Like an accident involving a chain of cars on a busy highway, one man's actions resulted in his death and forever altered the lives of others.

Laura wasn't sure how Ruth would react to this visit. Surely, her feelings were as complex as Laura's had been after Jed died. When she rang the doorbell, the curtains parted in the front window, and she heard footsteps in the entryway. Ruth opened the door, and Laura saw with relief that the bruises on her face had begun to fade, and the cut on her upper lip had healed into a scab.

"Guess you heard about Luke," Ruth said. In a flat voice, she added, "I bet you're glad he's dead."

"You just lost your husband, and your boys lost their father. I know how hard it is to suddenly lose your husband, no matter what the circumstances," Laura said. "My feelings about Luke are really complicated, as I'm sure yours are." She handed over the basket. "I thought there might be something in here that might taste good to you."

"That's real nice of you," Ruth said, peering under the cloth. "Would you like to come in?"

"Very much. Thank you." Laura greeted the two little boys who were playing with their toy trucks and cars. She followed Ruth into the kitchen and sat down at the small round table. Ruth filled a tea kettle with water and set it on the stove to boil. She flitted around, fixing a small tray of baked treats from several containers on the counter.

"I can imagine what happened was a terrible shock," Laura began. "I'm sorry."

Ruth turned around to face her. She seemed to be searching for the right words and finally blurted out, "Since he got out on bail, I haven't had a moment of peace. I was afraid to sleep. I thought he might kill me."

"Did he hurt you again?"

"He didn't hit me," Ruth said in a monotone. "I know husbands can do what they want with their wives . . . in the bedroom," she said in a halting voice. "As soon as he came home from jail, the first thing he did was drag me into the bedroom and lock the door. He, uh, he . . ."

"He raped you," Laura finished for her.

He's my husband. I don't think . . ."

"If he forced himself on you, it was rape." Laura stood and went to her. Ruth moved into the circle of Laura's arms and began to cry.

"There is never a good reason for a man to do what he did," Laura said, holding her close. "Husbands are supposed to love and care for their wives, not hurt them. You're safe now."

"Why don't I feel safe?" Ruth sobbed.

"I know. You feel like the fear is part of your body, in your bloodstream, part of your bones. You don't know how *not* to be afraid."

Ruth drew back and looked into Laura's eyes. "Was it that way for you, too?"

Laura nodded. "The fear will lessen with time, but you're going to need help. So will your kids."

Laura reached for a kitchen towel and gently wiped the tears from Ruth's battered face. She pictured Ruth as a child—the little girl who wore hand-me-downs and needed her tangled blonde curls brushed. Had anyone ever cared for Ruth?

"Everything is going to be okay," she reassured her. "You'll get through this. I know it doesn't seem like it right now, but you will. We'll figure this out together."

They sat down with their cups of tea. Ruth passed the tray of chocolate chip cookies and apricot and raspberry bars. The cookies were perfectly golden-brown, studded with chocolate chunks. There were also carrot cake squares with cream cheese frosting and tiny spice cupcakes with whipped orange frosting. "I just baked these yesterday," she said. "Before it happened."

"I would have sworn these came from a professional bakery," Laura said. It was true. She bit into one of the cookies. It was perfect, slightly crisp at the edge, soft and chewy in the center, with the right amount of dark chocolate chunks. "Mm, this is wonderful. Real butter."

She smiled at Ruth. "I came over here to make sure you were okay. But I had another reason—to thank you for going to the police last Friday and telling them what was happening—what you knew. I understand that what you did set things in motion, and Luke is dead as a result. But you showed how strong you really are. If you could do that, you can do anything."

"How will I pay the bills? Luke handled everything." Ruth rose to her feet, grabbed a dishcloth, and flitted around the kitchen, wiping up imaginary spills and crumbs. She reminded Laura of a scared rabbit—jumpy, unable to stay in one place.

"He probably had some life insurance through his job." Laura suggested, reaching for Ruth's hand as she wiped off the table for the third time. She stroked her cold fingers. "It takes a while for that to come through, though. You'll want to call his employer first thing and ask."

"We didn't talk about stuff like that. He was the man. He made the money and paid all the bills. There is a little bit of money in the checking account I can use."

"Can your family help out?"

"A little. My mom won't let us starve."

"There are financial assistance programs for widows and children. You'll qualify for medical benefits, too," Laura said. "But right now, you need something you can do to help yourself."

"I've got no real skills." Ruth looked as if she might start crying again.

"I'm here to offer you a job."

"At your store?" Ruth's eyes were wide as saucers. "Oh, no. I'm kind of shy. I don't think I could sell anything." She blinked, looking even more like a scared rabbit.

"Just hear me out. I'm opening a little coffee shop on the second floor of Serendipities. It won't be a very big place, just a half-dozen or so tables. People can take a break from shopping or get their coffee and a treat to go. I'm thinking of wraps and pita sandwiches, maybe pierogies, a daily soup, definitely quiche."

"That sounds good." Ruth listened attentively.

"Of course, what's a coffee shop without cookies like these?" She took another bite. "And cupcakes. Maybe some fruit hand pies."

Ruth put down her teacup. "You would do that for me? After what my husband did to your son?"

"Luke killed Michael. You helped make things right."

A shy smile formed at the corners of Ruth's mouth. "I can't leave the boys full-time yet, but my sister and mom might be able to help out a little."

"I think there's a way for this to happen even when you can't be onsite." Laura had already investigated state laws regarding home-based food businesses. The state of Ohio had a cottage food law allowing for some low-risk foods to be produced from a home kitchen. "You can make some of the food and baked items at home."

A look of wonder lit up Ruth's thin face. "I would love that. When can I start?"

"Why don't you start putting together some menu ideas and what you think it will cost to make them. I'll pay you for your time, of course."

AS OCTOBER'S MILDER WEATHER TRANSITIONED into November with occasional freezing rain and colder temperatures, Laura continued her weekly back-and-forth commutes between stores. It would have felt like wasted time if it weren't for podcasts and business audio books. She found the two-hour drives—what John often referred to as windshield time— helpful, even rejuvenating.

When in Parmenter, she spent nights at Marjorie's house. Laura still found Marjorie to be the best source of advice, professionally and personally. Now that Laura's mother was gone, Marjorie seemed to assume that role, as well. She was always willing to listen.

The original Serendipities store in Parmenter was doing so well in its first weeks under new ownership, Laura added another part-time employee. The coffee shop upstairs immediately brought more customers into the store, many lingering to shop afterward. Laura added greeting cards to entice customers to buy items as gifts. Serious readers couldn't resist low prices on used books Laura acquired from the library and the American Association of University Women.

Ruth worked mornings, arriving at seven a.m. to prepare soups, quiches, and sandwiches. The cheese and potato pierogies she made were a big hit. She baked cookies, cupcakes, cookie bars, and other treats from home. From all appearances, she and her children were doing well, beginning to heal from the abuse and fear, and leading happier lives.

Laura had arranged for counseling and assistance for Ruth from a domestic abuse organization. Her four-year-old was enrolled in a local pre-K program. The youngest boy, who had just turned three, was now receiving early intervention services for speech. Laura wondered if the problems the little boy had communicating were the result of being afraid to speak.

Jason and Dan, the men who caused Luke's death, were in jail awaiting separate trials. As more details emerged in the case, Laura learned that the three men, lifelong friends since their days in the church's elementary-secondary school, had argued repeatedly following Luke's release on bail.

Jason and Dan reportedly made a habit of following Luke in his truck, often trailing him as he drove to and from work, waiting outside for him. Luke's coworkers reported that he rarely left the building after arriving for work in the morning, and that he always brought lunches from home.

Despite not being prosecuted for Michael's death, Jason and Dan were angry. Luke had allowed himself to be tricked into a confession that ultimately involved them. They lost their exemplary standing in the community.

Luke's beating had been a vengeful act. But his attackers swore they only meant to teach him a lesson—hadn't known their savage kicks with their work boots to his head, face, and torso would result in his death. They were charged with manslaughter. Few people in Parmenter, aside from family and church friends, were sympathetic to their plight.

For the first time since Michael's death, Laura experienced a peace of mind that had eluded her for over ten years. With this semblance of closure, she could move forward. Perhaps it was time to think of what kind of life she wanted next.

As she turned the page on another new chapter in her life, Emily and Andrew moved forward on details for their Christmas Eve wedding. The ceremony would be a small candlelit affair at six o'clock, before Christmas Eve service at the Presbyterian Church in Dublin. It would be followed by dinner at a nearby country club where Emily's parents were members.

Laura was thrilled when Emily dropped by the store one afternoon and invited her to go shopping with her and her mother for a wedding dress. "We're getting down to the wire, and I haven't found anything that feels right," Emily said. "There are lots of beautiful gowns, but they don't feel like my dress. Maybe I need another set of eyes."

"I'm honored you asked," Laura said, her eyes filling with unexpected tears. "But isn't this something mothers and daughters and sisters do together? Are you sure you want me tagging along?"

"Well, you're going to be my other mother, right?" Emily let out a quick laugh. "My mom thinks you have exquisite taste. Please say yes."

"Yes!" Laura exclaimed, hugging Emily.

Between the upcoming holiday season, running errands, and making phone calls to help Emily and Andrew with their wedding preparations, plus the management of both stores, Laura's days were jam-packed. No matter what was going on, though, she made time for the Irish book club. It was her touchstone, an activity that anchored her schedule and kept her focused. Irish literature spoke to her soul, and not just because she was of Irish ancestry. They were stories so familiar, she felt as if she knew the characters. They brought insights that helped her process the events of her life.

With three additional members of the book club, seating had become too cramped at Serendipities Two. Jan moved the club's monthly meetings back to the library. "I'll try to provide treats, but they won't be anything like Laura's, and you probably won't feel as if you're having tea in someone's Irish country home," she apologized to the group.

John resigned from Ohio State. After gaining several new clients for his burgeoning law practice, it was time to launch. "It would be a conflict of interest to continue working for the university with my newest client," he told Laura. "To be honest, I should have done this much earlier. I feel as if I've been treading water for years. One step at a time, I guess."

It was good to see him happy and living out his dreams. But she had become accustomed to spending time with him regularly. Where once they ate lunch together each week and spoke almost daily, now they caught up less frequently.

With the resolution of Michael's murder investigation and the completion of her store purchase, they no longer had business reasons to meet. At times, she wondered if the entire reason for their reunion last summer had been fated. Had they been reunited for the express purpose of solving Michael's murder?

One day, as she sketched out decorating plans for the store for Thanksgiving and the winter holidays, Laura heard the bell on the front door of Serendipities Two. It was near closing time. She looked up and saw Larry, the man she had met on the dating website. She hadn't seen him since the library fundraiser in July.

"Hi, Larry," she said, delighted to see him. "How can I help you?"

"Hi, Laura. I came to take another look at that craftsman-style leather chair you have back there," he said, pointing toward a chair Laura thought was one of the nicest pieces of furniture she had ever offered for sale. "I hope it hasn't sold already."

"It's still available." She came around the counter to meet him, and they walked to the back of the store.

The chair had been an auction discovery. Laura loved it on sight, but the chair had some minor scratches. Refinishing the wood restored the chair to its former glory. She had been so pleased with the results she'd had half a mind to keep it for herself.

"How much do you want for it?" He ran his hand over the fine wood grain of the chair arm.

"Three hundred and fifty," she said, consulting the tag. "There is a tiny scrape on the leather under the seat cushion. I discounted a bit for that."

"That's fair," he said. "Can you deliver it?"

"Absolutely," she said. They went back to the counter as she began the transaction. Her cheeks reddened. "I'm sorry. I don't remember your last name," she said as she began filling in the information on the screen.

"Dillard," he said. "By the way, it's really nice to see you again. Everything good in your world?"

She grinned and let out a whoosh of air. "The short answer is yes. The longer answer would take more time than either of us have today."

"Maybe you could tell me about it sometime," he said. "Are you seeing anyone? I know you were on the fence about dating when we met last summer. I thought maybe we could try it again, if you're willing."

She startled for a moment, nearly hitting the 'cancel sale' button. Breaking into a shy smile, she thought about her response. She wasn't dating anyone else. What was the harm in accepting Larry's invitation?

"Hopefully, I'll do a better job carrying my end of the conversation," she answered with a chuckle. "You were so nice, and I was such a dolt."

"First dates are scary," he said. "I had an unfair advantage. I've been on dozens. You were new to the game."

She thought back to the last time she had seen him at the library fundraiser. "It's none of my business, but I thought you were seeing someone. I mean, I saw you at the gala with . . ."

"That was my second cousin—once removed. Gail. I didn't want to go alone. I do the same for her sometimes." He grinned. "If I had known you were going to be there, I would have asked you."

"And I would have accepted," she said, smiling at him. She completed the sale and handed back his credit card. "I can have that chair delivered Saturday morning. I've got another delivery in your neighborhood. Is between ten and noon good for you?"

"That's perfect," he said. He paused for a moment before continuing. "This might be short notice, but would you like to go out this Friday evening?"

She smiled at him. He really was a very good-looking man. "I can be done here by six-thirty."

"Six-thirty, it is. I'll pick you up. I hope you like Italian food."

"My favorite. I'll look forward to it."

Chapter Twenty-Nine

As Thanksgiving approached, Laura's days were defined by hectic long hours at the store, complicated further by last-minute store deliveries to customers' homes. Those details, along with seemingly endless lists of holiday errands, resulted in too-frequent meals-on-the-go. She also helped Emily and Andrew with wedding preparations, purchasing table decorations online at a discount and fretting over potential delivery delays.

But even when her list of things to do exceeded the number of hours in a day, Laura loved the feverish pace of the holidays. After closing up the store and running errands well into the evening, she often curled up on her sofa with a cup of lavender-chamomile tea. Wrapped in one of her mother's handmade crocheted quilts, she welcomed time to read a good book and listen to holiday music. The Irish book club had one more meeting in early December, when they would continue their discussion of Irish poetry. She could afford to indulge her desire for a Christmas romance novel.

Her favorite part of the holiday season was decorating Serendipities for each holiday, Thanksgiving through New Year's Day. After her first year in business, when a local newspaper featured gift ideas from Serendipities as part of its holiday circular, she made a special effort to make her store a holiday destination point for out-of-towners and locals. Every year, she could depend on the newspaper to take photos for their business and lifestyle sections. December, normally a prosperous month for any retail establishment, set new records each year at Serendipities Two.

It was all about ambience. She kept both gas fireplaces in Serendipities Two burning during store hours, providing a cheerful, warming touch. Cinnamon-infused brooms permeated the air with their aroma. This year, she had arranged colorful silk autumn leaves with branches of bright-red winterberries, white pumpkins, colorful gourds, and fresh autumn flowers around the store in preparation for Thanksgiving. In each room, dining room tables glistened with crystal, fine china dinnerware, and cloth napkins rolled and tied with raffia and ribbons.

"You have a knack for enticing people into the store and convincing them there's no place they'd rather be," Marjorie had said often enough.

It was fun to create irresistible displays of gift items that customers could imagine adorning their holiday tables—the more eclectic, the better. People often admitted to feeling overwhelmed at the prospect of creating holiday tables to rival what they saw in magazines and on design shows. Especially for women juggling careers and families, the pressure was intense. For this reason, it wasn't unusual for customers, upon seeing Laura's exquisite arrangements, to purchase the entire dining room set—complete with dishes, crystal, silverware, and table linens—to re-create the holiday perfection they could imagine through her expert eyes.

At the Parmenter store, the new Serendipities Café was doing a booming business. Ruth got into the spirit of the holidays by baking up trays of pumpkin muffins, frosted pumpkin-spice cookies, and an impossible-to-resist savory pumpkin-sage soup. She also created mouth-watering pumpkin-sage raviolis. Not surprisingly, the café soon had a booming takeout business.

Anyone could see that Ruth was content, intently wiping down already spotless counters, sweeping the kitchen floor to remove imaginary crumbs, and stirring steaming pots of fragrant soups and stews of her own creation. Her eyes were bright, her cheeks rosy, and her blonde hair had reclaimed its youthful shine and bounce. She had gained enough weight to fill out her formerly bone-thin frame and sunken cheeks. She reminded Laura of a tiny, graceful bird, hopping from one foot to the other, always on the move.

Only one topic caused Ruth's mood to turn somber. The two men responsible for her husband's death had not yet gone to trial, though there was no doubt they would eventually receive sentences for killing Luke. Laura asked one day how she was coping with the inevitable delays in the court system.

Ruth bit her lower lip and let out a long breath before answering. "Let it drag on. The longer they sit in their jail cells, the safer everyone else will be."

Laura and Larry saw each other at least twice a week, going out to dinner and a movie or for a drink and easy conversation. He was attentive and eager to please. It was touching, really, the respectful manner in which he asked questions of her—never intrusive, genuinely seeking to know more about her life and what she thought about news and topics of local interest. He had a deliberate way of expressing himself, choosing his words carefully. She was becoming fond of him.

If there was anything lacking, surely this, too, would develop over time. She had a vague sense of what it might be—something she could scarcely put into words without feeling shallow and slightly guilty. While Larry was ideal in many ways, the chemistry she had felt with Greg was lacking. Whenever Greg had touched her, she had felt an electricity and warmth long afterward. When he kissed her, even that first time on the cheek, Laura wanted more—so much more.

When Larry kissed her, it was pleasant enough. But she felt troubled at her lack of interest in anything more with him. Maybe it was the hectic pace of the season that kept her from being able to focus on him. Perhaps it was an overabundance of caution following the breakup with Greg. Whatever the reason, when she and Larry weren't together, she rarely thought of him. She was sure this was unfair. He was a kind and decent man.

She forced herself again and again to recall the miserable, humiliating outcome of those passionate feelings for Greg—physical feelings that had overwhelmed her best judgements. He had been dishonest, unworthy of her faith in him. It had been a humbling experience.

Clearly, Larry was a better choice. He was grounded and sincere, emotionally available, and respectful in his actions. His relationship with his adult sons was loving and close-knit. He would make a reliable partner if their relationship continued moving forward.

But it wasn't memories of Greg that were most troubling. Try as she might, she couldn't keep from thinking about John, of the enjoyable times they had together. They shared a history, could talk openly on any subject, and enjoyed many of the same interests. It had always been so easy and fun being with him. And when they brushed against each other or offered a friendly hug, Laura's imagination invariably took flight. She could picture herself with him in a much more intimate way.

John's role as her attorney for the purchase of the Parmenter store, and his advisory role in pursuing justice for Michael, had been the primary reasons for the amount of time they spent together in recent months. But even business lunches segued naturally into other more enjoyable topics. They were friends first. But there had always been the tantalizing promise of something more. This something, she sensed, had the potential to develop and deepen, given the right conditions.

When she spent time with him, even if they were at book club, she was aware of the nearness of him, his soapy-clean scent, the sound of his voice, his laugh, of the pleasant tingling sensation she felt when their hands touched. The hugs they shared when they saw each other were friendly, nothing more. But she could imagine more. When he was that close, it was far too easy to imagine a future with him.

Marjorie had suggested that John might be a kindred spirit, someone who might forever be in orbit around her. This was an unsettling thought. If the only possibility in their future was friendship, and if she continued to see him, wouldn't she always want more? Unrequited love often appeared in novels for a reason. It was incredibly common. It was also painful.

Whether the reason was work-related or the result of personal concerns, John was keeping her at arms' length. She let out a deep breath. It was time to stop focusing so much on John and open her mind and heart to Larry. It was the right thing to do.

THIS THANKSGIVING WOULD BE LAURA'S FIRST HOLIDAY without her mother. In tribute, she intended to make all of Eileen's favorite recipes. It was traditional fare, nothing fancy, but all the dishes were family favorites: turkey and herb stuffing, whipped potatoes, sweet potato casserole topped with marshmallows, green bean casserole, a dried-corn casserole that everyone raved about, and an assortment of pies.

When it came time to extend invitations for Thanksgiving dinner, Laura automatically included Marjorie and Terri, as she always did. Andrew had casually inquired if John would be invited this year. Laura pondered this for a moment before responding that yes, she would invite him. This was his first Thanksgiving holiday without Jackie. No doubt, he would appreciate a dinner invitation. If he had other plans, so be it.

Not surprisingly, he accepted gratefully. "I'll bring my famous chocolate chess pie."

She had decided earlier not to invite Larry to Thanksgiving. It would be awkward since they had only been on four dates. He didn't suggest it, and it seemed premature to introduce him to family and friends. As it turned out, he already had plans for dinner with his sons. Problem solved.

Thanksgiving Day dawned with the first hard frost of the season. Laura awoke at six to prepare the turkey, make stuffing, peel and dice potatoes for mashed potatoes, and assemble her mother's sweet potato casserole. As familiar smells filled her kitchen and the windows steamed up, she was transported to another time and place.

It was the first Thanksgiving without Michael. Like this one without her mother, she hadn't expected that first holiday without him to feel like a normal holiday. Nor was she adequately prepared for the assault of emotions she felt.

On that day, just three months after Michael's death, she put the turkey in the oven. The side dishes were made, and the house was spotless. She had bathed and dressed for dinner, carefully donning an apron over her blue housedress. Arrangements had been made for her to pick up Eileen at the nursing home at two-thirty so they could spend extra time together. Her mother liked to feel useful, and Laura had saved a few jobs she could do to help with dinner. After a lunch of soup and sandwiches, Jed went to church to work on his Sunday sermon.

Andrew, unusually quiet, had been in his room all day. She had taken up a sandwich and glass of milk at noon only to find him lying across his bed, face-up, one arm thrown over his eyes. She could tell he had been crying.

"I know," she said softly, setting the plate and glass on his bedside table. She laid her hand gently on his shirtfront. "I miss him, too." She tenderly caressed his chin. "You need to eat something, just a little to tide you over till dinner."

He sat up on the bed and glanced over at the plate. He looked sad and drawn, older than his thirteen years. "Thanks, Mom." Swinging his legs onto the floor, he leaned forward, elbows on his knees, head hanging down. The sight of her usually upbeat son so broken in spirit evoked Laura's most basic motherly instincts. Somehow, some way, she would help him.

"We'll make sure Michael is remembered today," she promised.

He nodded and offered a wan smile. "Thanks, Mom."

At dinner, Jed pronounced a lengthy Thanksgiving blessing, asking God to look down with mercy upon all his parishioners and anyone without family or a holiday meal. He ticked off the names of several elderly people who had recently passed away, those in the hospital, and a few others who appeared to have lost their way on their holy path. He thanked God for food and shelter, and for the meal that had been prepared for their nourishment in body and soul.

"Amen," he said and placed his cloth napkin on his lap. He waited for Laura to pass him the first dish.

Laura waited until he opened his eyes and sat back in his chair before adding her own prayer, "And, Heavenly Father, please look after our sweet Michael, and help us on this our first holiday without him. Amen."

Andrew looked at her gratefully. Laura reached over to squeeze his fingers. Jed raised his eyes, a crease appearing between his eyebrows. He spoke not another word. Dinner was mostly silent. The only words spoken were requests to pass serving dishes. Laura sliced homemade pumpkin and pecan pies topped with vanilla ice cream.

After dinner, she and her mother did the dishes, and then Laura drove Eileen back to the nursing home. She was tired but satisfied that everything had gone smoothly. The food was delicious, and there hadn't been any unpleasantness to mar their holiday meal. If Jed was silent throughout, well, that was for the best.

Returning home, she parked in the driveway and stepped out of the car, making sure to return the driver's seat to the exact position Jed favored. The night was cold, but it felt good on her face. Frost tipped each grass blade, creating an otherworldly silver glow across the front yard. Hundreds of stars shone in a clear navy-blue sky, adding to the beauty and peace of the night. She could imagine Michael as one of those stars. The air smelled of woodsmoke from a neighbor's fireplace.

Though the windows of her house were steamed, she could see the comforting glow of the reading lamp in the front room. Fitting her key in the lock, she opened the front door and sniffed appreciatively at the comforting aromas of turkey and pumpkin pie. She dropped Jed's keys in a ceramic dish on the hallway table and slipped out of her winter coat, hanging it in the closet. A cup of tea would be nice.

Jed sat in his chair, reading by the light of the lamp. He glanced up at her, frowning slightly, then placed his Bible on the table beside his chair, dimmed the light, and rose to his feet. Laura blinked in the low lighting and smiled. "Would you like another piece of pecan pie?"

He went to her and placed his hands on her upper arms, seemingly to kiss her forehead. Then his expression changed, and he shook her hard enough that her head smacked the wall behind her. She attempted to steady herself through the pain as he continued shaking her. "Jed . . ." she gasped, losing her breath.

"Don't you ever finish a prayer for me. Do you understand me? I had every intention of mentioning Mike. You never gave me the chance."

"I'm sorry. I'm sorry. I thought you were finished," she said, knowing full well that she had not misread the situation. He had said, "Amen" before she added her prayer. But the truth didn't matter, not now, not ever. She tried to raise her arms to protect her face, but he held them in place.

She heard a door creak open and footsteps on the stairs. Andrew moved swiftly toward his parents. He put an arm out, causing Jed to take two steps back, enough that Andrew could move in front of her. "Mom, if you hadn't said it, I would have," he said, staring defiantly at his father.

In a flash, Jed's hand was on his belt, yanking it out of the loops. Father and son stood face-to-face. Andrew was two heads taller than Jed and seemingly unafraid.

"Jed, it was my fault," Laura said in horror as he coiled the belt around his hand.

"Mom, *none* of this is your fault," Andrew said, squaring off, inching closer to his father. "Go ahead, Dad," he said. "Show Jesus what a good, loving father you are. 'He that spareth his rod hateth his son; but he that loveth him chasteneth him. Proverbs 13:24.'"

Jed halted as if he'd been struck. Laura stood frozen, waiting, watching. What was Andrew thinking?

"It is a father's job to teach his son the ways of God," Jed said, nodding at Andrew, unable to disguise his pleasure. "I'm glad you know your Bible verses." It appeared that some of Jed's anger had dissipated. Nevertheless, he held the belt between his hands, stretching it in a loop like a Cobra head preparing to strike. "You shouldn't get between your mother and me like that. She knows her place."

Laura felt her heart constrict, her stomach cramping, as Andrew stood still, shielding her. Laura's heart pounded in her chest, not sure whether or not to be relieved. Andrew wasn't going to strike his father, after all. Then Andrew turned toward her, bent slightly, and steeled himself for what was to come.

"No," Laura breathed in horror.

Jed raised the belt and whipped Andrew's back, twice, then four more times, six before he was satisfied. Andrew never uttered a sound. At one point, he moved slightly to the side so that the belt would not strike Laura as Jed lashed it again and again.

Jed backed away, red-faced and sweating, and threaded his belt through the loops of his trousers. He took in the sight of Laura, her hand fisted over her mouth, eyes wide with fear. "I believe I'll have some of that pie now," he said.

FLASHBACKS FROM THAT OLD LIFE IN PARMENTER had become less frequent over the past few years. It was easy to keep them at bay by staying busy, focusing on a list of tasks, checking them off. But when those bad memories struck, as this one had so suddenly, the swift and visceral reaction she had to the sights, sounds, and smells of those scenes threatened to undo all sense of stability and security.

She shook her head and took in long, deep breaths to clear the nausea that had overtaken her. She had to pull it together. It was almost time for her guests to arrive.

Walking through the living room, she stopped to plump sofa cushions and rearrange knick-knacks. She glanced out the front window as Marjorie and Terri emerged from their cars, greeting each other with hugs and kisses. Marjorie carried her overnight bag and a square Tupperware container filled with what Laura knew was her specialty, deviled eggs.

Laura hoped she could convince Marjorie to stay the entire weekend. There was so much to talk about. Hurrying down the stairs to the front door, she welcomed her friends, exchanging more hugs and kisses.

They came upstairs and got settled. Terri filled an ice bucket, removed wine glasses from the dish cabinet, and got to work setting up a small bar. Marjorie joined Laura in the kitchen. They lifted the enormous golden-brown turkey onto its serving platter and removed the stuffing to another dish. Everything looked and smelled delicious. Minutes later, Emily and Andrew entered the kitchen, carrying crusty rolls from a specialty bakery.

Just before five o'clock, John rang the doorbell. Laura hurried downstairs to welcome him. He produced an enormous bouquet of autumn flowers. "I brought pie, too," he said, juggling the bulky container on his other arm.

"Pie is always welcome here," she said, chuckling. "Come in and get warm." She shivered as a brisk wind nearly blew the door shut.

He kissed her on the cheek. "Thanks again for inviting me. Now put me to work."

"Could you slice the turkey for me? Andrew hates that job." She led the way upstairs to the apartment. "Terri is in charge of drinks. Marjorie is helping me in the kitchen with side dishes. We'll eat in about a half hour. Hope you're hungry."

From the kitchen, Laura could hear snatches of conversation: the winning floats in the Rose Bowl Parade, college football results, and wedding details. "John, I hope you can be there," Emily said. "The invitations just went out yesterday."

Laura exchanged glances with Marjorie. "I didn't say anything to him about going to the wedding, although I thought about it. Andrew and Emily don't know about Larry," she whispered. "We haven't been dating that long, and I wasn't sure what to do about inviting Larry to the wedding. If we're still dating in a few weeks, it might hurt his feelings if I don't ask him to go with me as my plus-one."

Marjorie looked thoughtful. "John is a family friend, and the kids want him there. Anyway, the cat is out of the bag. He knows about the wedding, and the bridal couple wants him there. Do you?"

"Um." Laura bit the inside of her cheek, considering the matter. "The easy answer is 'Of course.' The more difficult answer is, 'How do I finesse this?'"

Marjorie bit into a radish rose. "Does John know you're dating Larry? If so, he might decide he shouldn't attend. Let that be his decision."

"You're right. I'll see him at book club. We can talk afterward."

Chapter Thirty

"You haven't said much about Larry lately," Terri said, taking a cautious sip of steaming mulled wine. They sat at Laura's dining room table wrapping Christmas presents. "Is he still on your radar or have you met some other handsome, available man? You're, like, a total man magnet these days."

Laura nearly choked on her drink. "He invited me over to his house last evening for a drink. I said I couldn't." She raised her eyebrows. "He wanted to show me the chair he bought at Serendipities."

"That's nice of him."

"At his house," Laura stressed. "His house."

"A visit to his house to see the chair you sold him? Just like that? No foreplay?" Terri laughed and snipped the end of a ribbon. "Put your finger here," she said, shaking her head, a grin on her face. Laura held the ribbon in place with her forefinger until Terri tied it in a bow. "Just saying, it seems like a normal thing for him to suggest. He wants you to see the chair in its native habitat. It's his *house*, Laura. He didn't ask you to spend the night."

"I know. I just . . ." She thought for a moment. "I'm really busy, you know."

"I distinctly remember you saying there was zero chemistry with him when you met the first time," Terri pointed out. "Is that still the case?"

"He is such a nice guy." Laura twisted her mouth. "He's kind of perfect, really. Very good-looking, grounded emotionally, interesting. I don't know what's the matter with me. Maybe it's too soon after Greg."

"And maybe you just aren't that into Larry."

"Why not? I feel guilty for not liking him more. He is perfect boy-friend material."

Terri was quiet for a moment before responding. "If you don't like him that much, why do you keep saying yes to his invitations? You're sending him signals, and they seem to be 'Come hither' ones."

"It's the holidays. When he asks me out, I can't say no, even if I'd rather stay home. I'm supposed to go to an office party with him this Friday night." Laura flinched. "I can't say no. Who wants to go all by themselves to their office party?"

"I cain't saa-aay no," Terri sang with a perfect Oklahoma twang.

Laura smiled and shook her head. "Are you going to give me sage advice or what?"

"It's lonely at the holidays," Terri said more seriously. "It's that time of year when people are most aware that they're single. Showing up at a party by yourself *can* be hell."

"The truth is, I don't know how I feel about him."

"Seems like you do." Terri looked meaningfully at her. "If Larry really likes you, and I'm guessing he does, he will hope for more. For his sake, don't give him the wrong idea."

"I would never want to hurt him. You're right." Laura cut across another section of wrapping paper. "To be honest, when he first asked me out, I said yes because I didn't have a reason to say no."

"John," Terri said, emphasizing his name. "John is a reason to say no. What about *John*?"

"What *about* John?" Laura paused, scissors in mid-air. "He's a recent widower. We're friends. He is—well, was—my attorney. What we are not, at this moment, is a couple. And I don't want him to think I assume that we're going to be a couple, either. This is complicated."

"You and John are the only ones who don't know you're a couple," Terri muttered, rummaging through a box of ribbons and bows. "Quit hogging the green bows."

"We are *not* a couple," Laura protested, sliding the bows across the table to her. "There has never been any talk of anything more than what we have now."

"What is your definition of a couple, Laura?" Terri asked. "Couples support each other. They are there for each other in good times and bad. They have fun together. They take on projects together. That's the defini-tion of you and John. The two of you might be the last to know."

Laura watched out the passenger side window as Larry drove her home after his office party. He was a certified financial planner who worked for a large financial services company. This office party was the biggest party Laura had ever attended. From a lavish charcuterie board and full bar to an elaborate buffet dinner followed by a jazz trio, no expense had been spared.

Larry stayed by her side, introducing her to his colleagues and their spouses. She knew some of the women from Serendipities Two. As office parties went, it was fun. She was glad she had agreed to go with him.

Afterward, he pulled into an available parking space on the street in front of Serendipities and turned off the engine. She glanced at her Apple watch and saw that it was almost ten o'clock. He opened her car door and took her arm as they walked across the frosty grass and uneven sidewalk. When they reached the entrance, she started to unlock the door.

She would have preferred that he leave, but knew it was time to invite him inside. "Would you like a cup of tea? It's not a school night," she said in an attempt at humor.

"That would be nice."

They went upstairs to her apartment. He removed his coat, and she hung it for him in the hall closet. Turning on lamps along the way, she went to the kitchen. He followed her, standing companionably in the doorway while she filled a teapot with water and set it on the stove to boil. "Nice place," he said. "It's much bigger than I thought it would be."

"I was lucky this building came on the market when I was ready to open my store," she said. "The fact that it included this second floor living space cinched the deal. I love this place."

"You've never considered buying another house, somewhere away from your business?"

She sensed a deeper reason for the question. "To be honest, it has never crossed my mind," she said. "It's convenient being so close to work. When my mother lived with me, it was important to be close to her."

"But she's gone now. You could choose to live elsewhere."

What was he getting at? Her eyes met his. "Larry, I . . ."

"Laura, I'm going to lay my cards on the table," he said. There was no aggression in his stance, though his arms were crossed over his chest.

Laura recognized it for what it was: an unconscious attempt to protect his heart. She smiled gently and said, "Let's sit down."

They went into the living room and sat down across from each other. Larry looked directly into her eyes and said, "I've enjoyed getting to know you. If this seems premature, so be it. I want to be married again, and I have a beautiful home that I want to share with the right woman. I was hopeful that woman could be you. I'm not saying this to rush you. I just want you to know how I feel."

Laura nearly dropped the mug of tea she was holding. Although she might have expected him to say that he thought their relationship was going well, and he was enjoying time with her, she hadn't expected this level of candor. She met his gaze. "Larry, you are a wonderful man." She paused, taking in a deep breath. "I have enjoyed getting to know you."

"But?" He smiled gently. "I've begun to sense that you may not share my feelings." His eyes never left her face. What she saw there was acceptance. "Is there someone else? You deserve to be happy."

"There might be," she said, looking into his kind eyes. "I think I need to find out."

A PICTURESQUE SNOW FELL THE FIRST WEEK OF DECEMBER, ushering in the winter holiday season. Red, green, and white Christmas lights twinkled in Dublin storefronts, canned carols played in shopping malls and on the radio, and holiday fir trees sprouted overnight in parking lots. Laura decorated Serendipities Two and set up a hot chocolate bar with trays of cookies baked by Ruth that she brought back with her to Dublin.

She had boxes and boxes of them stored in a new basement freezer. She had come to think of Ruth's cookies as signature Serendipities treats. It wouldn't do to serve her shoppers anything less.

On Wednesday, the Irish book club discussed *Angela's Ashes*. Although the novel had been published in 1996, and everyone in the group had read the book after its release, they agreed it had been worth re-reading. Laura knew that her grandparents had lived in Ireland during the time that Frank McCourt's family was there. Hardships abounded. Her grandparents and their children endured poverty and political unrest in their homeland.

Her grandparents had left Ireland with two small children for a better life in America. From what Eileen had shared, life was better in the United States, but far from perfect, since Irish immigrants were often treated poorly. They moved to Parmenter, Ohio after Laura's grandfather got a job on the railroad.

Eileen married at twenty. Her new husband was a handsome man with a strong personality, seemingly lacking a sense of humor. Although Laura didn't recall any domestic abuse, her father had been conservative, traditional in his beliefs about a woman's role in a marriage. Still, her parents had loved each other.

However, her father had not always been respectful to her mother. Even so, Eileen had held her husband up as head of the household, never speaking against him. For this reason, Laura had been hesitant to share information about Jed with her mother that painted him as anything less than a good husband and father. That information came to light much later, when mother and daughter lived together.

She could see parallels of Angela McCourt's life in her own and in Eileen's lives. It didn't seem to matter the time, place, or culture. Women shared challenges in their roles as wives and mothers, and often as providers. Laura wondered whether she would have remained so long with Jed if she hadn't had Michael and Andrew. And yet, it had been her sons whose very existence made that time of her life worth all the trials. Motherhood, too, was bittersweet.

Times were changing, although Laura remained convinced that women's lives might be even more difficult now as more of them juggled high-powered careers with marriages and families. In many cases, they had no choice but to remain in the workforce when they started families. Emily would have opportunities to balance work and family with a strong partner. She and Andrew had the kind of relationship that would enable them to navigate through decisions about career and family. For this Laura was grateful.

After the group finished its discussion of *Angela's Ashes*, everyone headed to the Irish pub, where Terri and her band, Street, were scheduled to perform starting at nine o'clock. The pub's parking lot was full. Laura had trouble finding a spot big enough for her SUV. She circled the lot several times before giving up and parking on a side street. In her rearview mirror, she saw that John had the same idea.

"Seems like this is the place to be tonight," he said as they met on the sidewalk. "Shall we?" Laura stepped cautiously over a frozen puddle. John held out his arm. "Watch. It's slick."

"Thanks." Laura linked her arm through his as they made their way to the front door of the pub. Entering the crowded bar, Laura caught sight of other book club members. They had commandeered three booths and were in the process of ordering food and drinks. She and John slid into one of the booths.

"I'll have a Black-and-Tan," John said. "You?" He looked at Laura.

"Chardonnay. Thanks."

"Chardonnay," he said to the server. "Oh, and can we get an order of Super Spuds for the table?" Super Spuds were potato skins overstuffed with cheese, sour cream, bacons, and green onions. "All that discussion about Ireland made me think of potatoes."

Laura glanced over at the small, raised stage where Terri was doing a sound check, her band members in place. Terri tapped the microphone. "Good evening, everybody. It's great to see everyone out tonight. I spy my Irish book lovers over there." She shaded her eyes from the overhead lights. There was loud applause from the Irish book club. "Speaking of Ireland, we talked about a great book tonight. Some of you may remember *Angela's Ashes*." More applause from the bar crowd. "So, in honor of all things Irish, we're starting off with a classic tune, 'Whiskey in a Jar.'"

She began the intro on her fiddle, which was hailed by cheers and clapping. Laura scanned the bar area for anyone she knew. She felt a little nervous, realizing that she might see Larry or, worse, Greg. But the coast was clear.

It was close to eleven when she and John left the pub and headed to their cars. John turned up the collar of his overcoat and again, offered his arm to her. "Nice night," he said.

"It is. The snow is all sparkly."

"I meant being together tonight, listening to Terri sing, and feeling— I don't know—normal." He stressed the word. "It's been so long since I had the time or even the interest in doing stuff like this."

Now they stood in front of Laura's car. She clicked the key fob and unlocked the door, pulling it open. "You're right. It was fun, and I've needed some down time lately," she said. "Thanks for making sure I made it to my car."

"Hey," he began, tentatively. She waited for him to finish. "I haven't returned my wedding RSVP yet."

"Are you thinking you might not be able to make it, after all?"

He rubbed his chin, appearing uncertain. "I'd like to. I guess what I need to ask is whether it's really okay with you. For all I know, you might already be thinking of bringing someone."

"John, you have been a very important person in our family this year. You helped Andrew and me get justice for Michael. More than that, you're my friend. I want you there." She bit her upper lip.

"So, you're not seeing anyone?"

"I went out a few times with a guy." She hesitated. "But he isn't any-one I could imagine spending my life with—even though he is really,

really nice. Of course, not everyone you date has to end up being your true love or anything." She felt embarrassed as soon as the words were out of her mouth.

John offered a half-smile. "I'd imagine it's pretty difficult to date again at this age. People are set in their ways. They want different things."

Laura paused. Was there a message in this? "Well, I guess if you meet the right person, it's probably not so bad."

"The right person makes it all worthwhile." He put his hands in his coat pockets. "I'll send back my RSVP tomorrow."

"John?" Their eyes met.

"Thank you for saying what you just said. I hope we can always be honest with each other. I don't ever want us to have uncomfortable feelings when we're together."

"Didn't I just cause that?" He looked as if he wanted to say something more, then stopped. "Good night, Laura," he said, offering a half-smile before walking away.

THE FOLLOWING THURSDAY EVENING, Laura met Jan Armstrong for fish and chips at the pub. It was a tradition for them to exchange presents over dinner, away from the library or the Irish book club. Terri and Street were scheduled to perform at eight o'clock.

Laura gave Jan a personal teapot with a built-in tea strainer for loose teas. When she opened Jan's gift, she laughed. It was the same teapot.

"We know each other so well, don't we?" Laura laughed. "Teapots and books go so well together."

Jan agreed. She picked up a crispy potato wedge and bit into it before asking "So, how are wedding preparations coming along?"

"All set," Laura said. She sprinkled malt vinegar over her fish. "I finally found a dress. It's burgundy velvet, full-skirted and tea-length, with a square neckline that hits about here." She indicated the area beneath her collarbone. "Emily's mother is wearing a dark green suit, so I thought I'd go with an opposite Christmas color."

"Sounds pretty." Jan removed the tea bag from the stainless-steel miniature teapot the server had set before her. "A Christmas wedding is so romantic."

"They're going to the Bahamas for their honeymoon," Laura said. "Emily's parents and I went together on that gift. The kids deserve a nice trip."

At seven-thirty, Terri and her band began setting up. Catching sight of Laura and Jan, Terri left the stage and hurried over to their table. "Glad to see you both here tonight," she said, offering a shoulder bump to Laura. "Is anyone else from the book club coming?"

"Presumably yes," Jan said. They scanned the room looking for familiar faces. "Aren't they almost always here when you play?"

It was at that moment that Laura noticed Larry sitting at the bar. As if on cue, sensing her nearby, he turned and offered a friendly wave. Laura waved back.

"That's Larry" she said, and then added, "Jeez, don't both of you turn and look at him at once."

"Too late." Terri grinned. "He's way better looking than you've told me."

"He dresses really well, too. And, he smells nice." Laura grinned. "He's really wonderful."

Jan looked perplexed. Laura quickly explained. She had not told Terri about the last conversation she had with Larry. She had simply emailed to tell her that she and Larry agreed they would not continue dating, and she wished him all the best.

"I know Larry pretty well," Jan said. "He's been our financial advisor for years—and a good one."

"Did you know his wife, too?" Laura asked. Larry hadn't been forthcoming about his former spouse. He merely said she lived in New York City, and they had been divorced for several years.

"We met her a long time ago, but never really got to know her. She's in academic medicine. I seem to recall she's a pulmonologist by training, but she's also an associate dean of a medical school in New York City. They kept up a long-distance marriage for a while."

"He mentioned what his wife did and where she lived. But he never got into details," Laura said. "To be honest, when we were together, he was always focused on me. That was nice." She smiled. "He seems like a very honorable, good man."

"That he is. He'll make someone a nice husband," Jan said. "I've always thought that."

"Well, I'd better get back up there," Terri said. It was ten minutes till eight.

"I'm going over to say hi to Larry," Laura said. "Would you come with me for just a minute?"

"What for?"

"Because who doesn't want to meet the lead singer of the band that's playing? Besides, I've told him that you and I are friends. He's bound to be impressed."

Terri allowed herself to be led over to the bar. Laura tapped Larry on the back. He turned and smiled broadly. "Laura!"

"I saw you over here and thought I'd come say 'hi.' I want you to meet my friend, Terri."

"It's great to meet you, Terri," Larry said, getting off the bar stool to shake her hand. "I enjoy your music. It's really cool that you and Laura are friends."

Terri smiled—not the usual hundred-watt onstage smile she gave to her audience, but a shy, sweet one. "I've seen you here before," she said. "Thanks for supporting my band."

Chapter Thirty-One

Laura stood in front of the full-length mirror assessing her appearance. She wore the velvet burgundy dress she had selected for Andrew and Emily's wedding. She decided, after a few turns, that the cut of the neckline on the dress with its fitted waist and full, tea-length skirt complimented her figure and her neckline. She had chosen black pumps with a two-inch heel, comfortable enough to ensure she could dance the night away.

She fastened the buttons on her good black coat and made her way into the living room. Turning off the white twinkle lights on the Christmas tree, she glanced around at the room. Gifts were stacked under the tree for family members who would gather in the morning to open them and enjoy a traditional Christmas breakfast.

"Ready?" She peeked into the hall bathroom where Marjorie stood in front of the vanity mirror applying lipstick.

"As ready as I'll ever be," Marjorie replied, blotting her rosy lips with a piece of toilet tissue. She looked lovely in a blue-gray silk suit.

Laura helped her into her coat, and the friends went downstairs to wait for John. He had just texted to say he was on his way. The wedding was in less than an hour.

When he arrived, he helped them into his car. Laura sat in front. The temperature was in the mid-thirties, and two inches of snow lay on the ground with more expected overnight, ensuring a white Christmas. As they made their way to the church, they passed homes lit with holiday lights, Christmas trees, and wreaths adorning doors and windows.

Laura realized, with a lump in her throat, that by the end of the evening, her small family would grow with the addition of Emily and her extended family. There would be holiday gatherings. Children would be born to this marriage. A feeling of joy and love washed over her. This day was a dream come true.

She was ushered to her seat on the arm of one of Andrew's fraternity friends, Matt. There were two other groomsmen in the wedding party to match Emily's three best friends. John maneuvered his long legs across Laura to sit on one side of her while Marjorie sat on the other.

"Your son looks amazingly calm." He chuckled. "I was a nervous wreck when I got married."

Laura watched with motherly pride as Andrew stood at the front of the church with his best man, Josh. The two had been roommates their freshmen and sophomore years in college. Andrew and Josh and the groomsmen wore charcoal-gray suits with emerald ties. Emily had chosen emerald gowns for her maid of honor and bridesmaids.

The organist began playing soft Christmas music. Candles adorned the end of each pew. More candles were arranged on the altar.

Ten minutes before the ceremony, Terri arrived in the sanctuary accompanied by Larry. Laura motioned for them to sit in her row. As Larry arrived at Laura's pew, he winked and mouthed a silent thank you.

She smiled back and reached over to take his hand in a gesture of friendship. It was wonderful to see him and Terri so happy. They deserved the best life had to offer. Terri wore a black lace dress. Her waist-length raven hair was arranged in a sophisticated updo. Larry looked handsome in his navy-blue suit with a patterned burgundy tie. Looking closer, Laura saw tiny candy canes on his tie. From all appearances, Terri had found her Hallmark-style happily-ever-after love. Laura smiled at her friends' newfound happiness and silently wished them well.

"You look absolutely stunning," Laura said to Terri, hugging her tightly. "That dress is gorgeous." She leaned in to whisper, "I'm so happy—for both of you."

"He's wonderful." Terri's face beamed.

"Yes, he is." Laura smiled and squeezed her friend's hand. "He deserves someone as wonderful as you."

Laura had been delighted to learn that on the night she introduced them, Larry stayed at the pub until Terri finished performing. They had a drink together and enjoyed their conversation so much, he asked her on a date. They had gone out just about every evening since then.

"It might be too soon to say this," Terri had confided a few days earlier when she and Laura talked on the phone, "but I think I'm in love. I have never felt this way about anyone before."

"You need to invite him to the wedding," Laura said. "It's not too late to add him to the guest list. Tell him I insist. We'll all have so much fun together."

As the strains of Pachelbel's *Canon in D* began, everyone turned to watch as the maid of honor and bridesmaids made their way down the aisle, pairing up with the best man and groomsmen at the altar. Emily's attendants were her closest high school and college friends. "My besties," she had described them. They took their places along the communion rail as Emily and her father began their walk down the aisle toward Andrew.

Emily's gown, an A-line in white satin was adorned with an emerald velvet sash with a wide bow in back. The simplicity of the dress suited her delicate figure. She carried a simple bouquet of white carnations and holly with bright red berries.

The Presbyterian church was led by a female minister who ably served her congregation and was well-liked by everyone in the community. Emily and Andrew attended church regularly. Although Laura was not Presbyterian, she liked the minister and thought she might start attending there, too.

"Jed would roll over in his grave if he knew a woman was performing the ceremony," Marjorie said under her breath to Laura.

Laura giggled quietly and whispered back, "He'd probably argue it wasn't a real ceremony. They won't be married in the eyes of God—or something."

It didn't take long before Laura began to fumble for the stash of tissues in her purse. Thank goodness for waterproof mascara. Watching her youngest son standing with the woman he loved, and to vow to love and honor her, brought joy Laura could not have imagined.

Watching them together, she knew that Andrew's life might have taken a much different trajectory. He had been willing to have counseling to talk about life in a household where domestic violence was an ever-present threat. She knew that Emily and Andrew had been introduced their freshmen year at Ohio State. At first, Andrew was guarded in sharing information with his new girlfriend concerning his family's troubled history. Over the course of their relationship, it had been Emily's unconditional love and support that had gotten Andrew to a place where the likelihood of a lasting, happy marriage was not just a hope-for; it was a probability.

"We gather here today to celebrate the marriage of Emily Rose Hancock and Andrew Paul Fisher," the minister began. Laura was barely conscious of the words spoken as she watched her handsome son. His eyes never left his bride. "Will you, Emily, take Andrew to be your lawfully wedded husband? . . . Will you, Andrew, take Emily to be your lawfully wedded wife? . . . In sickness and in health, to love honor and cherish . . ."

As the minister pronounced the couple husband and wife, Laura watched as Andrew kissed Emily, a look of adoration on his face. In response, Emily placed her hands on either side of his face and returned the kiss. At that moment, John placed his hand over Laura's and squeezed her fingers. She took his hand. It was as natural as breathing.

When the newlyweds faced their guests, and the minister introduced them as Mr. and Mrs. Andrew Fisher, there wasn't a dry eye on either side of the aisle. The love expressed in a bride's kiss for her new husband was evidence of a love that could withstand any test. Andrew looked over, and his eyes met his mother's. In that look, Laura saw pure happiness.

For the next ninety minutes, the photographer took photos of the wedding party at the altar, followed by the bride and bridegroom with their families. As Laura watched Emily and Andrew with Emily's grandparents, she thought of her mother. How she would have enjoyed seeing Andrew marry Emily. Perhaps she could see now from where she was.

"Could we get just a few more pictures?" she asked as the photographer finished the bridal party and family shots. "I'd like photos of my circle of friends." She motioned to Marjorie, John, Terri, and Larry. Laura felt certain this photo would have a place of prominence in her home. These friends had become her life lines, people as dear as family.

It was snowing when they left the church. The crystal snowflakes glistened in the night air and fell to the ground, covering everything in sight. It was a short drive to the reception on the outskirts of Columbus. John drove through Dublin, past snowy fields and onto the curving drive leading to the country club.

The banquet hall had been transformed into a winter wonderland. Christmas trees decorated in white lights and colored metallic balls towered in every corner of the large room. White tablecloths set with forest-green cloth napkins were arranged on each table, along with sparkling cut-glass centerpieces of white candles surrounded by white carnations, holly, and berries.

Dinner was a prix fixe menu featuring the chef's specialties of crown roast, stuffed Cornish game hens, and honeyed salmon. As Laura ate her arugula salad, dressed in a lemon-olive oil dressing with freshly shaved Parmesan, she marveled at the elegance of their dinner setting. She had never been to such an elegant wedding, and was grateful that Andrew could be married in splendor. For the next hour, Laura and her friends sipped Champagne, enjoyed a leisurely meal, and talked.

Music for the reception came courtesy of a popular radio celebrity and disc jockey. He was Andrew's friend from college, and had promised to play favorites from every decade. After toasts to the happy couple, it was time to dance. Laura had never actually danced until she moved to Dublin. On a lark, she joined a ballroom dancing program and learned all the steps she hadn't been allowed to learn as a girl. She looked forward to stepping onto the dance floor with Andrew tonight for the mother-son dance.

As the bride and her father stepped onto the dance floor, Laura watched with joy as they twirled to a popular song about fathers and daughters. As the sweet lyrics expressed the bittersweet feelings of a father dancing with his little girl in the kitchen, Laura could picture Emily as a toddler, her tiny feet on his big shoes, as he twirled her around the kitchen.

The song ended, and Andrew beckoned his mother with a smile, holding out his hand to her. He led her onto the dance floor and kissed her cheek. Earlier, he had promised that his choice of groom's song would be a surprise for her. As she heard the first strains of "A Mother's Song," tears welled in her eyes, and she rested her head against her son's broad chest, loving him more than ever.

"Are you as happy as you look?" she asked him.

"Happier than I ever thought I could be," he said. "I'm not sure how I got so lucky or how I got to this place in life. But it feels right," Andrew said. "Thank you for everything you did to make this the best day of our lives."

"Something tells me this will be just the first of many more to come," Laura said, smiling. "We'll be all together here supporting each other. We'll celebrate your anniversary every year, and it will make Christmas that much more special."

"You're the perfect mother. You know that, right? I owe everything I am to you." She heard the catch in his voice.

"And I couldn't be prouder to call you my son," she said.

As their dance ended and a new song began, they stepped apart. Turning, Laura saw John approaching them on the dance floor.

"May I have this dance?" he asked, directing the question to Andrew.

"Thanks, John, but I think I'll find my bride and dance with her," Andrew quipped.

"Oh, you meant Mom?"

They laughed, and Andrew stepped away. John held out his hand, and she placed her hand in his. They moved easily together, talking and laughing as he led her around the dance floor. Dancing with John felt as effortless as if they'd danced together many times before.

"You're a very good dancer," she said.

"I was about to say the same about you. It's been years since I did this. I guess it's like riding a bike."

"Growing up, we didn't dance—I mean ever," she said. "It was forbidden in our church. I never danced at all until about two years ago when I took a ballroom dance class, just to see what it felt like to dance. I enjoyed it, especially the salsa dances."

"You'll have to teach me one of those," John said.

Laura turned to watch as Larry whirled Terri around. He was considerably taller than her. As the strains of "Unchained Melody" began to play, Terri laid her head against Larry's chest. He pulled her in more tightly, encircling her in his arms.

"I have a feeling those two will be the next ones tying the knot," John remarked.

"He's perfect for her," Laura said. "They're opposites, in many ways, but that only seems to heighten their attraction. He's ready for a serious relationship. She is, too. She just didn't know it until she met him."

"You knew Larry before they started dating?" John sounded curious.

Laura hesitated. She didn't want John thinking she was a serial dater. "I only went out with him a few times, but . . ." She shrugged. "He's the one I mentioned earlier."

"No spark?"

"Something like that. He deserves someone special. Terri was playing at the pub one night, and he was there, too. I introduced them, and they've been inseparable ever since."

"I guess when the situation is right, wild horses couldn't keep two people apart." He led her away from another couple that was about to bump into them before adding, "I disagree with one thing you just said."

"What's that?"

"You just said he deserves someone special. You're special." He led her to a less crowded spot on the dance floor.

"That's sweet of you to say." She was conscious of his hand on her lower back, the scent of his aftershave, the warmth of his body. She hoped "Unchained Melody" would go on and on.

"I don't know what I would have done these past months without your support."

"John, you've been there for me . . . twice," she said. She paused before continuing. "Have you ever wondered whether it's fate?"

"How so?" He leaned back, gazing directly into her eyes.

"I mean, I was in trouble when we met, and you helped me twice that day. Then, we meet up again years later at Glenview Gardens, when we're about to need help from each other . . ." She spoke carefully now. "We both needed support—you when Jackie was dying, me when I was trying to get justice for Michael. Then when my mom died, you were there, too. Meeting in the dining room at Glenview Gardens that day felt like it was meant to be."

"I considered that, too," he said. "Over the years, I thought about you sometimes—wished I knew where you were—you know, how you were doing."

"You did?" This amazed her. "If you don't mind me asking, what about that day made an impression? I was pretty forgettable in those days." She remembered how she had dressed the day she had first met him, in clothes that kept her invisible, especially to other men.

"You, forgettable? No way," John said, smiling.

"It was just one day in a life."

"It may have been just one day, but it stuck with me. I felt I should have done more to make sure you were okay. I dropped you off, and it was obvious that you'd been injured. Later that night, when I saw the ugly bruise on your neckline, I knew."

"He tore a muscle squeezing my shoulder," she said, wincing at the memory. "It took quite a while for it to heal completely."

He let out a deep breath. "Man, it couldn't have been easy those first few years after he died."

"I had a lot to learn, but I always wanted to do the work I'm doing now. And I had Marjorie to show me the ropes."

"I'm talking about the way your husband treated you. There had to be scars, and not just physical ones." John looked directly into her eyes. "After . . . what is it? Almost four years since he died?"

She nodded. "Almost."

"How do you feel now?" His question seemed to require a more detailed answer.

"The thing about scars," she began, "is that you can see those silvery-white lines where something painful once happened. If you think about it, scars are a sign that something has healed. Oh sure, there might still be an ache in that spot. But broken bones heal stronger than they were before. I had counseling, of course, to deal with the emotional scars."

With a shy smile, she held out her hand to John who took it and spun her. In the next moment, he drew her in, enfolding her in a way that felt familiar, as if they had held each other many times before. Looking over, she watched as Andrew danced with Emily. Her arms were linked around his neck, and they were conversing as if they were the only two people on Earth. At that moment, Laura realized that she felt the same way—as if she and John were alone.

"Look at those two," John said. "Their entire future is in front of them."

"It's nice to imagine what that might look like," she answered.

John was quiet, staring off into space, even as his hand tightened on hers. From his expression, Laura suspected he was thinking about Jackie. She hoped it wasn't sadness he was feeling.

"Are you thinking about your own wedding day?" she finally asked, hoping he'd share his thoughts.

"Sorry." He smiled.

"No need to apologize. It's perfectly natural."

"Do you think you'll ever get married again?" he asked, surprising her with the question.

She thought for a moment. "Yes, but my expectations will be way higher next time."

John chuckled. "Good answer."

"What about you?" she asked. "Do you ever see yourself falling in love again?" As soon as the words were out of her mouth, she regretted them.

"Jackie insisted on it."

"You actually talked about this?" Laura was fascinated.

"Several times," he said. "She had been sick for a long time and felt guilty for all that she couldn't do—what we couldn't do together." Laura could imagine that a physical relationship was high among Jackie's concerns. "At one point, she offered me a divorce. Of course, I said no way. At the time, I couldn't imagine . . . Well, I couldn't envision a future without her."

"She must have loved you very much. She wanted you to have a happy life, more than anything. It must have been so difficult for her to actually speak those words."

"She had no ability to speak at all toward the end, and she couldn't write her thoughts, either," John said. "I had to do all the talking. But I always knew by her reaction what she thought. When I told her I didn't want to live without her, she reacted almost violently. She blinked her eyes and made sounds that I knew meant she didn't want me saying anything like that."

"Only you will know when you're ready," Laura said.

"I imagine you're right," he said. "The truth is that I will never love another woman the way I loved Jackie." Laura's heart skipped a beat. "But," he continued, "it doesn't mean I can't love someone in a different way."

Laura was quiet, taking in his message. "It took quite a while before I could even imagine dating again," she said. "Terri pushed me into trying one of those internet dating sites. Actually, it's how I met Larry. But we weren't really a match. At least, I didn't think so."

"Hopefully, I won't need to go that route," John said with a chuckle. "Larry's already taken."

Laura laughed and lightly smacked his arm. Though she was reluctant to talk about her disastrous relationship with Greg Waters, she wanted the subject out in the open. John surely wondered what had happened. "I met that guy, Greg, at a library fundraiser. Now that I look back on it, I realize how naïve I was. He wasn't who I thought he was."

"He wasn't good enough for you," John said emphatically. "Guys know that about other guys."

"I could tell you didn't like him. The thing is, I never felt completely comfortable with him. It was a new experience, dating, and . . ." She faltered. "He wanted to move fast, and it felt like he was pushing me."

"I assume you're talking about a physical relationship. That needs to be a mutual decision." He was silent for a moment before continuing. "That makes me sound like I know what the heck I'm talking about. I'm no relationship expert. But I *was* a one-woman man for many years."

"I admire that about you," she said, and took in a breath as his hand tightened around her waist.

At that moment, dancing in his arms, conscious of the in and out of his breath, the low resonance of his voice, the way they moved together, Laura knew she was falling in love. Were her feelings obvious to him? Surely, it was too soon for him to share these feelings. But, as the song ended and they stopped dancing, he kept her in place a moment longer.

"Laura," he said, pausing for a moment before starting again. "Your patience and kindness mean the world to me." She nodded, understanding that other words might need to remain unspoken. Taking a breath, he said, "This is a process. I won't wait much longer to start living again. But for now, I'm taking baby steps."

Chapter Thirty-Two

"For those of you who have never been to Ireland, or for others who have been there and yearn to go back, I just learned of a tour in late July," Jan announced when the book club met the third week of January. "It's short notice, I realize, but there are still a few spots left." She looked around at her book club members. "Anyone interested in joining me?"

"I will!" Laura's arm shot up so fast, she nearly toppled her cup of tea. This was serendipity at its best.

After hearing so many stories of her Irish mother's homeland and reading Irish novels and poetry, she wanted to visit the land of her ancestors. As a child, her mother, two brothers, and a sister had emigrated with their parents from the seaside town of Kenmare. They had sailed to New York City, then traveled by train to Ohio in the early nineteen-forties. Though their lives were impoverished, there was another even more challenging hardship: discrimination due to their Irish heritage. Laura's grandfather worked on the railroad. Her grandmother took in laundry and ironing. Despite their hardscrabble existence, Eileen was proud to be an American citizen.

Although she had expressed homesickness for Ireland and talked often of favorite places, Eileen hadn't been interested in traveling back there, either by air or sea. Laura had offered to accompany her several times, but Eileen always declined the offer.

"My life is here now," she would say in her Irish brogue.

Three other members of the book club also expressed interested in the July trip. Laura glanced over at Terri and mouthed the word, "You?"

Terri shook her head no. With a name like McDonald, Terri's Irish roots clearly ran deep. But Laura knew that the summer months were Terri's busy season performing at summer concerts. There was also an issue of cost. Terri was on a tight budget.

"The tour starts in Dublin and continues south toward Killarney and around the Ring of Kerry. There is also a day trip to the Aran Isles—something you don't want to miss on any tour of Ireland." Jan handed out brochures with details and costs. "Just think: eight days of scenic Ireland, food, and fun."

By nine o'clock, Laura and Terri were ensconced on Laura's over-stuffed sofa, wrapped in fleecy blankets, a bowl of popcorn between them. They hadn't spent any time together since Andrew's wedding. Terri, it seemed, was busy with Larry nearly every evening. She kept Laura apprised of the progression of their relationship through frequent text messages.

The last one, received the night before, simply said, "He loves me."

"So?" Laura began, raising her eyebrows. "Will there be a wedding anytime soon?"

Terri grinned. "We rang in the New Year with all the fireworks, in more ways than one," she said and tossed a fistful of popped kernels into her mouth. "Not any time soon, but yes, I do believe we are heading toward the altar."

"I suspected as much." Laura said. "Watching the two of you is better than a Hallmark movie."

"If that movie was an epic story over decades with at least one hopeless bride-to-be," Terri quipped.

"You had plenty of opportunities," Laura corrected. "You were just being choosy."

Terri's face turned serious. "If I look back at other relationships that might have moved forward, I realize that even if a guy seemed nice, I was afraid to love again."

"Because of your ex-husband?"

"Royce is the reason I have my band. Street was his band, originally." She leaned over and picked up her wine glass from the coffee table, took a long sip, and set it down again. "Royce was one of those rare gifts, you know? He played the saxophone like it was an extension of his body, his very being. You always tell me when I play, I become the fiddle. Royce became the saxophone. I fell so hard for him."

"How long were you married?"

"A little over five years. I should have known it wouldn't last. We never had the kind of relationship that holds a marriage together. But what we had was good." She shook her head. "No, actually, it was more like being the best of friends who also happen to be roommates. I realized about four years into the marriage that we weren't having sex much, and that when we did, he was somewhere else . . . in his head. I blamed myself. I wasn't what he wanted."

"You?" Laura couldn't believe what she was hearing. "Anyone who looks at you sees this gorgeous, passionate, gifted woman who gives everything she has to her music. You're generous and kind. You're the best friend anyone could have. What was his problem?" She felt outraged on Terri's behalf.

"I wasn't what he wanted," Terri repeated, wrinkling her nose, a sure sign that she was fighting off tears. She looked at Laura. "The thing is, I wouldn't ever have been enough."

"Why? I don't understand."

"He was gay."

"Oh." Laura's eyes opened wide. "How did you . . .?"

"I came home and found him in bed with Max, a guy I thought was just a good friend of his. Later, after I stormed out and came back a couple of days later to pick up my stuff, he said he 'was exploring feelings he'd always had for Max.'" She made air quotes with her fingers.

Laura shut her eyes and tried to imagine the scene, could almost feel the emotions Terri likely had experienced walking in on her husband with another man. "I'm sorry. That must have been awful."

"It broke my heart," Terri said simply. She shrugged, stared down at the upturned palms of her hands. "Turns out, it was more than exploration. They had been lovers for a long time."

"But he must have cared for you when you got married."

"He did care for me. But I think . . ." She paused. "I think I pushed him into marrying me. We were together all the time. If we had broken up, I might have left the band. It would have been too uncomfortable for both of us to stay. I was the lead singer, by that time. Can't let personal stuff get in the way of the music, right? He didn't want the band to fall apart. And he wasn't comfortable admitting he was gay. So, he . . . faked . . . how he felt about me. It was an act."

"Surely it wasn't all an act. He must have loved you. I'm sure he did. People can't help who they are. It isn't a choice; I'm certain of that." Laura bit her upper lip. "It's sad that he couldn't have admitted sooner—to himself—who he really was. But, Terri, that can't happen again. You know it's not the same with Larry. He loves you. He said so."

"I do know Larry isn't gay." Terri let out a short laugh. "But it's complicated. At first, I was embarrassed so many people knew about Royce. It wasn't like I thought I could keep Royce from being gay. I knew that, at least." She leaned over and picked up her glass of red wine. "But it still hurt that my marriage ended the way it did. Since then, my life hasn't exactly been normal. My past isn't *anything* like Larry's. I wonder if he'll realize that one of these days and decide I'm not enough for him."

"I feel like the last person who should ever give love advice," Laura said, shaking her head. She leaned over and laid a hand on Terri's blanket-covered knee. "Haven't you always told me that hearts are stronger than they seem? That love can overcome any fear? So, what exactly is your fear?"

Terri took a breath and thought for a moment. "Larry is so traditional. He was married to a very successful woman. She's a doctor—a pulmonologist and head of a medical school in New York City. I couldn't be more different. Here I am, just this offbeat singer-song-writer-fiddle player from a small town. I barely make enough to pay my bills. I'm not like his ex-wife. This all seems too good to be true. What if Larry comes to his senses and realizes how far out in left field this all seems to be? What if his sons won't accept me?"

"You're just different from his ex, Terri, *not* less than." Laura had to help her understand. "What you have to offer Larry is very different. Maybe it isn't what he thought he wanted decades ago when he married his first wife, but you are who he wants now. You're perfect for who he is *now*." She paused. "He's perfect for who *you* are now."

Terri dabbed at a tear that dribbled down her cheek. She looked so grateful that Laura knew Terri's pain ran far deeper than she had ever understood. "Don't be afraid. You can do this." Laura chuckled. "Why, the nerve of me."

"What do you mean?"

"Here I am, giving love advice to you as if I know anything about it."

"You know way more than you think you do," Terri said. "So, where do you and John stand, at the moment?"

Laura stretched her arms out in front of her, hands clasped. "I have no idea. At the reception, he said he won't wait much longer to live again. But I guess I have no idea what that means."

"Well, if I were you, I'd continue to be hopeful. I think he might have been letting you know he sees you in his future. Maybe he wanted to see what your reaction would be."

"Time will tell," Laura said, changing the subject. "In the meantime, I'm glad I'm going to Ireland. I have something to look forward to."

JANUARY AND FEBRUARY BROUGHT HEAVY SNOW and ice that frequently kept Laura overnight in Parmenter. She stayed with Marjorie, always grateful for her friend's hospitality and cherished long talks. Laura brought her friend special hostess gifts and treated her to dinners at area restaurants. "I feel as if I ought to pay rent. I'm here so often," Laura said. "I hope you'll let me know if it's not convenient. I can always stay over at the B&B."

"Consider this your B&B. Truth is, I'm glad to have the company. Retirement ain't all it's cracked up to be," Marjorie said one evening. "You can only do so much needlepoint or watch so many stories on television. I thought I'd have fun catching up on soap operas, but . . ." She shook her head, looking thoughtful. "I wonder, could you stand having me around the store more often? I promise not to get in the way of how you do things."

"Are you kidding?" Laura couldn't believe what she was hearing. "You could never be in the way. I still think of it as your store. Of course, you can work more," she said. "It was such a huge part of your life for such a long time. I don't know how you stayed away this long."

"I don't need the money," Marjorie said. "I just want purpose again, a place to go every day. I could fill in whenever you need help."

"I'm happy to pay you whatever you think is fair. I've been looking for another part-timer. The café is doing so well; we have more business than ever. Let me work out a schedule."

"How is Ruth doing?" Marjorie asked, ladling vegetable soup into bowls. She set a salad plate in front of Laura. "This soup is hers, by the way."

"It smells divine. You know, she's really something." Laura tore apart a pretzel roll and buttered it. "It's as if she closed one really awful badly-written book—the story of her life—and decided to write her own book. Her mom has been helping her with the kids. Now, the two of them are cooking and baking up a storm."

CHAPTER THIRTY-THREE

BY MAY, THE SERENDIPITIES CAFÉ WAS SUCH A HIT, Laura urged Ruth to find another part-timer to help her. She had a feeling it would be her mother who was finding her wings, too. With the heightened demand, Laura placed a few more café tables on the front porch. Customers stopped at the café for coffee and a baked treat, or for lunch, and they often stayed to browse items in the store. The used book section located off the café was difficult to keep fully stocked—a nice problem to have.

Many people, she noticed, bought gift items on sight. She enticed them into the store with scented candles, handmade soaps wrapped in country fabric, and bric-a-brac that she arranged with furniture groupings. When she found a large Amish-made dish cabinet at an auction, she removed the glass doors and stocked Ohio-produced honey, infused vinegars, jams, and relishes. Her business forecasts indicated blue skies ahead.

It had been an emotionally tumultuous March and April for her and Andrew when the two men responsible for Luke's death received five-year prison sentences. They would be eligible for early parole. The defendants had wives and children. Both men had been active members of the church Jed had pastored. They had skilled jobs. They swore in court that they never meant to kill Luke. He was their friend. An argument while drinking at a nearby campsite led to a scuffle. Luke had no business being there. Jason and Dan were furious that Luke had blown the lid off what had happened the day Michael died. The three men had sworn each other to secrecy. After arguing at the camp site, Luke drove off, and they followed him. The fight continued farther down the road when Luke pulled over. On a dark, lonely road outside Parmenter, Luke met his end.

As soon as she heard about the light sentences for Jason and Dan, Laura invited Andrew and Emily over for dinner. She included John who, she hoped, might be able to shed light on the judge's decision. Although John was not one of the attorneys for the prosecution, having been a witness to Luke's confession, he continued to keep them abreast of what he knew. He was helpful in explaining the perplexing vagaries of criminal law and human behavior.

"Because of Ohio's statute of limitations laws, the time had passed for them to be charged as accessories in Michael's death," John explained. "Luke was the one, they swear, who hurt your son. It's true, they didn't do anything to stop him. But the only crime Jason and Dan could be tried for was beating up Luke and leaving him by the side of the road. He wasn't dead when they left him. That means the charge is involuntary manslaughter, which carries a maximum sentence of five years in prison."

"It's not fair," Andrew said, pounding his fist on the dining room table. "Those two assholes get about three years in prison—less for good behavior. Let's face it: they played a huge part in Michael's death. They could have tried to stop Luke . . . or tried harder to save Michael."

Emily rubbed the space between his shoulder blades. There was silence around the table as each of them fought an internal struggle to let go of the anger that permeated their every thought about the trial. Laura couldn't sit still any longer. She got up and served carrot cake—thick slices filled with carrots and dried fruit topped with a rich delectable cream cheese frosting. She had brought the cake back to Dublin from the café in Parmenter It was one of Ruth's specialties. She poured coffee all around.

"Strangely enough, if they had actually finished him off by the side of the road, they might have gotten away with it," John continued with a humorless laugh as they ate their desserts. "They would have been suspects, for sure. But there were no witnesses. Luke had other enemies." He looked at Andrew. "If Luke hadn't survived long enough to tell the police who did it, you could have been a suspect, Andrew. The angry brother who wanted justice."

"I know," Andrew said. "I wanted to get even with him. I wasn't going to kill him, obviously."

"It is possible, I guess, that they really didn't intend to kill Luke," Laura said. "He was a big guy. I'm sure it took both of them to bring him down. They probably never considered that someone that big and tough could be hurt badly enough to die." She blew out a long breath. "I guess we'll have to be content that the truth is finally known about what happened that day. Andrew and I always felt it wasn't an accidental drowning." A lone tear dribbled down her cheek. She brushed it away.

"Ironic, isn't it? Those two characters likely would have escaped punishment entirely," John said. "They could have testified against Luke as witnesses for the prosecution. Luke was going to take the fall, anyway. He was the ringleader. There is no statute of limitations on what he did. They had to be tough guys and settle a score. You can't fix that kind of stupid."

"It's over now," Laura said. "That was what I wanted: for everyone to know the truth, and for Luke never to have a chance to hurt anyone else, including Ruth. I will accept this."

After dessert, Andrew and Emily stood up to leave. "I've got an early class tomorrow and a test," Andrew said, stifling a yawn. "Think I'll go over the stuff one more time and get some sleep."

Emily winked at Laura and leaned in for a hug. "That's code for 'He approves of John,'" she whispered. "Hope you two can get a little quality time alone."

Laura smiled at her. Anything was possible. Her daydreams for months had revolved more and more around John. In her mind, she replayed the time they spent dancing at the wedding. It had felt magical, like the start of something that could be lasting love. In her daydreams, she couldn't keep from imagining they were dancing at their own wedding.

After Andrew and Emily left, John expertly rinsed off dirty plates and salad bowls while Laura loaded them in the dishwasher. "Why don't I wash and you dry?" he suggested, running water in the sink where a few pots and a skillet had been left soaking. "You're a very neat cook, by the way."

"Mom always said if you clean up as you go, it makes life easier," Laura replied, smiling. "But I definitely never turn down offers to help. Thanks." It occurred to her that she had never seen a man, other than Andrew, help with the dishes.

"It was nice of you to invite me to dinner," he said. "I really like Emily and Andrew."

"We think of you as part of the family," she said and instantly regretted the remark, realizing that she had unintentionally divulged a deeper desire. "I mean, you and Marjorie and Terri are like family to me."

He didn't answer, just handed her the skillet to dry. Neither spoke as Laura dried the skillet and stored it in a lower cabinet. When she turned, John was drying his hands on the kitchen towel. He faced her. "Could we talk?"

"Of course," she answered, her heart thudding in her chest. "Let's go to the living room." He looked serious.

"After you." He picked up their wine glasses and followed her, placing them on the coffee table. She sat on one side of the sofa. He chose a nearby arm chair across from her. "I've been thinking," he started. He placed his hands in his lap, one hand balled into his other hand, a gesture she had noticed on several occasions when he was nervous.

Laura watched his face, entreating him to say something that might give her hope for the future. Now she felt nervous, too, and picked up her wineglass for something to do with her own hands. She had never been good at hiding her feelings. Unspoken words flowed like a ticker tape across her forehead. Surely, he could see how she felt about him. She waited.

"This is hard," he began. "There are many things I want to say to you. You've been such an important part of my life this year. I couldn't have gotten through it without you. It's just . . ." He chose his words with even more care than usual. "I'm working through some stuff."

In a flash, Laura realized he could sense what she was thinking and feeling. Her cheeks reddened. Of course. He didn't want her to misunderstand his intentions.

"I understand," she said, swallowing the lump in her throat.

"I'm not sure you do." He reached across what felt like a growing chasm between them, and took her hand. As if reading her thoughts, he said, "Laura, you are an incredible woman. But this—what we have right now—is all I'm capable of."

"John, please don't," she said, lowering her eyes. "You have nothing to explain. You just lost your wife. I don't expect anything from you."

"This isn't going well," he said, wiping a hand across his brow. "It wasn't what I wanted to say."

She interrupted him. "You were so helpful in getting justice for Michael. You were wonderful to me when I lost my mother. That's what friends do."

She faltered, unable to continue, needing to distance herself from him before the tears came. Her throat tightened in embarrassment. As long as she spent time with him, she would wish for more. It wasn't possible, not now—maybe never.

He sat beside her on the sofa. "This wasn't how I wanted this evening to end. I'm so sorry. I've had the feeling lately that you deserve more from me." He cleared his throat. "It's just that . . . I can't seem to . . ."

"It's okay," she said quickly. She wanted him to leave. She stood up, and so did he.

"Thank you again for dinner," he said.

"You're welcome," she said, praying he wouldn't say anything more. She could feel hot tears forming. "See you at book club?"

"Yes," he said, his eyes crinkling in a smile. "I bet you're getting excited about the big trip coming up."

She smiled weakly. "Can't wait."

"Laura . . ." He hesitated, watching her. Then he pulled her gently to him, his eyes meeting hers. In the next moment, his lips were on hers, so gentle, fitting against hers as if they had kissed many times before. He brushed his fingers over her cheek to wipe away the tear he found there.

The kiss deepened. She allowed the kiss to continue, felt her heart beat wildly. There was no awkwardness, just a knowing. The scent of his aftershave, the feel of his mouth overwhelmed her senses. It was more than chemistry, this attraction. It was deeper and spoke of something far more important. He was the one. She was sure of it now.

He took a step back, his arms holding hers. He smiled. "Good night, Laura."

"Good night, John," she said.

He left quickly, promising to call her the next day. Afterward, her body thrummed with a sensation that confused her—part desire, part sadness. Even worse, she wondered if he had kissed her out of a sense of duty, seeing her tears, not wanting her to be upset, feeling that he owed her an explanation. She wished she had not invited him to dinner. Now, after this kiss, she would have to wait and wonder when or how, or even whether he would ever want more.

"It was not a mercy kiss!" Terri said later, when Laura called her. She had shared what had happened with John the night before.

"I'm sure he knew I wanted him to kiss me. Then I made him feel bad, and he had to do it."

"Men don't kiss like that, unless they want to. No, ma'am. He was not feeling sorry for you. He wanted to comfort you," Terri said. "He isn't saying never. He's just letting you know he's not ready yet. There's a difference."

"I love him, Terri," Laura said in anguish. "I love him, and I know I'll never measure up to Jackie."

Terri was quiet for a moment before speaking. "Remember what you said to me last week, when I worried that I wasn't as good as Larry's ex-wife? You said what I have to offer Larry is different, not less than. John had a happy marriage that ended tragically. There will always be a special place in his heart for Jackie. But she is gone, and you are here. And I believe he loves you, too."

Laura blew her nose and took a deep breath. "I have to pull myself together. I don't want to be sitting here every night, wishing for something that might take years."

"It might. I doubt it, though," Terri said. "You've got this trip to Ireland coming up, and I think it's exactly what you need. You've never traveled. It will be the trip of a lifetime for you."

"I'm going to scatter my mom's ashes there," Laura said. "This gives me a purpose."

"Laura, do yourself a favor," Terri said. "Life is not just about duty and purpose. It's about joy, happiness in the moments. You are always so focused on what has to happen next. I know, I know. You're a business owner. You have responsibilities. But your business, that money you earn *pays for your life*. Are you enjoying your life?"

Laura was silent, absorbing Terri's words. "You're right," she said. "I'm always focused on what other people need, what they want or expect."

"It's one of the nicest qualities about you," Terri said. "You are the most generous person I know. You think of everyone else before yourself. But you have to be generous with yourself, too."

Laura considered this advice. "It's not how I was raised."

"If your mother was here right now, I'm sure she'd say, 'I'm sorry if I ever raised you to believe your life always had to be about putting your needs last.'"

"My mother said many things to me while we lived together," Laura said. "She even apologized for allowing my father to dictate who I could marry. She was proud of what I became on my own."

"You are so much stronger than you know, my friend," Terri said. "Let go of the past. You gained a lot of life experience on the way to becoming the woman you were meant to be. All those things that happened to you made you deeper, stronger, more compassionate. Go to Ireland. Put your mom's ashes to rest—along with the past. Let yourself have the most wonderful time of your life."

"You think that will help me feel less sad about John?"

"I think once you realize that you can't continue to live your life always hoping and waiting, always wanting something that's in the future—not being happy in the moment—you'll be able to let things unfold the way they're meant to."

Chapter Thirty-Four

John Speaks

Driving home from Laura's apartment that evening, the steady thwack-thwack of the windshield wipers were a soothing backdrop for John's even louder thoughts. It had been an unusually hot, humid day for June. As a steady rain fell, mist rose from the pavement, creating a halo effect around Dublin's streetlamps. The cross-town drive to his house was only fifteen minutes, but he wished it could take longer. He wasn't especially anxious to get there.

The house he and Jackie had purchased had always felt too big and quiet for just him. At night, he had gotten into a habit of turning on the television for background noise, even while reading. He had intended to sell the house, at some point. But he had taken Laura's advice not to make sudden decisions the first year after Jackie's death. Anyway, where would he go?

Laura's invitation to dinner with Andrew and Emily that evening had been a welcome respite from the loneliness of spending another long evening at home. Her call had come at the perfect time. He had downloaded a different ringtone on his phone just for her so he would know when she called. As soon as he heard the electronic notes of "You've Got a Friend," he raced to answer her call.

He laid his head against the driver's headrest and pressed his lips together, thinking about the moment he had kissed her. It hadn't been intentional. That is to say, he hadn't meant to kiss her quite that way. He had started to give her a friendly good-night hug like the ones they usually shared. Kissing her had been spontaneous, surprising him as much as it did her. Funny, but he could have sworn he heard Jackie's voice in his right ear. *Go ahead. Kiss her.*

From the way she responded, he knew Laura had welcomed the kiss. But now, things would be different between them. He wondered if either of them would end up having second thoughts.

He had been relieved that Laura wasn't seeing Greg anymore. He had disliked the guy on sight—had known he was trouble. Laura had offered her tender heart to someone undeserving, not yet aware of the countless ways that her innocence was like bait for the Gregs of the world. No doubt, Laura had fallen prey to his well-practiced lines. Her husband had exerted power over her. Greg's power had been far more insidious.

She deserved better than someone who would use her. John felt that familiar stab to his own heart as he recognized that he cared for her as more than a friend. Of course, he had no right to an opinion about anyone Laura might see socially. He was a recent widower, a heartbreak waiting to happen if they weren't cautious.

He was a careful man, particularly in matters of the heart. While his wife was dying, he hadn't wanted to rely on others. It was his job to care for Jackie, to make certain all her needs were met. He had promised her he'd be there till the end. Yet, as she became weaker, when she lost her ability to speak, to eat, and finally to breathe without assistance, he had been forced to ask for help.

There had been a stream of nurses and home health aides, along with fellow teachers and his wife's girlfriends who brought food—for John— to the house. Jackie was on tube feedings by then. They offered to stay with her while he left the house to run errands or get some exercise. As the years dragged on, a few of them even offered their bodies to him, which always came as a surprise. Had he inadvertently given off some kind of signal?

He never accepted anyone's offer of sex, though he was painstakingly gracious in his refusals. Later, he would laugh at himself. Surely, one didn't turn down an offer of sex using the same words you might decline an offer of a casserole.

Laura had been completely transparent about her motives, never offering more than she believed he could accept without discomfort. She respected his marriage and had compassion for the grieving process. Even if she had no reason to be sad about her husband's death, she had lost her son in such a terrible way. She understood loss in ways that others didn't.

In a way, they were alike. Each was hesitant to take the next step because each of them felt broken in some way. They were unwilling to hurt someone else while they were healing from the past.

It was almost as if she made his grief her own, guiding him through a range of bittersweet emotions that allowed him to see a future without Jackie. She helped give away Jackie's clothing, a task he couldn't have handled on his own. She even took the money from the sale of the consignment furniture, and contributed that amount—and more—to the scholarship fund in Jackie's memory. He never would have known this if he hadn't seen the unusually generous gift on the quarterly fund statement. After calling the foundation's development office, he learned it was an anonymous donation. He asked Laura point-blank if she had been the contributor, wanting to thank her properly. To his surprise, she seemed embarrassed to have been found out.

His feelings for her had grown by degrees since that day they met unexpectedly in the dining room of Glenview Gardens. He thought he recognized her. But how could this attractive well-dressed woman be the same Laura Fisher from Parmenter? He approached her carefully, certain he was mistaking her for someone else and would end up apologizing. But when she turned to look at him, he saw those blue, blue eyes.

She was a different person, and yet not. It was remarkable to think of how much she had accomplished, personally and professionally, in just a couple of years. She clearly had a knack for design. Heck, she could probably host one of those television home design programs; she was that good.

All too often, he noticed how she downplayed her intellect. In reality, she had well-considered views on many topics. She also possessed a deadpan sense of humor, rarely even cracking a smile when she said something side-splittingly funny. He thought it was because her ability to make people laugh came as a surprise—to her. After all, there hadn't been much reason for her to laugh all those years in Parmenter.

It hadn't taken long for him to recognize how much he valued the easy friendship they shared. When he had something to tell someone, she was the first person he thought of calling. When he needed advice, her insights were spot-on.

Almost from the start, he knew their friendship had potential to grow into something more, even as he dismissed it as premature and inappropriate. His status first as the husband of a dying woman and then as a recent widower meant these feelings needed to be put on the back burner. How could he even be sure that what he was feeling was love and not gratitude for all she had done for him?

But as the months went by, he couldn't deny his growing attraction. She was a beautiful woman with no idea of the effect she had on men. It was just one of the things he loved about her.

Loved. Yes, he loved her. It would be a year in July since Jackie's passing. Her death had come after many years, a predictable, relentless downward spiral. When her suffering finally came to an end, he had been relieved, for her sake.

Even if he asked Laura out on a date, at some point, it was still important to allow their relationship to unfold in a way that wouldn't leave either of them open to a different kind of grief if things didn't work out between them. He wasn't willing to lose her as a friend. Though she had grown into a confident, successful businesswoman, Laura was fragile, too, in ways she couldn't admit.

His mind went back to the first day they had met, years ago, when he had seen her struggling to leave the store with all those heavy grocery bags. In the stifling heat, she had looked as if she might faint. Upon further notice, he could see pain in her eyes, and something more. It was fear.

He could tell from the conservative style of her dress that she was from one of the strict religious sects. If so, it might not be appropriate to offer her a ride. He was surprised when she did accept, albeit with hesitation.

There was an anxious air about her. He suspected she had a good reason. In his work in criminal law, he had seen enough women like her—women who lived as if they were invisible. Many were abused; some died. Was this woman one of them?

To his dismay, he learned in the car that she was married to the minister who had been suspected of inappropriate behavior toward a minor girl a few years earlier. The district attorney's office thought they had enough to charge him with molestation. But then, the girl recanted her story in a way that led attorneys to suspect she had been coerced by someone, likely her parents. They were members of that church. He doubted Laura knew anything about it.

The night her husband had been taken away by ambulance, John took one look at her and knew he was right about the abuse. Those ugly finger-like bruises creeping up her neck were the result of her husband's hands. No wonder she had been in pain. She was more seriously injured than she had let on earlier that day, and he swore to God, he was glad the bastard was dead.

It couldn't have been easy to recover from the emotional wounds Jed inflicted on her. And as if that wasn't bad enough, how much worse could it have been to live with the death of her son, particularly when she understood that his life had been considered expendable by some—even by his own father? That tragedy had marked her life in a way he couldn't possibly comprehend.

When she had first asked him about the possibility of reopening the investigation into Michael's death, he hadn't the heart to tell her it was unlikely justice would be served—not this many years later. But she was doggedly determined, having made up her mind to do whatever was possible. It was her good heart that ultimately fed into the serendipitous events that led to Luke's confession. She had worried about Ruth and wanted to help. If, at first, her intention had been to gain information from Ruth, it soon turned into a mission to save her.

When he realized how personal it was for Laura to help Ruth, he stayed in even closer touch with Laura, asking questions. On the day, he learned of her plan to go along with the delivery truck to deliver the beds, he knew she was putting herself in grave danger. It was how he knew he needed to be there the day Luke Forrest confronted her. The rest was history.

Without the legal work that had brought them together regularly, there wouldn't be as many reasons to see her. But he could hardly ignore what was happening between them on a personal level. She was authentic enough that she couldn't hide her feelings. Tonight, the pent-up longing on her face had been visible. Even worse, he knew that his inability to communicate his feelings was causing her more pain.

He hadn't intended to get into a discussion of what he knew was happening between them. But then, she made the remark that he was like family, correcting herself with embarrassment, and he knew. It seemed wrong, somehow, not to get it out in the open. But his efforts to discuss what might be happening hadn't gone well, and he could see the embarrassment he caused.

He had meant simply to give her a hug. But seeing the devastation in her expression, watching as the tears gathered, he couldn't help himself. He pressed his lips against hers. He hadn't expected it to feel so natural, as if he should have kissed her before this, as if they had already kissed many times.

It certainly wasn't her fault that she was beginning to entertain romantic feelings. Hadn't he given her a hint of what he felt when they danced at the wedding reception? Truth be told, he had wanted to do far more than dance with her. As he held her close, the aroma of her perfume rising from the heat between them, he had wanted to waltz her right out of the room to a place where he could make love to her.

These feelings had been building, deepening in intensity, until he wanted to speak the words in his head and heart. Yet it might not be the ideal time to make a promise to someone when he still felt so keenly the loss of one who had been his entire world. It was getting easier month by month as he created a new rhythm to his life. Starting up his law practice was helping him feel more like his old self. But Jackie was still there in so many moments of his day. How long would that continue? Would it ever stop? Did he want it to?

Jackie wouldn't want him to be sad and alone. When speech was still possible, she had nearly broken him in two by saying, "When I'm gone, I want you to find someone else to love. It's been too long that I've been like this."

After three years of being bedridden, when lovemaking seemed a distant memory, she had even suggested that if he had needs, he should find someone. This he could not do. And even if he had, she would know. Somehow, she would know. They could read each other that way.

When the time was right, he would ask Laura on a proper date. And with any luck, their relationship would be happy, and he would eventually marry her. It would be a different kind of love than what he had with Jackie. But he felt that Laura might just be the one to help him heal.

He shut off the engine and let out a long breath. Laura had suffered enough in her life. He needed to move forward with caution. Hopefully, she wouldn't lose interest or worse, meet someone else.

When he was ready to love again, he would give his entire heart and soul to her. For now, he hoped she would do more than understand his need to move slowly. He hoped she would wait for him.

Chapter Thirty-Five

"The line-up of bands for this year's Irish festival is the best we've ever had," Terri told the Irish book club at their June meeting. Her eyes shone with excitement. "We were lucky to get one of the best fiddle players in Ireland. He's usually on tour in Europe. Oh, and remember, you can still get tickets at a reduced price."

She needn't have mentioned the last part. Every member of the book club was an avid festival-goer with passes they purchased months in advance. Laura was glad she had been able to serve again this year on Terri's music selection committee. Despite all that had happened over the past year, she enjoyed reviewing all the entries.

Dublin's Irish Festival always drew a crowd for the long weekend due, in no small part, to the quality of the music performers on multiple stages. This year, Terri believed they would draw an even bigger international crowd because of the Irish fiddle player.

Laura couldn't wait to hear him play. As time for her Irish trip drew nearer, she googled a few of the Irish bands whose entries she had enjoyed most, and discovered that one of them was playing at a pub in Killarney while book club members were scheduled to be there in mid-July.

"We'll have to make sure we hear them," Jan agreed, when Laura told her. "Oh, we're going to have such a good time! I haven't been back to Ireland in eight years."

"I'm going to leave the group for one day when we get near Kenmare, the town where my mom was born," Laura said. "I want to scatter her ashes in her hometown."

"Oh, Laura," Jan said. "What a wonderful tribute to your mom."

The trip was in less than two weeks. Laura worked at a feverish pace to prepare both stores for business as usual while she was out of the country. She had never traveled before. Receiving her passport in the mail had been such a thrill. It would be her first real vacation since becoming a business owner, and she was nervous and excited. Thank heavens for Marjorie who said she would work full-time at the Parmenter store while Laura was away. Andrew and Emily would help out at the Dublin Serendipities Two store.

"You need this trip in more ways than you realize," Marjorie had said the last time they were together. "When you get to Ireland, I think you'll feel right at home."

"I hope so."

"You've seemed a little down in the dumps lately," Marjorie said. "Can I guess the reason?"

"You'd probably nail it on the head." Laura let out a deep sigh. "No matter how hard I try to let go of these thoughts in my head, the less successful I am. I've tried to just stay busy and forget about everything."

"You're in love. It's next to impossible to let that go." Marjorie took a sip of her coffee.

"Am I? How would I know?" Laura picked at the embroidery on the tablecloth. "I wasn't in love with Jed. I thought I was in love with Greg. Clearly, that wasn't real love. Would I even recognize real love?"

"What you were experiencing with Greg was lust."

Laura laughed. "I'll say. And look what that got me."

"No one knows at the beginning of a relationship how it will turn out. When you realized the truth about him, you did the right thing."

"I feel things more deeply with John. It's as if he already lives in here." She pointed to her chest. "But it hurts to feel this way and not be able to express it openly. I see him and want to say it. I remember the way we danced, how natural it felt to be in his arms. I remember the night he kissed me. Surely, surely, what I felt was real."

"I'm sure it was. And John is a good man. I'm confident that what he was feeling when he kissed you was very real, too. He's taking his time, that's all."

"I promised myself I wouldn't do this."

"Do what?"

"After Jed died, I promised myself I would learn to live on my own, become my own person. I don't want to become the kind of woman who can't live without a man."

"Haven't you lived on your own for several years now? Didn't you build a business and then assume ownership of another one? If you ask me, you have done just fine on your own. You just didn't count on meeting someone who feels like the one."

"The one. Yes, he does."

"Going to Ireland with Jan and your other friends from the book club is the best thing you can do. You'll see new sights, and you'll be in a different place." She pointed to her head. "You'll put yourself in a different mindset, and there won't be as much room for the sadness."

"I can't stop hoping for more." She felt the words catch in her throat.

"Hope is a good feeling. Without hope, we all feel lost. Give it time."

"I think maybe these sad feelings are happening because I see how happy Terri and Larry are now. I think 'That could have been me.' Except it couldn't have been. I never did feel the same way about Larry that Terri does."

"She's your dear friend. Aren't you happy for her?"

"Of course, I am. I introduced them because I thought they would hit it off. I'm glad they're together. I guess watching them, seeing them so happy just reminds me that I don't have what they have."

Terri and Larry's relationship had progressed to the point that they were discussing marriage within the next year. Terri had asked Laura for help in planning a simple wedding with just family and friends. "Nothing too elaborate," she said. "This is a second marriage for both of us."

"Why not? You deserve a nice wedding," Laura protested. "Do you two have a budget in mind?"

"Larry said I can have whatever makes me happy," Terri said.

"He's a keeper," Laura said, smiling.

"I know he's the one." Terri's face beamed. "I can't wait to marry him."

"I hope I can have that kind of love someday," Laura said with a wistful expression. "Ever since John kissed me, it's as if he's avoiding me. I've barely seen him except at book club and a few times at the store, usually on the fly. He stops by, and we run upstairs to the café to have coffee."

"Did you even talk about the kiss?"

"Um . . . not exactly." Laura thought for a moment. "I would say that neither of us has acted like it was anything more than it actually was."

"Which is . . .? Laura, he kissed you." Terri shook her head. "You're not making this up."

"I mean, it was a spontaneous kind of thing. I'm certain he hadn't planned to do it. I told him I was surprised that it happened, but I liked it."

"Oh, good! At least, you gave him some encouragement. Well, now the ball is in his court. At least, he didn't apologize and say it would never happen again."

"No, he definitely didn't say that. Even so, it was premature. I hope he doesn't come to regret it."

"I doubt that. I've seen the way he looks at you," Terri answered. "Anyway, isn't he super busy getting his legal practice up and running? You aren't the only one with too much on your plate, you know."

"True. He's about to take on another associate, I heard. He has enough clients from referrals that he needed another attorney. I'm glad he decided to leave the university and follow his heart. I think playing it safe didn't make him happy."

"Playing it safe rarely does."

ON SATURDAY, JULY SIXTEENTH, LAURA WAS AWAKE at five o'clock, too excited to stay in bed any longer. She had barely slept more than ninety minutes at a stretch all night. By tomorrow morning, the plane would touch down in Ireland. She got up, dressed, and finished readying the apartment for her time away. She watered plants, put out the trash, and adjusted the thermostat.

She carried her heavy suitcase down the stairs to the front porch and glanced at her phone. Jan had texted to say she was on her way in a ride share to pick her up. *I'm ready*, she texted back. Then she went upstairs to retrieve her carryon bag and the small purse she was taking with her. "Novel to read on the plane, check. Sunglasses, check. Passport and ID, check."

She had enough Euros to last at least a week. Jan had assured her of that. And, anyway, she could always get more. She had also exchanged a thousand dollars for traveler's checks and got a traveler's credit card that would allow her to save air miles for future trips.

"Ready for fun?" she asked her reflection in the hallway mirror, and blew a strand of damp hair off her forehead. It was hot and humid here. The more temperate weather in Ireland would be a welcome change.

She carefully locked her apartment door and came downstairs, waving at her two employees already hard at work. Serendipities Two was in good hands. "Text me if you need anything," she said.

"Have fun!" they called out. "Don't worry!"

For a moment, she felt disembodied. Was it possible that this was really her life now? Ever since childhood, she had dreamed of going to Ireland. Every time her mother talked about the village of Kenmare where she had spent her early childhood, Laura could picture the town in her mind's eye. How would she feel setting foot on the streets where her mother had walked to and from school? It seemed doubtful she'd find the house where her mother had grown up, but she planned to look for the street, at least. She could go to the Protestant church where her mother had attended services.

In all the years that she had been married to Jed, it had never once occurred to her that she could actually go to Ireland. Jed hadn't wanted to travel, had said America was good enough for him. And he wasn't spending his hard-earned money on frivolous trips. In his mind, the fact that he didn't intend to go to Ireland meant Laura wouldn't go, either.

"And I believed that, too." She murmured the words as the rideshare vehicle pulled up to the curb. "I don't believe it, anymore. I am going to Ireland!"

Jan bounded out of the car as soon as it came to a stop. "Can you believe it? The day has final come!"

Laura couldn't recall ever seeing Jan this effervescent. Jan Armstrong was many things: smart, capable, a veritable powerhouse of library science. What she was not was giddy. But here she was, grabbing Laura's bag as if she might carry it the whole way to Ireland on her own steam. The driver stowed Laura's heavy suitcase in the back, and Laura reclaimed her carryon bag, waiting for Jan to scoot over in the backseat.

"We're on our way!" Jan put on her seatbelt, a wide smile lighting up her face. "Got everything?"

Laura fastened her seatbelt and rechecked her purse. "Passport and ID, check. Cash, traveler's checks, Euros, check."

"You'll do that every few hours the entire time we're away," Jan said, grinning.

"Do what?"

"Obsessively check to make sure everything is in your bag. I do it, too."

"I just don't want to lose anything," Laura said. "I've never traveled before."

"Don't worry, it will be fine. You made copies of your passport for inside your suitcase and your carryon, right? Traveler's checks are replaceable. You have nothing to worry about."

Laura let out a deep breath. "I'm lucky to be traveling with you," she said. "You've been to Ireland and a lot of other places. I should just relax and let you lead me around."

"It's normal to feel anxious the first time you travel out of the country," Jan said. "But I promise, you'll start to breathe easier once we land in Ireland and you see the countryside. Every scene is as pretty as a picture."

When they arrived at the Columbus airport, Jan and Laura retrieved their bags. They went into the airport and began the process of checking in and going through security. It was all new to Laura, but she followed everything Jan did. Fifteen minutes later, they emerged from security.

"We're meeting everyone at the gate," Jan told her. "Hopefully, we can all sit in the same area of the plane." They walked to the gate where their plane to Chicago was scheduled to take off. From Chicago, they would fly straight to Ireland. Jan waved as she spotted the other three book club members waiting at the gate.

Laura smiled. She liked Carol and her husband, Jim, who had been members of the book club since its inception several years earlier. The other member, Josie, also a long-time book club veteran, was a high school English teacher and lover of anything Irish. This trip would be fun since Carol, Jim, Josie, and Jan were easy-going, always ready for a laugh.

Jan arranged her carryon bag and purse on the floor in front of her seat. She patted the seat next to her, and Laura sat down. "It will be at least an hour before they call us to start boarding," Jan said. "If you want a snack or a last-minute drink, now's a good time."

Laura took in all the sights of the airport as travelers wheeled carryon suitcases and briefcases, many obviously traveling for business. A young mother and father led their two small daughters, who dragged princess suitcases and stuffed animals into a corner where their mother handed out granola bars and juice boxes. An older man with an oxygen cannula in his nostrils sat with his wife who patted his hand every now and then. Laura watched them as they sat together in silence, comfortable being together, looking after each other. A couple obviously on their honeymoon exchanged kisses and handfuls of Fritos. The young woman wore a t-shirt that said *I'm the Bride*.

"We'll be at the hotel in plenty of time for afternoon tea," Jan said, relishing the role of travel guide. "Trust me, afternoon tea in Great Britain isn't like having a cup of tea in the U.S. It feels totally different."

"I hope so," Jim said. He looked at his wife and grinned. "Otherwise, we're spending a whole lot of money to travel somewhere to drink tea." Everyone laughed. "What I'm really looking forward to is a pint of Guinness."

"Me, too," said a male voice.

The voice was familiar. Laura turned to look at Jan. "Didn't that sound like . . .?"

Jan's mouth was gaping, her eyes wide. "Turn around," she said.

Laura stood up from her seat. There, smiling ear to ear, was John. He carried a black travel bag slung over his shoulder. "Hi," he said.

"John, what are you doing here?"

"I decided it was time to see Ireland. You don't mind if I tag along, do you?"

"Of course not!" Laura still couldn't believe her eyes. "But when did you decide to go? You haven't said a word about it."

"To be honest, the thought came to me a month ago. I wasn't sure it would be possible to get away, but my new associate said he could handle things while I'm gone. I called the travel agent, and she said I could still get a spot with this group. So, I figured why not."

Their kiss had happened a month ago. Now it all made sense. Laura smiled. "I thought you were regretting, well, you know."

"I wanted to do it again, to tell you the truth." They stood there, gazing into each other's eyes, until they heard someone clearing their throat.

"John, why don't you take this seat?" Jan moved her travel bag and purse one seat over.

"Would you mind watching our stuff for a minute?" John asked Jan. She shook her head, still grinning with surprise.

"Walk with me?" He reached out to take Laura's hand as they began walking through the long hallway in the terminal.

"I'm so surprised," Laura said. "I had no idea . . ."

"Neither did I—well, that is, until I kissed you that night. I drove home and couldn't sleep a wink. By the next day, I knew what to do. It's been a year. I've had time to process it all, and God knows, I've had enough years to grieve. It's time to move forward. If you're willing, I think we ought to take this relationship to the next level."

"And that's a trip to Ireland?" She grinned. "A restaurant would have been fine."

He laughed out loud. "Normally, I'd ask a girl out on a date before going to Europe with her." He shrugged, grinning in such an adorable fashion, Laura's heart fluttered in her chest.

Then he kissed her. With his hands holding her face so gently, his lips met hers and lingered there. It was a kiss that left no doubt in Laura's mind or heart that he meant what he said. He wanted to be with her.

Walking back to their seats at the departure gate, Laura could see flight attendants and the pilots going through the door to the jetway. "I'm a little nervous."

"About the flight or about us?" John asked, and squeezed her hand.

"The flight. I've never been on a plane before. You, I think I can manage."

John laughed. "I'm going to assume that we can arrange to sit together. I'll hold your hand the entire flight, if you'll let me."

"Here they are," Carol said as they returned to the group. "Twenty minutes until we board."

Laura looked around at her friends. No one said much, but they were all smiling. No one looked particularly shocked at John's sudden appearance.

"So, it was meant to be," Carol said with a sigh. She placed her hand dramatically on her heart. "Seeing the two of you, the way John showed up like that . . . . Why, this is way better than the end of any romance movie I've ever seen. We all wondered, *When will these two finally figure out they belong together?*"

Josie chuckled. "The book club could see this coming for months. Man and woman reunite after time apart. She captures a criminal. He is a witness to her bravery. Neither knows how the other really feels. She prepares to fly away. He shows up at the last minute. They kiss. It's classic."

There were laughs all around. Laura exchanged glances with John. "Well, when you put it like that, it does sound like the perfect ending of a novel or movie."

"Not an ending," Jan said. "It's only the first chapter of the story of Laura and John."

Epilogue

S HE HAD NO DOUBT; THIS PLACE WAS MAGICAL. Everywhere she looked, Laura took in breathtaking sights and sounds that awakened all of her senses. Ireland was dubbed the Emerald Isle for a reason, possessing an infinite number of shades of green, gold, orange, red, and blue.

From the vibrant emerald-green of grassy fields where sheep grazed to a rainbow of flowers in window boxes, household gardens, and parks, Laura felt as if her life had transformed from a nineteen-sixties black-and-white scene to technicolor. Even coffee, she noticed, smelled and tasted richer. A club sandwich made with creamy Irish butter and cheese, locally raised vegetables, and organic meats was far more delicious than anything she had ever tasted back home in Ohio. The sky above was a more brilliant azure-blue, the white clouds skittering like cotton balls across the horizon. Even the air smelled different here—cleaner, fresher, more fragrant.

Strolling along the nearly deserted beach in the town of Kenmare, Ireland, Laura brushed away a wisp of hair that the strong northern wind blew into her eyes. In her handbag, she carried a small metal urn containing her mother's ashes. There was no other place she could imagine sprinkling her mother's remains. This town on the scenic Ring of Kerry was her mother's birthplace. Though Laura had never heard Eileen request that her remains be scattered here, she knew that her mother would have been overjoyed at the thought.

This stretch of beach was pristine with light sand, banked by tall grasses. She picked a spot where she could safely wade into the bay before turning back toward town. The sun was already high overhead as she wiped perspiration from her upper lip. She planned to meet John for lunch at a nearby café.

As with so many of the seaside villages along the South West coast of Ireland, Kenmare had retained its historical charm but now exhibited a lively, modern culture. The town was picture-perfect with everything Laura could imagine to be happy. She had read in a guidebook that Kenmare's Irish translation, *Neidin*, meant "little nest."

In just a few short hours, she had come to understand that this place already felt like home. She loved it and planned to spend more time here. She also felt a deep sense that the creation of Serendipities Two had been a fated destination on a path set forth long ago, perhaps even before she could even identify her dreams.

To the north of Kenmare, Killarney National Park offered pristine views of the lakes of Killarney. Visitors to this region could enjoy scenic drives around the Ring of Kerry, stopping here and there for a meal, live music, or a quick shop for collectibles. Just as easily, they could venture out in a boat onto Kenmare Bay to fish or hike the mountains and forest trails. This morning, John and another member of the Irish book club, Jim, had gotten up early to play eighteen holes of golf on a recommended course outside Killarney.

Though this was her first visit to Ireland, Laura felt that she already knew the way as she walked the same streets her mother had walked. Armed with her cell phone, she had taken hundreds of photos to show Andrew and Emily. She would have liked to explore longer, but this was, after all, a mission.

Although she had enjoyed playing tourist with John and the others, Laura was secretly glad to have a few hours on her own to acquaint herself with the town where her mother had lived before emigrating to the United States. Stepping inside the hushed interior of St. Patrick's Church where Eileen had attended Protestant services with her family, Laura knelt at the altar where her grandparents made their wedding vows.

Kenmare was famous for its beloved lace. Eileen had told Laura stories about how women and girls in Kenmare were taught to make the intricate lace designs. Laura's grandmother had been highly-skilled in making lace. In those days, it had been expected that girls would contribute to their family's income by learning how to make the fashionable, highly-desired lace creations.

Laura had already purchased several of the more intricate designs she intended to display in frames. They were as much works of art as any painting or sculpture. In a flash of inspiration, she decided to make arrangements to carry Kenmare lace and other Irish products in both Serendipities stores. Everyone, it seemed, had a touch of the Irish in their soul. Especially in Dublin, Ohio, Irish products would be a big hit. In fact, she could devote an entire room of the store to Irish gift items, packaged food, teas, and biscuits.

She continued on, consulting a map for the street where her mother's childhood home had once stood. When she found the address, the house was no longer there. In its place was a series of shops. Disappointed that she couldn't see where her mother had lived, she made her way inside the small gift shop standing in its place. To her delight, she found that it included an art gallery featuring local and regional artists.

She talked with the shop's owner and left an hour later, promising to ship some of her mother's still life paintings to sell in the gallery. She had shared her mother's story and rediscovery of art during the last year of her life. The shop's owner had been excited when Laura showed him several photos on her phone of her mother's paintings.

It was only when Laura was told that two of the small landscape paintings depicted scenes from around Kenmare that she realized her mother had painted entirely from memory. Perhaps it was possible that sense memories of beloved places, triggered by music, beauty, smells, and tastes could be positive, outliving other memories. She wondered if this would be the case someday with her negative memories of Parmenter.

Sending her mother's paintings to her hometown would be a fitting tribute to the woman who had once dreamed of becoming an artist and was now home again, albeit posthumously. In a period of just a few months, Eileen had completed over forty paintings. Laura had already selected three of her favorites, including the painting of the three pears, that she intended to keep forever near her.

At noon, Laura met up with John at a café for toasted bacon-and-tomato sandwiches, a pot of strong Irish tea, and biscuits. He was there, waiting for her at a table in back. His face and neck were pink from the hot sun.

"How was your golf game?" she asked. "Did you and Jim play well?"

He laughed. "We did *not* play well. Actually, I'm not sure you could call what I played today 'golf,' but I did have fun," he said. "How was your morning?"

She told him about all the places she had visited and her idea for bringing Irish gift items to both Serendipities stores. "I'm glad I had the chance to see the town where Mom was born and raised. It makes what we're doing this afternoon even more significant. Kenmare isn't just a place I've heard stories about. Now that I'm here, it feels like home to me."

"Technically, it is your homeland. It's only natural you'd feel drawn to it," John replied. "There's more to see than I realized. It would be nice to come back again and spend more time here."

"I agree. One day isn't enough." She bit into one of the crispy cinnamon biscuits their server set out for them to enjoy with their tea.

Glancing at his watch, John said, "I'll get us a couple of bottled waters. It's going to get even warmer this afternoon, especially on the water."

She looked over at him. Bluish circles ringed his eyes. Jet lag had caught up with both of them the second day of their trip. It took sheer will power to keep moving on such a tight schedule without frequent catnaps.

It was nice of him to want to go with her for this pilgrimage to Kenmare. But she was worried that it might cause him sadness, remembering that it had been Jackie's ashes he scattered last summer. It was only fair to give him an out.

She reached across the table for his hand. "If you would prefer not to come with me this afternoon, I'll understand. You've already walked a lot today. You could go back to the hotel and take a nap."

He waved off her concern. "I enjoyed getting to know your mom over those last weeks of her life. It's an honor to do this with you, unless you'd rather be alone."

"It means a lot that you want to be there with me." She was grateful for his company in more ways than one. "I've already scoped out a spot on the beach."

John paid their check and they left the café, arm in arm. The sky was a vibrant cerulean blue, the perfect backdrop to the colorfully-painted houses and buildings all around them. Flowers bloomed in profusion in pots and gardens everywhere they looked. John linked his fingers in Laura's as they strolled through town to the waterfront. There, they stood for a few moments on a dock, watching as sailboats drifted languidly on the rippled surface of the bay.

As they made their way onto the beach, through grass and white sand, a flock of seagulls cried out overhead. Waves whooshed softly at the shoreline as Laura removed her shoes and laid them on a grassy mound. Cupping the urn in her hands, she walked carefully into the water, feeling the strong pull of the tide on her ankles.

"I'll be right here," John said, sitting down on the sandy bluff.

Laura uncapped the top of the urn. She took in a long breath that turned into a choking sob. She had prepared in her mind for this moment. But now, she hesitated, unwilling to let go of what remained of her sweet mother.

Taking another breath, she spoke the only words that were needed. "After so many years, you've come home again," she murmured. "I wish we could have been here together. I promise I'll visit again soon. I love you, Momma."

She tilted the container into the soft lapping waves and watched as the ashes dispersed on their way out to sea. Just as quickly as the sadness overcame her, a feeling of peace muted the sadness. At that moment, she could feel her mother's presence—thought she could even hear the lilt of her mother's Irish brogue. It was a song she heard.

As she felt the serenity of the moment and this place, she knew what to do. Lifting her head toward the sky, she sang the words she had just heard through her mother's voice. It was Eileen's favorite hymn, "Amazing Grace."

Her mother had loved the third verse most, and often sang the comforting words as she did her housework. "Through many dangers, toils, and snares, I have already come. Tis grace has brought me safe thus far, and grace will lead me home."

The wind picked up again as Laura finished singing. She returned to the spot where John now stood, patiently waiting for her. She walked into the circle of his arms and lifted her face for the soft kiss he planted on her lips. Leaning into him, she rested her head on his chest, feeling the beat of his heart. The security of his arms around her was all the comfort she needed, now and always.

Finally, they stepped apart. "Ready to go yet?" John asked.

She nodded. "Now she can rest in peace."

THE OTHER MEMBERS OF THE IRISH BOOK CLUB had taken a tour bus to Galway Bay and a few other points on the way back. They wouldn't return until early evening. Without the structure of the guided tour, Laura had no idea what she wanted to see or do next.

"You're missing all the places you wanted to see on the tour today,"

Laura pointed out as they walked back to town from the beach. "Some of your family came from Galway, didn't they?"

"They did. But it's okay. We can always come back."

"That would be wonderful."

She was thrilled at his suggestion of a next time. They had been in Ireland just four days, and she had no desire to leave. It was as if all sense of time had been suspended. Was it because their lives in the States were so harried and fast-paced?

Life in Ireland moved at a considerably slower pace. People exhibited a healthier work-life balance here, stopping for a cup of tea in the afternoon or joining friends for a pint after work or in the evenings. Pubs offered live music, which usually resulted in impromptu dancing. It seemed to Laura that the Irish were determined to enjoy each moment of their lives.

Here, she felt no reason to plan ahead. Now that she was in Kenmare, she wanted to stay longer. She began imagining that the cottages that had captured her attention might someday belong to her. Was this place destined to mean more in her life? She was already thinking that she could return, bringing Andrew and Emily, too.

During the flight from Chicago to Ireland, and over the past several days, she and John had begun talking about things they wanted to do and places they wanted to see together. Now they agreed that eight days in Ireland wasn't nearly long enough.

They hailed a taxi for their return drive to Killarney, and found themselves in the care of a Kenmare local, a talkative Irishman named Paddy O'Toole. He knew far more about life in America than Laura and John knew about Ireland.

"And might you be thinkin' that you'd like a longer driving tour?" he asked with an irresistible grin. "There are many wonderful places you'll not see on your bus tour. I promise to make your experience memorable."

They agreed immediately. Paddy was quick witted and knowledgeable on seemingly any topic, answering all their questions about Irish history, geography, and culture, along with the best restaurants and amenities. As they approached each location on the tour, he prepared them for what they would see, enticing them with Irish folklore and a knowledge of Irish poems perfect for every site. It seemed he had a poem or story for every place they saw and an uncanny ability to remember every line he had ever memorized. Laura was enchanted.

"This turned out to be the best day yet," she said with a happy sigh as they bade Paddy a farewell in front of their hotel a few hours later. "I thought I'd be sad this afternoon. But I think my mother had other ideas in mind. She wanted us to have a happy time, so she sent Paddy!"

"I wouldn't put it past her," John answered with a grin. "Your mother told me once that she wanted more than anything for you to have a good life with happier times." He put his arm around her.

"Well, if she can see us now, she must really be glad," Laura said. "She definitely would have approved of you."

"She tried to fix us up on a dinner date. Did you know that?"

"My mother did?" Laura was shocked. "No, I didn't know that. When did it happen?" she asked, laughing.

"It was while you were dating he-whose-name-should-never-be-spoken."

Laura laughed. "I never did tell Mom about him."

"Your mother suggested—very innocently, I might add, although I got her point—that she thought it was high time for the two of us to be getting better acquainted, perhaps over dinner,'" he said in a perfect imitation of Eileen's Irish accent.

"Oh my gosh!" Laura grinned, slapping her hand over her mouth. "What you must have thought. In her later years, she could be quite direct."

"I thought it was a good idea," he said. "Being direct is one of the best things about getting older, if you ask me. Anyway, it's good to know she thought we should take the next step." He glanced at his phone. "Hey, speaking of dinner, are you hungry? It's almost six-thirty."

"I am. What shall we try tonight? Maybe fish and chips at a different place?"

He studied her face for a moment. "While we've been on this group tour, all we've done is eat in pubs and the hotel dining room," he said. "There is a restaurant I'd like to take you to. It has great online reviews. No offense to the others, but it would be nice to have you to myself."

"I feel the same. I'll change into something nicer," Laura said. "Meet you downstairs in about an hour?" She lifted her face for the kiss he placed softly on her lips.

She showered and refreshed her hair and make-up. Then she selected a black sleeveless jersey dress and matching scarf from her suitcase. Slipping her feet into black ballet flats, it suddenly occurred to her that this was her first official date with John. Every other time they'd had lunch or dinner together, it had been as friends or as part of a group.

She glanced over at her bed and removed the discarded clothing she had tossed on it, storing them in her suitcase. Then she tidied the room, wondering if she should invite him in for a nightcap. She had stored a bottle of wine in the mini refrigerator.

She met him downstairs in the hotel bar, where he ordered chilled glasses of Sauvignon Blanc. "To us," he said.

"To us." She clinked her glass to his. "John, did you realize this is our first official date?"

"Why, you're right," he mused. He let out a quick laugh. "To be honest, it doesn't feel like that's possible, though. You're the first thought I have every morning and the last thought I have before I fall asleep at night. That is so amazing to me—as amazing as it is unexpected."

"I know what you mean. How is it possible that so much can happen in just a year?" She took a thoughtful sip of her wine. "It does seem as though there have been larger hands guiding us, at times."

"Perhaps more than one set." He took her hand. "Laura Fisher, will you go out on a date with me tonight?"

She laughed. "Yes, John. I would love to."

They finished their wine and left the hotel, headed down the street to a restaurant known for its excellent European cuisine, service, and ambience. They ordered crab claws for their appetizer followed by fillet steaks that were cooked perfectly. The steaks were served with the most delectable boxties Laura had ever tasted. Boxties were a traditional Irish dish made of grated potatoes in a thick batter, then pan-fried. They looked like a mixture of hash browns and pancakes. These boxties were light, crispy, and perfectly fluffy inside. She spooned sour cream over her boxty and tasted it.

"Food tastes so much better here, doesn't it? Boxties at the pub in Dublin, Ohio are good, but not like this."

As they shared a bottle of red wine their host promised would not disappoint, Laura and John enjoyed an unhurried evening together, talking easily about what they had seen that day and what they hoped to do for the remainder of the trip. John wanted more time to explore places he had seen along the drive. Laura wanted to show him the Kenmare Lace and Design Centre.

"Okay, I've got to say it: I wish we weren't on this group tour," John said as he cut into his steak. "Once I came to the decision to come along on the trip, I wished it had been just the two of us."

"The same thought occurred to me while we were sitting together on the plane," Laura admitted. "I've had a good time with Jan and the others. But you're right. It would be great if we could take at least another day or two this week to do more of what we did today, just you and me."

They shared a thick slice of chocolate cake with whipped cream and fresh raspberries and a pot of Irish tea. "I'm stuffed," John said. "What do you say we take a short walk around town before we head back to the hotel?"

He paid the check and took her by the hand, leading her outside onto the street. She loved the feel of her hand in his. This was as happy as she had ever been.

"I think you had a great idea," he said after a few moments.

"What's that?"

"I doubt anyone would care if we took another day to ourselves," he said. "Why not tomorrow?"

"I'd better let Jan know. We're supposed to be on the bus by eight o'clock sharp. What exactly did you have in mind?"

He pulled her into an embrace as they stood on the sidewalk. "Whatever you and I decide," he said. "Let's play this one by ear."

"I like the way you think," she answered.

John let out a contented sigh. "In my entire life, I don't ever remember doing anything this spontaneous." He shrugged. "I've always been a planner. I think of my time in terms of billable hours. This is completely unlike me."

"Me, too," Laura said. "By the way, I like this new you."

John laughed. "I'll try to be spontaneous more often. We should definitely play more, from now on."

She took in his choice of the plural 'we' and registered that again, his message pointed toward a future together. Squeezing his fingers, she said, "I'd like that. Let's decide which country we want to see next. Italy, maybe?"

They walked back to the hotel and up the stairs to the second floor. As they reached the landing on the second level, he placed his hand on her lower back, steering her down the hall to her room. His hotel room was three doors down the hall. Laura's heart fluttered wildly. Would he kiss her goodnight and proceed to his room, as usual? She hoped not.

As they stood together in the hall in front of her hotel room, she had an overwhelming sense that something magical was about to happen. She was breathless as he leaned in, his eyes meeting hers. He caressed her cheek with the back of his hand.

"Laura . . . I wondered whether . . ." He stopped, searching her face.

If, at one time, she might have second-guessed this kind of spontaneous, passionate decision, that was in the past. She welcomed his touch, had no hesitation or second thoughts. This was the man she loved. Desire pushed everything else from her thoughts.

He held her face between his hands and kissed her. This kiss was not like any other they had shared, even in recent days. This kiss spoke of passion, of wanting more.

"John." His name came out in a whisper. "I want you to make love to me."

His eyes shone with desire, and he nodded. "Are you sure?"

"Yes." She inserted her room key in the door and opened it, drawing him inside by the hand. And now, he kissed her more urgently. Wrapping his arms around her waist, he drew her to him.

Laura unbuttoned his shirt, loving the male scent of his skin and the spicy soap he favored. She ran her fingers through the fine hairs on his chest and then leaned in to kiss the spot over his heart. He raised her face to his and kissed her, then moved toward the place where her jaw met her neck. She shivered, even as heat built within her.

Without a word, he lowered the zipper at the back of her dress and slipped it off of her shoulders, bunching the soft fabric in his hands as he kissed the swell of her breasts. He dropped her dress to the floor, and she stepped out of it. Standing now in her black lace bra and panties, she felt her breath quicken as he reached around her back and removed the lacy bra.

"I want you so much," he said as he took in the sight of her. He quickly removed his clothing and beckoned to her.

He led her to the bed, pressed her gently onto the sheets, and drew her to him so they were facing. She could feel his heart quicken as they continued kissing. He worked his way from her neck down, kissing her. And then his fingers found the elastic waistband of her panties, and he lowered them from her body.

She had never felt this kind of desire, hadn't known she could ever feel such intense sensations. She placed her hands on his hips as he moved over her and drew him in. She let out a small, surprised sound of ecstasy. As he entered her, she cried out his name, pulling his face to hers and kissing him. The physical sensations she was experiencing in ever deepening waves were far more exquisite than anything she could have imagined. And then, she lost all sense of time and place.

At the same time, his breath caught, and she reacted with a cry of unrestrained delight as he arched his back, shuddering, out of breath. They were still and silent for a few moments, as close as two people could get. She wrapped her arms around him to hold him in place.

And then, she heard him speak the words she knew came from his heart. "God, how I love you, Laura."

Tears coursed down the sides of his face. She brought his head to her breast, wiping his face with her fingers, knowing they were tears of joy and healing.

She thought of all that he meant to her beginning with the day they met. He had been there for her then. He would be there for her now and forever. She had never known love the way she knew it with him.

Now she spoke the words she knew to be most true. "I have loved you for so long."

D'Lara Photography

AN AWARD-WINNING POET AND AUTHOR, Robin Strachan began her writing career as a reporter and features writer. Her girlhood dreams of writing novels took years to fulfill. But once begun, she was determined to continue.

Her novels include Manifesting Dreams, Designing Hearts, Listening for Drums and its sequel, Daughter of the Heart.

She makes her home in Darien, Connecticut, where she spends as much time possible reading, enjoying the charms of coastal Connecticut, and visiting the acclaimed Darien Library.